"YOU WOULDN'T DARE!"

"No? Maybe it's time that I should dare a lot more." Jacob dropped to his knees and reached for Dominique. "If you had been raised in this village, you would be the mother of many strong young sons by now. Perhaps you have remained a maiden for too long, crazy one." Keeping one strong hand firmly clasped around her arm, he reached up with the other and lightly brushed the backs of his fingertips across her cheek. "A night spent in the arms of a Dakota warrior will most surely soften that barbed tongue of yours."

Dominique's voice was weak with indecision as she said, "No, thanks. Just leave me alone."

"That isn't what you want. I can tell by the look in your curious eyes"—his middle finger traced her eyebrow—"the way your mouth trembles as you think about the heat of my lips against yours."

"N-no," she said through a sudden gasp. "S-stop it!"

Jacob's laugh was hoarse as he said, "Your voice and the look on your face do not match your words, crazy one. Let me show you what it is to be truly a woman . . ."

Dakota Dream

SHARON MacIVER

DIAMOND BOOKS, NEW YORK

DAKOTA DREAM

A Diamond Book/published by arrangement with
the author

PRINTING HISTORY
Diamond edition/January 1991

ISBN: 1-55773-445-3

Diamond Books are published by The Berkley Publishing Group,
200 Madison Avenue, New York, New York 10016. The name
"DIAMOND" and its logo are trademarks belonging to
Charter Communications, Inc.

PRINTED IN THE UNITED STATES OF AMERICA

10 9 8 7 6 5 4 3 2 1

To
my loving North Dakota hubby, Larry—
inspiration for all that I do
and
to the marvelous Carroll clan of Moffit, N.D.—
with many thanks

ACKNOWLEDGMENTS

Grateful acknowledgment is made to Farrar, Straus and Giroux, Inc., for the excerpts from *The Ladies' Oracle* by Cornelius Agrippa, copyright © 1962 by Hugh Evelyn Limited

and to

the *Bismarck Tribune,* P.O. Box 1498, Bismarck, N.D. 58502 for permission to use titles and verses from their cassette, *The Songs of the Seventh Cavalry.*

Special thanks to the North Dakota Parks and Recreation Department and the Custer Battlefield Preservation Committee.

Chapter One

Dakota Territory, early spring 1876

SHE WAS NAKED.

Dominique DuBois was as bare as a winter landscape and twice as cold. *How can this be?* she wondered, fighting her way to consciousness.

Her survival mechanisms jerked a tremendous shudder along her spine, spawning chattering teeth and limbs that twitched with rhythmic spasms. Dominique slowly lifted a frozen hand toward her mouth for a puff of hot breath, but on the way her fingers caught in a nest of warmth.

What had happened? Where was she?

Too disoriented to question the origin of the life-preserving heat, too thankful to care, she snuggled against it and pressed her face into silken curls.

"So it seems you will live, my golden treasure from the river."

The man's voice startled her.

Dominique opened her eyes, but could focus only on darkness. Was it the black of night, or a shuttered room of some kind? A bad dream, or had she died? She opened her mouth to speak, but could only manage a hoarse gurgle.

"Easy, golden one," the deep voice crooned. "Let me help your blood to thaw. Soon it will again rush through your veins like hot springs."

As he spoke, his powerful hands slid down her back and cupped her derriere. Squeezing her damp, frigid flesh with his strong grip, the stranger drew her against the length of his body as he lay down on top of her.

Mon Dieu! The man was also naked!

Gathering her meager strength, she pushed against the warm mat of chest hair. "Aahh, g-ge-e-t a-awa-a-y!"

His laughter taunted her as she struggled for breath and the energy with which to fight him. But in her condition, she was no match for her three-year-old godchild, much less a full-grown man. Dominique collapsed against the coarse blanket stretched beneath her.

"That is better, golden one. Relax," he instructed as he slid a muscular leg between her knees, "and I shall warm you in a way you've never been warmed before—in the Dakota way."

"D-Dak-kota?" she gasped, her head spinning.

"Ah, yes. Your life has been returned to you by a great Dakota warrior. I will help to grow strong again here in my tipi."

"Dakota?" she sputtered, trying to make sense of all this information as it merged in her mind. "Tipi? You're an *Indian*?"

He laughed, the sound dark and sinister, tinged with sarcasm. "Yes, woman. You lie in the arms of a savage."

Still confused, Dominique said, "B-but you speak English! I don't understand, I don't—"

"Quiet!" he ordered as he pulled an enormous buffalo robe across their bodies. "You do not have to understand—you need only to obey. Now let me warm you."

In a daze, Dominique acquiesced as the Dakota tucked the edges of the robe beneath her shoulders. She'd been rescued from a watery grave only to find herself captured by Indians? If anything she'd read in her secret collection of dime novels was true, this savage would be happy only after he managed to rape, torture, then kill her! Dominique took a deep breath and renewed her struggles. "Pffft. P-pfff-tt. *P-p-fff-t-tt!*"

The Indian's mocking laughter increased, telling her he realized that even though she'd swallowed gallons of Missouri River water, her mouth was as dry as the Great Plains in July. She sucked in her cheeks, drawing every drop of moisture from the inside of her mouth, and tried again. "Pffft. P-p-ffff-ttt!"

Jacob Redfoot wiped the tiny drop of spittle from his forehead and grinned. "If you wish to frighten me like a fierce mountain cat, you will have to do better than that."

Her flesh and spirit warming, her fear replaced by a growing indignation, Dominique folded her fingers into a half-fist and braced her elbows against his chest. "L-leave m-me alone!"

"If I do that, you will die. The river chose to spit you out and drop you at my feet—a sign you were meant to live. I must accept you, my gift, or offend the Great Spirit." He brought his hands up from beneath the buffalo robe and jerked her arms over her head. "Do not fight me. Let me do what I must."

"N-never, y-you—you . . . heathen!"

"Hah!"

Knowing if the woman didn't accept the heat from his body soon, her chances of survival would be cut in half, Redfoot maneuvered his knees and easily pried her powerless thighs apart. Then he slipped his hips in between them.

As he released her wrists and dragged his fingers through her damp hair, he whispered, "It is said a white woman would rather die than have an Indian put his hands on her. Is the heat of my flesh really so terrible that you would prefer to give up your life?" He punctuated the question by cupping her chilled breasts in his warm hands and gently brushing the tip of each with his mouth.

Peculiar sensations fluttered deep within her as the Indian's caresses grew bolder. Instead of finding the strength the icy waters had stolen from her, Dominique's body sank further into weakness. But her mind cleared.

"Unhand me, you brute! I—I swear, if you—if you even *think* about . . . violating me, my papa will have you drawn and quartered!"

Having anticipated her confusion and fear but not her anger, Redfoot leaned back and peered down at her shadowy outline. Did she think he meant to force himself upon her helpless body?

Amused, he laughed. "Your . . . papa? He owes me more than ten good ponies for pulling you from the river. Now still your wiggling tongue. I grow tired of your nonsense."

Catching the hint of hesitation in his voice, and an underlying gentleness, Dominique decided the forbidden novels had painted too simple and savage a picture of the Indians. She set her chin and tried another tack. "I demand you return me to Bismarck. At once!"

"You—you *demand*?" Redfoot gripped her shoulders, his patience with the golden-haired woman rapidly waning. "You will do as I say. And I say—be quiet!"

Dominique pursed her lips. "As you wish."

She tested the inside of her mouth again and found moisture had finally returned. This time, when Dominique spit at her captor, the sound of a target well splattered greeted her ears.

"Enough!" Redfoot raised his arm and brought his open hand across her cheek in a hard slap.

Refusing to cry out, Dominique bit her tongue and raked her fingernails down the side of his neck.

"Ayeee!"

The Indian pushed up on his elbows and knees as he prepared to jerk her up off the blanket. The maneuver gave Dominique a clear shot. She took it. She kicked upward and out, aiming for his most vulnerable area, then rolled out from beneath his body before he had time to react.

Amid his howls of agony, she grabbed the blanket, wrapped it around her nude body, then scrambled blindly across the rug until she bumped into a tipi pole. Making herself as small as possible, Dominique curled up against a wall of stiffened buffalo hide and sat shivering in the darkness while she awaited her fate.

"*Wi witko!*" he screamed as he struggled to his feet.

"A white woman is a crazy woman! The golden treasure between your legs is a prize only in your mind!"

Dominique's eyes grew huge and she bit her bottom lip. No one, but *no one*, had ever spoken to her in such a manner. Had she been right from the start? Did this brute mean to kill her—or worse? Drawing on her only resource of the moment, she kept her silence. Instead of issuing threats or delivering mournful pleas, she listened. To the clacking of stone upon stone. To the rustle of branches and twigs. And finally to the crackle of a small fire as it came to life a few feet from where she huddled against the mat of thick fur.

Squinting into the dim light, she picked out the Indian's nude form glistening through the soft flames. He was bigger than she'd imagined, but in spite of her new fears, he looked less savage and intimidating than she had expected. His back was to her, exposing the rigid curves of his firm, rounded buttocks. Dominique's cheeks burned with the messages her eyes conveyed to her brain, but still she couldn't seem to help but watch—this being her first glimpse of a naked man—as he stepped into his breechclout.

As he pulled on pants made of buckskin, the taut, hardworking muscles of his strong horseman's legs rippled in unison, coursing up to his slim hips and trim middle. Dominique noticed then how his flesh paled at his waist in stark contrast to the darker skin of his back. Why, she wondered, were Indians called redskins when their coloring so closely resembled her own? He turned then, exposing his thick chest and the cloud of sable curls funneling down to the band of his fringed pants.

She knew she ought to avert her gaze, should have done so the moment he exposed his naked body. She also thought she ought to throw herself at his feet and beg for mercy. But then, Dominique DuBois rarely did anything she ought to do. If she had done so more often, she probably wouldn't be in this predicament from which there seemed to be no escape. Her gentle father, the honorable

Judge Jacques DuBois, should have had *his* way for a
change and sent her off to yet another finishing school.
But no, she wouldn't hear of it. As usual, Dominique, the
judge's only offspring and sole reminder of his beloved
wife, Julia, had badgered him until she got what she
wanted. An adventure out west. The dream of a lifetime,
the opportunity to study herself on her own terms and
discover what the future might hold. No rigid finishing
school would tell Dominique DuBois what kind of person
she would become! Now it seemed that dream, that impulsive leap for independence, had turned into a nightmare. Would she escape it with her life? she wondered,
watching as the savage finished dressing.

The Sioux pulled on his leggings and moccasins, then
wrapped a buffalo robe around his shoulders as he approached her. She could feel his gaze bearing down on
her, hear his uneven breathing over the sputtering fire.
Dominique swallowed hard and raised her chin. Slowly
lifting her lids, she leveled defiant brown eyes at him. The
pale light from the fire illuminated only his leggings and
the knife dangling from its rawhide thong at his waist. His
torso was a shadowed outline, his features completely en-
gulfed in darkness save for the amused twinkle in his eyes.

Drawing on her feeble knowledge of the wild, she remembered what her papa had once told her, that an animal
could smell fear and that, once detected, the frightened
one might as well order a headstone. Hoping to save herself from such a fate, Dominique filled her lungs and lied
through her teeth. "I am not afraid of you. If anything, I
feel sorry for a man who is such a disgusting animal that
he must force himself on helpless females."

"And I"—he bit off the words, in no mood to correct
her opinion of him—"feel sorry for any man who must
listen to your wicked tongue! Perhaps," he said as he unsheathed his hunting knife, "you would be a better prize
if I relieved you of that offensive organ."

Dominique glared at him and drew her body into a
tighter tuck. "Do what pleases you, heathen, but know

that my papa will make you pay dearly for any harm you may visit on me!''

''Hah!'' Redfoot fingered the edge of the gleaming blade, then gripped the knife by its handle. ''Planting his seed and reaping one such as you is punishment enough for any man. I should seek him out and make him pay for fathering you!'' He stalked over to the fire and squatted with his back to her as he issued an impatient warning. ''Keep your silence, woman, and let me do what I must.''

When no protest or complaints were forthcoming, and only the rattle of her chattering teeth disturbed the calm, Redfoot grinned. This one would not be easily tamed. She would try to flee the minute he turned his back, he guessed; she would run even if such a foolish act cost her her very life. She needed warmth and rest. He knew of only one way to see that she remained calm and compliant.

Redfoot filled a small bowl with water from a pouch hanging close to the fire. After removing the soft wood stopper from a buffalo horn nearby, he tapped a measure of powder into the bowl, then used a wooden ladle to remove a cooking stone from the center of the firepit. Water sizzled and boiled up over the rim of the bowl as he eased the hot rock into the liquid. When the mixture of water and medicine had cooled to a simmer, he stood and marched over to his captive.

''Here,'' he said, offering the bowl. ''Drink this.''

Dominique turned her head away and pressed her lips together.

''I said drink this, woman! You may be warmed enough to fight me, but if you are to survive, you must rest your spent body. I offer you your life in this potion. Take it, crazy one. It will make all the difference.''

Dominique slowly returned her wary gaze to the bowl. ''What it is?'' she asked quietly.

''Medicine. It will warm your gut and make you sleep. Drink it. Then move to the fire and rest beneath the warmth of my robe.''

She peered up at him, but still his features were hidden by darkness. Trusting him, because of the hint of concern in his voice and because she hoped what he said about the medicine was true, Dominique reached for the container. Shivering, she lifted the warm bowl to her mouth. Steam rose, thawing the tip of her frozen nose, and she sniffed the aroma of something bitter, like the scent of a young sapling culled from the depths of a virgin forest. The heat of the remaining liquid comforted her. After the barest hesitation, she drank it down.

Redfoot wheeled around and strode to the entrance of his lodge. He tossed open the flap of hide, then looked back at the woman. "I leave you now. Do not try to escape. If you step out of this tipi, what you find in the forest will make you wish the river had swallowed you beyond my reach."

Still guessing silence was her best ally, Dominique kept her tongue and watched as he stepped through the opening and disappeared. After the flap had dropped back into place, she let out her breath in a long groan, then crawled to the center of the tipi and the beckoning fire.

Dominique sat rigid for a full minute, half expecting to drop over dead from the effects of the brew. When it didn't happen, she added a buffalo robe to the blanket shrouding her trembling body, then grimaced as its pungent odor reached her nostrils. What to do now? she wondered, her head feeling a little off balance. Her sheltered upbringing in Monroe, Michigan, had certainly never prepared her for anything like this. What chance did she have to escape, to survive, if she should find her way out of this . . . this— Where *was* she? Dominique's brain, suddenly and curiously sluggish, labored to remember.

The ferry! Her uncle's men had put her and her chaperon on the boat for the trip to Fort Lincoln. The river, the chunks of ice, a bump. That was it! She suddenly remembered, giving in to the insane urge to giggle like a schoolgirl. She'd fallen off the ferry shortly after leaving Bismarck. Or had the ferry fallen off of her? The giggles erupted again as her mind, fragmented and numb, supplied a cartoon of the ferry, bottom-side up.

Instinct and the will to live took over then, and Dominique found a way to ignore the strange sensations and colorful images flashing in her head. Determined to find out where she was and seek an avenue of escape, she crawled over to the entrance of the tipi. Carelessly tearing the flap away from the wall, she peered out at what appeared to be a campground and found her eyes would not focus.

Although her vision was blurred and nightfall shadowed much of her surroundings, she could see at least five more tipis arced around another lodge twice their size. She hadn't been kidnapped by a single Indian—she was in the middle of an entire village! Fear knotted in her throat.

"Mon Dieu!" she ground out, her voice sounding hoarse and guttural. But at the words, her fear dissipated and again she thought of her father, of his liberal use of his native tongue, French, and of the love he had for her mother even seven years after her death. Mother, she mouthed to herself, thinking of Julia's Custer blood and the fact that she was the youngest sister of the general himself, what would Mother do?

Julia Custer DuBois would have approved of Dominique's adventure, even to the point of wheedling Jacques into allowing her to accompany their headstrong daughter out to the wild frontier. Dominique giggled again as she remembered Julia's fiery streak of independence—and the day that streak had sent her to her own husband's court to answer charges of harassment and battery. A staunch supporter of women's rights, Julia and a small group of women had bound and imprisoned a terrified jupon manufacturer in a crinoline cage of his own making, then challenged him to wear one of his miserable creations for even a day. Beyond those few details, the incident was never discussed in the DuBois home, but Dominique knew all she had to do was mention the word "crinoline" and her father's cheeks would puff out like a squirrel's and turn as bright as her mother's flaming red hair.

She gave in to another fit of giggles, then suddenly felt maudlin and contrite. A bare six months after the crinoline incident, Julia had died, a victim of consumption. Dominique cast mournful eyes on the circle of lodges. In the darkness, with fires burning inside each dwelling, the scene was almost familial. Each small circle of flames, visible through the skins, looked pink and inviting and gave her an eerie sense of home—and a desperate feeling of loss. She watched, envious of the watery forms of the families as they moved near the fires inside the tipis, and she smiled drunkenly as she thought how much they resembled dancing shadows. Then she blinked, and they transformed themselves into glowing monsters.

Was she losing her mind? Dominique giggled as even that thought flashed a bizarre, yet terribly vivid picture to her poor confused brain. On hands and knees, lurching from side to side, she crawled back to the fire. Collapsing on the buffalo rug, she curled into a fetal position and willed her head to stop spinning, to stop distorting the images around her.

Dominique lay still, straining for lucid thought, searching for some understanding of what was going on inside her muddled head. Then her brain sent its final message just before she passed out: The odds of surviving this little adventure, or even the night, were as good as finding an orchid blooming on the snow-dusted riverbanks.

Chapter Two

JACOB REDFOOT SIGHED WITH SATISFACTION, THEN ROLLED over onto his back. He glanced over at Spotted Feather and smiled. A Dakota woman knew how to serve a man, knew when to speak and when not to. What arrogance made the crazy woman in his lodge think he would seek or find this kind of gratification with her—in the arms of a white woman—even if he *was* born of the same kind?

Surprised by the disturbing, unbidden thought, he clenched his fists in anger. *I am Dakota!* he grumbled inwardly. He had become one nearly twenty winters past on the day a Crow raid destroyed his family. Chief Gall of the Hunkpapa Sioux tribe had found him, a frightened trembling child, and taken him in as his own. Forced by circumstance to accept the Dakota life as a youngster, when Jacob grew to manhood, Chief Gall offered him a choice: to return to the people of his birth and make a place for himself in white society, or to remain with the Dakota and prove himself as a warrior. The choice had been easy. The Dakota were the only family he knew, the only people he trusted. Until he'd found the crazy white woman, he'd almost forgotten the physical differences between himself and his adopted family.

Shaking off the troubling thoughts, Jacob slammed his fist into the rug and growled, "I am Dakota!"

"Have I not pleased you?" a small voice whispered at his side.

"Yes, Spotted Father, you have pleased me well. Now silence your tongue if you do not wish to anger me." Half expecting her to make some kind of reply, Redfoot laughed at his own folly, then turned his back to her.

Although she'd been widowed only a few short weeks, already this berry-skinned woman was easing the pressure on many a warrior's loins, giving of herself, but never asking for anything in return. The complete opposite of the golden-haired woman he'd pulled from the river. How did the white men manage if all their women were like this "gift" he'd found along the frozen banks of the Missouri? *Why* had he bothered to save her from the icy grave?

But he knew, of course. It wasn't just that cloud of golden red hair floating among the chunks of ice that beckoned him, nor was it her white-skinned beauty. Redfoot would have pulled a worthless Crow warrior out of those icy waters—even if only to kill him later in hand-to-hand combat. That way, it would be a fair death, an honorable end to an otherwise useless life.

Angered as he thought of the Dakota's most hated enemy, the Crow, Redfoot allowed his mind to drift back to the woman, to her glorious multicolored hair. Red, gold, and yellow streaked her curls, as if the Great Spirit himself had dipped his fingers into a fiery sunset, an early morning's dawn, and a starlit night, then passed them through the silken strands of her hair. His breath caught as he thought of the locks so like the stars, the color of which reminded him of the woman he'd once called Mother.

His throat tightened. Redfoot swallowed hard and rolled onto his side. He'd been expecting this; yet still, memories of another time, another heritage, shook him, rolling his gut into a tight ball. How would he manage when the Dakota's plans for him finally reached a climax and he returned to the world of the whites? Would memories of this past life, of the gentle yellow-haired woman of long ago, cloud his judgment, jeopardize those he now called family? He wouldn't, *couldn't*, let such thoughts interfere with his mission. He would have to find a way to harden his mind and heart to the past and to the woman whose presence seemed to draw this forgotten part of him to the surface.

Redfoot closed his eyes and worked at forcing sleep, but still his mind refused to rest. Still he saw those golden curls bouncing down the woman's naked back, felt his fingers swim through waves of hair the color of maize at sunset, and he recalled the sweet scent of lilacs that seemed to drift up from her soft skin. Something about her—was it those defiant brown eyes coupled with the stubborn set of her chin even as it trembled with fear, or perhaps the way her lithe body twisted and writhed beneath him, or all of those things? Whatever the cause, sudden flames licked at the depths of loins he'd thought were sated.

Groaning his newest frustration into the buffalo robe, Redfoot knew he must make a decision. The crazy woman could prove to be a costly, if not deadly, distraction. But she was his gift, his responsibility. What was he to do with her? He considered offering her to one of the other warriors, but then he recalled the surprise and innocence in her eyes when he caught her gawking at him as he dressed. This one remained a maiden. Who but himself would have any consideration for her white flesh? None, came the answer. The others would tear and ravage the crazy woman's tender body with no thought to her discomfort or pleasure. What to do?

After a few hours of restless sleep, he awakened well before dawn, his decision made. The Hunkpapa, along with the six other council fires in the Dakota nation, were finally ready to send him back to his own kind on a mission that could bring great rewards—or an end—to the Dakota nation. This gift, this sharp-tongued woman, was an amusement he could not take the time to enjoy, much less groom in the way of the Dakota.

Redfoot dressed quickly, knowing he must be rid of her while the sun still slept. If the dawn's light touched his features and the woman was still his captive, he would have to kill her to ensure his identity would remain secret. Working even faster, he helped himself to a few articles of Spotted Feather's clothing, then hurried out into the night and back toward his own tipi.

As he approached the entrance, he made a decision as to which direction to ride. He'd been very close to the town of Bismarck when he found her. His task that morning had been to study the perimeters of the fort, to establish meeting sites for himself and the first in a series of messengers who would take information back to the Hunkpapa camp. But he'd wandered too far north, much too close to the town and its citizens. Again doubts plagued him. Had he been drawn to Bismarck by some forgotten link to the past or had he simply strayed off course?

Redfoot forced his thoughts to yesterday, to the boat and its occupants just before it lunged out of control and began tossing its cargo into the icy waters of the Missouri. All had been dressed in the clothing of farmers and townsfolk. None wore the uniform of the Long Knives. Armed with this logic, he decided the woman belonged to the town and not to the soldiers. He could safely leave her near the fort, and one of the general's eager soldiers could escort her back to Bismarck. Redfoot could not take a chance of approaching the town again. Satisfied with the new plan, he paused as he reached his tipi, then lowered his head to duck inside.

Coiled in the corner behind the entrance flap of the tipi, Dominique tensed in anticipation as she heard footfalls growing louder and closer. When a large figure stepped past her, she leapt from her hiding spot and sprang onto his back.

"Ayeee!" Redfoot cried as he spun in a circle, raising his arms and grasping at her loose curls.

Dominique clawed at the front of his buckskin shirt, but her fingernails glanced off the rows of porcupine quills sewn there. Panic drove her to wrap her arms around his neck and try to squeeze the life from his body. But she was too weak to do anything but hang on.

Redfoot caught her wrist and jerked her off his back. He held her for a moment, then flipped her to the ground as if she were nothing more than an annoying insect.

"Are you really so brave?" He laughed. "Did my little gift plan to use me to make coup? Perhaps you thought to to take my scalp and present it to Chief Gall in the warriors' lodge as well?"

Dominique squinted up at him in the near darkness, then squeezed her aching eyes shut and rubbed at her temples. "I—I thought you were a bear or a cougar or a m-monster. I thought I— I *can't* think," she cried. "What's wrong with me?"

Redfoot's brow bunched as he leaned down and tilted her chin toward the faint glow from the dying fire. He could barely see the woman's big brown eyes, but what he found in them startled him. They were swimming in rivers of fog and insanity, drifting in all directions with no set course. Her head wobbled then, and Redfoot caught her before she tumbled sideways into the fire.

Jerking her to her feet, he tried to reassure her. "I think I have given you too much medicine, crazy one, but you should be well again soon. Can you dress yourself?"

All night long, her manner and emotions had been changing at will. For some reason, his words brought forth the giggling schoolgirl. Dominique chuckled and stuck out her hand. "Of course I can get dressed by myself, you dolt. My gown, if you please."

"You have done *nothing* to please me since I set these weary eyes on you," he muttered as he collected the clothing he'd brought. "Now dress yourself. We must hurry."

Dominique reached for the clothing, then recoiled when her fingers touched buckskin instead of silk. "That's not my dress," she pouted.

Jacob thrust the garments into her arms, his voice rising with his temper. "That mountain of clothes you almost drowned in has been shared by the women in our camp. I am sure they thank you. *Now dress!*"

When she didn't move immediately, Redfoot lost all patience. He tore the buffalo robe and blanket from her shoulders, then slid the buckskin dress over her head before she could protest. He tugged at the garment, noticing it was too narrow for her curved hips and rounded bottom. Then she slumped against him and began to weave. With a final jerk, he managed to get the buckskin down past her knees. Straightening, he caught her by the waist and pulled her close to him. Her body was limp and unresponsive. Had she passed out?

"Crazy one?" he whispered. "Will you be sick?"

But her only answer was a feeble moan.

Gripping the back of her neck, he tilted her head toward the faint light, and again he gazed into her eyes. They were shrouded and glazed. Her thick auburn lashes skimmed the crests of her cheeks, bobbing open and closed like gentle summer waves teasing the shoreline of the Missouri. The crazy one languished in a dream state, the medicine still heavy in her brain.

Redfoot looked around for a safe place to prop her up while he finished dressing her, but the woman's lovely features and sudden lusty chuckle drew his gaze once again. Her mouth opened, her upper lip curling at the corner, her full bottom lip, just made for pouting, jutting out to its most tantalizing and appealing pose. Then she gasped a quick breath and sighed breathlessly from deep in her throat.

A fiery whip of desire uncoiled in Redfoot's gut and lashed at his senses. Stung by an urge more powerful than reason, he ignored all logic and took that provocative mouth with his own. *Soft*, he discovered where he'd expected rigid denial. *Lush*, he realized, surprised to find the white woman's lips riper, fuller, and more intoxicating than those of Spotted Feather. Expecting to be rebuffed, Redfoot plunged ahead, indulging his curiosity, dangerously igniting an inner passion he might not have the strength to suppress. Still she remained compliant. Still she moaned, the sound deep and throaty as she accepted his kisses.

Redfoot's control began to unravel then, and he knew that to indulge himself with this woman would be to condemn her to death. Dawn was just on the dark side of rising. He had to let her go—after one more taste.

Startled into as lucid a state as she was capable of, Dominique struggled to understand what was happening to her. Her mouth, her body, all seemed to be on fire. New, wonderful, frightening sensations throbbed inside her, coaxing foreign feelings from everywhere at once. Kissing, she realized. A man was kissing her. Who? Why? A thousand stars exploded in her head. A whirlwind gathered a field of dandelions, then scattered them in her brain. Her mind was cotton. And the man continued to kiss her.

Dominique's eyes flew open as she jerked out of his arms. Suddenly indignant, she slapped his face with as much strength as she could find. "Unhand me, y-you . . . cad! You don't know who you're dealing with. You are— Who are you?"

Redfoot's deep laughter was prompted as much by relief as by amusement. He gathered the other articles of clothing as a sense of urgency overcame his desire; then he approached the woman. She was weaving again. He had wasted too much time trying to reason with her. They must leave now if she was to arrive at the fort before daylight. Redfoot gathered her in his arms and tossed her over his shoulder like a sack of grain. Then he pulled a pair of knee-high moccasins onto her feet and adjusted a buffalo robe across her shoulders.

When she groaned as if to protest, Redfoot slapped her bottom in warning and made his way through the opening in the tipi. The bite of the frigid morning air nipped at his face, cooling his heated body, and he stopped long enough to inhale its crispness. Then he continued on his way, amused by the feeble pounding of her fists against his back. When he reached a string of horses, he loosened his grip and leaned forward. Dominique slid off his shoulder and landed in a thin patch of snow at his feet, a tangle of arms and legs.

Dominique's hands sank into the slush, and the cold air revived her enough to realize she was in danger. She swallowed hard and said, ''What are you going to do with me? Who are you?''

Redfoot ignored her as he separated his horse from the rest of the mounts and tied a rope around its muzzle. When he grabbed a fistful of the stallion's mane and launched himself onto the animal's back, the woman's demands grew louder.

''Well?'' she said, her tongue thick and unwieldy. Dominique glared up at the Indian's shadowy figure, but her eyes crossed as she strained to make out his features. She shook her head, then warned, ''Either you tell me what's going on here, or I shall have to—''

With a sigh, Redfoot reached down and gripped the back of the buckskin dress. Leaning farther away from the animal's neck, he gave a mighty tug, then draped her flailing body across the horse's withers as if she were his kill for the day.

When he gave the rope hackamore a sharp tug, the stallion wheeled around to the right, then reared before it took off at a dead gallop. As he'd hoped, the combination of surprise and speed stilled the fiery woman's tongue and ended her struggles as she clung to the horse with a death grip.

Knowing sunrise was near, Redfoot urged the horse on, never slowing the speed as they crashed through a thick stand of trees, and not even as he neared their final destination. When the clearing between the trees and Fort Lincoln was finally in sight half an hour later, Redfoot reined the stallion to an abrupt halt and slid off the animal's rump in the same movement.

Too breathless and disoriented to move or speak, Dominique inclined her head and followed the Sioux's silhouette with wide round eyes. He crept to the edge of the meadow and surveyed the countryside, then returned to the heaving animal and reached for his sputtering gift.

''Ow!'' she complained as he dragged her off the horse's back. ''You hurt me. I think my ribs are broken!''

"Be still," he muttered under his breath. "I will break a lot more than your ribs if you don't quiet yourself—*now*!"

Dominique opened her mouth to speak, but instinct and a growing sense of danger snapped it shut as her mind finally began to clear.

"That," he whispered, "is the first clever thing you have done. If I were as clever, I would have left you in the river to sink or swim and never thought of you again."

Dominique stepped toward him, hoping to get a glimpse of the mysterious savage, but he backed deeper into the shadows. She stamped an unsteady foot and said, "Why did you save me, then? Why *didn't* you just leave me in the river?"

"Because, crazy woman"—he grinned, unsure of the answer himself—"because . . . you have a spirit in you that is not ready to die, because I do not wish to be the cause of that spirit leaving your body."

Taken aback, Dominique felt off-balance, flattered, yet manipulated somehow. She averted her gaze, then noticed the clearing in the pale gray dawn. "Where are we? What are you going to do with me now?"

"There is a fort with many soldiers not far from here. I am sure your flapping tongue will make them return you to Bismarck."

Struggling to bring her eyes into focus, she peered out through the trees. "Fort Lincoln?"

"Yes, crazy one. Fort Abraham Lincoln. Do you think you can hold your tongue long enough for me to take you to its gates?"

"I—" Dominique looked to the Sioux, then back to the clearing. "I had no idea we were so close to the fort. We were just outside of town when I fell out of the boat."

Eager to convince her he and the Hunkpapa had been nowhere near Bismarck, he said, "You rode with the waters of the river for many miles. You are lucky your soul did not soar to the heavens during that long ride."

Watching as she drunkenly pondered this possibility,

anxious to be free of his burden while lingering shadows of night still hid his features—and his purpose—he said, "We must go now."

But Dominique snapped to attention and sidestepped him. "I think you've done more than enough," she said, suddenly delighted to know she was so close to her destination. "I can make my way across a little old field without your help. I suppose I ought to thank you for pulling me out of the river. Thank you for your gallantry, Mr.— I, ah, Mr.—"

"Redfoot," he supplied, his expression grim. "You cannot go to the fort alone. In this dress, a soldier will think you are a squaw. You will have—"

"Don't be ridiculous," she scolded, her mind clawing its way through the final mists to sanity. She flipped her long golden-red curls down across her shoulders and laughed. "With this hair? Who's going to think I'm an Indian?"

Relief dissolving any fears Dominique still harbored about the savage, she pressed her fingertips against one of the long thick braids he wore pulled forward and draped across his chest. "Thank you for saving my life, Mr. Redfoot. I'll be going now."

"You are welcome, crazy one." He sighed; then he drew back his fist and drove it into her chin.

Maybe he'd hit her too hard. Redfoot grew alarmed as the first slivers of sunlight snaked across the thin blanket of snow covering the meadow, and still the woman remained curled against the base of a leafless sapling. He'd darted across the clearing with her draped over his shoulder the second the sentry disappeared around the corner of the fort. After dropping her as close to the gates as he dared get, he returned to the cover of the trees. She'd had plenty of time to awaken.

Redfoot measured his chances—against the light of dawn, against the soldiers if he should return to check on the woman and be discovered. She wasn't worth the risk, he reminded himself. And yet something deep inside wouldn't let him just leave her there.

The crazy woman stirred, then sat up, relieving him of the dilemma. Still unable to leave her alone and vulnerable, he waited until the soldier reappeared and discovered the dazed woman stumbling about in the snow.

Redfoot watched a moment, his clear sapphire-blue eyes twinkling with mirth, as the Long Knife reached out to steady the woman. Then he laughed as she jerked her arm from the soldier's grasp and began flapping her tongue at him.

"Take this gift to your chief, the Long Hair," he whispered into the wind. "May she visit her craziness on him. May she also give him something to think of besides ways to rob the Dakota of what is theirs."

Then he wove his way through the trees to his horse and sped back to the Hunkpapa's temporary home. After caring for the stallion, Redfoot strode into a camp already bustling with early morning activities.

"Ah, so you return," called an old squaw as she glanced up from the buffalo skin she kneaded with dry cracked hands. "The Father looks for you in the warriors' lodge."

With a nod of thanks, he continued on toward the lodge in the center of the camp. As he passed by a circle of women heating stones with which to cook the morning meal, Spotted Feather fell in step with him.

She carried a parfleche filled with buffalo chips under one arm and a pouch swollen with water under the other. Small fires of jealousy lit her slanted obsidian eyes as she looked up at him and said, "What called you to the hills so early this morning?"

"A mission that is no business of yours, woman." Although he instantly regretted snapping at her, Redfoot, a true Dakota in his heart, didn't apologize. Instead, he relieved her of her burden. "Go and fetch me something to eat. I have the hunger of a grizzly." Then he turned, carrying the supplies he had taken from Spotted Feather, and stepped into the warriors' lodge.

"Ah, Jacob Redfoot." Chief Gall regarded his adopted

son and smiled. "We have been speaking of you—and of your golden-haired treasure. I see she leaves marks of her great passion for you on your flesh."

"Hah!" Redfoot rubbed at the scratches on his neck, then opened the buffalo-hide container and removed several dried chips. He tossed them into the fire as he eased into position at the side of the man everyone called Father. "This treasure was a curse, Father. I have returned her to her people at the fort."

"You have shown yourself to the Long Knives?" Sitting Bull, a shaman revered by all people of the Dakota nation, dropped the pipe he was carving and narrowed his close-set eyes. "You have risked our mission?"

"I was not seen by the woman or the Long Knives," Redfoot assured them all. "My identity is safe. I am known to no one but the Dakota."

The shaman's broad features sagged into a scowl, but he picked up his pipe and resumed carving.

The doubts of another warrior, one of the chief's natural sons, were not so easily assuaged. "So says he, Father! Does not the wolf raised by sheep turn on them when he is grown? Does he not gorge on the bones of those who sought only to protect him?"

"Silence!" Gall glanced around the room, daring any to side with the jealous son of his loins. He knew there would be doubts about this plan. He understood the temptations he would be placing at his white son's feet; yet instinct told him to continue on the course he'd set for Redfoot so many winters past. When his hunting party first found the boy, orphaned and alone, Gall had sensed that Jacob would fit well with the Hunkpapa, knew through his uncanny ability to glimpse the future that someday the loyalty of the white youngster would be of great benefit to the entire Dakota nation.

Now the time had come; now it was Jacob's turn to give back to the Dakota what they had offered to him—his very life. Gall turned to his son—to the tribe's hope for the future—and said, "What if this woman should recognize you when you become a soldier at the fort?"

"I am a shadow in the dawn to her."

"Even shadows have their identity, my son. Can you not tell the silhouette of a deer from that of a horse, a soldier from a warrior?"

Jacob frowned, suddenly doubting his judgment. "The crazy woman is from Bismarck." Then he thought back to the scene in the meadow when the soldier offered assistance to the woman. He laughed and added, "The Long Knives will take her back to her home before I go to the fort. Her tongue is a torment, even to them."

Redfoot regarded his father as the older man considered the possibilities, and his heart swelled with pride. Clad in his ceremonial dress for this, the final council before their plans were set in motion, Gall was a stunning figure to behold. His six-foot frame was draped in a shiny buffalo robe that reached the ground when he stood, and his head was adorned with a long headdress of eagle feathers that skimmed along the hem of his robe. The crown of this headpiece was finished with strips of prime mink, and the legs and tail of the animal hung down on either side of his proud, kind face.

Gall's features—softer, less angular than those of the others at the council—relaxed as he shrugged. "Then we shall hope it is so, and the woman can be forgotten. Now you must prepare to join the soldier we have borrowed from his people."

All the warriors shared a hearty laugh. Then Redfoot announced, "I am ready, Father."

Through a broad smile, Gall answered, "Then let us begin. I fear if you do not join this poor woman of a soldier soon, his timid heart may give out on him."

Little Wound, nephew of Sitting Bull, chuckled and said, "The Long Knife cries in his sleep! He fears that we plan to roast him over a large fire at dawn and feed him to our dogs."

Again the warriors laughed; then the small circle broke

up, and the men began to move about, this one opening the flap and retrieving the supplies the women had left outside for them, that one stripping Redfoot's clothing from his body, and yet another sharpening the blade of his knife on a stone.

Redfoot filled his belly with buffalo pemmican as the other warriors draped him in the clothing of an unfortunate homesteader who now rested beneath the soil he'd hoped to farm one day. When they'd finished dressing him, right down to a pair of too tight boots, Chief Gall approached him. In his hand he carried the newly sharpened knife.

Holding the weapon between their bodies, he addressed his son. "The Great Spirit, Wakan Tanka, shall watch over you. Little Wound will leave now and return to Red Cloud's camp in the Black Hills. He will inform the chief of our plans, and Red Cloud will send his thoughts to help you in your mission."

Chief Gall paused as Little Wound took his leave; then Sitting Bull joined him. The great shaman pulled a little medicine bag made of deer hide from beneath his breastplate of bear claws.

"This medicine," he announced, taking a small portion from the bag, "is made of eagle heart and brain mixed with dried aster flowers. It will protect you and bring you good luck." He rubbed some of this on Redfoot's chest and offered him the rest. "You must chew this, Jacob Stoltz, and you will have good medicine until you return to our camp as Jacob Redfoot again."

Jacob took the mixture into his mouth then slid the pouch and its leather string over his head. Tucking it well inside his shirt, he turned and faced his adoptive father.

"From this moment," Gall went on, "you are called by the name of your birth. My son Jacob Redfoot is no more. Now you are Jacob Stoltz." He circled behind him and sliced off his braids in two quick motions. "You are a white man and we spit on you."

Then the warriors set upon him. They spat on his flesh, punched at his body, and tore at his clothing until he became dizzy and his mind swam in darkness. When he regained consciousness, Jacob Stoltz was lying in the dirt at the back of the prisoners' tipi.

"Mister? Hey, you all right, mister?"

Jacob lifted a bruised and puffy eyelid and tried to focus on the man. "I—I do not know."

"Boy, those bloodthirsty Injuns really pounded the bejesus outta you. Maybe some of this water will help."

Jacob watched as the man made his way across the floor with the pouch, but he kept his swollen mouth closed. Instead of speaking, he moaned his gratitude as the stranger soaked a piece of material torn from his shirt and bathed his battered features with it.

"These danged Sioux are just plain loco, there ain't another word for it. They oughta do themselves and us a favor and go back to the reservation where they belong before we have to waste the lead and shoot em all!"

Jacob's fists tightened, but he kept his silence.

"Can you talk, fella? What's your name?"

Through barely parted lips, he whispered, "Jacob."

"Well, despite the circumstances, it's nice to meet you, Jacob. I'm Lieutenant Barney Woodhouse, Seventh Cavalry, at your service."

Jacob tried to smile at the man, but his lip cracked and a trickle of blood crept into the corner of his mouth.

"That's all right, Jacob. Don't try to talk yet. If you can, just listen and think. I've been here two days now—wouldn't be here at all if I hadn't been so stinking randy that I went across the river and got all drunked up at a hog ranch. These damn Sioux found me passed out in the back of a wagon."

"Y-you . . ." Jacob moaned, eager to get on with his lessons in the ways of the white man, "you were captured while stealing pigs?"

"No," Barney laughed. "Guess you ain't from around here."

Jacob shook his head slowly, carefully. "Black Hills."

"Oh," the soldier commented, wondering if this man

had been one of the gold-crazed prospectors who'd driven the Sioux from their reservations. "Anyways"—he shrugged—"a hog ranch in these parts is a bawdy house. You know—women and whiskey. I went over to the Dew Drop Inn—get it? Do drop in! Anyways, I guess I stayed a little longer than I should have." The soldier slapped his hands against his thighs. "General Custer's gonna skin me alive when he finds out what happened—that is, if these Injuns don't get to me first."

General Custer? The Long Hair! "I have heard this Custer's name spoken."

"Hell, who hasn't? I'm proud to say he's my commanding officer, and I answer to him personally—at least, I did."

Jacob smiled as he thought of how well Little Wound and Spotted Horse had chosen their random target. If he could strike up a friendship with this man, then convince him he'd saved his life as well, the Dakota would know the Long Knives' plans sooner than they had hoped.

This time suppressing the urge to grin, Jacob moved forward with his plan. "Have you thought of a way to escape?" he rasped through a groan. "We must find a way to escape."

"Hey, take it easy, mister. From here on out, you just nod yes or no. I'll do the talking."

Which was exactly what Jacob and the Hunkpapa had counted on. By the end of his ten-day confinement with the Long Knife, his superficial wounds would have healed and he would have refreshed his knowledge of the white man's language and learned the phrases used by soldiers at the fort. By then, if all went according to plan, Jacob would blend into life in the army like any other recruit.

In just over a week, Jacob Stoltz would be ready to take his place in a world he hadn't seen since his eleventh winter.

Chapter Three

DOMINIQUE WRENCHED HER ARM FREE OF THE SOLDIER'S grip, and even though she realized her anger was directed at the Sioux, still she was somehow unable to stop making the young soldier pay for her grievances. "I'm not injured or crippled, sir," she snapped. "I have been through a terrible experience indeed, but I'm just cold and desperate to get out of these stinking buckskins. Please take me to my uncle Armstrong at once, if you please."

"Uh, yes, ma'am," the sentry said briskly. "I—ah, I'd be glad to, I guess." Still shocked at having found a disheveled woman, *any* woman, floundering about in the frozen dawn as he completed his rounds, he approached her with a cautious inquiry. "Is your uncle with the infantry or the cavalry?"

"I don't know." Dominique rubbed her fingers across her swollen chin, then pressed them to her aching temples and groaned. "I think he's in charge of the whole blasted fort."

"In charge of the fort, ma'am?" He chuckled before asking, "Why don't you give me his full name? If he's enlisted here, I'm sure I can find him for you."

"Of course he's here! I may have lost my favorite traveling dress and the better part of the last two days, but I have not lost my mind." Or had she? She suddenly had to wonder as more wildly colored lights exploded in her head. With a sigh, she tried to explain. "Uncle Armstrong is a very important officer. Now, please, will you—"

"An officer, ma'am?"

"Yes, he graduated from West Point. His name is George Armstrong Custer."

"General . . . Custer? Brevet Major General Custer, ma'am?" the soldier gasped, clutching at his chest.

"Yes, I suppose that's what he could be called. Most of our friends just call him the General." She shivered as the young man struggled to get over his shock, then began stamping her numb feet. "Please take me to him before I freeze to death!"

"Yes, ma'am, right away, ma'am!" The officer snapped to attention, suddenly awed by his find. "You must be the gal General Custer has been so worried about. He's had his troops out looking for your body since yesterday."

"My body?" She sniffed.

"Well, that is, we assumed you'd drowned. He's going to be mighty glad to see you're alive." In his excitement, the soldier saluted her, then whirled on his heel and started for the gate.

Afraid he would leave her alone, exhausted and still fighting off the effects of the medicine, Dominique forgot her manners and called after him, "Wait for me, you nincompoop!" Then she lifted the fringes of her dress out of the slush and stomped after him. "You're not leaving me behind! Being the hostage of a band of savages once is bloody enough adventure for me."

Lieutenant Macky turned back, his thin features florid, his expression mortified. Again he saluted her, then stammered, "S-sorry ma'am, I meant—that is, I didn't forget you. I was just going after a buggy." He reached out to take her arm, but she waved him away.

"I can walk, Private."

"That's lieutenant, ma'am." He grinned, looking sheepish and uncertain. "I only wanted to help you."

"Oh, of course." She sighed. Ashamed of her waspish tongue, Dominique lowered her voice and assumed a more ladylike demeanor. "I know you're only trying to help. I'm afraid I'm a little on edge and not feeling too well after all I've been through. I also have a bruised chin and ribs that feel as if they're on fire. I'm sorry if I offended you, Private."

This time Lieutenant Macky didn't bother to correct her. He offered his arm again. "Please, then, allow me to escort you to your uncle."

But just as she was about to accept, Dominique had the strangest sensation she was being watched. She snapped her head around to the north and stared at the distant stand of juniper trees. Although she couldn't see them, she could feel the Sioux's eyes on her, watching, laughing.

Dominique lifted her chin and her buckskin skirt and sashayed on past the lieutenant. "I appreciate the offer, sir, but I'm feeling much better now. Which way to the general's quarters?"

The buggy turned out to be a mule-drawn cart with only two wheels and a hard wooden seat. It bounced and lurched down the mile-long hill separating the infantry garrison from the cavalry post situated in the valley below. By the time Dominique stood before the large wood-frame home, her backside was nearly as sore as her ribs. She quickly forgot her discomfort as she approached the front porch. A grand white stairway, built in the shape of a pyramid with the top removed, beckoned.

Dominique sighed as her moccasin touched down on the first tread. "Why, this is just like walking up one side of a fancy wedding cake! Is the rest of the house as grand, sir?"

"Oh, I wouldn't know, ma'am," he said as he knocked on the glass-framed door. "I've only been inside the parlor, but it's real nice. Real nice."

The wide door swung open to reveal a large colored woman. The maid stared through skeptical black eyes, then wrinkled her nose. In a voice that twanged like a southern guitar, she said, "What business y'all got here?"

"Uh, the lady, she says she's, uh—"

"Tell General Custer his niece, Dominique DuBois, is alive and well." Taking a step toward the threshold, she added, "Be *sure* to tell him I am standing here freezing in these filthy buckskins, too!"

Her manner, added to the family resemblance and name, startled the servant to action. She curtsied and backed down the hallway, "Yes, ma'am. Right away, ma'am. Come on in."

Dominique turned to her escort and managed a wan smile. "Thank you for seeing me to my uncle's home. That will be all, Private."

"Ah, yes, Miss Custer, ah, yes," he stammered as he slowly made his way back down the stairs. "Please be sure to remember me to the general—that's *Lieutenant* Macky. I'd appreciate it."

"Yes, of course. And my name is the same as my father's—DuBois." Dominique waved to the lieutenant, then spun around and waltzed through the front door. As she looked around the parlor, she heard approaching footsteps. The staircase creaked; then Elizabeth Bacon Custer burst through the arched entrance to the room.

"Oh, my stars!" she cried, her small hands cupping her girlish features. "It's true! You really are alive and well!"

"Aunt Libbie, am I glad to see you!" The women closed the short distance separating them and threw themselves into each other's arms.

"Oh, you poor thing!" Libbie went on, her relief sending a flood of tears to her throat. "Autie is going to be so happy to see you! I've sent one of the servants after him." Libbie stepped back and scrutinized her husband's niece. She pulled her fingers through Dominique's tangle of frizzy curls and cried, "How did you ever survive a dunking in that treacherous river? Where have you been? And *where* did you get those awful clothes?"

"It's a long incredible story," Dominique said with a

sigh, "but one that I cannot begin to tell until I'm clean and warm again."

"Of course, dear!" Libbie turned toward the kitchen. "Mary?" she called out. "You and some of the help draw a hot tub for my niece. Scoot along now and be quick about it. The poor girl's near to freezing!"

Two black girls scrambled out of the kitchen carrying large copper kettles, and the third, Mary, motioned for Dominique to follow her up the gracefully curved stairway.

But Dominique hesitated a moment and turned back to her aunt. "My goodness, are all these servants yours?"

Libbie grinned, enormously proud of her husband's insistence on keeping her in style, no matter what other hardships she might have to bear. "Yes, dear. Mary and her sisters go just about everywhere with the general and me. I don't know what we'd do without them."

Dominique raised her brows, nodding slowly as she made a fast perusal of the elegant home. Perhaps, she thought, her sparkling smile back in full bloom, this little trip would turn out to be the adventure she'd dreamed it would be.

Later, after a deliciously hot bath scented with her favorite perfume, lilac, Dominique sat huddled in front of a roaring fire in the luxurious living room of her uncle's home. Her hair had been washed, dried, and rolled into an attractive coil pinned to the back of her head. She was dressed in one of Libbie's warm flannel nightgowns and a voluminous robe.

Now, snuggled beneath two quilts made by the officers' wives, she tested a bit of barley soup from a steaming bowl. "Umm, that's wonderful. Thanks."

Libbie, her brow still creased with worry, said, "I wish we had some chicken to put in it, but we're at the end of our winter supplies." Dismissing the cook and self-appointed mistress of the servants, Libbie waved into the air, "That will be all, Mary. Tell your sisters I appreciate their efforts in warming my niece."

"Yes'm." The round woman began backing out of the room, muttering, "If y'all be needin' anything else, just you holler."

"We will." Libbie waited until the cook was out of sight before she turned to her niece, her blue-gray eyes bright with fear. "Mary says you're covered with welts and bruises. What's happened to you, Nikki? Has someone—your rescuers, perhaps . . . did they . . . violate you in any way?"

Dominique swallowed another mouthful of broth, then patted her mouth with Libbie's lace-trimmed napkin and shook her head. "No one hurt me in that way, but as for the rest, I really don't know what happened after the boat turned over. One minute I was swirling downstream in that horrid freezing water"—she paused and shuddered at the memory—"and the next thing I knew, I was lying on a buffalo skin in a tipi."

"A tipi? My Lord, you were captured by Indians?"

Dominique nodded as she took another spoonful of soup.

"Oh, my God," Libbie groaned, knowing full well how the inhabitants of the East Coast looked on the West and its abundance of "savages." "Your father's going to have apoplexy when he hears about this!"

Dominique's almond-shaped eyes flew open. "You haven't wired Papa and told him I was missing!"

"No, no, but just the same—" Libbie shook her head and took her niece's hand in hers. "I just know Jacques will never speak to me again. After all, I'm the one who begged and needled him to let you come out west to keep me company. I'm the one who's going to incur his wrath for bringing you out to the Dakota Territory before the spring thaw was fully upon us."

Even though Dominique was thoroughly warmed, guilt chilled an icy path up her spine as she listened to her aunt. It was she, not Libbie, who'd done the begging and pleading, she who'd enlisted the aid of everyone from the general's youngest sister, Margaret, to casual acquaintances in her quest to persuade her father to let her make the trip. It had sounded so exciting at the time—so full of adventure! The stuff from which the little forbidden books were made.

Dominique hung her head and quietly murmured, "Please don't blame yourself. I'm to blame for everything bad that happens to me. If I just wasn't so strong-willed and determined to get my way, these things wouldn't happen. Papa is right—not even a fine lady like you can teach me how to behave. You ought to just put me on a train and—"

"No more of that, Nikki. I've had enough of the general's nephews and nieces join us for your father to know he was right when he agreed to let you visit us. What I blame myself for is not waiting another month before sending for you." Libbie began to wring her hands as she thought of the near-disaster. "One never knows about that horrid, treacherous river when crossing from Bismarck to Fort Lincoln, but I was afraid if I waited any longer, the general's newest campaign would take us away before you could get here. I am sorry for the—"

A great commotion in the hallway cut off her words. Both women turned toward the arched entrance of the parlor as male voices grew louder. Then George Armstrong Custer burst into the room.

His very presence commanded the attention of all wherever he strode, transformed the atmosphere around him into awe. He wore troop boots reaching up to his knees and buckskin breeches with fringed sides. His shirt, rumpled and slightly askew, was dark blue and set off by a long red necktie. After removing the large felt hat he wore bent low over his forehead to protect his delicate skin from the sun, he shook his head, the thick red-gold curls brushing the tops of his shoulders.

"Dominique," he said in a tight voice. "Then it *is* you."

"Hello, Uncle Armstrong." Dominique's dark brown eyes flashed with good humor and began to sparkle as her playful nature slowly returned. "Papa sends his greetings."

Sharing a nervous chuckle with the ladies, Custer pulled a three-legged footstool up beside Dominique's rocking chair. "And now, finally, I can send my greetings to him and news of your safe arrival. For a time there . . ." He left the sentence unfinished and shook his head.

"Autie," Libbie cut in softly. "The poor dear was captured by Indians before being found by the infantry."

"Oh?" Custer cocked a thick cinnamon-colored eyebrow and studied her more closely. "How did you manage to escape from them, Nikki? You look to be in good health."

"I—I didn't really escape," she said, trying to sort through all the strange images her time of captivity brought to mind. "Everything is so fuzzy, I really only remember waking up in a tipi, then riding off this morning with a great big Indian. He took me to the woods outside the fort"—she caressed the bruise on her chin, scowling as she remembered the unexpected blow—"and one of your guards found me."

"You said *he*," Custer prodded, his clear blue eyes suspicious and calculating. "Did this Indian have a name? Did he mention the name of his tribe? Was it Crow or Mandan?"

"His name was Redfoot, and he said the name of his tribe meant Sioux in English."

"English? He spoke to you in our language?"

Dominique nodded.

Custer hesitated, then shrugged. "Not very unusual. Some tribes, the Sioux in particular, like to have at least one warrior among them who can understand a few words of English." His elaborate mustache twitched as his gentle questioning became more of an interrogation. "In any case, I'm sure you weren't in the company of a Sioux. This Indian's grasp of the language must have been poor, and you may have misunderstood the name of his tribe. Was he alone, or were there others with him?''

''But I'm sure he said Sioux,'' she insisted, her almond-shaped eyes wide and alert. Dominique pressed her fingertips to her throbbing temples and tried to remember the other details. ''I think I peeked outside once and saw more tipis, but I—I can't be sure if they were real or if I dreamed them up.''

Custer's brow rose even higher. He pulled his hat off and lowered his voice to a more fatherly, gentle tone. ''Think back, Nikki. I know you must have been very frightened, but try to remember. I need to know every last detail of your captivity in order to bring the those savages to justice.''

''Oh, Uncle Armstrong,'' she said, her voice close to a whimper. ''It's not that I was so frightened—I was a little scared a couple of times—but I just can't seem get anything straight in my mind. The Indian made me drink some medicine, and then . . . I can't explain it. My brain seemed to leave me, and all these colors—''

''You were drugged,'' he growled, his expression stern. He tugged on the end of his mustache, wondering how best to broach the next subject. Custer glanced at his wife, thinking of eliciting her aid, then looked beyond her to the entryway as the front door opened then slammed shut.

Captain Tom Custer stamped into the room. A few years younger, a couple of inches shorter, and several ranks below his famous brother, his florid complexion was due to exertion, not allergies. ''Nikki! Thank God! Are you all right?''

Accepting his hand as he approached, Dominique brought it to her cheek. ''I'll be all right, Uncle Tom.''

Impatient to get at the truth, Custer sliced into their greeting. ''You ever hear of a Sioux called Redfoot, Tom?''

''Redfoot? Humm, no, can't say that I have. Why?''

''Nikki says he saved her from drowning, then brought her to the fort. He said he was Sioux.''

"Huh?" Tom looked from his brother to his niece, then back to Custer again. "I didn't realize there were any Sioux left in this neck of the woods."

"There aren't supposed to be." Scooting the stool closer to his niece, Custer took her small hands in his. Stroking her soft flesh with skin ravaged by a sun allergy and years of outdoor work, he softened his tone as he continued his probe.

"Let's try something else. Surely you saw the Indian before he drugged you. Can you describe him? Can you remember anything he said to help us figure out who he really was?"

Shrugging, Dominique thought back to the night, to her first memory of the Indian who called himself Redfoot. "It was awfully dark, even with the little fire he made. I never saw his face. All I can remember is his long heavy braids and . . ."

She closed her eyes and tried to recall the last twenty-four hours. Fragmented thoughts, like damp grains of sand, fell in painfully slow particles through the hourglass of her mind. The image of Redfoot's nude buttocks glistening in the shadows appeared. Then she saw his torso, the sable curls enhancing the contours of his thick chest, and suddenly for some reason, she knew exactly what it felt like to be pressed against the length that hard muscular body. She shivered, yet felt a great bud of warmth bloom in her abdomen at the same time.

Popping her lashes open, she gasped as a blush crawled up the sides of her neck. "I—I can't tell you any more than that. I didn't get a good look at him."

Custer's gaze turned narrow, thoughtful. As he leaned even closer, the tip of his large, crooked nose came within inches of her cheek as he whispered, "If this Indian has hurt you in any way, touched you anywhere he shouldn't have, you can rest assured that Tom and I will track him to the ends of the earth and see that he is punished severely."

"No, Uncle Armstrong," she insisted, even as her fingertips went to her mouth, to her swollen upper lip. "He didn't hurt me at all. If anything, he saved my life." And then, as if to shield her from the memory of how her mouth received its bruises, her mind provided a forgotten word. "Oh! I remember what he called himself—Dakota. That's it. He said Sioux was a word we might use for Dakota."

Clearly disturbed by the information, Custer jerked to his feet. "Do you have any idea in which direction the Indian traveled when he brought you to the fort?"

"North—northwest, I think. Yes, I'm sure we came in from the northwest."

"Through the trees and up to the infantry post?"

"Yes."

Swiveling toward his wife, he said, "See that Nikki is fed and rested. Tom and I are going to gather a few troops and go on a little mission."

"Oh, Autie." Libbie started to rise, but her husband's gentle hand pushed her back in her chair.

"Don't worry, sunbeam. As usual, your boy will take very good care of himself." He kissed her forehead, then gestured to his brother as he strode from the room. "Run over to Company B and pick out three good men. I'll meet you at the quartermaster's."

Then, their boot heels clicking with precision, with purpose, the Custer brothers marched out of the room.

Turning back to her niece, Libbie did what she'd done a thousand times before: She shut out the image of her beloved husband walking away from their home and into danger, and concentrated on something else. "Warm enough yet?" she inquired with a smile.

"Finally." Dominique squirmed beneath the thick blankets and uttered a delicious giggle. "I never thought I could feel this warm or this safe again. It's a good thing Papa doesn't know what's happened to me since I left home!"

"And he's not going to know—at least not from me." Libbie's small mouth grew stern. "From your father's letters, I think he's grown enough gray hairs over you and your escapades. It would be prudent of us not to add to them.''

''This one wasn't my fault. Surely the boatman could have—'' The sentence died in her throat as she remembered the start of the journey on the river. ''What happened to Hazel and the others?'' she exclaimed, jerking upright.

''Calm yourself. Your chaperon is a little shaken, but doing just fine. Her biggest fears were about you and what your father would do when he found out you were lost.''

''Was she rescued by Indians, too?''

''No, dear. She and the soldiers managed to hang on to the overturned ferry until it hit another patch of ice. The boat was actually quite close to the fort when it snagged on a fallen tree. She wasn't in the water long.''

''Thank God for that.'' Dominique settled back into the chair, considering all that had happened, then remembered her reception at the Bismarck train station. ''I have to say, I was a little surprised by the escort Uncle Armstrong sent for Hazel and me. Why, not one of those men wore a fancy uniform or blew a bugle in my honor.''

''My dear,'' Libbie said through a chuckle, ''you have a lot to learn about military life. I'm afraid that soldiers, even officers, are considered less than socially acceptable in town. The men are very concerned with our reputations; they do not wear their uniforms when escorting us ladies to or from Bismarck.''

Dominique was astounded. ''But back home Uncle Armstrong is a hero! He wears his uniform everywhere, and the people—''

''I'm aware of that, Nikki, but we're not in Michigan or New York, you know.''

Dominique groaned, her hopes and dreams of an adventurous summer in serious jeopardy again. Libbie's next words pulled a sigh from her and scattered her dreams of excitement into the atmosphere along with her breath.

''Now . . . about my plans for you. If I'm going to

finish you properly, I suppose we should get busy. I have a reputation as a stern taskmaster to uphold, you know, and I've only a couple of short months in which to do it." Libbie smiled, but her tiny mouth was pinched and businesslike as she cautioned, "I intend to turn you into a lady your papa will be proud of if it takes me all summer."

Nearly two weeks later, George Custer strolled around the barracks of Company F as the troops put the finishing touches on their decorations for the evening's dance. All of the bunks had been removed from the enormous room and the normally pale gray walls were bright with colored flags and guidons.

Both ends of the long room glowed with cheer as huge logs burned brightly in the wide fireplaces, and arms were stacked against the adjacent walls. Above these weapons, long tables laden with refreshments and imitation laurel leaves beckoned revelers with their bountiful offerings. The theme of this impromptu ball was a celebration of Saint Patrick's Day, even though the date had already passed. In accordance, paper shamrocks and sprigs of green were attached to the walls and windows. Even the cracker-box boards had been cut into shamrock shapes for use as side brackets or candle holders.

Pausing in front of a makeshift table, Custer helped himself to a piece of hard candy from a cut-glass dish.

"General Custer, sir. If I may please have a word with you, sir?"

Turning to his left, Custer regarded the tall, gaunt soldier standing at attention. "At ease, Lieutenant."

Barney Woodhouse relaxed and smoothed his scant mustache. Even though he was a full inch taller than Custer's six feet, he weighed a good thirty pounds less. His face, long of forehead and chin, seemed to confine his dark features into small, narrow space, as if it had other plans for the bare expanses of flesh between his eyebrows and hairline, and between his mouth and Adam's apple. Even his mustache, sparse and thin, seemed pushed into an area too small to cultivate anything more than a few dark hairs.

Still stroking this pencil-thin adornment, Lieutenant Woodhouse stared openly at the thick rust-colored brush drooping down along the corners of his commander's mouth and said, "Do you have a moment?"

"For you? All night," he said, polishing the brass buttons on his dress uniform with his shirtsleeve. Studying the soldier, he commented, "I must say, you're looking a great deal better than you did yesterday morning when you stumbled into the garrison. It takes more than a few rabid Sioux to bring down one of my best men! What can I do for you?"

"I want you to meet that fellow I told you about—the one who saved my life." Gesturing over his shoulder at the man standing behind him, Barney explained, "He's so damn vengeful over what them redskins done to his partner that he joined up to fight 'em. I'd like you to meet Private Jacob Stoltz, sir. He enlisted this morning. Private, this is General Custer."

Jacob stepped forward and snapped off a salute, hoping the only greeting he'd learned was correct for a man as important as the general. "A pleasure, sir."

"The pleasure is mine if I'm to believe everything Barney's told me. A good Indian fighter is worth his weight in gold around here. Welcome aboard, Private."

Jacob accepted his handshake, struggling to keep the hatred in his soul from leaping out through his eyes as he stared into the face of the Long Hair. This was the moment he'd been preparing for, the beginning of the end for this foolish leader and all like him.

A spasm ricocheted up Jacob's spine as the reality, the enormity, of his mission overcame him. He pumped the general's hand, surprised at first to find the soldier shorter than he was and smaller of stature than Dakota warriors had assumed. But Jacob quickly realized that wiry frame hid a deceptive strength as Custer's grip tightened, cutting off his circulation. A test?

Equal to the task, Jacob increased the pressure of his own grasp and smiled broadly. He stared into the ice-blue eyes, made a note of the florid, splotchy complexion of a man whose skin was at war with the sun, and admired his thick, curly hair. That red-gold mane streaked with flaming strands and his bravado were the things that separated the general from all other soldiers. Jacob smiled into Custer's sharp features. When this was over, he would bring that colorful scalp back to his village as a gift for his father.

Custer stared into the private's eyes, gauging the man's intelligence. Pleasantly surprised by the soldier's tenacious hold on his hand, for most were too intimidated to respond to his challenge, Custer released his grip. As far as he could tell, the new enlistee was not lacking in any department. "Have you been thinking of joining the cavalry for some time?"

"No," Jacob answered easily. "I searched for gold until the Sioux murdered my partner and took me captive."

Custer stroked his mustache, appraising the man's talents, wondering where a strapping man like this would best serve the army. "If what Lieutenant Woodhouse tells me is true, you reduced a whole camp of Sioux warriors to whimpering women."

As he stifled the urge to snarl, Jacob's dark blue eyes glittered and he lifted one corner of his mouth. "I did little. We were lucky."

"You are too modest. Lieutenant Woodhouse tells me he was knocked cold shortly after you two sneaked out of your tipi. You dispatched the guard, then dragged your unconscious companion to the horses and made sure he was lashed down. I'd say that took a little more than *luck*. I'd say your actions were worthy, had you been in uniform, of a medal, sir."

Unsure how to respond to such accolades from the commanding officer, Jacob merely shrugged and averted his gaze.

Impressed by the soldier's modesty, Custer said, "Nev-

ertheless, sir, we are in your debt. I'd like to meet with
you for a full report on your abduction at a more conve-
nient time, Private. For now, I wonder if you can give me
some clue as to why the Sioux kept you alive for so long.
Barney's under the impression he was kept around as dog
food, but I hardly think that is the case. What purpose
could there be in keeping a soldier and a fortune-seeker
locked up in a tipi for several days?''

Again Jacob shrugged. ''Barney said the Sioux had escaped from a reservation in the Black Hills. Maybe they
hoped white captives would keep them safe from attack.''

''Humm, possible, I suppose. Yet still . . .'' Custer kept
the rest of his thoughts to himself and turned his attention
back to Barney. ''Lieutenant, see that your new friend has
his fill of refreshments. The ladies will be joining us soon.
I'd best be at the door to greet them.'' With a nod, he
made his exit. ''Private, I still want to have that long talk—
perhaps tomorrow. Lieutenant, enjoy yourself.''

The men saluted their commanding officer as he retreated. Then Barney excused himself, leaving Jacob to
wonder if Custer had believed his story. Was the Dakota
plan too feeble to get past a shrewd soldier like the Long
Hair? On edge, he pushed out a pent-up sigh, knowing
there was little he could do but proceed as planned and
hope his purpose was not discovered.

Jacob ran his hand through his short-cropped hair as he
waited for Barney to return. He was scarcely used to the
absence of his braids, and the trip to the post barbershop
that morning had left him feeling completely stripped, naked somehow. He smoothed the sides of his hair, amazed
to find several natural waves rippling through his fingers
as the lieutenant returned with refreshments.

''Cup of coffee?''

''Ah, thank you.'' Jacob accepted the steaming liquid
and waited until his new friend began sipping his own
brew before he dared put his lips to the hot cup. Wrinkling
his nose as the first taste of bitter coffee assaulted his
tongue, Jacob withheld comment.

"The gals ought to be pouring in any minute now," Barney observed as he scanned the room. "How long's it been since you saw a woman, much less danced with one?"

The image of the crazy woman, damp and writhing beneath him, came to Jacob's mind. He could almost feel her soft lush mouth opening to him, seeking his secrets as he probed hers, wanting him, even if her response was drug-induced. Angry with his wandering mind, concerned that he hadn't thought first of Spotted Feather, he grumbled, "It has been so long since I saw a woman, I cannot remember."

"Get ready, then. Your poor tired old eyeballs are about to get a feast fit for a king. We've got some of the prettiest gals on both sides of the Missouri right here! Only trouble is, they're all either married or about to be."

"That does not concern me."

"It doesn't?" Barney thought a minute, then laughed. "I get it. You're planning to sneak down to one of the hog ranches after the dance, aren't you?"

"No, I have not considered that either. I am content to observe this party."

"Well, I'm not. I'm going to grab any female who'll let me and dance till my boots fall off!"

Jacob chuckled along with the excited officer, then followed his gaze until he abruptly clamped his mouth shut and stood at attention.

"Here they come," Barney whispered under his breath.

The double doors swung open, and several women poured into the room. Most of them were dressed in plain gowns of navy blue or pale green wool serge trimmed with black braid or lace. Several had gone to the trouble of curling their hair, leaving the back loose and flowing, but the majority had wound their tresses into tight buns at the nape of the neck. All of them carried some kind of offering—a small cake, a few sweet biscuits, or a bag of hard candy.

Observing the parade, Barney turned to Jacob. "These

ladies are mostly from Suds Row, but if the river isn't too agitated, we get a few single gals coming in from Bismarck, too.''

"Is this town, Suds Row, near Bismarck?"

"Sorry." He laughed. "I keep forgetting you're not familiar with army life. Suds Row is up near the infantry post. It's the quarters for the company laundresses. Their husbands and beaux are usually from the troops, enlisted fellows like you."

With a short nod, Jacob returned his gaze to the ladies. Most had removed their wraps, revealing several low-necked, short-sleeved dresses of gauzy material. Noticing the red arms and rounded figures, the unmistakable signs of strength and a hardy constitution, he remarked, "These laundresses are very sturdy. They will make strong wives for the soldiers."

Cocking an eyebrow that was thicker than his mustache could ever hope to be, Barney laughed. "I guess they're strong, all right, but it doesn't matter around here if they're weaker than the coffee a day before the supply wagon's due. Women are scarce, and every one's a princess. Wait till you see the officers' wives if you think these gals are a sight for sore eyes!"

Making a brief survey of the women, Jacob decided he could wait, but he said, "So far, you brag with cause."

"I told you we had the prettiest girls!" Barney slapped his leg, then rubbed his hands together as the first of the officers' wives appeared in the doorway.

Wrapped in a thick wool coat of navy blue, Elizabeth Custer stepped into the room and accepted her husband's outstretched elbow. Several enlisted men immediately approached them, removed the women's wraps, and whisked the garments off to the first sergeant's room.

"That's the general's wife," Barney informed his new friend as they observed the proceedings, "but I've never seen the beauty coming in behind her! My God, would you look at that gal!"

His instructions were hardly necessary. Jacob stood

rigid, his accelerating pulse pounding hard enough to strain the buttons on the collar of his new uniform.

It was the crazy woman! Why was she still here? She should have been returned to Bismarck days ago. Jacob's jaw twitched as he ground his teeth in frustration. He'd been a fool to bring her here, a weak-hearted, dim-witted fool to have taken her to Fort Lincoln, of all places. He should have turned her over to the other warriors and never given her plight another thought. Now he might have to find a way to silence her in a roomful of soldiers.

Jacob took a couple of backward steps, ducking out of her view, but kept his gaze firmly trained on her profile. He struggled to consider his options, but his mind was preoccupied with the vision his eyes lavished upon him. When he'd plucked her from the icy waters, he knew he'd stumbled on a rare creature, a woman whose delicate features would be cherished by all, regardless of race or background.

But she'd been unconscious then, lacking any spark of life or intelligence. By the time the crazy one had awakened in his tipi, the sun had bedded down for the night, robbing him of the full impact of her beauty. Even from across the room Jacob could see the mischief, the twinkle in her dark brown eyes. Her magnificent golden-red hair, which had been wild and strongly curled by morning's light after he dropped her at the post, was now pulled high on her head and arranged in long spirals cascading down her back. She was alive with joy, robust, and full of good health.

She was stunning.

And more dangerous than any adversary he'd ever encountered.

Jacob could almost hear her gay laughter as she greeted the other guests, treating soldier and laundress with the same good-natured enthusiasm. General Custer, he noticed, stood very close by her, protective and solicitous. His hatred of the man growing along with his fear of discovery, Jacob continued to stare, transfixed, at the crazy woman.

Suddenly she turned and faced him.

Unable to tear his gaze away, he watched, horrified, as she whispered something to the Long Hair.

General Custer looked up at Jacob. Then the pair began walked toward him.

His eyes darting from side to side, desperately searching for an avenue of escape, Jacob backed against the refreshment table. Custer and the woman were directly between him and the only exit.

Feeling trapped, like a wild animal caught in a snare, Jacob clenched his teeth and reached for the scabbard at his hip. He hesitated, fingering the handle, then made a decision as the pair continued to approach.

Jacob pulled the blade from its leather sheath.

Chapter Four

Dominique shivered.

She could *feel* those eyes, could almost reach out and touch a gaze so intense that doing so would most certainly have scalded her fingertips.

She slowly scanned the crowd. Her fresh good looks, coupled with the fact that she was General Custer's niece, had drawn many a long stare since her arrival at Fort Lincoln. Scores of otherwise intelligent and mannerly gentlemen were falling all over themselves in an effort to gain her attention. But this was different. And this was almost frightening.

Her search came to an abrupt end. Dominique's gaze was drawn into a pair of sapphire-blue eyes glittering at her from across the room. Caught, unable to turn away, she felt as controlled and completely helpless as she'd been while swirling down the raging Missouri. Again she shivered.

He was simply the most overtly masculine man she'd ever seen. Those eyes, intelligent, intense, and thoughtful, seemed to look through her, *into* her. She felt unmasked, exposed. And utterly fascinated.

Turning her head, but unable to glance away from the intriguing soldier, she whispered to her uncle, "I'd love a cup of coffee. Do you mind if I meet the rest of the officers and their wives later?"

"Of course not, Nikki. You're here to enjoy yourself." Preparing to point out the refreshment table and give her

her leave, Custer looked up and noticed his newest recruit studying them from across the barracks. "Actually, a cup of coffee would suit me, too. Besides, there's a fellow over by the table I think you should meet. You two may have a few things to discuss." Then he started toward Private Stoltz with his niece following along behind.

The first thing Dominique noticed when she was finally able to look away from the man's mesmerizing features was the glint of a knife blade turning over and over in his palm. As she and the general approached him, her expressive brown eyes widened with alarm as much as with anticipation.

"Private Stoltz," Custer said as he reached Jacob's side. "I've brought someone to meet you. But first," he suggested, his voice barely above a whisper, "please be so kind as to sheathe your knife. I understand you're new to the post and may not realize how skittish the ladies can be when weapons are displayed. You'll notice our larger arms are stowed under the tables. You're welcome to retain your knife, but please, keep it out of sight."

Tiny rivulets of perspiration gathered on Jacob's forehead and began a slow tattletale march down his brow. Was the Long Hair trying to disarm him so he could gain the advantage? Had the crazy one seen enough of his features to recognize him and alert the post commander to the deception? He glanced at the stunning woman, expecting to find an accusing finger pointing him out as an impostor, but her demeanor suggested curiosity rather than animosity. Could it be that his identity was still unknown? If it was, how long could he hope for it to remain so?

In spite of his reservations, Jacob took the sanest course and returned the knife to its leather holster. "I am sorry, sir. I did not think of the ladies."

"You will before this night's over," Custer promised with a chuckle. Turning to Dominique, he brought her forward. "This is Private Jacob Stoltz, Nikki. He's one of the soldiers who escaped from the Sioux yesterday. I thought you two might have a few things in common."

Again he laughed, then completed the introduction. "Jacob, this young lady is the daughter of my oldest sister Julia, who has since departed. Her name is Dominique DuBois. She lives with her father in Michigan."

Jacob's newfound manners deserted him. He struggled to hide a gasp of surprise, then cleared his throat and collected himself. "She is of your blood?"

Custer raised a brow and said, "An interesting way to put it—but, yes, Dominique is my niece."

Jacob quickly extended his hand, his fingers board-stiff, and dropped his voice to an unnaturally low tone. "A pleasure."

Dominique cocked her head as she acknowledged his greeting. Why did he seem so familiar? she wondered, the fine down on her arm rising with foreboding. Had they met somewhere before? Dominique made the mistake of looking up into those riveting blue eyes for the answer, and suddenly she felt naked all over again. Stripped as bare as a winter landscape. But this time she felt no chill. This time her flesh burned with the heat of an August sun.

The stranger accepted her outstretched hand, but instead of lifting it to his lips as the other soldiers had done, he began pumping it in an awkward greeting. Dominique recoiled, stunned as the sensations increased twofold. She knew that touch somehow, felt the warm tingles of another time course through her body and down to her toes. What was happening to her? Were the effects of the Sioux medicine still wreaking havoc on her mind? Or was it something else?

"Nikki?" Custer said, his brow rumpled. "Are you feeling all right?"

The general's words gave her the strength she needed to look away. "I'm sorry, Uncle Armstrong. I was just feeling a little . . . woozy, I guess, but I'm all right now."

Custer glanced from Dominique to Jacob. "I'm afraid poor Nikki here was drugged by her captors. She's been quite disoriented since her arrival at the fort. Perhaps if you two talk, you can help her sort out the experience. Would you mind, Private?''

Jacob sighed, but realizing he had no choice, he said, ''I will do what I can.''

''Good. If either of you come up with anything that may be of value in hunting these dogs down,'' Custer said as he excused himself, ''be sure to let me know. For now I had best join Libbie before she comes after me with a buggy whip. Take care of my niece, Private,'' he added, his expression stern, the warning unmistakable. Then he clicked his heels and took his leave.

An awkward silence settled over the pair as Dominique waited for Jacob to help her sort through her experience. She blinked up at him with her most appealing smile, but still he remained silent. He just stood there staring, looking this way and that, then staring again. His gaze bored into her, but it was unlike any she'd endured since her arrival at the fort. The other cavalrymen openly gawked at her, told her how beautiful she was, made her feel like a queen. This one, apparently shy to the point of embarrassment, was no less open in his appraisal, but his opinion of her wasn't so easily read. His thoughts, whatever they were, seemed dark, obscure . . . feral somehow.

Her earlier feelings of unrest returned then, growing ever greater. Dominique chanced another look in his eyes and said, ''My uncle mentioned you were also a captive of the Sioux. Was it a dreadful experience for you?''

''Yes,'' he answered in that same flat tone.

''The brute who held me punched me in the face as if I were a man!'' She lifted her chin and pointed. ''See? I still have a bruise. Were you beaten, too?''

''A little,'' he said, barely controlling the urge to turn and run.

Dominique frowned. She wasn't reaching him. He seemed to be avoiding her for some reason, as if he thought she was somehow unworthy of his attention. And then she remembered the nasty rumors concerning her captivity, the lies she'd heard bandied about the fort. Had he, too, heard that she'd been ravaged by the Indian who abducted her? Did he assume she was spoiled for decent men? Others, mostly the wives of the enlisted soldiers, snickered and pointed behind her back, made rude comments about her virtue when they thought she could not hear. Apparently their vicious gossip had already reached the ears of the Seventh Cavalry's newest recruit.

Dominique inhaled, smoothing the silk skirts of her green and white candy-stripe dress, and flipped a long golden curl across her shoulder. Then she lifted her chin in defiance and said, "Excuse me, Private. I guess the general was mistaken—you and I have absolutely nothing to talk about. Good evening."

"No—wait!" Realizing that she was more offended than enlightened, convincing himself that to secure the Long Hair's trust, he must also court the goodwill of his family, Jacob feigned a timidity that was not part of his nature. "I do not know what to say to you. You are very . . . beautiful."

Words. They were just words she'd heard a thousand times before, but again those feelings of familiarity raced through Dominique's system, sending her mind back to chaos, leaving her body weak and trembling with something other than fear. She was drawn to him, compelled to remain standing before him whether he spoke another word or not. Eager to understand what these feelings meant, confused as well, she took a long breath and gave him a little pout as she said, "Thank you for the kind words, Private. I'll bet you say that to all the girls."

Jacob faked a sheepish grin, then glanced around the room. He was desperate to be out of her view, terrified her occasional thoughtful glances would suddenly turn to recognition. Soon, he feared, her memory would provide her with answers to the questions he could see in her playful eyes. When that happened, she would look at him and scream. What would he do then? Murder her? Kill himself?

"I realize you are a little shy," she said, determined to

get this bashful soldier to open up, "but the least you can do is answer my questions."

Jacob shrugged. "I do not know many women," he offered, hoping that would explain his silence. "I do not know what to say to you."

Dominique's gaze turned puzzled and introspective. She cocked her head as feather tips tickled the recesses of her mind. Frustrated, she blurted out, "You seem awfully familiar to me, private. Have you and I met before?"

Jacob tensed. "No."

"Are you sure?" As if drawn together by pouch strings, Dominique's eyebrows bunched. "How about your family? Do you have any brothers or sisters?"

As Jacob thought of ways to dissuade her and turn the conversation to her life at the fort, he suddenly saw a glimmer of hope in her final question. With another bashful shrug, he said, "I cannot be sure about my family."

"What?" she said, laughing. "Why wouldn't you know about your own family?"

Settling on a half-truth, he began with an accurate account of his own childhood. "The Sioux came into my life once before. My father and sister were killed by Indians many years ago. I was picking berries in the bushes away from our camp, and so my life was spared." Jacob paused here, surprised at the jolt of pain the memory still drove into his heart; then he finished with the lie that would best serve his purposes: "My mother was captured by the Sioux. If she survived the ordeal, I could have brothers and sisters I do not know of."

Dominique gasped, "Oh, dear—I'm so sorry to have asked such a personal question." As the implications of what he'd said sank in, she wondered—could she have been saved by a half-breed brother of the man standing before her? Was it possible the reason she thought she knew Jacob was because he reminded her so much of the Sioux warrior who'd rescued her from certain death? The voice inflections, the height and general build—everything about him was too like the Indian to be purely coincidental. It would also help to explain Redfoot's apparent ease in using the English language. But what could she do about it? She glanced up at the private, suddenly burdened by the suspicions she carried in her breast. How could she tell him that which she couldn't substantiate? What purpose would it serve other than to add to his obvious hatred of the Sioux?

Squeaks and groans of fiddles filled the hall as the musicians warmed up for the festivities. Dominique glanced at the band, then back at the soldier, and her shoulders slumped. Jacob's strong wide jaw was taut, and his intense blue eyes were narrow and thoughtful. Riddled with guilt for opening the wounds of his past, she reached across the distance separating them and placed her hand on his forearm.

"I'll bet a high-stepping reel will make us both feel better about our troubles with these savage Indians. What do you say, soldier? Care to dance?"

Jacob allowed her fingers to slip into his palm, too relieved over her apparent acceptance of him as a stranger to understand what she was talking about. As she led him toward the gathering crowd at the center of the room, he shifted his gaze to the end of the hall. The first sergeant was standing among the musicians announcing the beginning of the ball and the opening promenade. Jacob stepped back and shook his head. "I cannot. I do not know how to do this dance."

But Dominique was ready for him. "Private Stoltz," she chided, again slipping her hand in his, "Aunt Libbie warned me about you soldiers. She said it's sometimes difficult to get a man out on the dance floor when all his feet are trained to do is march."

The crazy one tugged at him, making it impossible for him to do anything but follow. Grumbling under his breath, Jacob allowed himself to be led onto the dance floor. He glanced around the room, looking for something, anything, to use as an excuse to leave her side.

But the music started, and Jacob was swept from his

thoughts into a swirling cloud of skirts and waving arms. Laughing gaily, singing along with the musicians, the crowd passed him from one woman to another, into a quick embrace or a fast spin, over and over again. Trapped in boots of stiff leather, his feet felt as if they'd been sucked into a bog, and the agile hunter tripped time and time again.

"Oh, turn her to the left and turn her to the right," the fiddler sang. "Twirl your partner all through the night. Turn those pretty pretty girls you were lucky to find, and forget those pretty little girls you left behind." When the music finally ended, Jacob stood confused and off balance.

"Well?" Dominique said with a breathless laugh. "How'd you like that?"

Jacob shrugged, looking for an avenue of escape. "I am not sure."

Dominique's expressive eyes lit up as she laughed and said, "Maybe later we can dance to a waltz. That might be more to your liking."

" 'Scuse me, Miss DuBois," a young soldier said from behind. "May I have this next dance with you?"

Vaguely irritated at the intrusion, Dominique whirled around and smiled uncertainly.

"Begging your pardon, Miss DuBois. It's me, Lieutenant Macky—remember me? I found you in the snow and brought you to your uncle?"

"Oh, yes, of course. Thank you—I'd love to." Again she smiled, then turned back to Jacob. "Thanks for the dance, Private Stoltz. Maybe I'll see you later."

And because he had no idea what was expected of him at this juncture, if he should or shouldn't allow the other man to interfere with them, Jacob bit his lip and offered a short nod. Then he averted his gaze, unable somehow to watch the lean soldier take his gift away from him.

Jacob forced his thoughts to the soldiers, to Custer in particular, and tried to regain his focus on the main objective: his mission. He was to listen to the conversations of the officers, ingratiate himself with those in positions of power, and learn whether the Long Knives had made plans for the capture of his people. That done, he and the council could determine how best the Dakota might avoid the soldiers' traps. Jacob was, in essence, the eyes and ears of the entire Dakota nation. Now he toiled to that end, determined to avoid thinking about or even looking at Dominique, but his gaze moved of its own volition, sifting through the crowd until it came to rest on her striking features.

She was dancing with yet another in an endless line of soldiers, this one an officer with many decorations on his dark blue jacket. Clearly the niece of the Long Hair was prized above all the women at the fort. And just as clear was the danger he would face if he allowed his fascination with her to get in the way of his mission. She stirred him and managed to bring emotions and memories to the surface he was better off forgetting—*she* was someone he would be better off forgetting. As Jacob worked to that end, his mouth puckered into a scowl, and dark thoughts shadowed his eyes. Looking for a distraction, he glanced away from the dance floor and made a casual appraisal of the weapons stowed beneath the refreshment table. He was counting the types of rifles when Dominique glided over near him and reached for a glass of punch.

"Whew," she gasped, waving a hanky in front of her face. "I need a rest. What has you in such a state of horrors, Jacob?"

He turned to her and said, "Horrors?"

At the repetition of her word, Dominique clasped her hand across her mouth and looked around for the Custers. They were not within hearing distance. "I'm sorry. That just sort of slipped out. It means you're looking in low spirits, but the way I said it isn't a proper phrase for a young lady to use."

Jacob shrugged. "Then maybe you are not a lady." He meant it in the nicest possible way, but at her gasp and look of indignation, he quickly realized he'd made a blunder. "I mean to say, you are—"

"That's all right, Jacob." She laughed. "You're not the

first to make such an observation about my manners, and I suspect you won't be the last.'' She looked into his eyes and smiled, but her grin faded as she asked, ''Have you been standing here beside this punch bowl all night? I haven't seen you out on the dance floor once since you and I danced the reel.''

Jacob looked away, pretty sure where this conversation would lead. ''I do not like dancing.''

''Oh, Jacob,'' she complained as the chords to one of her favorite tunes, ''Suzanne's Waltz,'' began. ''How can you know if you don't try it a few more times? Come with me. This is a beautiful song to dance to and much easier than the reel.''

When the crazy one reached for his hand, Jacob stepped back. ''I must say no.''

''Don't be silly.'' She marched up to him and took his reluctant hand in hers. ''All you have to do is hang on to me and go where I go.''

She turned with Jacob in tow, as if there was never a question in her mind as to whether he did or did not wish to dance with her. Again grumbling to himself, he allowed her to drag him to the center of the room. But this time, he promised himself, would be the last.

When she stopped walking, Dominique continued to hold one of his hands; then she positioned his other hand at her waist. After draping her dainty fingers across his shoulder, she began moving and counting in time with the music.

''One, two, three,'' she sang along, ''one, two, three—see how easy this is?''

Her big brown eyes flashed with pleasure as she stared up at him, and Jacob could feel the knot of fear in his gut slowly begin to unravel. She was a ray of sunshine, a breath of fresh air in the crowded building the Long Knives called home. In spite of the danger, he found himself wishing he could have thought of a way to keep her, to make her his own after pulling her from the river—to keep her and teach her to live among *his* people. She would have been worth the risk, he decided too late, definitely worthy of the challenge. Then he thought of the difficulties, the nearly impossible task a man would face in trying to tame one such as her, and Jacob laughed out loud.

"See?" She beamed. "I told you you'd like this dance. It's not hard at all, is it?"

Brought out from under his thoughts, but not her spell, Jacob smiled down at her, and relaxed for the first time since he'd left the Hunkpapa camp. "It is a very nice dance, Miss D-Der—"

"Please, Private," she said with a grin. "My name is Dominique. It's all right with me if you use it."

"Dominique," he whispered, testing the name, loving the sound. Caught by her beauty, her closeness, Jacob thought back to the night in his lodge, to the feel of her flesh beneath him. She was strong and agile, yet soft and yielding, as brave as any warrior and endowed with the vitality of the finest squaw—nothing like the image the Dakota had painted of white women. His eyes darkened, as much with desire as with anger and frustration at his hasty decision to release her when he'd had the chance to make her his.

Aware of Jacob's intense gaze, Dominique glanced up and met those deep blue eyes. Again a sense of intimacy swept through her, and again she was drawn to the past and into the mysterious night shadows of the Sioux's tipi. Her feet continued to move, to dance after a fashion, but the music sounded far off, as faded as the whisper of a summer breeze. The paper lanterns flickered emerald shamrocks against the barracks walls, but they were no match for the explosion of color and the steady glow in her mind. She stared at Jacob's mouth, but saw the lips of a savage named Redfoot. His were the lips, she finally realized, that had kissed her so well. Dominique trembled at the surprising memory, then shivered as hot fingers of desire skittered across her abdomen.

"Dominique?"

She heard a voice in the distance, the song of some

delicate bird; yet still she thought of the kiss, of the marvelous hypnotic effect it had on her, and she continued to drift along in her memories. She had not only allowed Redfoot to kiss her, Dominique realized; she'd kissed him back. And quite unashamedly at that. Her mouth had parted easily, and the savage had taken full advantage of her generosity by—

"*Dominique!*"

She tried to open her eyes and look for the person who'd called her name, but her lids felt heavy and languid, weighted somehow. Dominique's ears nagged at her, insisted the sounds of the party were all wrong, and then she realized the problem wasn't the kind of noise, but more the lack of it. The music had stopped. Peering through her lashes, she noticed the other dancers had made their way to the refreshment tables or were standing in clusters talking.

"Dominique—look at me!"

Finally recognizing the sound of her chaperon's voice, she turned and focused her eyes on Hazel Swenson's round, motherly features. She was upset. "Is something wrong?"

"I'd like a word with you, if I may."

"Of course." Dominique looked back at Jacob and smiled. "Thank you for the lovely waltz. I hope we'll have another before the night is over."

Jacob bowed. "Thank you for the lovely lesson."

Dominique's invitation had been automatic, a courtesy she had offered to countless young men who hoped for the thrill of another dance with her. Now as she stared into the deep blue of Jacob's eyes, again a shiver skittered throughout her. Surprising herself, she whispered, "I really hope we do get another dance, Jacob."

Again uncertain about what was expected of him, he glanced at the older woman and smiled to acknowledge her presence. Hazel scowled and narrowed her eyes in return. Understanding that he had no place in a conversation between two white women, Jacob clicked his heels together and retreated to a far corner to observe the proceedings.

Keeping her voice low, Dominique repeated, "Is something wrong, Hazel?"

The widow held a finger against a mouth that was cracked and dry from thirty-seven hard years of life and said under her breath, "I have some sage advice: Your behavior is not becoming to a lady of your breeding, and it's definitely unbecoming to a young woman with the Custer name in her background—especially here on an army post."

Dominique blushed, not sure exactly what she'd done, aware only of the vivid memories of her captivity. "I—I don't really know what I've done. I feel as if I've been sleeping or something."

Hazel pressed her fingertips against her waist and took several shallow breaths. A tight corset strained to harness the extra helpings of potatoes and pie she'd eaten to combat loneliness over the past six years, but still she felt bloated and uncomely, and more than a little faint. Her fingertips moved to her brow as she scolded her young charge. "You were much too close to the private while you were dancing. That was bad enough, but when the song was over, instead of taking your leave like any proper lady, you remained in his arms, staring up at him like a lovesick cow. It won't do, Dominique. It simply isn't proper behavior."

"Oh, Hazel, I'm sorry." Dominique assumed a repentant posture and murmured, "Maybe I'm still feeling the effects of the drugs I was forced to take. I had no idea I was making a display of myself. I'm sorry I got you all upset."

"Oh, don't worry about me, dear." Hazel wiped her brow with the back of her hand and took another breath. "I'm all right, really I am. I think I may have let Mary lace me up too tight."

"Is it all right if I stay and dance some more, then?" Dominique's eyes, bright and full of life, had regained their natural sparkle.

Hazel worked to press her lips together in a show of disapproval, but a smile filtered through in spite of the effort. Envious of the girl's youth and spirited nature, for she had lost her zest for life when her spirit was broken along with her husband's back during a violent storm on Lake Erie, she gave in and said, "Of course you can. Just make sure you choose your partners wisely and dance with them modestly. There are plenty of officers waiting in line for a chance to take a turn with you. Mrs. Custer said you are not to waste any more of your time on common soldiers."

"Oh?" Dominique pursed her lips and glanced around the room. She spotted her aunt chatting with a few of the better-dressed ladies and surmised they were officer's wives. As sweet and lovely as she was, Libbie Custer had definite ideas about the rung she occupied on the social ladder. In her short stay at Fort Lincoln, Dominique had learned that the divisions between rank were clear and on several distinct levels. But why did they have to extend to her, an outsider, a visitor?

Dominique frowned and turned back to Hazel. "Please tell Aunt Libbie you informed me of my breach of protocol and that I will do the best I can to behave from here on out. I will make sure to dance with a wide variety of Uncle Armstrong's men."

Hazel studied her young charge's expression, taking special interest in the mischievous glint in her dark brown eyes. "Dominique," she warned, "have a good time, but do remember your manners. I will be making weekly reports to your father, you know."

"Yes, ma'am," she said, properly contrite as she noticed a tall, gaunt soldier approaching them. "Oh, excuse me, Hazel, here comes a suitable partner for me. An officer, if I don't miss my guess. Shall I ask him to dance?"

The older woman looked over her shoulder, then quickly snapped her head around. "Why, ah, y-yes, he is an officer. I suppose Libbie couldn't object to him."

"What about you?" Dominique's grin was scampish, secretive. "Won't you mind? Or did you think I hadn't noticed you clinging to this particular officer like a spit curl on a lady's brow?''

"Dominique! Your language!" Hazel's amber eyes widened, as much with shock as with the realization that Barney Woodhouse was standing directly behind her.

"Sorry," Dominique said through a giggle.

"Miss DuBois," Barney said with a short nod, "Mrs. Swenson. I ain't—'Scuse me, I mean I'm not interrupting you ladies, am I?''

"Goodness, no," Dominique said. "Why, Hazel and I were just talking about what an excellent dancer you are, Lieutenant.''

Bright color crawled up Hazel's neck. She tried to spear Dominique with a pointed gaze, but found she'd lost control of her eyes. They darted back and forth between Barney and Dominique as if they couldn't quite decide on which person to land.

"It's Mrs. Swenson and who's the excellent dancer, Miss DuBois. She could make a blind man with a peg leg look good on the dance floor.''

The blush deepened and crept up past Hazel's cheeks. "Now, Lieutenant, I'm not that proficient.''

"Why don't we see if you can prove me wrong?" Barney extended his elbow. "I just asked them to play another reel. Maybe I can show you a thing or two." When Hazel grinned and accepted his arm, Barney nodded to Dominique. "Miss DuBois, have yourself a real good time now, you hear?''

"Oh, I intend to, sir.''

Then Dominique Custer DuBois made out an extensive mental dance card, a lineup that would keep her on her toes all night long. She also made damn sure there wasn't one officer on her list.

From across the room, Jacob watched, still fascinated, but no longer uneasy about being in the company of the crazy one. In fact, he thought, pleased and encouraged now that she seemed to believe he and Redfoot were two separate people, he might even find the time to know her better, to taste the tempting delights she so richly displayed. His smile—and his expectations—grew huge as he remembered how quickly her naked flesh had warmed under his touch. Yes, he would make the time, he thought, his loins stirring. He would—

"Evening, Private. You're new here, ain't ya?"

Jacob glanced at the intruder, a woman whose features he gazed on, but didn't see, and said, "Yes, ma'am."

"Got a surprise for ya, then." She laughed, exposing a row of crooked, stained teeth. "Have a swallow—but don't be surprised if it don't taste like coffee, soldier."

Jacob accepted the mug and peered at the contents. "What is this?"

The laundress, aged beyond her years, glanced around the room, then whispered, "Hard cider. Stir it with this and take a sip. It'll warm the cockles of your heart and a lot more!"

Jacob accepted the short length of wood, slipped it into the liquid, and stirred the cider. Skeptical, but careful not to offend anyone at this critical period of acceptance into white society, Jacob lifted the mug to his mouth. His senses were assaulted by the sharp scent of heavily spiced yet bitter fruit. He tapped the stick against the edge of the cup, then brought it to his nose: cinnamon, his memory supplied. He stood there, as if frozen in time, while his mind raced to the past. The woman he once knew as mother had served him apple dumplings. They were sweeter and warmer than the drink he held in his hand, but the aroma was very close to the same, and the scent of the cider evoked vivid images of a life he'd long since ceased thinking about.

Jacob struggled to return to the present, but felt himself slipping back in time, crawling through layers of a past he didn't dare think about. Without warning, his mind's eye supplied the image of a pretty blond woman with sparkling blue eyes. She was humming a tune, reaching out to hug him, smelling of spiced apples. Her name was Christina and she was German like his father, the immigrant Joseph

Stoltz. Jacob blinked his eyes and saw his baby sister crawling on the bed of their covered wagon. Then he blinked again and saw the orphaned daughter of a fellow homesteader, a young girl with eyes the color of a stormy day, but whose name escaped him. The girl had made it her personal crusade to tutor Jacob, who spoke in curious and halting sentences comprising both German and English, in the proper use of the King's English. She promised to instruct his awkward fingers to write it one day as well. But before that could happen, a Crow arrow slammed into her throat. And a lance found a home in the heart of the woman who smelled of spiced apples. Mother.

The mug crashed to the wooden floor. Hard cider splashed over Jacob's boots. The laundress cried out as the soldier brought his hand to his temples, his features twisted into a grimace.

Stumbling blindly, pushing his way through startled revelers, Jacob ran from the hall.

Later that night, Libbie Custer sat at her dressing table going through her nightly routine. "Seventy-seven, seventy-eight, seventy-nine . . . eighty." She rested her arm on the edge of the table and waited for the blood to rush back into her fingertips before picking up the ivory-handled hairbrush and finishing the job. "Eighty-one, eighty-two—"

"Surely your locks are shiny enough for this night, my precious sunbeam," Custer murmured as he approached. Reaching the back of her chair, he stared into the mirror and fondled a lock of his wife's silky chestnut hair. "We need to talk."

Libbie glanced into the looking glass at her husband's reflection. Lines of dejection, of weariness, cat-tracked from the corners of his eyes, aging him beyond his thirty-six years. She dropped the brush and rose.

"What's wrong, Autie? Have there been some complaints about the ball?"

"No, sunbeam." He pulled her into his arms and

stroked her shoulders through the soft flannel of her nightgown. "I received new orders this morning, but didn't want to trouble you with them until after the party."

"Orders? But your orders are to wage a summer campaign against the hostiles right here. You have your orders."

"Had," he corrected with a kiss on the tip of her nose. "I have to report to Washington at once."

Libbie pulled back and tried to push out of her husband's arms, but he held fast. "That can't be!" she cried. "We've just returned from New York in the dead of winter. Don't they have any idea what they're asking of us?"

"They probably do, but it doesn't matter. The official dispatch says I'm urgently needed so that the building of new forts on the Yellowstone River can be discussed and implemented. It seems that President *Grant*"—he spit the name out as if it were sour milk—"has found one thing he likes about me—that I do seem to know my Indians and the particular problems they present."

"Oh, Autie, I can't believe he'd make you go all the way back to Washington so soon. Do you have to go?"

"Keep control of yourself, precious. This may work in my best interest. Grant's term is almost up. With a little luck and some intelligent voting, what he thinks or does may no longer be of any consequence to my career. Besides"—he smiled, winding the tail end of a pink satin ribbon at her throat around his finger—"if we can live through the next four years of a new administration, don't be surprised if you find *my* name on the ballot in 1880."

"Oh, Autie!" she gasped. "Do you really think it's possible?"

"It's more than possible, my precious." Custer gave a tug on the ribbon, releasing the bow at her neckline. "It's almost a fact. Now, then, we have only tonight to last us for the next few weeks. How would you like to drop your drawers for the future President of the United States?"

Chapter Five

JACOB SWUNG THE SHOVEL AND TOOK A SWIPE AT THE pile of manure. The movement startled the general's favorite horse, Dandy. The stallion reared, striking out with his hooves, and narrowly missed Jacob's temple.

"Waicpia," he murmured, reaching out to calm the horse. Then, realizing what he'd said, damning the lapse into the Dakota language, Jacob corrected himself. "Easy, brave one. No harm will come to you. It is your master who must have the eye of the eagle and vision of a shaman."

Grinning at the thought, Jacob continued his work. He'd accomplished much over his first three days as a soldier and had made several friends among the officers. These new friends, Barney in particular, would be of great service to him and ultimately to his people. It had taken him only one day to demonstrate to the Long Knives his prowess with the horses. In less than a week, he hoped also to show them how valuable he could be as a scout.

He'd done much toward fulfilling his mission in a very short time, he decided, congratulating himself. Jacob repeated that thought, hoping to convince himself that these accomplishments were all that mattered, that the recurring thoughts and dreams of his dead white family would eventually fade, and that his undeniable attraction to the crazy one would ease after his return to the Dakota camp—and to Spotted Feather's arms.

Footsteps, the rustling of petticoats, and low voices alerted him to the approach of visitors. He threaded his fingers through Dandy's mane and turned toward the barn door as three figures passed through the opening.

"Afternoon, Stoltz," Barney Woodhouse called. "I have a new assignment you might be interested in—one that's bound to be a heck of a lot more fun than stable call."

Jacob noticed the lieutenant squired Hazel Swenson on his arm, but his attention was riveted on the woman at her side—Dominique DuBois. His spirits lifting in spite of his doubts, Jacob nudged Dandy back into his stall and knotted the rope gate. Wiping his hands on his blue regulation trousers, he approached the trio.

"Afternoon, ladies," he said with a tight smile. "You have work for me, Lieutenant?"

"When we're not at assembly, I'm just plain Barney to the man who saved my life, Stoltz." He gestured toward Dominique, then turned back to his friend. "The general's niece has a hankering to learn how to ride a horse. Captain Ruffing says he's mighty impressed with your work, says he's never seen a man so smooth with the mounts. Says— and begging your pardon if I don't quite believe it—that you could give Iron Butt a run for his money any day of the week."

"Iron Butt?"

Barney choked, and his scant mustache puckered with his upper lip until it almost couldn't be seen. "Begging your pardon, Miss DuBois," he muttered, tugging at the bright yellow scarf knotted at his throat. "Iron Butt is an affectionate term some of the soldiers use for your uncle. It is an honorary title, to be sure, since the general's horsemanship is legendary, but, well . . ."

"But Uncle Armstrong doesn't know about the nickname?" She laughed, struck by the ludicrous image of her uncle wearing trousers of lead.

"Ah, I don't know for sure, but just in case—"

"Don't worry—he won't hear it from me, Lieutenant."

"Ah, thank you, Miss DuBois." Quickly turning his attention back to Jacob, he said, "Do you think you can teach the young lady how to ride? I might be able to wrangle a little more than your basic pay out of it for you."

Jacob's brow wrinkled as he considered the lieutenant's request. While the idea was as tempting as the beautiful woman herself, he hesitated; was this honorable work for a soldier or better left to those too cowardly to confront the enemy? If he accepted, would helping the crazy one interfere with his mission or make it more bearable? His main objective was to get close to those included in the Long Hair's council. Barney Woodhouse was one of those soldiers. Could he chance the lieutenant's disapproval if he chose not to give the lessons? Perhaps this chore could actually work to his advantage, even gain him favor in the eyes of Custer, should he hear of Jacob's obedience upon his return to the fort.

Jacob shrugged. "I can try to help her."

If Barney missed the underlying tension, the hesitation, in Jacob's words, Hazel didn't. She cleared her throat and stepped forward. "Maybe this isn't such a good idea. I can see you have work to do, Private Stoltz, and I'm sure Dominique doesn't want to interfere with the operations of the fort. Perhaps we'll just—"

"I really don't see the problem, Hazel," Dominique cut in, worried all her planning would be for naught. Ever since Jacob had disappeared from the dance, she'd schemed to see him again, hoped that more time in his company would help her to separate the feelings she had for him from those she harbored for Redfoot. To that end, she laughed gaily and said, "Why, even Uncle Tom said the riding lessons would be a welcome break from the tedious busywork the soldiers must do. Why don't you and Barney go ahead and finish your walk? I'm sure Private Stoltz and I can manage my lessons without an audience."

Hazel trained a thoughtful amber eye on Jacob. "Well . . ."

"Come on, Mrs. Swenson," Barney encouraged. "She's right, and Stoltz knows exactly what he's doing with the horses. This lovely spring day demands we take advantage of it and go for our walk before a surprise storm hits.''

She shrugged. ''Oh, all right, but do be careful,'' she admonished both her charge and the soldier. ''Dominique has never been around horses, you know. She needs lessons from the ground up. Don't let her walk behind a horse lest it kick her, and be sure—''

Barney pulled her hand into the crook of his arm and marched toward the door, jerking the words from her mouth. ''She'll be just fine, Hazel. You should worry more about where you walk than where your niece does.''

Hazel squealed, sidestepping a fresh pile of droppings; then the pair disappeared out into the sunshine.

Her dark eyes sparkling with laughter, Dominique spun around to face the soldier. His gaze had never left her. Caught off guard by the calm intensity in his deep blue eyes, the sense of purpose in his expression, she found she had to look away to regain her composure.

Jacob sighed, again questioning his judgment, then stifled the urge to laugh when he noticed the rhythmic tapping of a small foot beneath her long navy-blue skirt. Impatience and a very strong will ruled this one, he decided, reinforcing his original opinion of her. Too bad they were not in the Dakota camp, he thought, swallowing the urge to laugh. A fast lesson astride his mount, the spirited Sampi, would teach this impetuous beauty a few things about the value of patience.

Dominique smiled up at him. ''Well? Where do we start?''

Jacob furrowed his brow and stared down at the hem of her dress. ''You must start by going to your quarters and changing your clothing.''

''Changing?'' She drew her fingertips down the sides of her navy wool serge riding suit. ''But my Aunt Libbie brought this back from New York not two months ago. She had it altered to fit me only yesterday.'' She lifted her chin, then draped one hand across the brown leather straps decorating the jacket. "This is the newest, most fashionable riding habit available anywhere."

Incredulous, he said, "You wish to ride a horse in this dress?"

"Of course." Dominique lifted her right arm, revealing the leather strap surrounding her wrist, which was connected by a thong to the hem of her skirt. The higher she raised her arm, the higher the skirt rose, until it rested above the toes of her boots. "Shall we?"

Uncertain, wondering if he should believe her, Jacob removed his trooper's hat and scratched his head. "I do not think you will fit on the back of a horse in this dress."

Dominique puckered up her mouth and frowned. "But Aunt Libbie rides in one just like it. This must be the correct attire." With her free hand, she reached up and adjusted her hat, a matching square fillet with a long ivory illusion veil that circled the crown and trailed down from a bow at the back. Then again she smiled and repeated her request. "Where do we begin?"

Jacob grinned. "With a horse."

"Of course." She laughed. "Why didn't I think of that?"

Caught by the sparkle in her playful brown eyes, Jacob indulged himself with a long look into them before he gestured for her to follow him. "I have come to know all the animals in the barn. There is a mare who will be very gentle with you."

"Oh?" she sighed, disappointed. "I assumed I would be riding my aunt Libbie's horse. She talks about that animal as if it were human."

Jacob stopped in front of a stall and began to untie the rope. "I have heard that Mrs. Custer has ridden many times with the general. Her mount is spirited, meant only for a rider with much experience. This mare will serve you best."

Dominique opened her mouth to protest, but one quick look at the animal in the stall kept her reply in her throat. Good Lord! Did she actually have to climb up on that monster's back in order to keep up this charade? Could she really go through with the riding lessons, with this suddenly insane excuse she'd dreamed up in order to see Jacob again?

Unaware of Dominique's attack of nerves, Jacob attached a leather lead line to the mare's halter, and led the animal out of the stall. "This is Peaches. Come to her, Dominique. Let her get to know your voice, your scent. Talk to her in a gentle voice. Be kind to her and she will be your friend for life." He handed the lead to her and added, "I will get a saddle while you become friends."

Alarmed, Dominique stood there looking at the length of leather resting in the palm of her gloved hand as Jacob walked away. Then she glanced up at the horse. Peaches began nodding her head, and her lush black mane moved back and forth across her long neck like a pendulum. For the first time since Dominique had come up with the idea, the enormity of what she'd gotten herself into dawned on her. A horse was a very *big* animal—much bigger than she. Why, if the beast chose it, it could simply walk right over her and crush her into the ground as if she were nothing more than a sapling.

Terrified Dominique stepped back.

Peaches followed.

"Stay," she ordered, her voice wavering as she took several backward steps. Frantically searching her mind, she tried to remember the words liverymen used to make a horse do as it was told, but she could remember only the plush leather seats and the comfort of the carriages her father hired to take her from place to place.

The horse began nodding again and resumed trailing after her new mistress.

What had started out as a lark, as a way to pass the time and learn more about the intriguing soldier called Jacob, was rapidly becoming another of her follies. Frightened almost as badly as she'd been when the ferry capsized, Dominique dropped the line and backed down the dirt and straw aisle. "S-stay, horse—*p-please?*"

Peaches tossed her head high and emitted a shrill whinny. She punctuated her song with a resounding snort, splattering her new mistress in the bargain. Then she resumed her forward march, curiosity prompting her to pick up the pace.

Panic replaced fear as the mare bore down on her. Dominique wheeled around, determined to race from the barn and never return. Instead, she tripped over a rake and fell flat on her face.

The plodding of hooves against the hard-packed dirt floor resounded. Clip-clop, clip-clop. The noise grew louder as the mare approached her prone body. Dominique covered her head and screamed, "H-help me! *Help!*"

The pitiful pleas reached Jacob's ears as he stepped out of the tack room with a saddle slung over his shoulder. Inclining his head, he slowly approached the woman whose cries were now reduced to unintelligible whimpers. Peaches stood directly above her, nickering softly in her ear, nuzzling the knot of hair at the back of her neck.

A grin tugging at one corner of his mouth, Jacob dropped the saddle and hunkered down beside her. "This is a very strange way to become friends with your mount. Peaches will think you are afraid of her."

"I—I am, you . . . you nincompoop! Get her away from me this instant!"

Jacob laughed.

"Get her *away!*" Dominique demanded, her jaw taut.

Realizing now that her panic was real, Jacob stood up and reached for the halter, but before he could catch the leather with his fingers, Peaches snatched Dominique's hat between her teeth and began shaking it as if it were a clump of grass. Laughing to himself this time, he pulled the tattered ruin from the mare's mouth and tied her to a nearby post.

Still paralyzed with fear, Dominique remained prone, her arms up over her head, her eyes shut. Jacob dropped back down to his knees and whispered, "You are safe. I have restrained the dangerous beast."

Dominique peeked over her shoulder. Satisfied the horse couldn't reach her, she sat up in a huff. "I thought you knew these horses!" she said, trying to sound brave as she dusted the dirt off her bodice. "That animal came after me. I think she meant to stomp me!"

"Peaches's only wish was to be your friend." Impulsively, he reached out and brushed away a smudge on her cheek.

Dominique slapped his hand away. "I still think she wanted to hurt me. Oh," she cried, reaching for her hat, "look what she's done! Isn't there a gentler horse for me to ride—one who will listen to what I say?"

Jacob grinned at her, amused to find this sign of weakness in one so brave. Choosing the method he felt would best reinforce that inherent courage, he issued a challenge. "No. You will learn to ride Peaches or you will not learn to ride at all. Perhaps your day would best be spent with the other women up on Suds Row instead of in the stables."

Dominique's jaw snapped shut and her eyes grew round. A sudden burst of temper running her tongue, she said, "We'll just see about that, you nincompoop! Please help me to my feet."

Jacob stood, offering his hand as he asked, "What is this you call me—nincompup?"

As Dominique smoothed her skirts and brushed the dirt from her jacket, she blanched at her lapse in decorum. Stammering, she shrugged and said, "Oh, ah—haven't you ever heard anyone say that before?"

Jacob shook his head. "My German family struggled with English. Then, after they were gone, I trapped and prospected—two very lonely ways to survive. I apologize for my poor English."

She waved him off with a nervous chuckle. "You do just fine, and nin— Well, that word is just a slang word; it doesn't mean much of anything."

But he persisted. "Much of what?"

She expelled her breath in a long sigh and mumbled,

"It's just another word for . . . soldier. Now, can we get on with my lesson?"

Jacob stared at her for a long moment, reasonably certain she'd been less than honest with him, but he opted to let it go. "If you wish to learn to ride, you will do as I say. Can you do that?"

"Absolutely." Dominique regarded the ruined hat, muttering to herself, then tossed it aside. Smoothing her mussed hair, she checked the back of her head and found it was still wound into a bun and held securely in place by a wide-looped hair net. "I'm ready," she announced.

"I hope Peaches is." Jacob laughed as he started toward the horse.

Dominique stayed one step behind him, peering over his shoulder as they approached the animal. He turned, taking her hand in his, and softly said, "I am going to raise your fingers to her nostrils. She must smell you to know you, feel your touch and know that it will be gentle. Do not make any sudden moves."

"I understand," she breathed, wondering how on earth the warmth of his hand could affect her so, even through the leather of her gloves.

Then he pulled her forward so she could reach the animal, and Dominique brushed up against Jacob's broad back. She stood there, a captive of sorts, and found herself mimicking the mare's fascination with her fingers. She breathed deeply, absorbing, learning, identifying Jacob by his scent, branding his unique aroma into her brain, wondering if it would ever stop reminding her of the Sioux, Redfoot. Once again she felt those odd sensations, grew giddy as feather tips from the past brushed her memory, and sensed a kinship with the private she'd tried to understand but couldn't seem to reconcile in her mind.

"Very good," Jacob softly encouraged, unaware of the turmoil behind him. "Stroke her with tenderness, show her you are not afraid."

On their own, for Dominique had no idea what her hands were doing, her fingers massaged the horse's jaw, then slid up along the lines of her round cheeks and slithered down her long silky neck. She continued the movements, but Dominique's gaze was fastened to the expanse of muscles across Jacob's back, watching as they strained against the smooth material of his gray flannel shirt. She could feel the mare's muscles bunching and expanding at her touch, and she wondered if Jacob's reaction would be the same if she were to manipulate and stroke his shoulders in a like manner.

Pleased by Dominique's progress, Jacob turned to comment on her quick reversal, but instead, he noticed the glazed look in her eyes, the slightly parted lips—so full, so pink, so inviting. Memories of their softness, of the lush texture and eager response, took him by storm. Jacob's breath caught in his throat and his mind could concentrate on only one mission—to find a way to make this woman his own. The mare forgotten, he leaned forward and took her face in his hands. "Dominique, I—" His throat slammed shut, cutting off his words, his air, as reason whispered in the recesses of his mind: *You cannot jeopardize your mission over this woman—over any woman.* But still he could not seem to release her.

"Jacob," she breathed with difficulty, drawn to him by something equally frightening and thrilling, unable or unwilling to consider the impropriety of what she was doing. She found herself wondering instead if his kisses would be like those of the Indian, if the memory of Jacob's touch would heat her, then linger in her body even as she slept. He pulled her closer to his tantalizing mouth, and Dominique knew that the answer to those questions would soon be burning on her lips. Bolder than she'd ever been in her life, Dominique slid her tongue across her bottom lip, closed her eyes, and inclined her head to receive him.

Peaches had more sense than either of them. With a shrill whinny, she bobbed her head and slammed her muzzle into Jacob's back. He lurched forward, crashing into Dominique. She went flying across the aisle.

She kept her balance as she stumbled, and for a moment, Dominique thought she would also keep her footing.

But then the heel of her boot connected with a pile of fresh horse dung.

Dominique shot backward, scattering, and then landing in the manure Jacob had carefully raked into a small mountain earlier that morning.

Later that evening after the nine-thirty lights-out, Jacob tucked his blankets around pillows he had formed into the shape of his own body. Then he crept silently out of the barracks. He made his way on foot to the meeting spot in the trees to the north of the fort, where he found a tethered horse waiting for him. It was his old friend, the stallion, Sampi. Jacob launched himself on the animal's back and dug his heels into the horse's flanks.

He rode in a zigzag fashion for five miles before reining his mount to a halt at the crest of a small butte. Leaning back on the stallion, he pointed his chin to the moonless sky and uttered the staccato signal: "Yip! Yip! Yip!" He followed this with a perfect imitation of the howl of a lone wolf.

And then he waited.

When he heard an echo of the signal from the west, Jacob wheeled the horse in that direction and rode until he came upon another rider. After the warrior recognized the horse and the soldier it carried, he raised an arm in greeting and led the man dressed as a Long Knife into the Hunkpapa camp.

Chief Gall stood outside the warrior's lodge and waited for his son to greet him. When Jacob approached, the two men clasped hands and stared into each other's eyes before the elder finally spoke: "It is good to see you my son. Are you treated well?"

"Well enough, my Father."

"Come, then, let us hear the news you bring." After opening the flap to the warriors' lodge, Gall stepped through and waited for his son to enter before he took his place of honor and sank cross-legged onto a buffalo rug.

Following his father's lead, Jacob eased onto the rug at his right and removed his cavalry-issue hat. Sitting Bull passed him the pipe the men had been smoking, and even though the acrid smoke stung his eyes, Jacob took a puff and handed it to his father.

"And now, Redfoot, what news do you bring us?" the Father said.

"Much information, but little news, I am afraid. The Long Hair left on a journey to his Chief's home in Washington two days after I came to the fort."

Chief Gall grunted and pointed to a young warrior who had just earned his way into the warriors' lodge. "Little Dog has made coup on a worthless soldier from the Seventh Cavalry. The soldier wandered too far off course during his duty as a guard. See the feather in Little Dog's hair to show his first victory over the enemy? Is this achievement to be the only tale for us this night, my son?"

Jacob slowly shook his head and began repeating the story Barney had told him only hours ago. "A message came to the officer in charge this morning. On Saturday, three days past"—*as I was spinning the beautiful niece of my enemy around in my arms,* his troubled mind added, and Jacob swallowed hard and went on—"a company of Long Knives led by Colonel Reynolds attacked Crazy Horse and his village at the Little Powder River. More than one hundred lodges were destroyed and many were killed. I am told that Crazy Horse survived, but now he will be hunted fiercely."

"As we are," Gall amended.

"As we are." Jacob regarded the thin yellow braid stitched along the outside seams of his trousers, then made an observation. "From what I have seen and heard, these Long Knives will not be happy until all warriors, regardless of nation or tribe, are lying in their final resting places."

His expression grim, Gall slowly nodded, then asked,

"Was the Long Hair, Custer, fooled by the camp you led him to after your escape?"

Jacob regarded his father, suddenly unsure how much he ought to reveal. Dominique was paramount in his mind. Was he honor bound to mention her name? Should he give the Dakota the true identity of the crazy one? Should he tell them how fragile his disguise had become and that the mission might be in jeopardy? He thought back to his rescue of Dominique, to the night in his tipi, and he remembered her fire and spirit. In peril, she had spit on him, issued threats he didn't understand, and told him she was not afraid. But then he thought of her lying in the barn only a few hours past, trembling with fear as a timid mare nuzzled behind her ear. He thought of her reaction when she'd fallen into the horse droppings, how she'd sputtered, all fire and spirit again, and he nearly laughed out loud.

Jacob admired and desired her, but he feared the power she held locked in her mind. She intrigued and enticed him, yet she represented all that he'd come to hate. How could he explain these feelings to Chief Gall when he wasn't sure he understood them himself? One day, perhaps soon, he would have to speak her name, reveal her threat to their mission. For now, Jacob took another puff from the pipe and relished the light-headed sense of freedom it gave him.

Too soon, his head cleared, and he knew he must answer his father. "I led the Long Hair to our camp myself. He thought I was a good scout and said so many times. I am certain, too, that he believed it when I said the Hunkpapa had fled the area. He also thinks I will make a good scout when the soldiers begin their war against us."

"That is good to hear, my son." Gall sucked at the wooden pipe as he mulled over his worries, and finally said, "What have you learned of the troops who were searching the area while you were confined to the prisoners' tipi with the Long Knife? Did so many seek one missing soldier, or was there another purpose?"

Dominique. But what was he to say, what could he do?

Jacob looked into the kind onyx eyes of the Dakota chief and slowly shook his head. Then, for the first time in his life, he lied to his father. "I—I do not know."

Sensing Redfoot was troubled, Gall's wide slashing mouth softened and the corners turned up in an understanding smile. "We have stirred your brain like a pot of stew in our hurry to gain knowledge of the white eyes. Rest, my son. Tell us what you have learned as it comes to you."

But the words didn't comfort Jacob; they added to his burden of guilt, his sense of betrayal. "I do not need rest. I have come to inform. Inform I shall." He took a deep breath and condensed the story of his first few days as a soldier in the United States Cavalry. "The soldiers have very strange ways. Everything they do must be done by a timepiece like this."

He reached into his shirt pocket and pulled out gold watch and chain. He passed it to Gall, who examined it and then sent it on to the other warriors. Jacob explained as each man studied the shiny object. "Each morning before the sun has awakened, a soldier blows air into a long metal horn to rouse the others. Then we are obliged to stand and have our names called before we are sent to a long room. In this room"—Jacob grimaced—"we are forced to eat what is called breakfast."

"Is this breakfast an animal the Long Knives have tamed?"

Jacob laughed. "It is the name of a meal, like *tankapa*. The food they force us to eat at all meals is not fit for our dogs. They make stew and hash with beans and molasses. Each meal seems to be made with these things, and each has a different name. All of it angers my belly."

Sitting Bull spoke up. "I will prepare a potion for you to ease your pain."

"Do not bother. Your medicine will only make my belly think all is well, when I know I must return and feed it more of this poor food. It will be better for me to continue this way." Noticing the men were through looking at the watch, he took it from the blanket and checked the time. Soon he must return to the fort or be discovered.

"I must finish my story and return." The others quieted and urged him to continue. "The soldiers spend much of the day doing women's work when they are not filling their bellies. For one hour they practice what is called a drill. This is their only preparation for war, and all they do is march around the fort on foot and sometimes ride the horses. They do not fire their guns. When I asked for instruction in this, I was told it was not necessary and a waste of bullets."

Gall's thick eyebrows leapt to his forehead. "They do not want you to know how to shoot a gun?"

"They seem not to care if any of their men can shoot or hit what they aim at. They think all they have to do is ride into our camps and frighten us away like scared women and children."

At this, the entire council broke into boisterous laughter.

When ordered was restored, Jacob jackknifed to his feet and motioned for the rest to remain seated. "I must leave and return to the fort now before the soldiers discover my trick and accuse me of taking what they call a French leave."

All nodded farewell and murmured good luck prayers, but none except the chief rose to join Jacob at the entry flap. Gall drew his ceremonial buffalo robe around his shoulders and stepped into the chill night air. "Then all goes well with you, my son? There is nothing more you wish to discuss?"

Walking beside him, his head bowed, Jacob said, "Perhaps next time I will have more news. Their chief, Custer, is due to return to the fort in less than one moon. I will know more about their plans then."

"And nothing else troubles you?"

Again he lied: "Nothing."

Too perceptive to ignore his instincts, Gall persisted as they approached the tethered horses. "What of the Long

Knives' women, my son? Do they offer relief, or are the rumors we hear true—that white women favor their men only for the purpose of breeding?''

Squatting, Jacob removed the buckskin thongs from Sampi's hooves. Then he rose and shrugged. ''I do not know. The soldiers have not spoken to me about this part of their lives. What I have learned is that some of them go to a small building across the river and trade their coins to women in return for relief. This is where I will say I have been should I be discovered upon my return.''

''Perhaps you should stop and take your relief here. Spotted Feather longs for you. She—''

''No.'' Jacob shook his head, curiously uninterested in that which he thought might cool his desire for the crazy one. ''I have no time for such things.'' Then he pulled himself onto the stallion's back and stated his candid opinion of the soldiers: ''You should be happy to know that the Long Knives I have met, officers and common warriors alike, do not seem to be burdened with a great many brains.''

With a nod of approval, Gall said, ''Let us hope they all prove to be so simpleminded.''

Jacob's thoughts immediately went to the Long Hair. Custer was anything but simpleminded; he possessed an intelligence and drive even Chief Gall would admire. But that information did not require discussion, at least not on this night. The Dakota had faced Custer and his men before. His cunning and abilities were well known to them. Also known and understood was the fact that one man, no matter how clever, could not bring down an entire nation determined to survive.

Jacob glanced at his father and waved. ''Until the new moon.''

''May the spirits guide and protect you.'' Gall pressed his palm against Jacob's thigh and squeezed. ''Soon I am sure a rider will bring news of Crazy Horse and where he has fled. When you seek us next, we will both have much information. Ride to the tree-that-lives-in-death. Call the signal there and you will be directed to our camp.'' Then he backed away, adding an unnecessary warning to the son he'd trained himself: ''Take care that none of the soldiers follow you.''

''Hah!'' Laughing at the improbability of that happening, Jacob felt confident and at peace for the first time since he'd left the fort.

''Do not trouble yourself with such thoughts, Father.'' He wheeled Sampi toward the southeast, assuring the chief as he rode off, ''When nature's call must be answered, those nincompups are lucky if they can find their own man parts.''

Chapter Six

✦

"I WANT THE ANSWER TO QUESTION NUMBER SEVENTY-one: Ought I oppose the projects of my husband?" Libbie Custer squeezed her eyes shut and twirled her index finger before pushing it forward and spearing a spot on the page. "What have I chosen?"

"A single black triangle." Dominique snatched her book, *The Ladies' Oracle,* off the coverlet and furiously flipped through the pages. When she found the corresponding answer to her aunt's question, she howled with laughter and fell over on the bed.

"Nikki, stop it! What does it say? I have to know." Libbie reached for the book, but Dominique clutched it to her bosom. Libbie sat back on her heels and waited for the hysterics to subside.

"Oh," Dominique gasped, her eyes filling with tears. "It says, 'Yes, you may oppose your husband's projects—if you wish to ruin him, that is!' "

"Oh, pooh!" Libbie stuck out her tongue. "That book is filled with nothing but nonsense. I can't believe you were issued such a thing in a proper girls' school."

Dominique's expression sobered and she sat up. "I never said it was school *issue.* I merely mentioned that I got it at Miss Annie Porter's School for Girls."

"Nikki!" Scandalized but nonetheless intrigued, Libbie scooted closer. Whispering, even though she and her niece were alone in her bedroom, she asked, "Who gave it to you?"

"I bought it from one of the other inmates in boarding school. Her mother felt her education wasn't complete without this book and a couple of others whose titles I can't mention."

"Oh, *Nikki!* What would your father say if he knew we were having this conversation?"

"Mon Dieu! J'ai élevé une traînée!"

Libbie's brows collided. "What did you say? I can't speak French."

"I know." She laughed, but at the older woman's stern expression, she made the translation. "All right, he'd probably say, 'My God! I've raised a harlot!' "

"Oh, my Lord." Libbie fell back on her pillow and fanned her brow with her hand. "No wonder your father sent you out west to finish you." She took a deep breath and went on, "I've spent the last ten of my twelve years of marriage lamenting the fact that the good Lord has denied Autie and me the joy of parenthood. Now and not for the first time, I feel I can see the wisdom in his judgment."

Dominique rolled over on her tummy and propped herself up with her elbows. "Aunt Libbie," she began, her tone serious. "Please don't think me rude or indelicate, but I have no mother to teach me these things, and asking father is, well, it's just out of the question."

Libbie turned her head and looked into Dominique's wide sable eyes. "I know, dear, and I've a confession to make: I'm not quite the laced-up old biddie you might think I am. But I'm also not given to talking about my personal life. These things are deeply private matters as far as I'm concerned."

"Oh," Dominique said in a tiny disappointed whisper.

Feeling empathy for her niece, remembering how bereft she felt when her own mother was snatched away while she was but a young girl, Libbie sighed. "All right. I will answer any questions I can, dear, but do not press me if I feel they are too personal.''

"Oh, thank you, Aunt Libbie!" Dominique's mind raced, but it was suddenly a blank. The best she could do was "Why can't you and Uncle Armstrong have children?"

"That's easy enough. I have no idea; it just never happened. Not, of course, that we haven't''—Libbie softened her voice and lowered her lashes before she said the final word—"tried."

"Tell me about that!" Dominique said, her mind suddenly full of questions. "Tell me about—"

"Not for all the silk in Paris. That subject is definitely too personal. In fact, I am growing weary of this entire conversation. Where's that cute book of yours? This time you ask it a question.''

Dominique collapsed her arms and allowed her head to drop to the pillow. It was no use pressing her aunt any further. The subject had been closed just when her heart was beginning to open. She wanted so to ask Libbie about the incident in the stable with Jacob, tell her how close she'd come to kissing him right out there in the open with no thought to her morals. What did it mean? *Was* she a harlot? Or worse?

Dominique pressed her lips together. She didn't even know if there was anything worse than a harlot—and if there was, what shameful name a woman like that might be called. How would a sporting woman have reacted to the near kiss with Jacob? Would it have affected a more experienced woman as strongly as it had affected her? She remembered her very first open-mouthed kiss—with the gardener's son—as if it were yesterday, even though it had happened several months ago. He had kissed her, all right, and quite thoroughly as far as she could tell. Why did merely the *thought* of kissing Jacob excite her ten times more than the experience back home? And *why*, she wondered, frustrated, wouldn't Libbie talk to her about these things?

"Nikki? Have you fallen asleep?"

Lifting her head from the pillow, she propped it up with her hand. "No, I'm sorry. I was daydreaming."

"Get your little book," Libbie urged, sensing that Dominique was upset about something. "I'm dying to hear what it has to say about your future love life."

With less enthusiasm than she usually had for the oracle, Dominique lifted it off the coverlet and studied the list of one hundred questions. When she got to number thirty-three, her spirits lifted considerably. "Here's the one I want an answer to: 'Shall I cease to be a virgin before I marry?'"

"Dominique Custer DuBois!"

"But, Aunt Libbie, it *is* a question—see?"

Libbie looked at the page. "So it is, but it is not—"

"Oh, please? What harm can there be? Just let me choose my sign from the table and you read the answer. If you think it is much too vulgar for my delicate ears, simply keep it to yourself."

"Oh, all right." Libbie spread the book open to the sign table and waited for Dominique to close her eyes and make her selection. When her finger finally landed on three black circles, Libbie quickly consulted the numbers chart to find the answer. She read it once, screwed up her features, then read it again.

"Well?" Dominique demanded—her good friend, impatience, ruling her tongue.

"Hold your horses, miss." Libbie narrowed her eyes and read the small print. "It seems innocent enough. It says, 'No, as you will be married sooner than you expect.' Is there someone you haven't told your uncle and me about?"

Perplexed by the answer, Dominique ignored Libbie's question and reached for the book. "Are you sure you have the right page? Did you look under three black circles or two?"

Backtracking over the instructions and her choice of sign didn't change a thing; the answer remained the same.

Dominique would retain her virginity until her wedding day. "I'm doomed," she groaned, "destined to live a life of boredom."

"Oh, Nikki," Libbie encouraged. "It's not that bad. It only says you'll be getting married, as any young lady should. You will be chaste and pure on that special day— what's so terrible about that?"

Dominique shrugged. "It doesn't sound very exciting, especially when you consider I don't even have a beau." She immediately thought of Jacob, of his smoldering gaze. Here, she supposed, was a man who could burn the innocence from her body with only a dark, roguish glance, answer all of her questions with his fiery touch. Here was the kind of man who could teach her to be a woman. Dominique shivered at the thought.

Unmindful of her niece's indecent musings, Libbie offered a suggestion. "Now, don't think I'm rushing you into anything—marriage or any kind of courtship—but you must be blind! Haven't you noticed the streams of husband material lining up for a chance to court you?"

"Husband material?" Dominique wrinkled her nose. Is that what she really wanted—a husband? She glanced at Libbie and sighed. Her aunt was a woman who'd groomed herself to be the perfect complement to her man. What skills did she, Dominique, have to offer a man—an artistic flare, the ability to turn a blank canvas into a thing of beauty? Of what possible use could that feeble talent be? Again she sighed. "I'm not interested in finding a husband, Aunt Libbie. I don't think I'll ever get married."

"Why that's ridiculous! Of course you'll get married. And soon, I'll bet! Just last night in the parlor I noticed Captain Ruffing swooning, even if you didn't. The man is positively smitten, Nikki. Why don't you give him a chance?"

She thought of the long-haired officer and rolled her eyes. "I noticed him, but I don't like men who fawn all over me like that. I swear, he reminded me of Uncle

Armstrong's staghound, Cardigan, drooling all over me the way he did.''

"I doubt he was that bad, but even if he was, you can't blame a man for admiring you.''

"I can so. That's not what I want from a beau. I like . . . I mean, what I really want is . . .'' *Jacob.* "Oh, bloody hell, I don't know what I want!''

"Nikki! I simply will not permit that kind of language in this house!''

"Oh, Aunt Libbie, I *am* sorry! I meant no disrespect.'' Knowing she must sound ungrateful and ill-mannered, Dominique sighed. "I don't know what comes over me. Sometimes it's as if my mouth runs all by itself—and such language! I realize this is no excuse, but I think I must have picked it up from Grandpa Custer.''

Libbie's sparrowlike features softened, became girlish and nonjudgmental again. "Don't be too hard on yourself, dear. Grandpa Custer does have a penchant for foul language, and he's not particular about who's in the vicinity when he spouts off.''

"Just the same"—Dominique hung her head and took an exaggerated breath—"I don't deserve to live in a fine home like this. You would be completely within your rights to pack me up and ship me off to—to the ends of the earth. *California*, even.''

"Now, darling.'' Libbie scooted closer to her niece and slipped her arm around her slumped shoulders. "That's enough. You'll make yourself melancholy with these thoughts. We were having such a good time. All is forgiven. Let's talk about other things. Perhaps there is something special you'd like to do tonight.''

The devil, who found a very comfortable home there, sprang back into Dominique's eyes. "Well,'' she hedged, knowing exactly what she wanted out of her aunt—and from the evening, "I did enjoy yesterday's card party tremendously. Maybe we could have a few people in again tonight. And I adore listening to you play the piano.''

"Then it's done.'' Her smile bright, Libbie hopped off

the bed. "We'd better send out a few notes of invitation right away. Remember, this night is for you and your enjoyment. Is there anyone special you'd like to ask?"

Dominique made a great show of considering the guest list. With an air of nonchalance, she finally said, "I can't think of a soul. You choose the guests; you're so good at filling a room full of compatible people. I can't imagine how I can add to the list—unless, of course, you think it would be proper to ask Jacob Stoltz."

"Stoltz?" Libbie pressed a finger against her temple. "I'm sorry, Nikki. I don't seem to remember him."

"He's the soldier who is giving me riding lessons. I'd like to thank him for his patience by having him join us this evening. Is that all right with you?"

"Oh—him." Libbie bit her lip. "I think it's commendable you want to thank the young man, dear, but have you forgotten that he's only a private?"

"I realize that, but I do feel sorry for him. He's quite backward, you know. Why"—Dominique laughed, hoping to lighten her aunt's mood—"the poor soul has never even seen a sidesaddle. He actually thought I should learn to ride Peaches *astride*! Have you ever?"

The women shared a laugh and Libbie shook her head. "I understand he's from parts west. Lord knows what they expect of their ladies—if there are any requirements at all, that is."

"Exactly my point." Dominique pushed off the bed and bounced over to her aunt. "Think what a kindness it will be for us to open your grand home to a young man who can never have hoped to see anything like it. Why, you'll go down in history as a kind and generous bearer of the great Custer name."

"Nikki, please." Libbie blushed, but her mind was busy mulling over the idea, loving the thought. At last, she raised her brows and her tone. "I suppose it wouldn't hurt. Autie is always after me to make sure I don't offend the common folk or allow myself to get carried away with the other officers' wives in our evaluations of those less fortunate. Yes," she said with a resolute nod. "I think Autie would be pleased if I were to entertain this unfortunate soldier in his absence. Would you like to write his note yourself?"

Her heart soaring, Dominique swallowed hard and took a breath. "Since we're having guests this evening, I really should be seeing to my toilet, but I suppose I could take the time to make the private feel truly welcome. All right." Fighting the urge to skip, she forced an easy stroll on her way to the writing table. "When the note is finished, I'll have one of the servants take it to him."

"That's a very kind gesture, Nikki. Your uncle will be very proud of you. I'll leave you now. I suddenly have a lot to do!"

Dominique blew her aunt a kiss and waited until she'd passed through the doorway before she allowed herself to celebrate. She raised her arms above her head and sang a silent song, wriggled to the imaginative tune, and tapped her toes against the hardwood floor before she set about her task. When her heartbeat returned to normal, Dominique took a piece of pale pink parchment and dabbed the corners with lilac toilet water. Then she put her quill to the paper and, using her best script, jotted the invitation in a few short sentences.

As he brushed Dandy's sleek coat, Jacob hummed one of the new tunes he'd learned since joining the cavalry. Tonight he would ride the line, take his first turn at sentry duty. If he proved to be reliable, useful even, he could look forward to this post as a regular part of his responsibilities. And gaining the job as sentry for the Seventh Cavalry could be a critical maneuver for the Dakota's plans.

Smiling to himself, Jacob hummed louder, cutting off the outside world.

"Ya'll Private Stoltz?"

The voice startled him. Dropping into a crouch as he whirled around, he assumed a position of combat. When he spotted the "enemy," Jacob let the brush fall from his hand, then resumed an upright stance.

"Take it easy, fella," the servant cried out as she took several backward steps. "I brung you this here note from the Custer house. I don' want no trouble." She sailed the salmon-colored envelope toward the private, then turned and ran from the barn.

"Forgive me," Jacob called after the dark-skinned woman, "I did not hear your approach. I—" He cut off his own words when he realized he was the only one listening to them. Glancing down at his feet, he regarded the note, then bent over and took the thick paper between his fingers. As he lifted it to his line of vision, the scent of springtime, of prairie flowers, reached his nostrils. Dominique.

Anxious to know what she had sent him, he carefully peeled open the seal. Inside he found more paper. His enthusiasm turned to despair when he unfolded the parchment and found a scribbled message inside. She'd written him a note. In English. The language he'd never really had the time to learn to read, with an alphabet he'd hadn't seen in nearly twenty winters.

Not knowing what to do, afraid to show the Long Knives yet another of their customs and rituals with which he was unfamiliar, Jacob blew out a heavy sigh. Why had she written to him? To thank him for a job not yet completed? Or was this some kind of summons, an order relieving him of his duties where she was concerned? If it was the latter, he could hardly blame her or the men in command. The soldier who taught an important woman like Dominique DuBois should at least have some idea what kind of saddle she would prefer! Jacob laughed as he recalled the odd leather seat with not one but two horns, and the strange unnatural way a lady was expected to sit upon it. Then he looked down at the note again. What was he to do?

He folded the paper and put it back in the envelope. Then he slipped the fragrant pink note inside the shirt pocket nearest his heart.

* * *

She'd floated down the stairs one hour ago. Her frock was second in elegance only to the gown she'd worn to the Saint Patrick's Day ball. Made of white gauze of an incredibly silky texture, the dress was trimmed in rich grass-green satin and accented with a wide sash of the same material. Even her shoes, fashionable to the point of having the newest high heel, were lined in green silk and woven in shades of green and black on a creamy background. Dominique tapped one of these shoes against the mahogany rocker of her aunt's favorite chair, and peered out the window.

Jacob was late. Etiquette demanded he arrive over an hour ago, as the invitation instructed. It wasn't every private who was invited to the general's quarters, so where was he? Dominique turned toward the sounds of high-pitched laughter and managed a wan smile. The honored guests were enjoying themselves tremendously—or at least pretending they were. Libbie was seated at her precious piano, turning the pages of a music book. Her dress, a respectable black silk, was set off by black jet beading on the basque and around the hem of the polonaise. The ensemble, several stylish levels above the costumes of muslin and gingham her guests wore, represented Libbie's set of stripes and brass, an identifying uniform of sorts for the wife of the post commander.

Again irritated by the conventions of the military hierarchy, the distinct separations between social levels, Dominique turned back toward the window. The scenery remained unchanged. By the gentle, sleepy glow of dusk, she could look out over the kitchens and mess hall to the stables. Beyond that, the Missouri raged past, tamed enough now by the spring thaw for reasonably safe navigation. The muddy waters pushed onward, twisting as they collided with the mouth of the Heart River, and drove toward their final goal, the great Mississippi. All was as it should be—as far as nature was concerned, anyway.

Averting her gaze, ignoring what ought to have been a

tranquilizing scene, Dominique stabbed the needle through the sampler she'd been trying to embroider since her arrival at the fort. She hated needlework of any kind, especially when it was done only as busywork. She looked down at the material and regarded the message she was trying to embellish with lengths of colored thread: "Home is where the heart is." For some maybe, she thought with an inward grumble. But what about *her* heart? Would it ever be stolen, fulfilled—broken? For tonight, it didn't seem likely that any of those things would ever happen to her.

Even though she realized she ought to be mingling with her aunt's other guests, Dominique continued to stab the innocent square of yard goods. This time her aim was off, and the needle pierced her tender flesh. "Ouch!" she cried, bringing the injured fingertip to her mouth.

Boston Custer chose just that moment to join her. "Why are you off in the corner poking holes in yourself instead of singing with the rest of us, Nikki? We miss your sparkling smile and infectious laughter."

Dominique stared up at him, her finger still in the care of her soothing mouth, and shrugged.

"Let me have a look at that." He reached over and took her by the wrist.

Twisting away, Dominique shook her head. "I'm all right, Uncle Bos, really I am."

"Then join in the gaiety. Our guests look to fun-lovers like you and me to set the pace. I believe if Millie Huffman doesn't find something to laugh about soon, she'll shrivel up and fall down inside that stiff collar she has hugging her righteous neck!"

As always, Boston Custer found a way to untie Dominique's laces and make her laugh. She grinned up at him, giggling under her breath, as she pictured Major Huffman's wife trapped inside her very proper and voluminous dress. Of the three Custer brothers serving their country at Fort Lincoln, Boston was the least military minded. Although Armstrong and Tom were both endowed with a playful sense of humor, Boston made a career of it. All he seemed to think about was the pursuit of fun and beautiful women. He was physically dissimilar as well: both older brothers had red-blond hair and blue eyes, but the youngest Custer sported a head of coffee-colored locks and looked at life through hazel eyes.

Feeling a kinship and warmth for Boston that was more brotherly than anything, Dominique pushed herself out of the rocker. "All right, you win. First let me stop by the kitchen. I'll join you in a minute."

"The kitchen!" Boston's eyelids popped open, and he brought his palms against his cheeks with a resounding pop. "God almighty, little girl! Haven't you been paying attention to your illustrious uncle, the boy lord general?"

Dominique stood on tiptoe and peered over his shoulder to see if the other guests—or Libbie—had heard. Satisfied Boston's irreverence hadn't crossed the threshold, she released her pent-up laughter.

Pleased to see his niece acting like herself again, Boston added a startlingly accurate imitation of the general's voice to his words as he went on. "He'd say, 'Why, Libbie, you cute little sunbeam in this boy's heart, if I've told you once I've told you a thousand times—I can't stand to see my little girl even *pass* by the kitchen door. Those sweet hands are much too delicate for such work! Yes, ma'am, they're better suited for brushing my long golden curls and massaging my neck, which has grown weary from carrying my oversized head around, and they're just made for polishing my boots, cleaning my horse's hooves, oh, and digging—' "

"Uncle Bos!" Dominique choked the name out through a fit of laughter. "Why, if Uncle Armstrong knew how you spoke of him, he'd have you court-martialed!"

Laughing along with her, Boston said, "It would be worth it to see you laugh. A girl as pretty as you should never have cause to frown. Come on, now—let's join the old hens and see if we can't ruffle their feathers."

Dominique bit her lip to keep from laughing as she

strolled by the ladies. She gave each of them a short nod, explaining as she passed, "I have something to attend to in the kitchen, but I'll join you all in a moment. Aunt Libbie? I'll be speaking with Mary. Is there anything else you need by way of refreshments?"

Libbie took a fast inventory and shook her head. "We're all right for now, but do ask her to warm the cobbler. "Oh," she added as an afterthought, "and don't dawdle too long—you know how Autie feels about his girls going into the kitchen."

Trying to catch Dominique's attention, Millie Huffman waved her hanky and said, "Tell Mary not to fix any cobbler for me! I'm fairly straining against my stays as it is after last night's sweet cake!"

Millie giggled, but her laughter sounded more like cackles to Dominique who was already strangling on Libbie's words. The sudden image of a great white chicken flapping about in the yard—wearing Millie's dress, no less—tested her mettle and challenged her to keep a sober expression on her journey from the drawing room. Once in the hallway, she leaned against Libbie's new French satin wallpaper and took huge gulps of air. Her fragile control renewed, she continued on her way and found Mary laboring over the business end of a mop.

"Pardon me?"

The servant looked up from her work and dragged the back of her hand across her brow. "Yes'm?"

"The letter I gave you yesterday—did you make sure Private Stoltz received it?"

"Oh, yes, ma'am. I give it to my sister Annie. I know she give it to him, 'cause she says he scairt her half to death!"

"And she's positive it was Private Stoltz and not some other soldier?"

"Annie is one worthless free gal, all right, her being born after President Lincoln signed them papers an' all, but her stories is always wider than they is tall. She axed his name, she did, before he turned and made like he was gonna git her. It was Stoltz, all right.''

''Thank you, Mary. Oh, Mrs. Custer wants you to warm the cobbler now.''

Her heart heavy, Dominique retraced her steps, stopping at the same spot in the hallway. This time, instead of fighting convulsive laughter, she battled a dull ache within. Unused to the sensation, disliking the feeling intensely, she stabbed a freshly manicured fingernail at the maroon border running along the edges of the buff-colored wallpaper.

Jacob Stoltz would pay dearly for this breach of etiquette. He would rue the day he had chosen to ignore an invitation from Dominique DuBois, by God! She would see to it that Uncle Armstrong gave him the most disgusting, most often avoided jobs in the entire army! She would have him sent into Indian territory on imaginary missions! She would see that his arrogance was rewarded with a thousand arrows to his heart! And a thousand more to his backside.

Buoyed in spirit as she plotted her revenge, Dominique straightened her shoulders and lifted her chin. She was determined to join the ladies and gentlemen in the other room, and equally set on giving them the cheerful young woman they'd become accustomed to. Walking stiff-legged, she marched toward the drawing room.

Just before she stepped into view, Dominique manufactured the biggest smile she could. Then she brought her fingertip to the corner of her eye and wiped away a tear.

Chapter Seven

"STOLTZ? YOU IN HERE?"

Jacob stepped out of the feed room carrying a bucket of flax and molasses. At the sight of his ranking officer, he paused and touched the brim of his hat. "Morning, Captain."

"At ease, Private." Edgar Ruffing pulled a cheroot, the last one in the package, from his shirt pocket and slowly drew it across his upper lip. Closing his eyes, he indulged himself with several deep breaths of the rich tobacco, then struck a match and lit the small cigar. Through a long stream of smoke, he finally said, "Got a real plum of an assignment, if you're interested, Private."

Barely keeping a hot glare of loathing from his eyes, Jacob studied the haughty officer. This was a man the other soldiers described as "full of himself." They said his hands were callused from patting himself on the back. When Jacob had looked for calluses and found the captain's hands smooth and soft like those of a white woman, he understood the joke the other men made of their commanding officer.

He also came to understand the deep respect Ed Ruffing had for General Custer and recognized that his life was a poor imitation of the Long Hair's. Since their commander's departure, Ed had allowed his yellow hair to grow long, down to his shoulders. On Custer, whose red-gold hair was thick and curly, the effect was dramatic. On Captain Ruffing, the imitation was laughable. Pale almost to the point of whiteness, his hair hung in long, unkempt strands and made him look like the backside of a mare after a long, fly-ridden summer.

To Jacob, the captain's personality, or lack of it, showed most when he walked. His gait, alive with exaggerated hip movements, made him look as if some invisible string tied to his man parts tugged at him as he walked, led him, as it were, to his destination. Jacob's smile was genuine when he suddenly realized the major role he would play in determining that destination.

"I am interested in anything that will help the Seventh, sir," he said with a bright grin.

Ed took a deep drag of the cheroot, inclined his head, and blew out six perfect circles of blue smoke. Then, even though he was approximately the same height as Jacob, he managed to look down on him. "That's the attitude to have, Private. How'd you like to go to town?"

"To Bismarck, sir?"

"All those muscles, and brains, too! Of course to Bismarck, soldier—where else?"

In spite of his vow to hide his true feelings, his purpose, Jacob's eyes dulled. "Of course," he echoed, "where else but Bismarck?"

Did he have a choice, and if so, should he accept? He hadn't been to one of these places called towns since he was a very small boy. Only in the past few days had he become comfortable with cavalry life, confident that his identity would continue to be a secret. Would it remain so in Bismarck? He thought back to his youth, to the few visits his family had made to the towns dotting the wild country on their ill-fated journey west. He remembered best the large buildings called stores. Jars of candy, child-sized crackers, and cookies came to mind, filled his senses with the ghosts of their inviting aroma and sweet, comforting taste. Going to town held only good memories, drew no disturbing reminders from his past. Was it worth taking a chance to find out if Bismarck would reward him as the towns of the past had? Was it worth the risk of declining the invitation and finding he'd insulted his commanding officer?

Jacob considered the captain's proposal and recognized the generosity behind the invitation. The officer acted as if he'd offered Jacob his freedom, his very life. As much as he hated to think of the obstacles he might face in town, he knew he'd be a fool not to accept.

Calling up some of the English phrases he'd been practicing, Jacob kicked the soft ground with the toe of his boot, and said, "Golly, Captain, I am truly obliged to you, sir. Thank you kindly."

Ed's brows rose, then knotted as Jacob spoke. After a thoughtful drag on the cheroot, he snapped, "It's time you got busy, then. We'll be using the buckboard. Make sure it's clean, and pad all the seats with blankets. There'll be a couple of women along."

Women? The invitation was yet another foolish waste of his valuable time! This assignment would not help him to learn of the soldiers' plans *or* reveal the date of Custer's expected return. This trip could only serve to lower his status among the recruits. But how could he decline now that he'd accepted the Captain's invitation—or was it an order?

Loosening his collar, Jacob grimaced and said, "Women, sir? I don't—"

"Women, you know—they're the ones with the high-pitched voices, round little behinds that wiggle when they walk, and big round titties just made to fit in these." Ed stuck the cheroot in his mouth, then cupped his hands and drove them toward Jacob's face. Oblivious of the murderous thoughts behind the private's blank stare, he puffed out his thin chest and went on, "I'll be escorting the general's niece to town."

"Dominique?" Jacob blurted out, his fingers instinctively going to his shirt pocket and the ridges of the envelope it concealed.

Ed's smug grin reversed itself. "That's Miss DuBois to

you, Private! And yes, the pretty lady has chosen me to accompany her.'' He flipped his cheroot over near Jacob's boot, then rubbed his hands together. "That lucky little gal doesn't know what a treat she's in for—assuming I can find a way to get rid of her homely old chaperon and Lieutenant Woodhouse, that is.''

Wishing the captain's head was beneath his heel instead, Jacob ground the cigar into the soft earth. "And if you get rid of the others?'' he asked, his jaw tight.

Breaking into a burst of obscene laughter, Ed cupped his hands again and leered. "I'll be filling these—and maybe a whole lot more.''

Jacob stood rigid, his fists clenched, as the captain laughed and enjoyed his carnal fantasies. Only one thought kept his hands from circling the man's throat: When the day of reckoning occurred between the soldiers and the Dakota—and more and more it looked as if the confrontation couldn't be avoided—he would find a way to make certain this Long Knife was the first to die.

Ed straightened his jacket. "Now get busy, Private! Finish feeding the stock; then put the lead team on the buckboard. When you're done with that, pick out a couple of good mounts—one for you and another one for one of the Indian scouts. You two'll ride shotgun. Now get to it,'' he ordered as he spun on his boot heel and marched toward the barn door. "Miss DuBois wants to leave on the hour.''

"Yes, sir. Right away, sir.'' *Anything you say, you dog whom I will cut into so many pieces the spirits will never find enough of you to take you to your final rest.* Only slightly mollified by the thought, Jacob finished his chores. Then he hitched the horses to the buckboard and adjusted the plank on which the women would ride.

As he went to gather the other supplies, he tried to find some positive thoughts about his forced trip into town. Dominique. He hadn't seen or heard from her in nearly two weeks. Not since he'd received the note. Jacob took the envelope from his pocket. The scent of lilacs lingered, drawing his mind to thoughts best left to one such as the arrogant captain. The crazy one was trouble. She could mean the difference between success and failure for him, between life and death. Yet thoughts of her had filled his lonely hours and tortured his restless nights. Was there no way for him to get her out of his mind? With something akin to anger, he jammed the letter back into his pocket and began smoothing a blanket across the plank.

Ed Ruffing returned then, stepping out of the morning light and into the stable. Brushing Jacob aside with a wave of his hand, he began an inspection of the rig to make certain it met his specifications. "At ease, Private."

Jacob clasped his hands behind his back and spread his legs. He noticed the captain had changed into civilian clothing, dark blue trousers and jacket, and strutted about like a young warrior wearing the symbol of his first coup. He doubted the shiny medals the captain usually wore could be as significant. A few of the ribbons may have been earned, but the balance were most likely given on the field of battle during the War between the States. It was said a man had only to show up on the battlefield to win a medal at that time. The honors were more of a courtesy—not unlike the courtesy title of general bestowed on Lieutenant Colonel George Armstrong Custer in that very same war.

Amused by this, Jacob shook his head and looked away. White soldiers had very strange ways. To a Dakota, a chief was a chief, a warrior, a warrior. Never was a warrior called chief simply because he'd done a good job or shown extraordinary bravery. He fought the urge to sneer and turned back to the captain. "Shall I drive the buggy to the Custer house, sir?"

"No. I'll pick up the ladies myself. Everything looks in order here. Take the extra mount and ride on over to the Ree camp. Pick up Long Back, then head on down to the river. Wait for us there. Oh, and don't bother changing into your uniform. We have the ladies' reputations to think about."

Although he didn't understand what the captain meant, he said, "Yes, sir. Right away, sir."

With counterfeit exuberance, Jacob wheeled around and marched to the other end of the barn where the horses stood waiting. He mounted the large sorrel gelding he'd chosen for himself, then wrapped the reins of the smaller roan mare around his hand. He rode out one end of the barn, all military precision, as Captain Ruffing cracked the whip and drove his team of horses out the other.

Jacob headed up the long hill between the cavalry and infantry posts, consumed by the reality of his newest task. At the top of the hill, he would have to confront the Arikaree scouts in their own quarters—an encounter he'd managed to avoid until now.

Although he'd never actually seen a member of the hated Arikaree tribe before, on many occasions, the main topic of conversation during the Dakota council fires had been these same Indians. The discussion always centered on ways in which to spill their blood.

Grumbling to himself, but feeling no malice, Jacob wondered if Gall had any idea of the trials he would put his son through when he'd conceived this mission. Had he known that Jacob would have to face not one but *two* of the Dakota's most despised enemies? Or that his son would have to act like a friend to these mangy dogs?

Compelled to do no less, Jacob wore a smile as he approached the log buildings of the Ree camp. He slid down off the sorrel, hampered only slightly by the leather seat he was forced to use, then tied the animals to a log railing. Walking directly to the largest structure, a long, low building, he pushed the door open and stepped inside.

"I come for Long Back," he announced, his senses assaulted by the pungent odor of smoked venison and tanning hides.

Illuminated only by huge logs burning in the center fireplace, several shadowed figures stirred. One stepped forward. "I am Long Back."

Heavily jowled and broad of cheek, the scout was

neither Indian nor white, warrior nor soldier. He wore buckskin breeches with heavy fringe sprouting out from the sides. Around his neck hung a string of bear claws, their points denting the gray flannel of his regulation army shirt. The leather straps of the scabbard for his government-issue rifle crossed over his chest, but then, so did his waist-length plaits.

The thing that caught Jacob's attention, that which interested him the most, was the headband the Ree wore—and the feathers protruding from it. The number and color of the feathers combined with the way they were cut told of the warrior's many coups. Long Back had killed and scalped enemies and received many wounds in the bargain. A very impressive display. How many members of the Hunkpapa were represented by these symbols? Jacob wondered. How many killed or wounded by the two-faced Ree standing before him?

Once again calling on all his restraint, Jacob kept his features expressionless and said, "I am Private Stoltz. Captain Ruffing waits for us down by the river."

"I am ready."

The two men mounted their horses and rode down the long hill in silence, each entertaining private thoughts about the other. When they reached the designated meeting spot, they split up without another word between them.

From the background, Captain Ruffing raised his arm in greeting. "Welcome to you, Long Back. How."

"How." The greeting, a universal greeting or toast known to white man and Indian alike, regardless of tribe, was accompanied by the Ree's raised hand.

His required courtesy out of the way, Ed Ruffing got down to business. "Long Back, I want you and Private Stoltz to guard our flanks. Ride about a hundred yards ahead of us and keep a sharp lookout. The entire area is supposed to be free of hostiles, but I don't trust those damn—oh, excuse me, ladies—those Sioux. We don't want to alarm the women in any way, now, do we?" He twisted in his seat, gesturing to the dozen lucky men from Company B who'd been chosen to follow along behind with the supply wagon, and hollered, "Head on out."

Jacob tried to look into Dominique's eyes, but she refused to meet his gaze. What he saw in her expression— indifference mingled with something he couldn't identify—disturbed and hurt him more than he ever could have imagined. He touched the shirt pocket nearest his heart, then coaxed the sorrel into a gentle lope. The note. This sudden change in her attitude had to have something to do with the note she'd sent him. Jacob spent the rest of the morning not looking for hostiles he knew weren't there, but searching for a way to make things right between himself and the crazy one.

She'd felt Jacob's eyes on her, knew he was trying to attract her attention, but Dominique's sense of justice had to be served. Two weeks. Almost two weeks and the ungrateful private hadn't even had sense enough to send his regrets or his apologies. Now he expected her to *look* at him, pretend the breach of etiquette didn't matter—didn't hurt?

Dominique straightened her shoulders and drew her fur-trimmed pelisse closer to her bosom. She gave Ed Ruffing a sidelong glance and said, "How long before we reach town?"

Shifting the reins from his right hand to his left, Ed said through a broad grin, "Maybe three, four hours. Depends on the river crossing and how often you want to stop. You see something pretty like those flowers over yonder, you just holler and we'll pull up and give a look."

"That's very thoughtful of you." Dominique inched closer to the edge of the wooden seat and peered out across the sun-kissed meadow. A few patches of anemone splattered the new grass, their soft gray petals and bright blue centers contrasting with the spring green. To a bored Dominique, the smattering of flowers looked like a field of tattered army blankets. The last thing she wanted to be reminded of was the army or its officers—and certainly not its enlisted men. "This is a close enough look for me, Captain. I'm in a hurry to get to town."

"Whatever you say, little lady. I'm here to see to your pleasures."

From behind, Barney cleared his throat and said, "Have you heard from your uncle in the last couple of days, Miss DuBois? When's he due back?"

"I don't know. Aunt Libbie got another letter just yesterday saying he'd been delayed again. It seems that every time he thinks he's ready to return, someone from the Senate summons him and makes him testify against the secretary of war or the Indian traders, or both—I'm not sure. It's all so tiresome. Seems to me he could have simply written a letter to the government stating his observations and been done with it."

Barney opened his mouth to set her straight, but Hazel silenced him with a finger pressed against her lips. "Hush, now," she cautioned in a whisper. "You must remember Dominique's unfortunate childhood—or lack of it, shall I say?" Glancing up to make sure her impetuous charge couldn't hear, Hazel went on. "She lost her mother at a very impressionable age, you know, then spent her growing years in a succession of boarding schools. If she seems a little, well, spoiled, it's only because the schoolmasters felt sorry for such a lovely motherless child. Do be gentle when conversing with her."

"Sure, Hazel. Whatever you say." But he had no real interest in Dominique's troubled childhood. All Barney's attention was heaped on Hazel and her mesmerizing amber eyes. For nearly forty years he'd managed to stay clear of Cupid's, if not the Sioux's, arrows. Then the indomitable, even-tempered, and highly sensual Hazel Swenson had literally waltzed into his life. She'd been a dream to hold at the ball, a fluffy dumpling of mature womanhood whose capacity for satisfying his appetites he could only imagine.

Vaguely uncomfortable, Barney shifted against the blanket. She was a widow woman, most likely well versed in the ways of lovemaking. The thought sent a delicious shudder slamming into his loins—and a spurt of sheer terror up his spine. What if their relationship progressed? What if she actually . . . if she *wanted* him—*him*?

He wouldn't know what to do, how to act—how to *touch* a woman of her breeding. Crimson wings of shame fluttered along his neck as he realized the full scope of his inexperience. His knowledge of women had never been anything more personal than a business transaction. How could he ever hope to claim a fine woman like Hazel Swenson as his own?

"Barney?" she whispered, concerned about the deep furrows between his thick eyebrows. "Did I say something wrong? I only wanted you to understand about Dominique."

"It's not you," he finally said, brushing off her apology. "I—I was just thinking ahead, wondering how the boys are gonna make out, this being their first time in town since winter and all. I'd sure hate to have the general come back and find half the troops in jail!"

"I heard that." Ed Ruffing spun sideways on the seat, intentionally brushing the back of his hand against the bodice of his silent passenger's dress. "Do you really think the men will be a problem once we get to town?"

Drawing her wrap tight against her breasts, Dominique moved as far away from the captain as she could get without toppling over the edge of the buckboard. Her tone icy, she cut into Barney's reply before he could even voice it. "This trip to town was planned by me, *for* me, Captain, even if you do plan to fill the supply wagon. The main purpose is for Hazel and me to purchase some yard goods. I strongly suggest you speak to your men and let them know my uncle will not be pleased if one of them should ruin this little outing for me."

"Of course, ma'am." Ed glanced at the haughty woman, and grumbled under his breath. The general's niece was proving to be a real uppity bitch, too good to even sit close by him. She'd been hanging on the edge of the buckboard since they'd left the fort, even stayed put during the ferry ride across the river, clinging to the wooden slats as if her precious virtue depended on it. As far as Ed Ruffing was concerned, she could die unspoiled. She wasn't worth the trouble, or the risk to his career should the general find out his intentions were less than honorable.

Turning back to the horses, he made the decision that would best serve his military future. "I expect I'd best stay with the troops just to make sure they behave themselves, Lieutenant Woodhouse. Bismarck is a pretty rowdy town. Think you can handle these two women by yourself?"

"It'd be a pleasure, Captain."

Ed didn't bother to hide his sneer or the snicker as he steered the rig onto Main Avenue. Barney Woodhouse wouldn't know pleasure if she ripped off his pants and raped him. He laughed to himself. But Ed Ruffing did. And Ed Ruffing planned to find himself some hot, willing flesh if it took all day. He glanced to his right and grimaced. He sure as hell wasn't going to find it with the ice maiden sitting next to him.

Ed made his plans for the afternoon as he guided the buckboard down Main Avenue and steered it toward a series of logs fashioned into hitching posts across from the shops and stores of Bismarck. By the time he'd jumped from the seat and tied the horses, his blood was boiling for a good time.

"Lieutenant, we can't afford to miss that last ferry. You see those ladies are back here at least two hours before sundown." He spun on his heel and marched over to his guides. "You're free for the afternoon. Just make sure to stay out of trouble. Long Back, you know the rules—no whiskey. Stoltz, if you want a drink or two, go ahead, but don't get so drunk you can't stay in the saddle on the way back. Understood?"

Jacob nodded, watching as the captain sauntered on across the wide dirt road. Then he turned to question Long

Back about the town, but the Ree had disappeared. Jacob spun back to the buckboard. Barney was helping Hazel and Dominique out of the rig. Laughing together, with never a glance in his direction, the trio dodged horses and buggies as they made their way across the street. Then they disappeared inside one of buildings.

Jacob was suddenly alone in what might as well have been a new world. Impulse and his survival instincts told him to flee, to run for cover in the cottonwood trees along the riverbank. Common sense told him to stay put. With a tremendous effort, Jacob willed his pulse to slow, then he shoved his hands in his pockets in an effort to still their sudden tremors. Forcing an expression of nonchalance, he glanced around at the town, searching for something, anything, that might bring him comfort or at least some sense of safety. A long seemingly endless row of buildings threatened him from across the street. All of them bore large hand-painted letters above their openings, but none of them made any sense or spelled a word he could understand. A group of horsemen rounded the corner, whooping and hollering as they galloped on by him, splattering his boots with mud in the bargain. Wagons and buggies bobbed along, crisscrossing the deep ruts in the road, adding to Jacob's confusion.

Then he noticed the sign above the doorway of one of the buildings. Although he couldn't make sense of the letters, Ihle & Braun Mercantile, something about their shape and arrangement seemed familiar.

He decided to take a chance. Avoiding the mud puddles in earth still damp from the spring thaw, Jacob made his way across the street and stepped inside the large wooden store. The rich scent of leather goods and expensive fabrics greeted him, but he passed by the yard goods and piles of furs just purchased from trappers, and headed for the counter laden with sparkling glass jars.

He was staring at a jar containing something that looked like bees frozen in honey when the clerk said, "Kin I hep ya?"

Jacob snapped his head upward. "Ah, yes. Some of those."

"How much? A pound?"

Jacob offered his palms and shrugged. "Sure."

Using a big metal scoop, the clerk dug several pieces of the candy out of the jar and dropped them into a bag. "There ya go. A pound of horehound drops. Anything else?"

His eyes suddenly bright and childlike, Jacob nodded. "Some of those, and . . . how about a pound of these, too." He made his way down the row as the clerk followed along filling bags with licorice, chocolate drops, and peppermint balls. He was eyeing some small cookies cut in the shape of stars when he bumped into another shopper. "Pardon me—"

"It's no—" Dominique stared into the deep blue of Jacob's eyes, caught for a moment by what she saw in them, stunned by the fact she could see *in* them at all. Usually shuttered, the windows to his soul were wide open, if only for a moment. She saw laughter, delight, wonder, and awe. She saw the child Jacob, the boy who'd never had a chance to live. Too soon he looked away.

"That be all, soldier?" the clerk asked.

"Yes." Jacob handed the man several coins, hoping he'd brought the correct amount of money, then accepted the bags.

Unable to resurrect her earlier anger, Dominique laughed as he collected his candy. "That's some sweet tooth you have, Private. Aren't you worried your teeth will fall out?"

Feeling awkward, embarrassed, Jacob took the change from the clerk's hand and fumbled for the right words, "I—I like these candy drops. I—my teeth— I am not . . ." Unable to finish the sentence, he gave her a sheepish grin and shrugged.

His candor and that odd look of innocence spread like a warm poultice across her breast. Dominique reached out and impulsively pressed her fingers against his broad shoulder. "Why, Jacob?" she blurted out. "Why did you ignore my note last week? Why did you ignore *me*?"

"Your note?" he said, acutely aware how near her hand was to that very object.

"Don't play the innocent with me, Private. I know you received it. You've had almost two weeks to explain yourself. Why didn't you at least send your regrets?"

He paused, going over the story he'd settled on during the ride, then wondered if the truth wouldn't serve just as well. But he said, "You mean the note was from you?"

"Of course it was from me. Can't you read?"

Any thoughts he'd entertained about telling the truth vanished at her words. Stiff and guarded again, he lied. "I never had the chance to read your letter. It seems Peaches likes you and anything you have touched a great deal. She ate it before I had the chance to open it."

"Peaches? Oh," she said laughing, "that's right. She did eat my hat. That means you didn't get a look at the contents?"

"No. Was the message important? I thought if it was, whoever sent the note would have come to me by now."

"Oh, yes, I—I suppose I should have checked back with you, but I've been so busy of late . . ." Chagrined, Dominique let her words and feeble explanation die out. Not convinced that she owed him an apology, however, she waved a gloved hand. "Then I guess we've just had a little misunderstanding. The note contained an invitation to join me and my aunt in her parlor for an evening of music and refreshments. It's a pity you couldn't make it. We had a delightful time."

"I am sorry I missed it." He lifted the bag of horehound drops, but before he could offer one, Barney and Hazel approached them.

"Private." Barney greeted Jacob before turning to Dominique. "Have you finished your shopping, Miss DuBois? Hazel and I are thinking of going over to the Korner Kafé for some pie and coffee."

"I thought I'd look at the furs a little closer. Why don't you two run along? I can take care of myself."

"Oh, Dominique," Hazel clucked. "Bismarck is a very dangerous place for a young lady alone. I'm afraid you'll have to stay with us."

"I have no plans," Jacob said. "I will be happy to escort Miss DuBois around town and see that she is safe."

"Well . . . I don't know." Warming to the private, but not entirely certain he could be trusted, Hazel looked to Barney. "Do you think that will be all right?"

"I believe Private Stoltz can handle the assignment." Barney directed a narrowed eye at Jacob. "Captain Ruffing was right. Bismarck can be a little rowdy, son. Stay close to Miss DuBois and don't mention you're a soldier to anyone. Townsfolk, even the lowest of them, think we're on the same level as the savages we fight. Your duty today is to make certain the lady's reputation remains intact. And see that no harm comes to her, hear?"

"Yes, sir."

"Oh, and make sure you stay away from Murderer's Gulch. No telling what kind of trouble you'll find there, but find it you will."

"Where is this street called Murderer's Gulch?" Jacob asked.

"Sorry, I keep forgetting you're not from around here. Fourth is the name of the street. It's nothing but saloons, gambling halls, and . . . other places not fit for a lady's eyes."

"Or for a gentleman's either," Hazel tossed in.

"Right," Barney agreed, careful to avoid her gaze. "Or for a gentleman's. You ready to go, Hazel? I can smell them app—those apples from here."

Laughing, she looped her hand through the crook of his arm, and the pair strolled out of the store. Jacob stuffed the bags of candy onto his pockets, hoping when he came across Fourth Street he would be able to read the sign. When the bags were all tucked away but one, he offered it to Dominique. "Would you like some candy before you shop?"

Intrigued by Barney's description of Murderer's Gulch, she shook her head. "No, thanks. And if you don't mind, I'd rather go outside and take a walk around town. I'm tired of being trapped inside, and there really isn't anything else I have to buy right this minute. We have the rest of the day."

"Then let us explore this town of Bismarck." Jacob smiled and mimicked the gesture he'd seen Barney make to Hazel. He bent his elbow and extended it. When Dominique slipped her hand through the opening, Jacob's chest swelled, and he escorted her out the door.

Once in the fresh air, they strolled north toward the end of town. As they paused at the last building, the Northern Pacific depot, a sudden *whoosh* caught Jacob's attention. Fascinated by the sound, he lurched in that direction, dragging Dominique along beside him.

"Ah," he sighed when he rounded the corner and came upon a steaming locomotive. Tentatively, he reached out and touched the shiny black paint. "So this is the fire breather, the iron horse."

"The fire-breathing *what*? You sound as if you've never seen a train before!"

Undaunted by her observation, Jacob kept his gaze fastened to the locomotive. "I have seen these trains in the past, but only from a great distance. I have never been close enough to touch a machine of such power."

Dominique jerked her hand away from his elbow and rested it on her hip. "I swear, Jacob, I'm beginning to think you were raised in a cave!"

"Pardon me?"

"I don't mean to be impertinent, but there are so many things you don't seem to know about. It's like you come from a foreign land sometimes."

"Sometimes I feel that way. That and stupid," he said absently.

"Oh, please don't say that. I didn't mean . . ." Dominique took a deep breath and let it out slowly, wondering when she would ever learn to hold her reckless tongue. She had no right to talk to Jacob that way, probably had him confused with that secret half-breed brother of his, that mountain of a man who'd both saved and terrified her. She shivered. Then she tried to undo the damage. "Look, what I meant to say is—"

"I think I know what you meant, Dominique, and I do understand. In many ways you do come from a different world than mine. The Stoltz family were prairie people. We traveled in wagons and kept to ourselves, stopping only in small places where the railroad had not yet reached." Until the family was no more. Until of necessity, as Jacob Redfoot, he was forced to stay away from towns and areas where the iron horse roamed.

"That's no excuse for the way I talked to you. Just because I come from a big city, it's not right for me to assume everyone has had a train ride. That makes me the stupid one."

"Please forget about it."

He'd called a definite end to the conversation, if not by words, then by manner. Feeling guilty, as if she'd stepped into a part of his life to which he issued no invitations, Dominique glanced around for some kind of distraction. At the other end of Main Avenue, she found one.

"Come on, Jacob," she said, hoping this had something to do with the fabled Fourth Street. "Let's go see what's causing the commotion at the other end of town!"

Still fascinated by the hissing engine, he touched the hot metal one more time, then allowed her to drag him back down the street. Halfway there, after passing his mount and the buckboard, Jacob finally noticed the throngs of townsfolk. Like a swarm of wasps, they gathered around a wildly painted ox-drawn wagon. Concerned about displaying any further lack of knowledge Jacob kept his questions to himself.

Intrigued by what lay ahead, the pair crossed Fourth without realizing they had. When they stopped near the wagon, Dominique leaned against Jacob's shoulder and whispered, "What do you think it is?"

"You mean you don't know?"

"I'm not sure. Let's get a better look."

In need of no encouragement, he reached for her hand and pulled her into the crowd. Using his broad shoulders as ramrods, Jacob cleared a path to the front of the assembly. Before them, a tall silver-haired gentleman, obviously of fine breeding, gestured for the congregation to gather around. Flapping the sleeves of his colorful Chinese mandarin robe of satin, he used exaggerated hand movements to pull a yellow silk scarf from inside the folds of the garment, then waved it toward the audience.

When he was certain the crowd was with him, the man used the scarf as a blindfold, and tied it over the eyes of a beautiful Oriental girl standing beside him.

"Step right up, folks!" the silver-haired man called. "Come close and watch the mystical, magical sorcery of Princess Ling Ling, Queen of the Poppies."

Enthralled, Jacob leaned in toward Dominique and whispered in her ear. "What are they doing? What is their purpose?"

Dominique shrugged. "I don't know for sure, but it might be one of those medicine shows. My father would never let me go to one. I think I'm about to find out why."

"A medicine show?" Jacob glanced at the man, then returned his gaze Dominique. "And this is a medicine man?"

"I suppose so. I don't know what else he could be called."

Hugely impressed, thinking he'd finally found something the Dakota had in common with the white man, he casually slipped his arm across her shoulders and squeezed.

For a moment, the show was forgotten. Dominique and Jacob stared into each other's eyes, touched by the knowledge they were poised on the same level of discovery, intensely aware of their close proximity. Afraid he might have gotten too familiar, he sidestepped, apologizing, "I should not have done that. Please forgive—"

"It's all right, Jacob. You make me feel . . . safe." Her smile shy and self-conscious as his strong arm again surrounded her shoulders, Dominique turned back to the man in the robe as he launched into his routine.

"Who among you would like your fortune told for free by this lovely lady of the Orient? Step forward. Avail yourself of Professor Harrington's specialized services. It won't cost you one thin dime, not one shiny penny to learn what your future has in store for you. Step right up."

As if cued by the final words, the doors to the back of the bright red and white wagon burst open and an Indian wearing a banjo strapped to his chest hopped out. He let out a war whoop and shook a pole with a series of bells attached to it as he made his way to the professor's side. Then he jabbed the pointed end of the pole into the soft earth and slipped the toe of his boot into a halter near the bottom. When he began strumming the banjo, he tapped his foot and jingled the bells in rhythm with the song. Captured by the infectious beat, the crowd joined in and clapped along with the music.

Their heads swiveling in unison, Jacob and Dominique cast furtive glances at each other as they observed the strange proceedings. But they did not clap along with the music. Jacob's arm remained across Dominique's shoulders, and her hands stayed clasped in a tight ball at the front of her gingham dress. Even though they studied the entertainers, their concentration centered on each other's touch. Then the Oriental girl in the scarlet Chinese gown managed to capture their attention as she ran her finger across a farmer's palm.

In a high, squeaky voice, Princess Ling Ling proclaimed, "I see a record crop in the next harvest." She paused, allowing the crowd their oh's and ah's, then continued. "But I also forcast bouts of debilitating illness for you and your wife, too." She tore off the blindfold and widened her almond-shaped eyes. "You must take the proper precautions to guard your health. If you don't,'' she warned, waving a two-inch fingernail in his face, "I fear you will not live to see your abundant crops reaped!''

Several women gasped as others made their way forward and had their fortunes told. The words varied, but the princess always ended with dire warnings about expected sicknesses. Alarmed, Jacob pulled Dominique closer to question her about these illnesses just as another farmer stepped forward. He waved off the free palm reading and turned to the crowd, silencing them with his announcement.

"It's not as bad as it sounds! I know, I speak from experience!'' He spun around to the wagon and its owner. "You still make that tonic, Professor? It saved my life more than once last year, and I'm sad to say I'm almost out. I'd be right grateful if you'd sell me some more.''

"Why, as luck would have it, I do believe I still have a bottle or two left.'' The professor pointed to the Indian. "Chief Nogasackett, would you please have a look at our supplies?''

Jacob and Dominique exchanged curious glances, and he whispered, "What is a tonic?''

"Medicine of some kind.''

Jacob touched the small pouch beneath his shirt wondering if the professor's medicine was as powerful as that mixed by Sitting Bull, if it could cure illness of the mind as well as of the body. Then the Indian strolled back to the front of the crowd, his broad grin exposing several crooked, stained teeth. Although uncommonly white for a red man, Chief Nogasackett had the expected braids hanging down his back and a large feather protruding from a bright red headband, but he wore the baggy trousers of a miner. Sewn to the legs of these pants were large pockets bulging with glass decanters of the mysterious tonic.

Taking one of these bottles from the chief, Professor Harrington held it high above the crowd. "The life-saving formula our friend and neighbor speaks of is contained right here in this vial, this elixir of life. I have observed the authenticity of this product firsthand!'' he proclaimed. ''I have accompanied Chief Nogasackett on many an excursion as he picks just the right herbs and roots, blends them with his own specially grown herbs, and adds them to the mystical power contained in Princess Ling Ling's secret extract of poppy.''

He paused, taking a breath, and gave the crowd a chance to absorb the information before he made yet another proclamation: ''I stand behind this product with a guarantee no other can offer—Professor Harrington's Nature Cure and Worm Syrup will heal liver ailments, eliminate all suffering from the pain of a toothache to the agony of childbirth, and restore health to those who must endure any number of maladies.''

Again he paused, this time giving the chief a chance to resume his tunes. As the music built to fever pitch, the professor made his final claims. ''More than a spring tonic, able to purify and strengthen even the weakest of blood, this miracle cure and worm syrup can be yours for just one dollar. One small coin between you and the best health you've ever had. Step right up, folks. Get yours while the supply lasts.''

The chief resumed his banjo playing as the farmer came forward and bought two bottles of the murky liquid. Again, Jacob and Dominique exchanged glances.

''This must be very powerful medicine,'' Jacob breathed.

''I have to admit that it does sound kind of . . . interesting,'' she said, thinking of the dreadful cramping she was having from her monthly miseries. ''Maybe I should try some. I do have a—a stomachache.''

''And if it works the way the man says it does . . .'' Jacob answered, pushing his hand against his belly and the constant agitation he'd had since joining the army. He stepped forward and addressed the professor. ''Will this medicine work on an angry belly?''

''Indigestion, you say? You hear that, folks? The man wants to know if the professor's cure will relieve his indigestion! Hell, son, I don't even mention an ailment as simple as that. 'Course my tonic can cure a sick gut. That goes without saying!''

The professor turned as if to speak to someone else, but Jacob reached over and gripped his arm. "Then I would like to have two bottles, please."

The professor paused, regarding the large hand circling his biceps, and said, "Why didn't you say so? Chief, give the man his potion. That'll be two dollars, sir."

Jacob paid him, then turned to Dominique and escorted her back through the excited crowd. Alone on the board-walk, they ducked out of the afternoon sun under the bar-bershop awning. There Jacob handed her one of the bottles.

"Thanks, Jacob, but I can't pay you until Hazel gets back. I'm afraid I—"

"There is no need. I bought this as a gift for you. Please accept it."

"But, Jacob! You can't afford to spend a whole dollar on me. I know what the army pays, and it's not near enough."

"It is for me. I have no use for money. Let us see what I have spent these worthless coins on." With that, he reached over and twisted the cap off her bottle, then did the same to his own.

Jacob sniffed at the liquid. Tilting his head, he took a large gulp. He shuddered, wondering briefly why the med-icine tasted so familiar, then took another swallow.

Dominique observed his reaction. "Well? What do you think?"

Jacob frowned as the potion flowed throughout his sys-tem melting cords of muscle at will. "It tastes, it *feels*, a little like whiskey."

"Oh," she poohed, "don't be ridiculous. This is med-icine." With that, she eased a few drops into her mouth and grimaced at the bitter taste. She waited a moment, noticing that her tongue was growing warm and numb.

"It reminds me a little of my father's couch medicine. How bad can that be?"

Always careful to keep a ladylike demeanor, she averted her face from the crowd and took a large swallow of the syrup. Soon after, her entire body grew warm, glowed from within. Her cramps rapidly numbing, she waved Jacob and his objections away and indulged in another, larger dose of medicine.

Hazel and Barney took one last stroll through the mercantile store, but there was still no sign of Dominique and Jacob. Where could they be? As they hurried back out into the street, panic began to replace worry in the anxious pair. Barney checked the setting sun, wondering how much time they had left. That was when he spotted Captain Ruffing and his men heading toward the wagon. Time had run out.

Thinking fast, Barney turned to Hazel. "I'll take you back to the buckboard. When the captain gets there, try to stall him while I check a few other places."

"Oh, Barney! This is all my fault. Dominique is my responsibility. I should have—"

"That kind of talk isn't going to do us any good," he encouraged as he helped her across the street. "Just keep calm and don't say a thing about this to the captain. I'll explain to him if it's necessary when I return to th—" The words stuck in his throat as he noticed a long red-gold curl hanging down over the rear slat of the buckboard.

He straight-armed a very surprised Hazel. "Stay here. Don't move." Drawing his gun, Barney cautiously approached the wagon and peered inside.

Dominique pushed her chin upward, and gave the lieutenant an upside down grin. "Hi, Barney! How's you?"

Jacob rolled over on his side and jackknifed to a sitting position.

Barney demanded, "What the *hell* is going on here?"

Seeing there was no danger, Hazel joined him and looked inside the back of the wagon. "Dominique!" she cried, her hands to her cheeks. "What are you doing in there? What's *he* doing in there with you? My Lord, girl, have you no sense of propriety?"

"I fine, Hazel, reedy I am." She pushed up with one hand, trying to sit up, but toppled over on her face instead.

Jacob turned up his palms. "I tried to tell her about the med—"

"*Quiet*, soldier!" Barney glanced up the street, checking the captain's progress, then circled the buckboard. Reaching inside, he grabbed the back of Jacob's shirt. "I don't know what you could have been thinking about when you got that girl drunk, but right now you'd better listen and listen good."

Jacob's eyes swam in a murky, bitter haze, but his mind was clear enough for him to realize his best defense was silence.

"Get your butt on that horse now and find a way to stay on it. Don't say a word to anyone. Just ride on down the road and pray to God that animal knows the way home. Understand, soldier?" At Jacob's slow nod, he added, "You and I will have a little talk about this later. Now, git."

Knowing he had no choice but to obey, Jacob hoisted his long legs over the side of the wagon, mounted the sorrel, and rode to the edge of town while Barney and Hazel tried to extract Dominique from the buckboard. Their efforts were wasted.

Every time they pulled her into a sitting position and tried to get her to her feet, Dominique burst into raucous laughter and fell over backwards.

"This isn't going to work," Barney complained as the captain neared. "We'll have to think of something else." Reaching inside the wagon, he smoothed Dominique's dress, then covered her with the blanket from their seat.

Barney had just helped Hazel onto the wooden plank when the captain arrived, demanding, "Everyone ready to go? Where's Miss DuBois?"

Barney held a finger to his mouth as he climbed on board beside Hazel. "Shush. I'm afraid the young lady has taken ill. Too much sun today. She's resting in the back, but we really should return her to her aunt in all haste.''

Ed Ruffing raised his brows, took a quick look in the back, and vaulted onto the driver's seat. "Head on out, boys. We got a sick one with us.''

The wagon lurched to life, then made a large arc as it turned homeward. The movement disturbed Dominique's sense of equilibrium. Again she tried to sit up.

Like a doily spread across the back of a sofa, warm fingers covered her face and pushed her back down in the straw.

That hand was the last thing Dominique remembered during the long ride home.

Chapter Eight

"YOU'RE A MAN RIDING FULL OUT TOWARD THIRTY YEARS of age, and I got to tell you"—Barney stopped his pacing and looked the private straight in the eye—"it's damn hard for me to believe you didn't know what was in that elixir."

Jacob brought the tin cup to his mouth and took a sip of coffee. Groaning at the bitter taste, he said, "The professor told us it was medicine. Other soldiers were at his show. They will tell you that I am speaking the truth."

Barney slammed his fist into his open palm. "And stop talking like that! You sound like a goddam Indian."

Jacob lifted his head and tried to shoot the lieutenant down with a fiery gaze, but a stabbing pain behind his right eye rendered him unarmed. His head drooped down toward the table again as he tried not to think about the awful taste in his mouth.

"Sorry," Barney mumbled. "I don't mean to add to your considerable troubles by insulting you, but I'm kinda worried about my own hide. If Mrs. Custer gets wind of this and tells the general, we'll all be court-martialed."

"And would that bring us trouble?"

Barney's laugh was bitter as he explained, "I suppose that depends on your point of view. Me, I plan to stay in this man's army until I retire. That means I want leave the cavalry when it's my idea, not theirs. You got no stake just yet. I suppose there's lots worse things that could happen to you than getting thrown out of the army."

"No! That cannot happen!" Jacob struggled to his feet and lurched forward. Using the table for support, he said, "Please tell me what I have to do to make everything all right. Who can help me?"

"Now, take it easy, Private. Sit a spell—you're looking a little pasty-faced."

"But I must remain a soldier in Custer's army. Please tell me who can help me. What should I do?"

"Jacob, take it easy." Alarmed, Barney circled the table and gave him a reassuring pat on the back. "I didn't know a career in the cavalry meant so much to you. The situation's probably not as bad as I thought. Hazel's pretty good with words. I think we can assume she's been able to convince Libbie that Dominique was just a little sick."

"I cannot assume anything. I have to go to her and make certain all is well."

Barney laughed. "That's real brave of you, soldier, but you can't just go waltzing up to the Custer house and expect to be welcomed."

"I think I am welcome." He reached into his pocket and handed the note to Barney.

Even though the invitation was issued nearly two weeks ago, it was undated, as Jacob hoped. "Well, I'll be damned if you ain't welcome," Barney said as he read the delicate script. He scratched his head and returned the note. "I'd give my left arm for an invite to that house, and they go and ask you instead—a private, for chrissake!"

"I am sorry, Barney, but I must go."

"Hell, you got no need for apologies—unless that girl wrote the invitation when she was drunk! That it? Better tell the truth, Private."

"No, no. Miss DuBois gave it to me before we left for town."

"Then go on, get on out of here before you insult them by being late." As Jacob smoothed his hair and reached for his hat, Barney added a footnote. "Be sure to give my regards to Mrs. Swenson if she's there, hear?"

"I will." After popping a peppermint ball into his mouth, Jacob ambled out of the barracks. He slowly made his way past the officer's quarters, preparing and discarding speech after speech, then labored up the white steps to the Custer home. He stared at the glass panels surrounding the door for a long moment before he was able to bring himself to knock.

Upstairs, Hazel offered a steaming bowl of lentil soup to Dominique.

"Ugh, no." Turning her head, she tried to wave her chaperon off, but Hazel was insistent.

"Now, you listen to me, young lady. If you weren't past twenty-one years of age, I'd turn you over my knee and spank you. Now sit up and eat before your Aunt Libbie gets back from Major Kennedy's and guesses the state you're in."

"But, Hazel, I can't," she groaned. "It will make me sicker than I already am."

"Humph. You should have thought of that before you decided to swill a whole bottle of the devil's own brew."

With a low moan, Dominique collapsed against the pillows on her bed. "That's not fair. I didn't know what it was. I thought it would ease my miseries." And it had for a while. Now her cramps were back, stronger than ever, second only to the roaring pain thundering against her temples. "Please, Hazel. Just let me go to sleep. Tell Aunt Libbie that I took sun-sick like you told everyone else. *Please?*"

"I shouldn't let you off the hook so easily. What I ought to do—" A couple of sharp raps against the door cut into her thoughts. "I'll bet that's your aunt now—oh, dear! What shall I tell her?" Hazel slid off the bed and hurried to the door. When she opened it, Mary stared back at her.

" 'Scuse me, miz, but they's a soldier wanting to see Miss Nikki. Says it be mighty importan'."

"Oh? Did he leave his name?"

"Stoltz. Private Stoltz."

"Jacob's here?" Dominique bolted off the bed and stumbled over to the looking glass. "Tell him I'll be right down, Mary. Oh, dear Lord, I look a fright! Hazel, quick, help me with my hair."

With one raised eyebrow, Hazel nodded to Mary. "Tell the private *I'll* be down in a moment." Then she closed the door and stalked over to the dresser. "You can't seriously be thinking of entertaining the swine who got you in your cups this afternoon!"

"Hazel, please. Fix the back of my hair." She pinched her cheeks, then gave each one a hard slap. "And kindly stop saying that. Jacob didn't meant to get me drunk. He thought the elixir was medicine, too."

"Of course he did, my dear." Hazel blew a long low whistle as she finished knotting Dominique's hair. "Boy, do you have a lot to learn about men."

Some of Dominique's sparkle returned as she winked at Hazel's reflection. "You're right, of course, but how do you expect me to finish my education while standing in here with you? Shouldn't I be downstairs—with one of *them?*" She twirled, brushing a few lingering bits of straw off her blue gingham dress, and started for the door.

"Not so fast, missy." One step behind her, Hazel went over the rules. "First off, it's highly improper of you even to see a fellow who doesn't have an invitation to visit you. Second, you will not be seeing him alone. I shall accompany you."

Dominique stopped in her tracks and spun around. "It's not as if I'm some young schoolgirl, you know. I think I can manage the private all by myself."

"As you did this afternoon in the back of the wagon?"

Dominique pursed her lips. "I told you that was an accident. Why won't you listen to me?"

"Oh, all right. I'll compromise. I'll greet him with you, and then I'll disappear into the drawing room to work on my crocheting. Just be warned—if it gets too quiet out in the parlor, I shall have to return."

Dominique rolled her big brown eyes.

"Take it or leave it, girl," Hazel said firmly.

"I'll take it."

Raising the hem of her skirt, Dominique made her way down the long curving stairway, then carefully strolled into the parlor. "You wish to see me?" she said to her guest as she entered the room.

Jacob nearly dropped the carved ivory elephant he held. Replacing the statue on a small occasional table, he faced the women. "Yes. I came to see if you were well."

"No thanks to you, Private." Hazel advanced on him, but stopped her progress at a scathing glance from Dominique. Backtracking, she excused herself. "I'll just be in the other room. I trust your visit will be brief, Private. Miss DuBois needs her rest."

"I will not stay long." As soon as Hazel was out of sight, Jacob studied Dominique for signs of ill effects. Other than a general appearance of fatigue, she looked as beautiful as ever. With a sheepish grin, he said, "Your friend sounds as if she is quite angry with me."

"Don't worry about it, Jacob. She's none too pleased with me, either."

"Are you well?" he asked softly, concern reflected in his sea-blue eyes.

"As well as can be expected, I suppose. I have a dreadful headache and feel as if I may be sick at any moment. How about you?"

"I have definitely felt better," he said with a quiet laugh. "Perhaps what we need is a shot of Professor Harrington's elixir."

"Oh, Jacob!" Swaying against him, Dominique brought her hand to her mouth in an effort to stifle her laughter. She caught her breath and whispered, "I was afraid you might be mad at me for getting so silly after I drank that awful stuff."

With a quick glance over his shoulder, Jacob satisfied his sense of privacy. Then, in a bold move, he cupped her face between his hands, forcing her to look into his eyes.

"I am to blame for any harm caused to you this afternoon. It is I who beg your forgiveness."

He was so close, she could feel the warmth from his breath, catch the faint scent of peppermint it carried. Again she swayed, but it had nothing to do with illness or potions, the miseries or a sense of propriety. It had everything to do with Jacob, the man. "P-please don't say that. You've done nothing to forgive. You tried to keep me from taking too much of the potion, and even after it was too late, I-I know how difficult it must have been for you to—to handle me."

Her words were almost too much for him. If only she knew how badly he longed to handle her, to touch her. If they were back in his lodge, in the camp of his father, it would have been a simple thing. Dominique would have been his by now. She would share his tipi, his life. This he knew, this he believed without a doubt. Thinking not of their uncertain future, but only of the moment, Jacob raised his fingers to her brow and brushed a lock of golden-red hair aside. "You were no problem," he said in a throaty whisper.

But she knew she had been. Ever since her return to the house, vague, disturbing glimpses of her adventures in town had been popping out of the shadows in her mind. She remembered the potion, Jacob's warnings, Jacob's dark blue eyes, the way he smiled down at her with playful desire as he tried to comfort her in the wagon. She'd guessed it was desire because she felt the same thing, wondered if those feelings were there because of, or in spite of, the elixir. She remembered wanting to kiss him, had an idea she might even have asked him if he would do her the honor. Dominique's cheeks grew fiery at the thought. *Had* she verbalized her desires?

"Oh, Jacob, I—I'm afraid I said some terrible things to you, asked you to—to do some things a lady would never—"

"You are wondering if you asked me to kiss you?" He smiled, allowing one hand to fall down from her shoulder to her waist. "Yes, you did. But I also know the medicine made you say the words without your permission. Do not feel ashamed."

Dominique blushed. "I don't feel shame, Jacob. I feel embarrassed because I asked you to do such a thing, because with or without the medicine, my lips had my permission. Because," she added, looking up at him with languid eyes, "it's something I've been wanting to do for a long time. If I feel anything, I feel cheated because it didn't happen."

His breath caught as his heart thundered against his throat. "This is the way you feel now?"

"Now more than ever," she said, leaving her lips moist and slightly parted.

And because he was only a man at that moment, neither Sioux nor soldier, savior nor avenger, Jacob accepted her invitation without another thought. His arm tightened around her waist and he drew her against the length of his body in one swift movement only seconds before he claimed her mouth with his.

Startled at first by the near violence of his kiss, the force with which he came to her, Dominique went limp and compliant under the onslaught of his kisses. Then passion—honest and heady, a genuine sensation, no longer just a word in a forbidden book—welled up inside her. A new awareness lapped at her senses, roused in her a curiosity and an enormous need, enticed her with a siren's wail from deep within. Her hands moved of their own accord, explored the ridges of his muscular shoulders, followed the hard valley of his spine, and massaged the softer flesh protecting his ribs.

Then suddenly, as abruptly as he'd come to her, Jacob tore his mouth from hers and backed away. "Someone is coming," he said, his voice thick with desire.

As she reeled in the strange new world of passion, Dominique's lashes fluttered and she wobbled when she tried to make her way to the rocking chair.

Reaching out to steady her, Jacob gripped her arm until he heard the front door open, then slam. He released her and stepped back into the shadows just as Elizabeth Custer passed under the high archway.

"Nikki!" she greeted. "How was your trip to town?"

Dominique remained standing, even though she'd reached the rocker, and worked at catching her breath. "Fine, Aunt Libbie. Private Stoltz"—she gestured toward the corner—"was good enough to show me around the city."

Libbie spun on her heel, surprised to learn she and her niece were not alone. "Oh, Private—I didn't realize Nikki had company." She looked back to Dominique, one eyebrow raised, and asked, "Does the private have some special army business here?"

"Not exactly." Dominique picked at a hangnail, struggling to find one of her usually quick retorts, and finally said, "Private Stoltz just stopped by to inquire about my health. I took sick on the ride back home today."

"Oh, Nikki! Why wasn't I informed? I was only two doors down." She rushed to her niece's side and promptly pressed her palm against Dominique's brow. "You do seem a bit warm." Leaning back, she took in her niece's appearance. "Oh, and look at that high color. Why, you're positively flushed, girl. You should be in bed."

Not even trying to control her reaction to Libbie's observations, Dominique exchanged glances with Jacob, then lowered her head to hide her sudden grin. "I'll be all right, Aunt Libbie. I was just in the sun too long."

"Well, whatever the cause, you should be upstairs resting. Now run along."

This time Dominique bit back the impulse to argue, knowing that to push any more tonight would only rouse suspicion. She exhaled loudly and nodded. "I think you're right. Thanks again for the lovely afternoon, Private. Maybe we can do it again some other time."

"I would be honored, Miss DuBois."

Dominique curtsied, whirled around, and took one dramatic step toward the hallway before she stopped. "Oh, Aunt Libbie. There is one other thing. Private Stoltz is the soldier I invited to join us a few days past. It seems his invitation was destroyed before he ever had a chance to read it. Do you suppose it would be all right to extend him the same courtesy, oh, say . . . Friday afternoon?"

"O-oh, well, Nikki . . . I don't know. We may be—"

"It would be such a wonderful gesture. He was so helpful when I was ill this afternoon and all. I don't see how we can let him go unrewarded."

"Well, in that case . . ." Libbie faced the private. "Would you care to join us around four o'clock on Friday afternoon for tea and cakes, Private? We usually sing some songs or play cards."

Jacob's smile was broad, directed not at Libbie, but beyond her to the vision of cunning beauty in the doorway. "I would be honored. Thank you. I wonder if I might ask Lieutenant Woodhouse to come, too. He helped to care for Dominique this afternoon."

"Lieutenant Woodhouse?" Again Libbie looked toward her niece. "Isn't he Hazel's new friend?"

Grinning, she said, "Why, yes, I believe he is." From the other room, Dominique was sure she heard a small gasp. She continued, "Barney Woodhouse is quite some gentleman too. I think you ought to get to know him better, Aunt Libbie. He's a good one to have around."

"Hummm." Libbie turned back to Jacob. "Very well, then. Go ahead and extend the invitation to the lieutenant as well."

"Thank you, ma'am, but I have one more request."

"I'm sorry, Private, but I cannot invite any more strangers into the general's home in his absence. I'm afraid you—"

"It is nothing like that. I would ask that your invitation be in writing. Some of the soldiers play jokes on each other and I do not want Barney to think this is what I am doing to him."

"Oh." Libbie shrugged and crossed over to her small

marble-inlaid desk. She pulled a slip of her personal stationery from the drawer, scribbled a few lines on it, then folded the paper and handed it to the private. "There. That should convince him of the authenticity of my invitation. Until Friday afternoon, Private."

"Thanks, ma'am."

Her duty finished as she saw it, Libbie nodded and glided over to Dominique's side. "Now, then, let's get you upstairs."

"Good afternoon," Dominique called to Jacob as she and Libbie passed under the archway.

"Afternoon, ladies," he replied, hat in hand. After the two women left the room, Jacob followed along behind them, turning left in the direction of the front door as they headed right toward the stairs. When he reached the threshold, he stopped when he heard Libbie's excited voice cry out.

"Oh, Nikki. I almost forgot—I have just the thing to perk you up! One of the major's men was in town today, and he bought a few bottles of a brand-new cure-all. Why, I'll bet all you need to feel better is a dose of Professor Harrington's Nature Cure and Worm Syrup!"

Chapter Nine

ON FRIDAY, ONCE AGAIN WEARING THE WHITE GAUZE dress with the grass-green satin trimming, Dominique twirled before her full-length looking glass. She leaned forward, tugging at the fabric and encouraging her breasts to swell out over the square-cut neckline, then straightened. After spinning from one side to the other, she gave her reflection a nod of approval and strolled over to her bedroom window.

Through the large gabled window frame, her gaze swept the commanding view of Fort Abraham Lincoln and its Missouri River backdrop. Beyond the cottonwood trees lining the banks lay the wild, untamed Dakota Territory and the Indians fighting so mightily to keep this land as their own. Her thoughts, as they seemed to do more and more, reverted to the night she had spent in the Dakota camp—to the savage Dominique had come to think of as Jacob's brother—the man whose kisses had fueled the fire Jacob had ignited so well in the parlor.

Tonight she would inform him of his mother's fate. She would make it her duty to let him know of the existence of the man who carried his blood in his veins. Again Dominique thought of that man, of the savage whose naked body had warmed, then returned life, to her frozen limbs. His voice, the husky laugh that was so like Jacob's, stirred her memory, her heart. She couldn't let another day go by, allow another shared intimacy to pass, without telling Jacob about the man called Redfoot.

Dominique glanced over at the barracks. Friday afternoons left the fort looking deserted, as the common soldiers cleaned the facilities in preparation for their weekly Sunday inspections. Not a soldier stirred outside the barracks—with the exception of Private Stoltz and Lieutenant Woodhouse. This privileged duo, she noticed with delight, sauntered along the path of Officers' Row on their way to the grand centerpiece, the Custer house.

Ducking out of sight, Dominique gave her cheeks a final pinch before bolting from her room and down the stairs. Once in the hallway, she lifted her chin and modified her manners. Strolling quietly into the parlor, she found a member of her family over by the sideboard.

"Good afternoon, Uncle Tom. I didn't know you were coming by."

Thomas Custer jumped a foot, spilling the ill-gotten brandy down the front of his dress shirt. "Oh, ah, Nikki. I didn't hear you come in."

Unaware of his distress, she approached him. "Sorry if I startled you. Is Uncle Bos coming, too?"

"Uh, I don't know, sweetheart." Working with his back to her, Tom managed to hide the small glass behind Libbie's collection of fine silver before he faced her. "You know Bos," he said with a forced laugh. "He's a civilian and thinks he can march to his own drummer. I don't know where he is today."

"Tom, Dominique," Libbie greeted as she hurried into the room. Dressed in a plain brown wrapper the color of her chestnut hair, she looked unusually drab and stern. "Did I hear you mention Boston? Is something wrong?"

"No, dear." Tom reached for her hands. "I was just explaining to Nikki how hard he is to locate since he really doesn't have to answer to anyone."

"He has to answer to the general, Tom."

"Yes, of course, but more as a brother than as a soldier.

After all, Libbie, a civilian guide is hardly bound by the rules of the United States—''

"Tom!" Libbie blurted out. Sniffing, she stepped closer. "My stars! You *reek* of brandy. Oh, Thomas, you promised the general, you promised us all you wouldn't—''

"Shussh! Libbie, please." Tom inclined his head toward Dominique. "I hardly think this needs to be discussed in front of an audience. After all, it was just one little shot of brandy. You're carrying on as if I'd gone out and gotten all liquored up."

Libbie glared up at him, biting her tongue, checking her temper. She'd promised Autie and Grandpa Custer she would keep a close watch on Tom and help to ensure his sobriety whenever temptation reached out to him. And so she had. Or at least, she thought she had. How many times had he broken his pledge behind her back? Had he been fooling her all along? The sound of voices filled the entry-way, making it impossible for her to ask him any questions until some more private time.

Libbie leaned toward him, whispering, "You and I are going to discuss this later, Tom, but discuss it we will. Now, if you please, I'd like you to help me greet our guests." Then she took his outstretched arm and walked to the archway as the first of the ladies stepped into the parlor.

Dominique, forgotten and left standing by the side-board, contented herself by staying in the corner. She had no more interest in her uncle's drinking problem than she had in the officers or their high-and-mighty wives. Her only concern this night was for Jacob—and his opinion of her now that she'd allowed him to see the wild, undisciplined side of her nature. Would he think her common and cheap, try to take further liberties whether she encouraged them or not? Or would he ignore her altogether, think her less than worthy of him or of any decent man?

Suddenly more nervous than excited, Dominique bit her bottom lip and began to worry the split at the side of her thumbnail. Then Barney strode into the room. Jacob was one step behind him. After shaking the hand of hostess and saluting his host, the private made straight for her.

"Good afternoon, Miss DuBois," he said in a loud, clear voice. Then, making sure they weren't overheard, he added in a lower tone, "I hope you have had time to recover from your sickness caused by Professor Harrington's cure-all—or did your aunt force you to drink another bottle of this famous medicine?"

Dominique gasped, laughing as she said, "You heard her?" When he nodded, she went on, still giggling. "I spent the better part of the night convincing her I had suddenly become well. She was determined to test the effects of that horrible stuff on me! Ugh!"

Jacob chuckled as she mimicked an exaggerated shudder, then said, "I do hope you are well at last."

"I am." She looked up at him and smiled. His return gaze, the caress in his deep blue eyes, turned her insides to mush, her mind to soup. What was it she wanted to talk to him about?

"Do you intend to continue your riding lessons, Miss DuBois? Peaches misses you."

"Huh? Oh, yes, I do wish to go on with the lessons. Tomorrow, in fact." Dominique glanced around, looking for the most private seating, then took his hand. "Come and join me on Aunt Libbie's new sofa."

She led him to the low-backed Elizabethan couch of flowered damask and eased onto the edge of the cushion. When Jacob sat down beside her, she quietly broached the subject she'd been avoiding for so long. "Before the music starts, I thought we might take a moment to talk. There is something I should have told you before now, but I couldn't find the words. I should have said something right off, but I wasn't sure until—until, well, I can't say that I'm sure now, but I have a feeling that what I'm thinking is . . . I mean, if it's true—and, believe me, I'm not saying that it absolutely is a fact or anything—"

"Please," he sliced in, rubbing his fingertips across his

forehead, "tell me your news while I can still understand what you are saying."

"Oh," she said with a laugh, "I'm sorry. I get carried away when I'm nervous or upset."

"You want to talk to me about something that upsets you? Have I done something wrong?" His mind raced back to the burning kiss they'd shared, that treasured moment he knew he'd never forget, and panic gripped his heart. Had she confessed to her aunt? Was he—and therefore his mission—in jeopardy? Jacob prepared to leap from the sofa as Dominique slid her hand across the back of his.

Her voice hesitant, she said, "I've been afraid to mention this because I thought it might upset you, Jacob."

His confusion complete, he said, "Please, go on. Tell me what this terrible thing is."

"It has to do with my experience in the Sioux village when I first arrived in the Dakota Territory—my ordeal with a warrior called Redfoot." She looked into his eyes and watched them widen, then close as her words sank in.

He'd known this might happen. After all, hadn't he planted the seeds for this story himself? Somehow he wasn't quite sure he was ready to deal with it, with her feelings about it. When Jacob opened his eyes again, their azure depths twinkled with animation as he said, "We never did have a chance to talk about our lives as captives. I am very interested in what you have to say about this dreadful savage, but I think it would be best for you to forget it and never speak of it again."

"Oh, but I don't mind. I want to talk about it."

"Wasn't it a terrible thing to be held prisoner by this savage?"

"Terrible? Oh, no, he was very . . . awfully . . ." The word she sought wouldn't come to her, at least not a word that could be considered ladylike and decent. Memories of her few hours with Redfoot conjured up many words, many feelings, all unsuitable for the unmarried niece of General Custer. She fought against a sudden blush, and tried to explain. "What I'm trying to tell you has nothing to do with me, Jacob. It has to do with . . . you."

"Me?" he exclaimed, knowing exactly what she was trying to tell him. But even though quills of guilt poked at his gut, he went on with the deception. "None of the Sioux spoke to me. I was captured, beaten, and tossed into a tipi with Barney. I know nothing of a warrior called Redfoot."

"That's not what I was trying to say." She slid closer to him, choosing her words carefully. "Redfoot is someone I think you *should* meet. Oh, Jacob, I don't know how to say this other than straight out—I believe this Indian may be your brother."

Surprising himself with a sudden urge to laugh, Jacob pressed his hand across his lips and worked to twist his mouth into a grimace. His words muffled, spoken through his fingers, he said, "That is ridiculous. I suggest you forget about this Indian and never think of him again."

"But I can't! Don't you understand? These Sioux may be the savages who took your mother years ago. They may have . . . She might— This man was too much like you *not* to be related, Jacob! He had your—"

"Enough!" His anger real, just as sudden and unexpected as his amusement, Jacob bristled inside. How stupid he'd been to lead her down this path! He looked into her big brown eyes, so trusting, so innocent, so much like those of a newborn foal, and he wanted to scream. What a fool he'd been! Her heart was aching for him, burdened by this filthy lie, and filled with compassion for a man who deserved nothing but her scorn. He'd been wrong to think he could be her friend, insane to consider for a moment that she might someday be his, mistaken to believe he could live this lie and not feel the pangs of his own conscience. There was only one thing to do. He would leave this house and never see or speak to the crazy one again.

Dominique shrank against the cushions as Jacob's features twisted with rage. Had she told him too much too soon? Should she had been a little more discreet, fed him the information in small doses instead of shoving it all down his throat in one big scoop? She reached for his hand, murmuring words of comfort. "I know I've given you a huge shock, Jacob. Why don't you think about what I've said for a few days, and then, if you want to ask me any questions, I'll be happy to answer—"

"Dominique?" Libbie marched up to the couch, her expression pinched. "Aren't you and the private planning to join us at the piano? I don't think you should confine yourselves to this corner. It's not polite."

"Oh, sure, Aunt Libbie. We'll be right there as soon as I finish telling the private about his—a . . . a story."

"We're starting the music now, Nikki. Please join us."

The set of Libbie's chin, the lifted nose, said much more than her words. Dominique gave her a short nod, and rose. "We'd love to, wouldn't we, Jacob?"

Plotting a hasty departure as he stood up, Jacob decided to wait until the general's wife was seated at the piano before he feigned a sudden headache.

They'd only taken a few steps across the room when an ashen-faced Lieutenant Woodhouse clicked his heels together and saluted a figure behind them. "General Custer, sir! Good to see you again, sir!"

Libbie whirled around, her full skirts billowing out behind her, swinging to and fro like the eager tail of a devoted collie. "Autie! Oh, thank God!"

Catching his wife as she flew into his arms, Custer gave her a brief hug, then addressed his guests. "Greetings to you all. As you were. I'll just be cleaning up, and then I'll join you."

"Autie?" Libbie looked into the general's bright blue eyes, noted the hard dark centers, and fought a tremor. "What's wrong? Why haven't I heard from you for the last three days? Why didn't you tell me you were coming home?"

"Later, sunbeam." He kissed the tip of her nose and

released her. "We have much to talk about later, but for now, I see we have guests to entertain."

"Yes, but they can wait. We have—"

"Chin up, bunky. Give us a smile and go play something special on the piano. I'll return in a moment. Tom? Join me upstairs."

The order had been given, and there was nothing Libbie could do but force her leaden feet to march over to the piano and choose a song. As her fingers fumbled to find the correct chords, she urged her guests to gather around and sing along.

Dominique and Jacob moved in at her right, but neither of them attempted to sing a note. Dominique was too wrapped up in worrying about the Custers' strained embrace, the general's obvious anxiety, and Jacob was too busy plotting his questions for the general should he be given an opportunity to ask them.

Three badly played tunes later, the Custer brothers returned to the parlor. Libbie abandoned the piano and hurried to her husband's side. She stared at him for a long moment, wondering why he looked so different, thinking his uniform and slouch hat seemed too big for him. "You look so very tired, Autie. Why don't I send everyone home now so you can rest?"

"An excellent idea, but first I must speak with a couple of my officers." His eagle-eyed gaze scanned the room, landed on Jacob, then returned to his wife. "Why, may I ask, do I find a *private* in my home, availing himself of *my* refreshments and indulging himself in conversation with *my* niece?"

"Oh, well, I . . . Dominique thought it would be all right. She—ah, the private has been giving her riding lessons. She wanted to thank him, and I didn't see any reason why—"

"Has the girl lost the ability to exercise her remarkably glib tongue? A simple thank-you would have sufficed."

"Yes, that would have been the better option. I don't

know what I could have been thinking. I'll just go dismiss him.''

Custer held out his arm, pressing his fingers into the hollow of his wife's shoulder. ''Don't trouble yourself. I'll see to the private myself. You gather the ladies' belongings. They'll be more than ready to go to their own quarters after I make my announcement.''

Then he straightened his jacket and marched over to where Dominique and Jacob stood. ''Nikki, my dear, I'm surprised to see you're still here. I halfway expected you to have boarded a train and fled back to your papa in Monroe by now.'' He lifted her fingers to his mouth, gently kissing them, but never took his gaze off Jacob.

''*Au contraire*, Uncle Armstrong! I'm really beginning to enjoy life at the post. Why, only yesterday—''

''We'll talk later, dear.'' Custer turned his full attention on Jacob, completely dismissing his niece. ''It's Stoltz, isn't it?''

''Yes, sir.'' Jacob saluted. ''Welcome home, sir.''

''Thanks, Private.'' Custer narrowed his gaze and studied the soldier intently. ''Have you been doing much scouting in my absence? Found anything out of the ordinary?''

''I have been on detail at least three or four nights each week, sir. I have found no further evidence of hostile . . . of—'' Jacob struggled to remember the word the officers discussed at every meeting, and finally said, ''Of hostile infitation.''

''Infiltration, Private?''

''Yes, sir.''

''Well, speaking of infiltration, I wonder if you realize what an honor you've been afforded here tonight?''

Jacob cocked his head. ''Sir?''

''Privates, enlisted men, are not usually permitted at the social gatherings on Officers' Row, much less in my home. My niece has bestowed a great honor on you, but I think now would be a good time for you to say good night. We don't want the rest of the men to get jealous, now, do we?''

"Ah, no, sir.''

"Good. Allow me to escort you to the door.''

"I'll join you,'' Dominique said, elbowing her way back into the conversation. "I invited Private Stoltz. The least I can do is bid him good evening.''

"Very well, Nikki.'' Custer made a sweeping gesture with his arm, then led the pair down the hallway. As he walked, he continued questioning. "Are you finding military life at the post to your liking, Private? Are you enjoying yourself as much as my niece seems to be?''

"Why, yes, sir, I believe I am. As you know, I am very fond of horses and working with them, and I also like scouting duty very much. It is a good life, sir.''

They'd reached the entry. Custer gripped the doorknob, but before he turned it, he said, "What about recreation, Private? What have you been doing in your spare time?''

Jacob hesitated, not certain what the general wanted from him, then said, "I have traveled some. Two days past, I rode into Bismarck with a few of the other nincompups. We had a very good time.''

Custer's hand slid off the doorknob, and the corners of his mustache drooped on down past his jawline. "Nincom*pups*, Private? What the devil are you talking about?''

Jacob's eyes darted between Dominique and the general. "Ah, I went to town with—''

"He went to Bismarck with me and a few of the other soldiers, Uncle Armstrong,'' Dominique explained with a sheepish grin. "I had some yard goods to pick out, and they decided to fill the supply wagon, since we needed an escort anyway.''

"Yes, standard operating procedure,'' Custer said as he turned back to the private. "Now let's talk about the name you called the men. "Nin—''

"Uncle Armstrong, you really should let the private get back to the barracks. Look down the hallway—I think your officers are ready to leave.''

Glancing toward the parlor, Custer frowned. "Thanks, Nikki. I have a very big announcement to make. Ah, good evening, Private." He opened the door, calling after the soldier as he stepped across the threshold, "I'll give you a little advance notice, Private. Reveille will be at five instead of six in the morning. I suggest an early lights-out tonight."

"Thank you, sir, and good night." Jacob snapped off a salute and disappeared down the long white stairway.

Turning to his niece, Custer took her by the elbow. "Come along, girl. You might as well hear what I have to say."

He strode back into the parlor, his chest puffed, his jaw tense. After sending Dominique to her aunt's side, he called for quiet. "Gentlemen, we have our orders, and this time they are firm. We leave for our summer campaign in two weeks. Our preparations must begin immediately."

The men voiced a lusty cheer, but the women were noticeably silent and cast furtive glances at one another. When the celebration died down, an officer spoke up. "Does the campaign have a clear goal, then, General, sir?"

"We will have the usual purpose, Major, but this time, we will not tolerate anything less than full containment of the hostiles. The entire objective of this mission is to ferret out, then completely subdue those heathen Sioux once and for all. Either they will accept our terms, agree to inhabit the land we set aside for their reservations, or they will be"—he glanced around the room, noting the wide-eyed women, and amended his speech—"exterminated."

Another rousing cheer erupted, but this time Custer discouraged the response. "Gentlemen, please. We have much to accomplish in little time. Our men are to join General Terry's troops, the Montana Column, as quickly as possible. We will be known as the Dakota Column."

"And everyone knows," Tom Custer cut in, "the Dakota Column alone can wipe out the entire Sioux nation!"

Again the men cheered, and this time, Custer let them.

When they'd quieted to a few murmured conversations, he finished his speech. "Please inform your men and all the barracks that reveille will be at five from now until we leave on May seventeenth. Tomorrow I'll call a general officers' meeting, and we'll go over our strategy and plot our route. For now, I've just finished a very long journey. I'm exhausted. Good night, ladies, gentlemen." He bowed, then saluted, and his guests filed by, responding in kind.

As the men and women stepped off the porch and navigated the impressive staircase on the way to their homes, none of them noticed a private crouching behind a Juneberry bush. His hands worked the soil around the base of the plant, dusting the particles away as if he were looking for something he might have dropped under the parlor window of the Custer house. None of the officers paid any attention to this same private when he casually strolled away from the house and stole back to the barracks of Company C, either. And no one but Jacob grasped the full implications of the speech General Custer had just made.

After the last of the visitors said their farewells, Custer took his wife's hand and led her down the hallway, commenting as he walked, "I imagine you and Nikki haven't had your supper yet."

"No, dear, but I'm sure Mary's cupboards are full. She's just started working on a fresh saddle of venison. There's plenty for you!"

"I have no appetite, sunbeam. I would ask, however, that you have Mary hold your meal until you and I have a chance to talk. Then I must get some rest."

"Of course, Autie. Go on up. I'll be right with you." Libbie stood and watched her husband climb the stairs, her heart heavy when she noticed the lack of enthusiasm in his step, the heavy-footed gait. She turned to go back into the parlor, but Dominique was already at her side.

"I overheard you and Uncle Armstrong. I'll tell Mary

to hold your meal, but do you mind if I eat without you? I'm starved!''

"Go ahead, Nikki." Libbie glanced up the stairway and softly added, "I may be a while." Then she lifted the hem of her skirt and followed the footsteps of the only man she had ever truly loved.

When she stepped into the room they shared, Libbie found her husband stripped down to his trousers and socks. He stood, leaning against her dressing table, staring into her looking glass as if seeing himself for the first time. Tiptoeing across the carpeted floor, she stole up behind her love and slid her arms around his waist. "Oh, Autie. What is it? What troubles you so?"

With a weary sigh, he straightened and turned around in her arms. "I'm afraid your boy didn't quite make a very good impression on the President."

"Oh, Autie, what has he done to you this time? If he's—" Libbie cut off her own sentence as she finally realized what had been nagging at her since her husband's return. "Autie! Your hair! What have you done with your curls?"

His smile cut deep lines around his tired eyes as he said, "I had them cut. I hoped a new look might boost the Senate's opinion of 'the boy general with the golden curls.' I meant to bring my hair back for you to weave into a memento, but I was so upset by the time I left Washington, I'm afraid I left it behind."

"Oh, my darling," Libbie cried as she rested her head on his smooth chest. "What have they done to you?"

"Nothing much," he said. "Nothing but castrate me in front of my men, render me impotent as their leader."

Libbie jerked back, her brow knotted. "*What?* Oh, please, Autie, please tell me what that swine has done to you."

With great difficulty, Custer swallowed the steel ball of hatred in his throat and said the words he would have to repeat time and time again over the next few days. "I've been relieved of my command."

Libbie broke free of his arms. "You can't be serious!" She cupped her palms over her ears and shook her head. "I won't listen to another word until you tell me the truth!"

"Telling the truth is what put me in this position." He ground his teeth and reiterated: "President Grant relieved me of my command. General Terry is the commander of both the Montana Column and the Dakota Column. I wasn't even supposed to be allowed to join in this campaign."

"B-but downstairs, you told the men . . . You said—"

"I know what I said, and it wasn't a complete lie. Generals Terry and Sheridan know what we're up against, even if Washington doesn't. They convinced Grant that my experience was badly needed in this campaign, so he relented, but I'm only to head up my own regiment. The entire command is under Terry."

"Oh, no," she choked out through a sob. "Oh, God, no."

"There now, sunbeam. Chin up." He pulled her back into his arms and pressed her trembling head against his shoulder. "I'll come out of this all right. You know I'll find a way to make them pay, to sit up and take notice of the best damn military man the cavalry has ever seen."

Libbie took several deep breaths, fighting off the sobs, and said, "B-but why? Why was Grant so angry with you?"

Custer pressed his face into her warm brown hair and shrugged. "Because I'm an honest man. Because when he asked this forthright man to testify in congressional hearings on what I know about fraudulent practices out here on the frontier, he didn't like my answers. I guess he didn't *really* want to know how the government was being cheated—or by whom. That's why."

"Oh, Autie, there must be a way for you to convince them they're wrong. They simply can't treat you this way!"

"Apparently they can treat me any damn way they like, but I don't intend to tell them another thing. From now

on, I'll show them." Custer narrowed one steel-blue eye
and stared off into an imaginary future only he could see.
"I'll show them on the field of battle, where I have no
equal."

Encouraged by the change in his tone, Libbie stepped
away from her husband and stared into his eyes. Trancelike, illuminated by fires of imagination, they revealed his
skills as a great craftsman, a man whose talents were no
less creative than those of a fine artist. His canvas was the
uncharted territories into which he would lead his men;
his paintbrush, uncanny skills in strategy and the tenacity
to pull off miracle after miracle. A landscape, when
George Armstrong Custer finished with it, was no less
than a masterpiece that could be viewed as a graphic mon-
ument to man's fascination with war.

Libbie observed her husband and trembled with desire.
He was beyond the reach, past the understanding, of mere
mortals at this moment. Above even her. But when he
broke out of that spell, when she knew he could be approached as a man, as *her* man, she would make him
forget his trials in Washington; she would ease the pain of
his loss. She would show him her own creativity, those
areas in which she could only hope she had no peers.

Back to reality, Custer shook his head and yawned.
"That's my sad tale, precious sunbeam. And please believe me when I say I will not discuss it again."

"As you wish, Autie." She stretched up on tiptoe and
pressed her lips to his. The kiss—a brief, gentle caress—
ended when Libbie slid her hands to the front of his trousers and began to tug at the buttons.

"No," Custer said, "not like that. I'm in need of
comfort tonight. Strip and get into bed."

"Oh, Autie," Libbie breathed with a shudder of
excitement, "whatever you want."

She helped herself to another quick kiss, then began to
remove her clothing. Making sure her movements were
slow and deliberate, Libbie kept one eye on her husband
as she disrobed, hoping to see that he was as excited as

she. By the time she slithered between the sheets, her mouth watered in anticipation.

"Well, General? What are you waiting for?" She curled a seductive finger and beckoned him.

Custer peeled off the rest of his clothing and climbed into bed beside her. When she rolled toward him, he pushed her back against the mattress. "I said I'm in need of comfort tonight. Be my best girl. Hold me, take care of me."

"Of course, darling. Whatever you say, you know I'll do anything you want." Unsure what he expected from her, Libbie forced herself to remain still even as her hot blood raced through her system, heating her loins, driving her mad with longing. Impatient for his touch, she waited for the next instruction wondering what new game he'd thought of.

Sliding down on the mattress until his head was level with Libbie's breast, Custer curled into a fetal position and rested his newly shorn head in the crook of her arm. Then he took her rosy nipple into his mouth and began to suckle.

"Oh, Autie," she gasped, "that feels so-o-o-o good."

But he didn't reply. Custer squirmed, nestling his head deeper in the valley between her arm and ribs and curled himself into a tighter ball. His mouth worked furiously against her breast, then slowly eased to an occasional pull at her nipple. A random cry, muffled, pathetic, broke the silence. Soon, his lips ceased to move.

"Oh, my poor, poor boy," Libbie whispered against his golden hair.

But there was still no answer. As the rhythm of her husband's light snoring reverberated in her ears, tears swamped corners of Libbie's stormy blue-gray eyes.

Chapter Ten

THE NEXT TWO WEEKS PASSED IN A FLURRY OF ACTIVITY as the troops made preparations for their long journey. Dominique spent most of her time helping Libbie sew new silk flags for Custer and the troops to carry, and spent the rest of her hours fretting.

She'd hardly seen Jacob since the evening he'd spent with her in the parlor. If he wasn't off scouting, sometimes two or three days in a row, he was busy with the rest of the soldiers. Only twice had he found a few moments to give her additional riding lessons, and during those precious minutes, she had found him guarded, indifferent. She'd hope for some different lessons, a few stolen moments to further her education as a woman. Now it looked as if that would never happen—not with Private Stoltz, anyway.

Tomorrow the Seventh Cavalry would pull out. Jacob and the troops would head for the hills of Montana. There they would spend the entire summer in pursuit of some naughty Indians while she withered away at the deserted post. By the time Uncle Armstrong and the men returned to Ford Lincoln in the fall, she would be back home with her papa in Michigan. She would never see Jacob again. It just wasn't fair.

"Pooh! Pooh! And bloody hell double pooh!" Dominique kicked a spindle-backed chair across the room, then collapsed in a heap as a scorching pain shot from her big toe to her knee. "Owwweeee," she cried, cradling the injured foot in her hands.

"Nikki?" Libbie rushed into the room and knelt by her side. "What's happened? I heard a crash and then your cry. How did you get hurt?"

"It's nothing," she fibbed, biting her bottom lip. "I—I stumbled against the chair, that's all."

"Let me see." Libbie pushed Dominque's hand away. "Oh, my, honey—you're bleeding. I think you've torn your nail." Libbie got to her feet. "Stay put. I'll get a bandage and, oh! How about some of the professor's tonic for the pain?"

"No! I—I mean, no, thanks, Aunt Libbie. It doesn't hurt anymore. I don't even think I need a bandage."

Libbie cocked her head. "Are you sure, dear? It's no trouble."

"I'm positive."

"Well, all right." Libbie clasped her hands together and swung them like a pendulum. "I think I may have some news to turn that frown of yours into a great big grin."

"It will have to be awfully wonderful news. I'm afraid I'm not in a very good mood today."

"This should cheer you up. Autie says the men have done a splendid job of preparing for the campaign. He's giving the entire post the day off to do as they please." She lowered her voice, then went on. "Hazel and I had a long talk this morning—she's taken with Lieutenant Woodhouse, you know—and she thought a picnic would be great fun. Would you like to go along with them?"

Dominique wrinkled her nose. "Just me?"

"No, dear. That's where the good news comes in. Don't think I haven't noticed your interest in Private Stoltz."

Dominique gasped.

Libbie paused, clucking her tongue, then went on. "Since the odds of you seeing him again after tomorrow are nil, I don't see the harm in inviting him to go along for the ride. The buggy seats four. Now what do you think about the picnic?''

Dominique jumped to her feet, unfazed by the jolt of pain in her toe. ''I think it sound wonderful! Thank you Aunt Libbie!'' She gave the older woman a hug, then saw her riding boots out of the corner of her eye. ''Do I have to go in the buggy? I do so love riding Peaches, but I'm not good enough to try her on my own after the troops leave. This will probably be my last chance to go horseback riding.''

''Oh, you'll have other chances, Nikki. All the men aren't leaving, but if you'd rather ride, I don't mind.'' She started for the doorway, adding, ''I'll run downstairs and have Mary prepare a basket of food, then send Annie with a message to Barney and Private Stoltz. They'll probably be at the door by the time you get dressed.''

Jacob tugged on the lead, coaxing Peaches up alongside the big sorrel he was riding. A sense of foreboding swept over him, but unlike his earlier feelings of doom, this had nothing to do with the bad blood between the cavalry and the Dakota. It had everything to do with the crazy one. He'd worked hard over the past two weeks, alerting his people to the upcoming confrontation, gathering information about the types of weapons the soldiers planned to use against his people, and studying the most likely routes the soldiers would take in their quest.

During that time, he had avoided Dominique as much as possible, and had managed to keep their meetings to a minimum. Now this picnic threatened to ruin what was left of his sanity. This ''day of fun'' could be his undoing. How would he be able to endure an entire afternoon of looking into those lively brown eyes, of hearing her infectious laughter—of wanting her?

Jacob jerked on the line and instantly regretted the excessive force he'd used. ''Sorry, Peaches.''

''What's that you say, Stoltz?'' Barney called from the buggy.

"Nothing, Lieutenant. I am talking to the horse."

Barney laughed, then said, "I'm telling you, Stoltz, you should have taken my advice and run down to the Dew Drop Inn last night. Gonna be a long time fore you see another woman. You might fall in love with that horse and think of doing more than just talking to her fore this campaign is over. You still got tonight. Better run along while you're still thinking clear, son."

Jacob chuckled under his breath. "I have not noticed you taking your own advice. Do you plan to visit this hog ranch tonight?"

Barney puckered his mouth, forcing his mustache up under his nose like a small piece of black string. "Shucks, Jacob. You know how I feel about the widow Swenson. I don't have any interest in other women."

Neither do I, Jacob thought, nearly vocalizing his feelings, but he said, "Maybe tonight I will make that trip for us both."

"There you go. Now you got the right idea."

They'd reached the house. Jacob remained seated on the gelding while Barney went to collect the women. When the trio returned burdened with baskets and blankets, his sense of gloom increased as Dominique dropped her bundle in the back of the buggy and walked over to Peaches.

"Good morning!" she said with a bright smile. Shading her eyes with the back of her hand, she looked up at Jacob, and her grin widened. "Beautiful day for a picnic, isn't it?"

Helpless when she was near, he smiled back in spite of his qualms. "Perfect. May I help you mount?"

"No, don't bother," she said, taking the reins from his hand. "So far, this is the only thing I've been able to master by myself." Slipping the toe of her new black riding boot into the stirrup, Dominique gracefully lifted herself onto the saddle. "There, now," she said, gently patting the mare's neck, "that wasn't so bad. We'll do just fine today."

"Maybe you will," Jacob said, proud of her progress.

"Why don't we get a move on?" Barney shouted. "Time's awasting!" He clucked at the pair of bay geldings hitched to the buggy and slapped the reins across their backs, calling out his orders to Jacob as the rig pulled away from the house. "You and Miss DuBois ride on a ways ahead of us. Keep a lookout for any stragglers or renegades, and make sure you don't get out of sight of the blockhouse."

Jacob nodded as he wheeled the sorrel onto the path. "Where do you want us to stop?"

"A ways past the juniper trees and just this side of the river you'll find a meadow. You two pick a nice shady spot somewheres along in there."

"Yes, sir." Glancing at Dominique, Jacob asked, "Are you ready?"

"Let's go!" She bumped Peaches in the flank with the heel of her boot, intending to wake her up, but the startled mare reared, nearly unseating her instead.

"Easy, girl!" Jacob said to the animal, his tone deceptively cool. "All is well." He calmed the mare, then took her reins in hand. "I think it would be best if I lead her out of the garrison."

Her teeth chattering with fear, Dominique nodded and allowed him to lead Peaches down the road past the officers' quarters and post storehouses. Once in the open, Jacob returned the reins to her and issued a warning: "Be careful not to make any quick movements this time."

"Don't worry about that! I intend to sit as still as a mouse all the way to the meadow."

Jacob's only reply was to nudge the sorrel a few steps ahead of Peaches, making certain Dominique was no longer in his peripheral vision. He would have to find a way to maintain control of his mind, concentrate on the mission and the new demands it would make of him at dawn. He would have to forget the beautiful woman riding beside him. Maybe if he couldn't see her, he thought, knowing he was asking the impossible of himself, he wouldn't think of her.

They rode like that, silent and brooding, for nearly a mile. Finally unable to stand it any longer, Dominique clucked softly and carefully urged Peaches to catch up to the gelding. "Good morning again, Jacob. Why aren't you talking to me?"

"No reason. I am scouting."

"Oh," she said, lifting her chin. "I see." But she didn't. And she didn't like it one bit. She nudged Peaches sideways until her knee brushed Jacob's thigh. "When tomorrow comes, you'll be gone. I shall miss you Jacob. Will you miss me?"

He waited a long time before answering, and when he did, he kept his gaze on the box elder trees ahead. "I will think of you often."

"You'll write me often, too, won't you?"

"Write you?" he said, finally turned to face her.

"Yes. Friends usually keep in touch."

And because he couldn't see the harm in adding one more lie to their already tainted relationship, he said, "Sure. I will write you every day."

"Really?" She beamed.

He looked into her expressive sable eyes, saw the hope and genuine affection, and expelled a heavy sigh. How could he add to the hurt he had already caused her? How could he live with his conscience? Unable to bear the thought of the pain she would feel when the expected letters never arrived, Jacob altered his story. "No, Dominique, not really. I am sorry, but I will be very busy over the next few weeks. I will not have time to write to anybody."

"But of course you will! Aunt Libbie says the general writes to her just about every day when he's away, no matter where he's gone."

"I believe we are going into battle. I do not think that will be possible, even for the general."

"Yes, it will!" she insisted. "She says Uncle Armstrong even writes her from the field of battle, so now you don't have any excuse. I shall expect a letter at least every other day.''

"Do not expect anything from me! I will not be writing to you. Please understand that.''

"B-but, I thought we were . . . friends.''

"We are, but I simply cannot write to you. Please don't ask me to do so again.''

Reckless anger gripped her. Controlled by a rage she'd never known, unable to recognize its source, Dominique felt her temper flare. "Don't worry about that or about me, Jacob! I won't be asking a damn thing of you ever again!'' Then she drove a furious boot into Peaches's flank and jerked on the reins.

Unused to such treatment, the mare squealed and bolted, nearly tossing her rider to the ground before she broke into a dead run. The sudden movement tore Dominique's foot from the stirrup. With one knee hooked around the saddle horn and her hands wound into the horse's mane, she clung to Peaches, alternately cursing and begging the animal to stop.

"Whoa, Peaches! Oh, God—please stop,'' she screamed into the wind as the mare gathered speed. Her new bonnet was torn from her head as Peaches swerved, changing directions, and again, Dominique nearly fell to the ground. Instinct drove her to press her bosom against the animal's body and throw her arms around the thick neck. Then she squeezed her eyes shut and prayed, no longer able to scream or speak.

Behind the fleeing horse, Jacob spurred the gelding on, whipping the animal as he'd never whipped a mount in his life. He saw Peaches swerve and prepared to witness the worst, but Dominique surprised him by keeping her seat. The big sorrel was finally gaining ground on the smaller, faster bay, but would they be in time? Could he catch the terrified beast before she stumbled and fell, tossing and perhaps killing her burden in the process? Would Dominique's strength give out before he could prevent the inevitable fall?

The gelding leapt over a small bush and accelerated as his rider leaned forward and encouraged his progress. As they approached the foaming mare, Jacob slid down to the right side of his saddle, then encircled Dominique's waist with his arm as he raced by her flying skirts. Scooping her off Peaches and veering away from the mare in the same motion, he straightened in the saddle and shouted, "Put your arms around me, Dominique! Hang on!"

Her fingers clawing at the fabric of his shirt, she managed to cling to him, dangling from the side of the slowing gelding until it skidded to a halt. Then she released her grip and slid to the ground.

Jacob sprang off the horse and shooed him away. He dropped to his knees and cradled her in his arms. "Dominique, are you all right?" he gasped, out of breath, wild with concern. "Come on, tell me you are all right."

Her lashes fluttered lazily. Her eyes popped open. With a start, Dominique pushed herself up to a sitting position, then scrambled to her feet. She stumbled in a blind circle trying to get her bearings. "Oh! *Mon Dieu!*"

Jacob got to his feet and pulled her into his arms. "Easy, crazy one. You are only frightened. Your confusion will pass."

She allowed him to comfort her, and she gradually forgot her terror as his strength seeped into her. Snuggling her head against his chest, she sputtered, "Oh, J-Jacob, I was s-so *scared*! Peaches wouldn't stop! I—I yelled at her. I said everything you taught m-me, b-but—"

"Hush, now. The horse is stupid. You are not to blame." He kissed the top of her head and rocked her, surprised at the depth of emotion welling up inside him. "You are all right now," he crooned. "Nothing can harm you when you are with me."

"Oh, Jacob! How can you say that now?" she cried, lifting her head off his shoulder. "You're leaving tomorrow and I'll never see you again."

Her doelike eyes glistened as she looked up at him, and her rosy lips beckoned with a need he hadn't the strength to fight. Ignoring the voice of reason calling him from somewhere down inside, Jacob lowered his mouth to hers and took his fill of her sweetness.

The kiss was incredibly soft and nurturing as he came to her, but when Dominique parted her teeth and invited him inside her sanctuary, a sudden surge of passion combined with the anticipation of tomorrow drove them deep inside each other. Tongues entwined, hearts united as one, they grasped at the moment, at the only chance they might ever have to know what they could be together. She encouraged his loss of control, mimicking his movements, matching them, and surprised herself with a few of her own. Today was all that mattered. This moment would be the sum total of their short time together. Dominique suddenly wanted it all.

She pulled back from his fevered lips and drew her fingertips across them. "Oh, Jacob," she sighed. "If only you weren't leaving, if only—"

"Don't," he whispered hoarsely. "We should not have done that. It will be best for us both if we do not speak of this kiss, or of tomorrow, again."

"Oh, stop it! I'm tired of hearing you go on about what we should and shouldn't do. I want to be with you, and I know you feel the same way about me." She looked into his dark blue eyes, waiting for some kind of acknowledgment, but the shutters were firmly in place. "Well, don't you, Jacob? You do want me, don't you?"

Still holding her in his arms, his hips pressed against hers, he was surprised she had to ask. Attributing the question to her inexperience, he allowed himself a hint of a smile as he said, "I do not have the right to want you. It is foolish for either of us to think that I do."

He tried to push away, but Dominique kept her arms locked around his waist. "Is it because you're a private? If that's all, don't give it another thought. I couldn't care less about rank and who's who."

"No, that is not—"

"I've heard enough from you," she said with a pout.

"Stop fighting me. You're out of excuses. I know you must care for me. I've seen the way you look at me, and sometimes when we're talking, I can tell by the way you gaze into my eyes and touch my hand that—"

"Stop it," he said, breaking free of her arms. "This is no good. It cannot work."

"Of course it can! If you feel the same way I do—"

"I don't want to know how you feel. Please do not tell me."

"Then you tell me, Jacob. Stand there and tell me you don't care. Tell me you hate me and wish I'd go away!"

"What do you want from me, Dominique? What do I have to say? That I love you and I always will?" he raged. "That I've loved you from the first moment I saw you floating down the river? Fine! I will say it, then! I—"

"The river?" she cut in, her face ashen. "*The river*, Jacob?"

His heart beating wildly, no longer with passion or anger, but with fear, he said, "I—I do not know why I said that, I—"

"Crazy one?" She took a backward step. "You called me crazy one, too! I don't understand. How could you know that name? When could you have seen me in the— Oh, my God!" She took another, larger backward step. "You're not Jacob at all, are you? You're—"

"Dominique, please." He started toward her, his hand outstretched as he glanced beyond her to judge their position. Peaches had led them farther from the fort than he'd first thought, around the bend in the river and down to a small grassy valley hidden by a row of oak and elm trees, out of sight of the blockhouse and the guards. Barney and Hazel were at least thirty minutes from finding them, maybe closer to an hour in the slow-moving buggy. Was it enough time to convince her she was wrong?

Dominique's mind worked frantically as the implications of what she'd stumbled over came into focus. "Why are you doing this?" she demanded. "What do you have to gain? Are you some kind of spy for the Indians, or—"

"Please, I would like to—"

"I don't care what you'd like. I don't care about you! When I think of all the lies, the filthy rotten—"

"Dominique, you must believe me when I say I never meant to hurt you. I have done nothing—"

"I'll never believe another thing you have to say, you miserable heathen!" she sputtered, still backing away. "You tricked me! You lied and pretended to be someone you're not!" As his deeds piled up, as she recalled some of the things he'd said, she became more enraged, and continued to list her grievances. "And to think you let me go on and on about a brother you never had! You really had me feeling sorry for you and that clabber-headed behemoth who never existed, didn't you! You are lower than—than the soles of my shoes! Why, you're so low, I can't even *think* of anything low enough to be on the same level with you!"

"Dominique," he said softly, following along in her tracks.

"And don't call me Dominique! Don't you ever speak my name again, you no-good Indian half-breed snake, or whoever in the hell you really are."

"Please. If you will just listen to me, I can explain."

"*Explain?* Hah! That's a laugh. You'll explain all right, but it will be to my uncle, General Custer, not to me. I don't want to hear another thing you have to say."

"In that case," he said with a quiet sigh, "I am sorry."

"*Sorry?* You think you can pull a trick like this, sneak into the cavalry for God knows what purpose, *trifle* with me, and then brush it off with an 'I'm sorry'?"

"No, crazy one," he said with a heavy heart. "I am not sorry for any of that. I am sorry for this."

Then he drew back his fist and drove it into her chin.

Barney urged the team of horses up the small hill, careful not to whip them into a speed they couldn't handle, then pulled the rig to a halt at the crest. "I can't understand it," he said, scanning the valley below. "We should have caught up with them by now. I wonder how far that crazy mare got?''

''Oh, Barney, do you think Dominique's going to be all right?'' Hazel twisted her hands as if she were wringing a load of laundry.

''Don't worry, sugar. Jacob's the best damn horseman I've ever seen. He'll catch up to that skittish animal and see that Dominique's safe. Don't you worry.'' But he didn't really believe the words himself. He slapped the reins across the horses' backs and started down the hill, knowing they couldn't go much farther. Not alone. Not in the flimsy buggy. And not under these suspicious circumstances. If he didn't find some sign of Dominique and Jacob before he reached the bend in the river, he would have to turn back and round up a search party. Then he spotted an odd-looking sapling standing alone in a clearing a few yards ahead. Guiding the buggy to the spot, he squinted, then his eyes widened as the tree came into focus. What he had assumed to be a sapling was a large branch stripped of its leaves, stuck into the ground to resemble a pole. An unmistakable Dakota warning.

Handing the reins to Hazel, he whispered, ''Get a tight grip on these. I'm gonna check that tree ahead. If I turn and holler, you hightail it outta here. Understood?''

''But, Barney, I'm not going to drive off without you. If you—''

''Do as you're told, woman. I don't have time to explain.''

''Y-yes, Barney,'' she said as he climbed down off the buggy and stole over to the clearing.

Glancing from side to side as he approached the branch, his eyes and ears fully alert, Barney made a fast study of the piece of fabric hanging from it. Then, his eyes bulging, he spun on his heel and raced for the buggy. Vaulting onto the seat, he motioned for Hazel to remain silent as he whipped the horses into action and turned the buggy back up the hill. When they'd passed the crest and were in view of the blockhouse again, he relaxed his tense muscles, but kept the horses going at top speed.

"Why was that branch stripped of its leaves, Barney?" she said against the wind. "What was hanging from it?"

"It was a little message from the Sioux."

"Indians?" she gasped.

"Don't be alarmed," he said, even though he knew he was telling her an outright lie. "It probably doesn't mean a thing."

And it didn't. As long as she didn't understand the challenge represented by the strip of cloth tied to the branch like a flag. As long as she hadn't noticed the lock of Dominique's hair fastened to that flag.

Chapter Eleven

WHEN DOMINIQUE CAME TO, SHE WAS FLOPPING TO AND fro, though a strong hand gripped her waist. She struggled for breath. Jacob? The powerful aroma of moist horse hair told her that her face was pressed against the shoulder of his mount. Then she became aware of a series of familiar pains; a fiery agony flared in her ribs, and a steady throbbing hammered at her chin. She opened her eyes and saw the ground racing past at a dizzying speed. Her mind spinning, she raised her head and saw that Peaches was attached to the gelding by a rope and was galloping along behind. Directly ahead, hooves thundered, kicking up clouds of dust. Through the haze, she could see a half-naked Indian, a Dakota, she supposed, on a black and white pinto. Where had he come from?

Dominique groaned as her memory jolted her. Jacob had hit her—*again*, she remembered as she merged him with the Indian called Redfoot. Apparently after that, he'd flung her over his mount like a sack of grain. Grimacing as the galloping horse jolted her bruised ribs, she clung to the sorrel, praying Jacob's strong hands would keep her across its withers long enough for her to regain her strength. Then, she swore to herself, she would kill him. The horse jumped over a clump of brush, landing with a mind-jarring thud before resuming its breakneck speed. Dominique blacked out again.

The next time she regained consciousness, she was in

semidarkness. Her incredulous, bleary eyes told her she was standing next to a cylindrical beam of light that seemed to sprout from the earth. Someone slapped her face, forcing her to stand on legs that seemed to have no bones.

"Come on, Dominique! You must wake up now. I have no time for this!" Unable to hit her again, sickened by the bruise he'd been forced to raise on her chin, Jacob turned his head to call for water.

Dominique saved him the trouble. "You! How dare you touch me!" She spun out of his arms and lurched into a buffalo-skin wall. Snapping her head upward, Dominique saw that the beam of light shot down to, not up from, the earth. She was in a tipi.

"No!" She whirled around, facing Jacob like a spitting wildcat. "You can't do this to me again! I demand that you return me to the fort at once!"

If his plight hadn't been so dangerous, he would have laughed, for her words prompted a memory of the first time they had met. She'd made nearly the same request then, in almost the same tone. His answer this time had to be different.

Forcing an anger he didn't feel, Jacob buried his feelings of compassion. "You are in no position to demand anything!" he snarled, gripping her arms. "You are lucky to be alive. Remember that—"

"I remember plenty, you bully! I intend to make sure—"

"You will still your tongue now, or I will have to still it for you," he shouted, causing her to cringe. Satisfied that she understood how deadly serious her situation was, he went on with his instructions. "I have no time to explain anything to you right now. I must get back before the soldiers come."

"Oh, they'll come, Jacob, and when they do—"

"If you interrupt me again," he warned, squeezing her arms so tight he feared he might snap them, "I will have no choice but to kill you now and spare you the torture the others will put you through. Which will it be?''

Dominique glared up at him and saw instantly that the shutters in his eyes were thrown wide open. There were no illusions, no signs of deceit. If she didn't obey, he would break her neck as easily as he would a twig. She pressed her lips together and nodded.

''That is very wise.'' Jacob relaxed his grip, but kept his big hands wrapped around her arms. ''I have time to say this only once, so listen carefully. You are in my Hunkpapa camp with around seventy Dakota Indians. There is no chance for escape, and if you try this foolish thing, you will surely be killed. Your death, should you take this risk, will be very unpleasant. Do you understand?''

Tears sprang into the corners of Dominique's eyes. She'd heard terrifying stories at the fort about the Sioux and their particularly nasty forms of torture. She understood only too well. Swallowing the lump in her throat, she whispered, ''Yes.''

''Good. I cannot take the time to explain the customs of the Dakota people to you now, but pay close attention to what I am about to say. This wiggling tongue of yours can be very entertaining, but in this village, only to me. If you choose to flap it around the women in this camp, they will remove it for you.''

''Remove it?'' she gasped.

He gave her a solemn nod, then lifted a length of her hair. ''They will be jealous of this golden crop also. Braid it and try to keep it out of sight. They will want to remove it, too.''

''Oh, Jacob,'' she cried, tears spilling in earnest. ''I'm frightened. Please take me away from here.''

''I would if I could, but that is impossible. You will be safe enough for tonight and tomorrow. Just remember to keep that wagging tongue of yours still around the women in camp.'' He released her and stepped away. ''There is one other very important thing. If you want to keep your life, make sure you do not mention the general or the fact that his blood fills your veins. Say nothing about this to *anyone*.''

''They—the Indians know about my—my Uncle Armstrong?'' she said through a sob.

''They know the name Custer very well. The Dakota consider him their greatest enemy.'' He turned and walked toward the opening in the tipi, reassuring her as he departed. ''I will try to return by tomorrow night, and surely by the night after if that isn't possible. You will be all right if you do as you are told and say nothing.''

Dominique hiccuped, watching him through fearful eyes as he opened the flap. When he lifted his foot to step out into the camp, away from her, panic seized her. ''Wait!''

Jacob halted in midstride. ''What is it? I have no time to spare in conversation.''

''I—I was wondering . . .''

''Yes?''

''If—if I'm so much trouble, if all anyone around here is going to think about is ways to torture and kill me, I was wondering—why didn't you just murder me out on the trail and be done with it?''

Jacob stared down at his troop boots for a long moment, then raised anguished blue eyes to her. ''Because, crazy one,'' he murmured, his voice barely above a whisper, ''I love you.'' Then he was gone.

After tying a rope around his waist, Jacob called to his good friend, Drooping Belly. ''Go now, see that your horse is quick.'' Then he allowed himself to be dragged through the rocks and brush outside the camp.

He spun over and over like a leaf in the wind as the pony raced across the plains, but Jacob endured the pain, found a certain satisfaction in it when he thought of it as a punishment. He deserved worse for bringing the crazy one to camp, for loving her. And now that he had done so, he was responsible—for her life, for the peril her presence might bring to his people.

For now, all he could think of was Dominique. She'd looked so frightened, so vulnerable, when he walked away from her. If anything happened to her, if she should . . . Unable to continue the thoughts, Jacob turned his head to the pain hoping it would somehow bring him solace. When the pony stopped, then backtracked to where he lay, Jacob remained motionless, still doing penance.

"Redfoot, my friend, have I done too good a job?" Drooping Belly inquired as he slid down off his horse. "Can you not rise?"

"I am thinking about it." With a heavy groan, Jacob pushed himself to his hands and knees, then accepted his friend's outstretched hand as he struggled to his feet.

Drooping Belly stood back, surveying his handiwork. "I have done a good job," he pronounced. "You will not be doubted by the Long Knives."

"Then"—Jacob winced as he rotated his shoulder joint. "I thank you, friend. When I am feeling better, I promise to show my gratitude by trapping you in the den of a mother grizzly with a bad tooth."

"Ha-hah!" Drooping Belly slapped his thighs with delight. "Your flesh is bruised and torn, yet still you make jokes. You are very brave, my friend."

"No, I'm thinking that I am very stupid."

Still laughing, the warrior returned to his pony and unsheathed his lance. Turning back to his friend, he took a deep breath, then finished his job. Before Jacob had time to realize Drooping Belly was rushing at him, the warrior sprinted on by, slashing his arm from wrist to bicep as he passed.

Jacob let out a startled yelp, then grabbed the wound. "Not this arm, you nincompup! I must *use* this arm."

Drooping Belly whirled around, chagrined to see his friend angry. "I am sorry, Redfoot. I forgot to think about that. Perhaps if I cut the other . . ."

Startled, Jacob looked up. The two men exchanged glances, then a bout of hearty laughter. After binding the wound with a strip of cloth torn from his shirt, Jacob walked to the pony, grumbling good-naturedly as he stood at the animal's side, "Well? Come and help me on this pitiful horse. Some nincompup has made the arm I would use to mount him completely useless."

Still chuckling, Drooping Belly vaulted onto the back of his pony, then pulled his friend up behind him. They rode until they reached a spot just past the clearing where Jacob had left the stripped branch.

"This is far enough," he warned, sliding down off the pony. "I will see you in a day or two in the new camp. Have a safe trip back, my friend. And please see that Chief Gall protects the white woman. Let no harm come to her."

"What is this woman to you, Redfoot? Have you decided you prefer your own kind?"

"No! My kind are the Dakota. This woman is a . . . a friend. I wish to see that she is protected."

Drooping Belly raised one eyebrow, then waved his hand in farewell. "It is done, my friend." Then he rode off and disappeared into the trees.

Not ready to be discovered just yet, Jacob scrambled to the grass-covered banks of the Missouri and slowly eased himself into the frigid water. Thoroughly soaked and shivering, he climbed back onto dry land and began the long journey back to the post.

He'd gotten halfway to Fort Lincoln from the spot where his friend had dropped him when he noticed a lone rider and a packhorse heading his way. When the soldier was close enough for identification, Jacob saw that it was one of the younger men, lured into the cavalry, no doubt, by promises of great adventures. The lad looked more frightened than thrilled as he pulled to a stop in front of Jacob.

"You Stoltz?" the kid asked.

"Yes. I am very happy to see you."

"Tell me about it later. Get on this packhorse and let's ride. There's some renegade Injuns running amok out here."

Jacob knitted his brows, wondering if the soldier was

blind to his raw flesh and bleeding wound, or just too scared to care. "I have already made the acquaintance of a couple of the renegades. They were in a big hurry after they cut me down and stole my horse. I am sure they've left the area."

"Yeah, I can see they took a real liking to you. But I'm not taking any chances. You can stay out here all day if you want—I'm heading back to the barn."

With that, the kid slapped his horse's rump and took off at a dead gallop. "Thank you," Jacob called after his fleeing figure, "for helping me onto this fine animal."

Jacob regarded the packhorse, a palomino no longer fit for service, used only for very short outings when a lady felt the urge to ride around the fort. Apparently, he decided as he jerked his aching body into the saddle, the horse was deemed expendable should the kid be overtaken before he had a chance to complete his mission.

Exercising as much caution for the animal's advanced years as he did for his own physical discomfort, Jacob took his time returning to the fort. When he arrived at the stables just before dusk, Custer, Libbie, Barney, and Hazel stood at the door anxiously awaiting his return.

"My God, Jacob." Barney dashed over to the horse and gingerly helped his friend dismount. "You look like you're barely alive. What happened to Domi—"

"I'll take over, Lieutenant," Custer said, brushing Barney aside. "Where is my niece, Private? How did you manage to lose her?"

Resisting the urge to smash his fist, bad arm and all, into the thick part of Long Hair's mustache, Jacob slowly told the tale of the runaway horse, then finished with a fabrication: "Peaches must have run into the trees and stumbled upon the Indians. I never saw Dominique or her horse after that. I do not know if she is dead or alive. I looked for her and any signs of a trail, but they did a very good job of hiding their tracks. I am sorry."

"Oh, no," Libbie wailed. "Autie, whatever are we going to do? What shall we tell her father?"

Beside her, Hazel joined in, her voice cracking with emotion. "The poor dear! If she's still alive and those savages have her, I mean—Lord almighty! How will she survive, how can she ever be the same again?"

Custer turned his head, snapping out an order over his shoulder. "Ladies, go on back to the house."

"But, Autie," Libbie cried, "I'm so very upset and worried about Nikki. Can't we stay—"

"Back," he said, the word shooting out of his mouth like a bullet from a pistol, "to the house—*now*! Understand?"

Swallowing a sob, Libbie nodded and took Hazel by the hand.

Assuming they'd left, but not watching to see the women trudge back up the hill, Custer directed his wrath at Jacob. "Just what kind of horseman are you, Private? How could you have let that silly little mare get away?"

"She was startled by something, sir. I did not see what. When Peaches bolted, the sorrel was no match for her speed." Jacob paused, waiting for the general to make some critical comment, but he merely gestured for him to go on. "I followed the mare into the trees. That's when I was hit by a lance. The blow knocked me off my horse, and I rolled down the hill and into the river. That is the last thing I remember."

"The Indians must have left you for dead," Custer deduced, fondling the end of his mustache. "You never heard Nikki scream or anything?"

Jacob paused, pretending to try to call up a memory, then shook his head. "Nothing, sir. Just me and the river after that. I must have tumbled downstream quite a ways because I have been walking back to the fort for a very long time."

"Hell and damnation!" Custer aimed a wad of spittle at the toe of Jacob's boot. "I guess that's that." He checked the position of the setting sun. "We haven't got the time or the manpower to go out looking for my niece now. The troops are all in town or dead drunk. We'll just have to keep a lookout when we take off in the morning. About all we can do is hope to hell she's already dead." He leveled an icy blue eye on Jacob and added, "If you were any kind of soldier, you'd have seen to that when you realized you couldn't save her from them."

Sure he must have heard him wrong, Jacob said, "Sir?"

Custer swiveled to Barney. "Hasn't this man had a proper introduction to soldiering in this neck of the woods, Lieutenant?" Not bothering to wait for a reply, he informed Jacob of his sworn duty. "If ever a soldier's lady is in jeopardy of being captured by savages, orders are to shoot her before the Indians get the chance to grab her. If the soldier is unable to perform the deed, he is to turn his weapon over to the lady so she can carry out the act herself."

Jacob's mouth was hanging open. He *knew* it was hanging open, but he couldn't seem to close it. This order, this crazy story, couldn't be true. But he could find nothing close to mirth in the general's eyes. He was dead serious. He actually would have preferred that Jacob had shot his own flesh and blood. Unable, unwilling, to curb his instinctive reaction to the horrible policy, Jacob shuddered.

"I see you have no stomach for the work, soldier," Custer commented, his opinion of that deficiency concealed behind his steel-eyed gaze.

"Do *you*?" Jacob blurted out. "Could you shoot your own wife, sir?"

"You're impertinent, Private!" Custer looked to Barney, practically shouting the order. "See that this man's wounds are tended to. Then have the physician inform me if he will be fit for duty tomorrow."

"I will be fit," Jacob insisted. "I not only plan to ride out with the Seventh in the morning; I feel it my duty to ride on ahead, to scout for those devils who were foolish enough to kidnap your niece."

"Oh, you'll ride, Private. If there's any way at all, you'll ride. I'll have to think about whether or not I trust you enough to put you back on scouting duty, however." He faced Barney, clicking his heels together, "Lieutenant, see to your orders." Then he stomped back up the hill, never bothering to return Barney's salute or notice if Jacob had followed suit.

"This man, this leader of his people," Jacob grumbled, "is a nincompup."

"Jesus, Stoltz!" Barney said in a strangled whisper. "You musta beat your head against a few of them rocks in the river. You can't call the general names!"

"I don't care. He is not a good leader. He is no better than any one of us. He is a nincompup."

"Stoltz!" Barney winced, checking to make sure they weren't overheard. "You got to stop that unless you want to get bounced from the cavalry. And what the hell is a nincompup, anyway—a baby nincompoop?"

Jacob stopped. "Poop? The word is nincom*poop*?"

Barney nodded his head and prodded Jacob along. "Yes, Private. Remind me while we're with the doc to make sure he examines your head. I think you mighta got your load of powder wet when you fell in that river."

"Poop," Jacob said, savoring the word. "Poop. Nincompoop." Still forming the syllables over and over, he burst into laughter as he walked into the dispensary.

Several miles to the west, the Hunkpapa roamed, searching for a new and better-hidden place in which to erect their temporary village. A line of heavily armed warriors led the march. Behind them, the women, children, and old people clustered like a flock of birds playing follow-the-leader. On both sides of the flock and to the rear, more warriors protected the nucleus of their Dakota family. All rode on horseback but one.

Dominique Custer DuBois was a beast of burden. The minute Jacob left camp, the Indians had begun to dismantle the village. Much faster than she'd had believed possible, the tipis had been taken down, rolled into tubes, and strapped to several travoises fashioned from rawhide and long poles, which were harnessed to the strongest

horses and dragged along behind. The rest of the Indians'
belongings were stuffed into buffalo-hide parfleches and
added to the travois loads. The plains, when the Dakota
broke camp, were returned to nature, looking as if they'd
never been disturbed.

Dominique shifted the load on her back, a parfleche
filled with cooking supplies, and grimaced. They'd been
traveling for hours over the worst trails imaginable. Once
so proud of her new black riding boots, Dominique now
roundly cursed them with each step. Blistered and swollen, her toes begged for release from their tight leather
bindings, and she dreamed of finding relief for her feet in
an icy pond.

She shrugged, hoping to encourage the wool serge riding habit to release her skin, but it clung to her sweltering
body as if glued. Dizzying little flecks of light danced
behind her eyelids as she grew weak with exhaustion. What
would these heathens do to her if she fainted? Dominique
shook her head to clear it, then stopped to rub the ache in
her back. A long, tapered pole cracked her alongside the
head. Dominique whirled around, the sound of the blow
reverberating in her ears, and ducked as a berry-skinned
woman took another swing at her.

After nearly falling off her pony in her failed effort,
Spotted Feather righted herself, shouting at her enemy,
"Move your legs, white she-devil! You have not been told
to stop. Walk faster!"

Again, she raised the pole, but Dominique dodged out
of her range and bumped into the mount of a warrior on
her right. She staggered, surprised at the collision, winded
by the force. A strong hand gripped her shoulder, steady-
ing her wobbly legs.

"Cling to my pony, Golden Hair. Rest."

Unable to do anything else at the moment, Dominique
leaned against the dapple gray stallion. As she caught her
breath, she listened to the exchange between the man and
the woman.

"Why do you protect her, Father?" Spotted Feather

complained. "She is not worthy of your help. Her evil
flesh must not touch yours."

"Join the other women," he answered. "Do not trouble
yourself with things that do not concern you."

Dominique waited for the woman's reply, but those few
words were apparently all she needed to obey. Intrigued
to see the man who commanded so effortlessly, Dominique looked up into the kind onyx eyes of Gall, chief of
the Hunkpapa Dakota.

He sucked in his breath, startled by her lovely features,
her large, expressive brown eyes, and the hint of the magnificent explosion of color to come when her hair was freed
from its restraints. After forty-four winters and many
years, Gall was considered an elder, not expected to fight
or even appear on the field of battle. But even as a mature
man, he realized, gazing down at the comely woman, his
fires still burned bright enough to feel a twinge of envy
toward Redfoot, and the others who might enjoy the trea-
sures this one would have to offer.

"So," he said, his deep voice surprisingly soft and low,
"you are the woman Redfoot calls the crazy one."

Remembering Jacob's words, for after the breaking of
camp and the sneers and taunts of the other women, his
warnings were burned into her mind, Dominique kept her
silence. She nodded, then averted her gaze.

"Do not be afraid. Redfoot has asked me to protect you
from harm. I will do what I can."

Dominique glanced back up at him, daring to hope she'd
found a safe harbor in her suddenly turbulent world, but
the Indian motioned to someone behind her, then shouted
an order.

"Bring a pony! This helpless white woman slows us."
Then, never acknowledging her thank-you or even the fact
that she stood beside him, Gall rubbed his heel against
the stallion's belly and loped to the head of the column.

Later that night, Dominique lay huddled in a crudely
erected tipi barely big enough to contain her. Her shelter

stood near the center of the temporary village where the
large warrior's lodge commanded center stage. Curiosity
and hunger had driven her to poke her head outside the
flap only once. The act drew hoots and filthy comments
she couldn't interpret, but understood very well. How
would she ever return home? Who would save her? She
certainly couldn't manage to get away from the Sioux
alone. To even *think* of escape was an exercise in futility.
And exercise of any kind, at the moment, was out of the
question.

Dominique was exhausted, parched, and starving. She
drew her knees up to her chest, hoping to ease the pain of
back muscles pulled to the limit. Instead, her thighs and
tender bottom protested the movement. Just the couple of
hours she'd ridden astride a horse, rather than sidesaddle,
had left her legs and behind so bruised and swollen that
she didn't think she could have sat in a chair even if she'd
been offered one. How long would she have to endure
these indignities?

The flap to her tipi suddenly flew open. A brown hand
jutted through the hole and deposited a bowl of steaming
liquid. Then the flap dropped back in place, leaving her
in darkness. Dominique pulled the container closer and
inhaled. Although she couldn't identify the scent, she
found nothing offensive in the aroma. Too hungry to care
what she was fed, she lifted the bowl to her mouth and
slowly consumed the contents. It tasted flat and greasy,
devoid of the seasonings her educated palate had come to
know and relish. But it eased the ache in her stomach.

Drowsy by the time she'd swallowed the last of the soup,
Dominique dropped into a deep sleep, too weary to give
her plight another thought. Unable to face the terror of
reality, her mind soothed her as she slept, replaced the
primitive tipi with dreams of her cozy home overlooking
Lake Erie, and convinced her she rested in front of a
crackling fire.

Platters of hot, steamy muffins, thick, juicy steaks, and
smoked oysters paraded through her head. She could see

herself presiding over fine meals of leg of mutton smothered in caper sauce and baked pickerel in wine sauce. Her mind did an excellent job of convincing her she was well fed and safe.

An enormous slice of plum pie swimming in thick sweet cream was her undoing. Dominique awoke, ravenous for a taste of the sweet. The pungent odor of the dirty tattered buffalo robe filled her nostrils instead.

Dominique fell back asleep with only the salty taste of her tears to flavor her mouth.

Chapter Twelve

Fort Abraham Lincoln, May 17, 1876

THE MORNING DAWNED BRIGHT AND SUMMERLIKE. A GENtle breeze, as wispy as a baby's first locks of hair, warmed the men of the Seventh Cavalry and set them to joking and laughing.

At the front of the column, General Custer sat astride his most treasured mount, Dandy. Preparing to call the order to move out, Custer surveyed his troops. The regiment stretched out for nearly two miles and included seventeen hundred animals—pack mules, horses, and cattle. These were accompanied by twelve hundred men and wagons filled with supplies and artillery.

Through the morning mist, the column appeared shrouded and ghostlike, premonitory somehow. Custer blinked, and when he opened his eyes, the men seemed to be rising off the ground toward the heavens. Scattered among them, several Sioux warriors rode, waving tomahawks and bloodied scalps.

Custer shuddered and turned to Libbie. Perched on her mount, shading her eyes from the glare, she was no vision, but an oasis, his link to the real world. She would accompany him, as she often had, to the first campground a few miles away from the post. There she would stay overnight, then say her final good-bye and return to the fort the following morning. Would it be just that—the final goodbye—this time? He opened his mouth to speak, but again, a feeling of gloom, some ominous forewarning, washed over him. Perhaps it was because of Dominique and the fact that a handful of renegades had been able to snatch her almost before his very eyes. Then again, maybe it was something else.

Swallowing hard, Custer lifted his chin and swiveled to his right. The company bugler sat rigid awaiting his orders to sound the signal. Usually Custer couldn't wait to get going. What held him back this morning? Shaking off the feelings as nonsense, he prepared to give the order, but the band struck up his favorite marching song, "The Garryowen." Custer sat back in his saddle, relieved at the delay, and listened to the boisterous lyrics: "We'll break down windows, we'll break down doors, we'll let the doctors work their cures, and tinker up our bruises. We'll drink down ale, no man for debt shall go to jail, for Garryowen and his glory. Wherever we go they'll dread the name of Garryowen and his glory."

In mid-column, oblivious to the band and its music, Barney stood with Hazel. Gazing down into her amber eyes, he searched for the words to express what she'd done for him, what she'd come to mean to his very life. "It don't matter what happens to me now, Hazel. If I got to die in battle, I can die a happy man."

"Now, stop that!" she said in a harsh whisper. "I can't stand it if you talk like that. You've got to stay alive, if for no other reason than to help find Dominique."

"Aw, I didn't mean it literal. 'Course I'll find Dominique! Don't you worry your pretty head about her one more minute. I just know we'll find her safe and sound."

"Oh, Barney, do you really think so?"

And although he didn't believe it for a minute, he said, "Sure."

"Well . . ." She hesitated, slightly disgusted with herself for thinking of Barney and the wonderful evening they'd spent together when poor Dominique was in such peril. But unable to stop herself, she went on. "Then why did you say that about dying? I—I thought I gave you a reason to come back to me. You sound like a man who'd rather not."

"Oh, no, Hazel! That's not what I meant at all. You know I—" Again he struggled, wondering how he could possibly explain what last night had meant to him, what he hoped it had meant to her. He'd gone to her fearful and hesitant, unsure of his abilities as a man. Somehow she'd convinced him that he'd known what to do all along. She had tutored him, yet made him feel like the instructor; she had shown him how a man pleased a woman, but made him feel as if he was the only one who ever had. She'd given of herself—and shown him what it was to love. "I don't know how to say it, but I want you to know that last night, well, being with you was the best, the most—"

"Barney," she whispered, her eyes moist, "the only thing I want to hear from you today is that you'll be coming back to me."

He gulped, looking away for a moment, then said, "If it's the last thing I'm able to do, you know I will." He screwed up his lips, working his mouth until his mustache was completely out of sight. Sounding as if some giant hand squeezed his throat while he spoke, he said, "If'n you would, if it pleases you, there's something I'd like for you to do while I'm gone."

"Anything Barney."

"I—I never done this before, so I'm not right sure how to go about it, but, well . . ." Barney twisted his hat in his hands, spun it in a circle, then rumpled the brim as he gathered his courage. "What I'd hoped . . . I mean, when I get back, if you think you'd like to, if the army life don't seem too bad to you, I thought maybe, I—"

"I'd be honored to be the wife of a fine man like you if that's what you're trying to say, Barney."

"That'd be it!" he choked out, the hand suddenly releasing his throat, then swamping it with tears. Embarrassed, unused to such unmanly reactions, he jerked her into his arms and buried his face against her hair.

Glancing around at the others, Hazel saw the same scene

repeated over and over as husbands and lovers said their good-byes. Somehow, even though many of the other unions were of long standing, she knew her own was more poignant. She pulled away, intending to tell him how much she loved him when the bugle sounded the farewell.

"That's it," Barney muttered, his voice constricted. "I got to mount up. Bye, Hazel, I—"

"Barney, I think I know what you're trying to say, and believe me—"

He pressed a gentle finger against her lips and shook his head. "Thanks, sugar lump, but I got to say this myself: I love ya, Hazel. I love ya like I never knew love could happen. Take care of yourself for me. We got a whole lot of catching up to do when I get back."

"Oh, Barney," she said through a sudden rush of tears, "I'll wait here forever if I have to."

After swinging up into the saddle and adjusting his scabbard, Barney straightened his shoulders and smiled down at her. "I can't imagine the wait being that long, sugar. Shouldn't take the general more than a couple a months to find a few renegade Injuns and wipe 'em out. I'll be back in your arms before the fall air crisps your apple cheeks."

The column began moving then. All Hazel could do was wave good-bye as the horses and wagons thundered on past her, creaking and groaning and kicking up dust to mingle with the damp morning air. When Barney was out of sight, Hazel turned her attention to the final song the band played. As she listened to the words, and really heard them for the first time, her tears flowed.

In hurried words her name I blessed
And to my heart in anguish pressed
The girl I left behind me.
The hope of final victory, within my bosom burning,
Is mingling with sweet thoughts of thee and of my fond
    returning.
But should I ne'er return again,

Still with my love I'll find me
Sweet girl I left behind me.

Uninterested in the songs or the great show of military precision as the regiment finally departed, Jacob nudged his new mount, a black gelding called Hammerhead, out of the pack and up to his commanding officer.

"Captain Ruffing, sir," he said with a crisp salute. "May I have permission to ride up to the front?"

"What for, Private? We haven't even left the damn garrison."

"I know, sir, but I understood that the general may want me out beyond him and the regiment as a scout. I am fit this morning."

"You don't look so fit. In fact, you look like hell. Why don't you tie your horse to the back of a feed wagon and toss your mangy body on a sack of grain? You'll have plenty of time to be a target for the hostiles later."

"But, sir—"

"That's an order, Private, and on this campaign, orders will not be questioned or disregarded. You will do as you're told, or you will be shot. Understood, Private?"

"Yes, sir." Jacob snapped off another salute, then wheeled Hammerhead around and headed for one of the supply wagons. Although his mind resented the order, worked at finding a way out of it, his body longed for the relative comfort of a sack of grain. He and Drooping Belly had done a good job of making him look as if he'd been attacked by Indians—too good a job. It seemed as if every muscle in his body had been pulled or pummeled, scraped or torn. And the cut on his arm—his *right* arm, he grumbled to himself—felt as if a thousand bees were driving their stingers into it. Perhaps another day of rest would serve him and the Dakota purpose better than a journey back to the village.

Jacob slid down off the saddle and tied the horse to the back of the wagon. As he climbed and gingerly stretched out among the flour sacks, his thoughts returned to Dominique. She would have to spend another night alone in his tipi. He would have to spend another day hoping Gall had the patience and desire to keep her safe.

Most of all, he would have to pray the other warriors did not become overwhelmed with her golden beauty and force her to succumb to their demands. A white woman, especially one of any beauty, was a great prize, something to be shared among the most deserving of warriors. A woman like Dominique would be a very tempting morsel for even the most lowly of his brothers.

Jacob pounded a fist already sore with weeping wounds against the wooden floor of his prison.

Nearly twenty miles to the west, the Hunkpapa village bustled with activity. Buffalo had been sighted earlier in the morning, and now the women were hard at work processing the two bulls killed by their best hunters. Dominique, transferred to a larger tipi at dawn, sat huddled in a corner of her new lodgings, listening to the excited voices, wondering how long she would be left undisturbed and unmolested.

The answer appeared at the flap of her tipi in the form of a squaw who could no longer be called a maiden. "On your feet, white devil. We have much work to do."

Dominique glared up at the woman the others called Spotted Feather. "Leave me alone!" she snapped, in spite of Jacob's warnings.

"So, the crazy one does have a tongue." Spotted Feather drew a knife from the folds of her dress and stepped inside the tipi.

Bolting to her feet, Dominique backed away from the squaw, threatening, "Stay away from me! I mean it! You get away, or I swear, I'll—I'll—"

"You'll what, white filth? Fall on your knees and beg me to spare your stupid life? Or is it your plan to fight me?" She leaned her head back and howled with laughter, then sobered and said, "You are no match for me, stupid one. You are no match for a crippled sparrow."

With fright and her temper leading the way, Dominique snapped, "Get out! Get out and leave me alone this instant, you stinking savage!"

"Wi witko!" the Indian raged as she flew at her. "You will die now and then I will boil your tongue for the dogs!"

Dominique lunged to one side as the knife arced past her head. Spinning around, she flattened herself against the wall of the tipi, her eyes darting around for an avenue of escape. Spotted Feather circled, standing between her and the flap. She grinned, exposing her square blunt-edged teeth and the yellow gleam in her black eyes. And Dominique read the message. The woman not only meant to kill her—she couldn't wait to do so. Why hadn't she listened better to Jacob? Why hadn't she *believed* him?

Her hands still pressed against the buffalo-skin wall, Dominique edged toward the opening. "Look, I didn't mean a thing I just said, I swear. And really, I don't mind a little honest work. What do you want me to do? Just tell me. Wash the clothes? Cook a little? I'm not too good at sewing, but I can—"

"Silence!" Spotted Feather gathered a mouthful of spittle and fired it.

Although she raised her hand and ducked, the wad spattered the side of Dominique's head and dampened her fingers. "Ugh!" she complained, wiping at her hair and shaking the mess from her hand.

Taking advantage of her victim's disgust and the resulting distraction, Spotted Feather leapt across the short distance and knocked the unguarded woman to the ground. As the pair rolled across the dirt floor, the knife found a mark on its own.

"Owwww!" Dominique cried out as the blade scraped the flesh between her ribs. "You tried to stab me!" she cried out, incredulous. "You bloody heathen, you actually tried to *stab* me!"

Bent on her objective, Spotted Feather replied with a low gutteral laugh, then renewed her attack. She grabbed one of Dominique's sloppily plaited braids and jerked it hard, hoping to hear a rewarding crack of the woman's neck. Instead, a foot stomped down on her fingers.

"There is no time for fighting," Gall said in a deceptively casual tone. "We are hunted and must do our work quickly and with little confusion. Come, prepare the meat that will fill our bellies and the hides that will keep us warm."

"Yes, Father." Spotted Feather scrambled to her feet and brushed her hair out of her eyes. "I would ask that the crazy woman help us. We have much to do."

Gall narrowed his gaze, sending a message to the squaw, then said, "She is weak and not much good, but you may use her." His gaze shifted to Dominique, searching her for injuries, then he turned to leave. "See that she works, but return her to Redfoot's tipi if she falters. This one could slow us and interfere with our plans."

"I will see that she works quickly."

Satisfied, Gall stepped through the opening. Before Dominique had a chance to react, Spotted Feather grabbed her braids and jerked her to her feet.

"You are fortunate, one who wears a coat of porcupine quills on her tongue! Next time you will not be so lucky." She smiled, then slowly licked her lips as she brought the knife between herself and her victim. "Next time, my knife will do more than prick your precious white skin. The next time you dare to speak to me, I will cut out your heart and dance upon it."

Raging inside, Dominique managed to keep her silence and therefore her life. She meekly hung her head and allowed Spotted Feather to drag her outside to a camp filled with activity.

"You will care for the hides," the squaw laughed as she led her captive through the village to the outskirts. There, four old women toiled over two bloody buffalo hides that were nailed to the ground by a series of pegs. With a none-too-gentle shove, Spotted Feather pushed Dominique to her knees. "These women will show you what to do. Do not move too slow or try to leave. You will die if you do either of these things.''

Keeping her gaze pinned to the hides, Dominique pressed her lips together and nodded. Then the squaw spoke to the others in their native tongue. Once during this discussion, the women burst into laughter and murmured among themselves, pointing and waving at Dominique. Then Spotted Feather spun on her moccasin and marched off toward the cooking bags, leaving the hide-tanning group to themselves.

An old, especially wrinkled woman grinned, showing off her only front tooth, and tossed Dominique a scraper fashioned from a buffalo horn. Showing her new helper the movements, she began scraping the meat and fat off the hide, urging Dominique to mimic the maneuver.

Swallowing her revulsion, Dominique sat back on her heels and began to scrape the gruesome hide. She rocked as she worked, trying not to inhale the aroma of death and the stench of buffalo hair matted with mud and feces. When she thought her back might break from the exertion, the old woman reached over and snatched away her buffalo-horn tool.

Expelling a heavy sigh of relief, Dominique leaned back and stretched. Then she discovered her retirement was premature. The old woman tapped on her knee, muttering, ''Work, Tongue with Many Quills. Work.'' Then she handed her a finishing scraper, this one made of stone, and urged her to continue.

Dominique spent the entire day in this manner, stopping only to nibble on a few strips of jerky and a handful of chokecherries. When evening came, she staggered off to Jacob's tipi and consumed a meal of broiled rabbit and persimmons. Then she collapsed for the night.

The following morning found her jerked from her sleep in much the same manner.

''Get up, Many Quills!'' Spotted Feather barked through the opening in the tipi, ''The hides await you!''

In no condition for a repeat of yesterday's battle, Dominique struggled to her feet and followed the woman out into the morning sunlight. Again she was led to the outskirts of camp, and again she was instructed to kneel at the edge of a hide. This time, instead of scraping the hides with tools, however, she was ordered to spread a gelatinous substance on the buffalo skin.

"Get to work!" Spotted Feather ordered. "You will rub this mixture into the hide with your hands."

Dominique leaned forward and sniffed. When the foul odor assaulted her nostrils, she forgot her vows and grimaced, blurting out, "What in bloody hell is this stuff?" She instantly regretted the impulsive comment, but when she glanced up at Spotted Feather expecting to receive a blow of some kind, the Indian surprised her with a grin.

"This is good stuff, Tongue with Many Quills. You will like what it does for your white skin." She laughed and pointed. "See the old women? See their pretty hands?"

Dominique looked at the other workers as they held up their gnarled fingers, and gasped. Stretched over the crooked bones was skin dry enough and tough enough to stand on its own.

Laughing, Spotted Feather explained. "Pretty, are they not? You, too, will have such hands after smoothing the hides with this magic we make with cooked brains, liver, and urine."

"Oh!" Dominique wrapped her arms around her stomach and leaned away from the hide. She fought the retching, struggled to retain some measure of her pride, but her senses were too offended. She collapsed in the dirt, heaving up the remnants of last night's supper.

In her misery, she could hear the women's mocking laughter, their cruel taunts, but Dominique no longer cared. She wished only to die, to have the ground swallow her and take her to the bowels of hell if necessary. It had to be a better place than this.

"Get up, weak-hearted one." Spotted Feather grabbed a handful of her captive's wool serge dress and pulled her upright. "Enough of this nonsense. Work now. Do not stop until the old woman says you can.'' She released her, and although wobbly, Dominique remained sitting. With another laugh, Spotted Feather went on her way.

Her stomach finally resigned to the sickening odor, Dominique fought tears of despair instead of nausea as she worked into the late afternoon. When the old women released her, she stumbled back through the village, her eyes downcast, her ears barely hearing the taunts and remarks the warriors made as she passed by. No longer caring what they said or thought, she continued on her way. One particularly randy warrior reached out, tugging at her skirt, and grabbing at his crotch. Beaten, she paid him no heed and staggered on toward the tipi. Back inside the shelter she walked to the far wall and sank cross-legged onto the rug.

Dominique stayed there in a trancelike state, her eyes glazed, for an hour before her troubled mind slowly directed her back to the present. After reviewing her predicament she let her shoulders slump. Tears pooled in her eyes. Her bottom lip began to quiver uncontrollably. Dominique took a breath that was more of a sob just as the flap to the tipi opened and someone stepped across the entrance.

Jerking her head up, Dominique tried to shield her eyes from the setting sun, but she could only identify the fact that her visitor was a man—a savage who wore only a breechclout. The exposed parts of his body—his massive chest and long muscular legs—glistening in the eerie glow of sundown, threatened and fascinated her at once. But, more frightened than anything, Dominique opened her mouth and screamed.

''Hush, now,'' he soothed, ''there is no need to act the crazy one now. It's me, Jacob.''

She'd just filled her lungs for another bloodcurdling scream when she realized what he'd said. Scrambling to her feet, she peered through the rays of the sun. ''Jacob? Is it really you?''

''Yes, Dominique. You have no need to be afraid now.''

"Oh, Jacob," she sobbed, stumbling across the buffalo rug and throwing herself into his arms. "I swear to God, I can't stand another minute here. Please, please," she cried, her arms outstretched. "I beg you to take me away. I'll go anywhere, do *anything*, but you've got to get me away from these savages!"

"Hush, now," he said into her tangled hair. "It can't be that bad."

"Oh, b-but it is!" she insisted, renewing her outburst. "You can't believe what they made me do, what they made me *eat*! Oh, Jacob, I don't even know what it *is* they've been feeding me, but I've been sick since you left me here."

"As I've been sick since joining the cavalry," he said, stroking her hair.

Something snapped. Dominique jerked out of his arms. "That's hardly the same! I mean I've really been sick! Why, if you knew the things I've done. My hands—" She held them out, palms up, for his inspection. "Just look at that!"

Jacob took her hands in his, his brow creasing as he studied the cracks and welts in her shriveled skin. "What have you been doing?"

"Rubbing some horrid stuff into buffalo hides, sticking my beautiful—"

"You have been tanning hides?" he said, incredulous.

"I guess so. All I know is that the stuff I had to work with made me sick to my stomach, but that squaw, the mean one, made me do it anyway. Oh, and she tried to kill me, too! She almost stabbed me right here!" Dominique raised her arm and pointed to a tear in the fabric of her bodice. "If it wasn't for my corset, I don't know wh—" She cut off her words when she realized she was discussing her undergarments with a man. If she hadn't been so upset, she might have laughed when she realized that man had been raised by Indians and probably had no idea what she was talking about. "Well," she sputtered instead, "it really doesn't matter. What does matter is that I'm here and I hate it. I really must demand you take me back to the fort.''

"You know I can't do that," he said softly, wondering which squaw had attacked her, pretty sure if he guessed Spotted Feather, he would have the correct name.

"But, Jacob," she cried, panic edging into her voice, "you've just got to! I'm *begging*. Please take me back! I swear by all that's holy I'll never tell a living soul about you being a spy. Not one person. You can trust me, really you can," she added, her brown eyes round and pitiful. "Please, Jacob?"

"You are very convincing, but I'm afraid the answer must be no. Taking you back to the soldiers or to the fort is impossible. You must remain here with me."

"With *you*?" she spat, twisting away from him. "This is all your fault!" She drew her arm back, preparing to slap him with all her might, but as she swung around, he caught her wrist in midair.

"Careful, crazy one. Hitting me, or any Dakota, is not a good idea. You will be repaid for such an insult in ways that would pain me to describe."

Jerking her hand free, she jutted her chin out. "What do you care about me? You've hit me with your fist, not once, but twice! I'm the one who owes you pain!"

He raised his brows, then shrugged. "Perhaps you are right." Dropping the bundle he carried, he spread his legs and placed his hands on his hips. "Go ahead. Hit me twice. You deserve to have your vengeance."

Grumbling deep in her throat, Dominique curled up her fist and pulled her elbow back, but as she stared up into his deep blue eyes, her anger melted to reveal a core of despair.

"Oh, Jacob," she sighed, dazed, "I don't want to hit you. I want to go home." Her arms dropped to her sides and her chin trembled. "All the way home to Michigan. I want my papa." Then tears began to sprinkle the front of her dress.

Unraveled by a sight a Dakota warrior rarely witnessed, Jacob felt his brave stance waver, leaving him rigid and awkward. "Please, Dominique. Don't do that. I cannot help you if you do that."

"Wh-what?" she sobbed.

"This crying." He wiggled a finger at her damp cheeks. "I do not like this. Stop it at once."

"Stop—stop c-crying?" she gasped, amazed at the request. "First you kidnap me, and nearly break my jaw. Th-then you f-force me to live like an animal with these heathens, and now—now y-you tell me I can't go home or even c-cry about it?" Her anger grew as she spoke, and she damned the tide of tears that fell without her consent. "Why, you miserable—y-you clabber-headed—"

"Nincompoop?" he supplied, hoping to lighten her mood.

"You're a nincompoop, all right, but you're worse, too! You're the scum of the earth, a two-bit no-good lousy—" She struggled to think of a word bad enough to describe him, yet filthy enough to wake up God and make him take notice of her dilemma. She finally came up with one. "You're a no-good *bastard*, Jacob Stoltz Redfoot whoever-the-hell-you-are! And what's more, I hate you, and I'll hate you until the day my uncle Armstrong shoots a hole through your thick head!"

Jacob's eyes narrowed, and his mouth spread into a long grim line. "Dress yourself in this." He pointed to the bundle he'd dropped, adding in an icy tone, "You will find travel and work more comfortable. Put it on now. Soon you and I will take food with the others." Then he turned and stepped out of the tipi.

Dominique's heart constricted. She started after him, abruptly pulling up when she reached the opening. Looking out through the flap, she watched his retreating back, saw the other warriors greeting him and slapping his strong shoulders. He was out of her reach now, out of her world. Her sobs returned as she whispered, "I didn't mean it, Jacob. Really I didn't. I just . . . I want to go home."

But he couldn't hear her, couldn't hear anything but the dull beating of his heavy heart. He, not Dominique, was the crazy one, he muttered to himself. What ever had made him think she could be happy here, that she could adjust to life in the village?

Jacob announced himself as he approached the medicine lodge, then stepped inside for treatment of his wounds. When he emerged several minutes later, his injuries were soothed, but his heart still ached. What could he do? When would his mind ever rest again? Knowing the answer to that question had something to do with Dominique, unwilling to see just what that answer would lead him to do, Jacob pinched the angry cut slicing into his biceps and gave his mind something else to think about.

His arm still throbbing, he reached the flap of his tipi, and called out, "Are you dressed? We must take our meal with the others now."

"I'm not coming outside in this!"

Jacob blew out a sigh and tore open the flap. She stood near the entrance. With a quick movement, he reached inside and grabbed her arm. "You stretch my patience as if it were the hide you tanned. Let us eat." Then he jerked her outside.

"Jacob!" Horrified, Dominique tore free of his grip, then bent at the waist. She crossed her hands in front of her knees and looked around. "Are you insane? I can't be seen in this."

"I don't understand." He stood back, studying the dress, appreciating the intriguing body beneath it, then shrugged. "You look beautiful. You must also be more comfortable. Come. Let us eat."

"Jacob! I can't. This dress doesn't even cover my knees!"

"It covers all it needs to. Look around—you show no more than the other women."

"But I'm not like the other women! They are . . . well, they're Indians. I, on the other hand"—she raised her chin a notch—"am a lady. I simply cannot show my arms and legs, especially in front of you."

Jacob stood back and crossed his arms over his chest. Spreading his legs, he began a slow, lazy grin, saying with his eyes what he didn't dare speak in words.

It took Dominique only a moment to read the message. He'd already seen her legs—and much, much more. She thought back to the night in his tipi, the frozen encounter that seemed so long ago, and remembered how the heat from his naked body had brought life back to hers. He knew her almost as intimately as a husband. She closed her eyes and shuddered at the vivid memory, then fought the blush rising up from her breasts.

"Come, now," he encouraged softly. "My friends will be so fascinated with your hair, they will not even notice your legs."

Unable to meet his gaze as images of their first meeting continued to appear in her mind, Dominique allowed him to lead her to the campfire. When he said to sit, she dropped to the ground, tucked her legs beneath her, and took the bowl of food he offered. She did all of this dutifully, without so much as a glance at him or at the other savages gathered around the fire ring.

"Dominique," he said under his breath as he sat cross-legged beside her. "Look up. Greet my people with a smile."

Lifting her lashes ever so slowly, Dominique glanced around at his companions and offered a short nod before she dropped her gaze back to her lap. A few women remained, apparently waiting for a good look at the curious white slave. All of them stared at her as if she were some kind of freak. Then one by one, they faded back to their own lodges, no longer interested in the stranger. Spotted Feather stayed, spearing Dominique with an angry glance every time she got the chance.

"Eat your stew," said Jacob, keeping one eye on the warriors. To a man, they stared openly at Dominique, displaying an interest that went far beyond curiosity. He was going to have to make some decisions soon, lay down some rules, and try to make his friends understand that this white woman could not be community property.

"Jacob," Dominique whispered under her breath as she stared down into the bowl, "what's in this?"

"It is harmless. A little buffalo meat, some wild peas, and a root called prairie turnips. Stew. It is good."

Cautiously, she lifted the container to her mouth and took a small sip. The flavor, while nothing fancy, was surprisingly good. She tilted the bowl and captured a piece of meat with her tongue, then noticed the heated gaze of one of the warriors sitting near her. She chewed her food, never taking her eyes off the aggressive Indian, then whispered to Jacob. "I don't like the way your friend is staring at me. Make him stop it."

"Do not look at him." Jacob glared at Chatanna, knowing he would try to do a lot more than stare at the golden vision the next time opportunity struck. Would Gall be able to prevent the inevitable? Did he even have the right to ask his brothers to forgo taking what they felt was their right? Beside him, Dominique squirmed, nudging him with her complaints.

"Forget Chatanna and eat. He means no harm," Jacob lied, hoping to ease her fears, even if he couldn't relieve his own. "You will soon feel at home."

Unable to play the obedient captive any longer, Dominique slammed her bowl on the ground and turned on him. "Never! I could never feel at home under these barbaric conditions, and I cannot survive eating this—this slop!"

"Then don't eat," he snapped back, his anxiety beginning in earnest, his patience at an end. "Starve to death if you wish. It no longer matters to me."

Turning his back to her, Jacob began to stuff chunks of buffalo meat in his mouth, swallowing them along with the lump in his throat. When he finished his meal, he jerked her to her feet in spite of her unfinished supper, then marched her back to his tipi.

"Stay in here and go to sleep. Do not come outside

again tonight.'' Dominique opened her mouth, but Jacob closed it with a well-placed finger. ''We'll speak no more this night. Do as I say and you will be safe.''

Then he closed the flap and headed for the warriors' lodge. He'd run out of time, used up nearly all of his options. And he couldn't go on like this. As long as Dominique was in camp, as long as his friends expected to have what was rightfully theirs, he could not complete his mission. His concentration—the considerable lack of it since he'd met the crazy one—would soon become a problem, if it hadn't already. His full attention was crucial to the Dakota survival. Jacob could think of only one way to regain the concentration he so badly needed.

The time had come to take some drastic measures.

Chapter Thirteen

JACOB LOOKED ACROSS THE DYING FIRE AND INTO THE eyes of his father, Gall. He continued trying to put into words that which he really couldn't explain. "But, Father, you saw her hands. You know what the other women have forced her to do. The crazy one is too young to tan hides. That is a job for old women. What else will they make her do if you and I cannot protect her in some way?"

The wise chief regarded his white son a long moment before he spoke. "I agree she has been treated badly, especially by the one who would hope to be yours, but I believe there is something more here. Something that has nothing to do with the other warriors or this white woman's wrinkled hands. Speak to me of it now, or this council is over and we shall not mention the crazy one again."

Jacob drew a long breath and stared into the flickering embers. How much should he confess? Would a complete explanation garner his father's understanding or earn his disdain? Too much discussion of Dominique, of her family, and of the reasons for her visit, would bring up the Custer name. Jacob didn't need his imagination to know what the council would do with that information. He suppressed a shudder and settled on a half-truth, taking the only option he knew would be respected and, he hoped, understood by all.

"I wish to have the crazy one as my woman alone. I ask for your permission to marry her."

"Ah." Chief Gall nodded, as if he'd been expecting the announcement. "I feared this change in you. I suspected once you were returned to the people of your birth, you might wish to become one of them again."

"No, Father. That's not it at all. I spit on the soldiers and what they stand for. My feelings for Dominique have nothing to do with her white skin." He flattened his palm and pressed it against his chest. "They have to do with what I feel in here."

Again the chief nodded. Gall took a long pull on his pipe and closed his eyes as he thought back to long ago. Then he asked, "Are these feelings like those you had for Lame Fawn?"

Jacob expelled his breath in a low groan. He should have been expecting the question. It was honest enough, especially coming from the chief of the Hunkpapa. It was only natural that Gall would want to know if Jacob felt the same love for Dominique that he'd once had for the woman he'd taken as his wife. What was his answer?

No. Surprised—not by the thought, but by the rationale behind it—Jacob averted his gaze so Gall couldn't see the confusion and the surge of insight flickering in his eyes. Where was the pain he used to feel whenever he thought of his days with Lame Fawn? He'd used that pain, the sense of emptiness, over the last four winters, as a kind of punishment for the part he'd played in her premature death. Now it was gone, save for the remnants of a guilt he would never shake.

But what of love? Why had his mind instinctively told him this new love was nothing like the love he'd had for Lame Fawn? His feelings for the Indian maiden had been deep, but never filled with the intensity of those he had for Dominique. This niece of Custer was constantly in his mind; she rendered him nearly helpless, with a loss of control so complete that at times it terrified him. Life and love with his wife had always been quiet and dignified, a simple thing. With the crazy one, he was in constant turmoil, either wildly happy or insanely angry. He couldn't even imagine what life would be like as her husband. Suddenly he couldn't wait to find out.

Choosing his words carefully, he looked across the dying fire again and said, "My feelings are very much the same, Father. I cannot explain it better than that."

Gall narrowed his eyes and nodded, then continued with his questions. "The crazy one has no people here. Who will bless her union with you and give permission for this marriage?"

"I was hoping you would give it along with my own permission."

Gall nodded, deep in thought. "Then what of her people, her own mother and father? How will they feel about their loss, about the fact that she is being held captive in a Dakota camp? Will they turn their backs on her? Will they increase their persecution of us?"

Jacob walked a very narrow ledge. Any more discussion of Dominique's relatives would put the Custer name foremost in his mind and on the tip of his tongue. His inherently honest nature would be sorely offended if he had to tell his father any more lies. Then inspiration struck, and he used the words he'd recently heard spilling from the general's mouth: "It is no problem. She is dead to her family already."

"Then it is done. I wish you happiness, son, and hope this marriage does not interfere with the success of your mission."

Feeling cleansed, as if he could finally speak with a refreshing splash of honesty, he said, "Once we are wed and I no longer have to worry about the crazy one, my total concentration will be on our mission. That is a promise."

"I hope it is one you can keep." Gall gestured for Jacob to rise. Then he followed suit and walked with him to the opening in the lodge. He turned to his son, his mouth twisted into a sideways grin. "Since this woman has no family and I am to represent them, I hope you do not expect me to deliver gifts at your door in the morning."

"No, Father," Jacob said, with a chuckle of relief. "I think we can forget that part of the ceremony. Taking the crazy one as my bride will be gift enough."

"From what I have seen, taking the crazy one for a wife may be more burden than gift, my son. My present to you is a wish for much luck."

"Thank you, Father," Jacob said through his laughter as he stepped into the night air. "I believe I can use all the luck I can get."

Still laughing, he made his way across the small village and stepped into his own lodge. Dominique sat in the middle of the tipi near the fire. His uniform lay beside her in a heap. In her hand, she held the letter of invitation she'd written him several weeks past.

Her dark eyes flashing accusations, she held the paper out. "So Peaches ate it, huh? Is everything you've ever told me a lie, Jacob? Can I believe anything you have to say?"

His good humor a distant memory, he stalked across the floor and snatched the note from her hand. "This is no concern of yours."

"It most certainly is. You lied to me. You said—"

"Enough! I did not say you could look in my clothing. Now lie down and go to sleep before I am forced to put you to sleep permanently!"

Dominique jerked her head back in a huff. "How dare you threaten me!"

All thoughts of tenderness, of explaining their upcoming marriage and the reasons for it, vanished. Jacob rumpled the paper into a ball and threw it to the ground. "You still don't understand, do you? Perhaps I should throw you outside where many warriors will be happy to do much more than threaten you!"

Dominique crawled to the edge of the rug, her eyes wide. "Y-you wouldn't d-dare!"

"No? Maybe it's time that I should dare a lot more." Jacob dropped to his knees and reached for her. "If you had been raised in this village, you would be the mother of many strong young sons by now. Perhaps you have remained a maiden for too long, crazy one.'' Keeping one strong hand firmly clasped around her arm, he reached up with the other and lightly drew the backs of his fingertips across her cheek. ''A night spent in the arms of a Dakota warrior will most surely soften that barbed tongue of yours.''

Wondering how serious his intentions were, she felt equally outraged and intrigued by the idea of their union. Dominique's voice was weak with indecision as she said, ''No, thanks. Just leave me alone.''

''That isn't what you want. I can tell by the look in your curious eyes''—his middle finger traced her eyebrow—''the way your mouth trembles as you think about the heat of my lips against yours''—then down along her lower lip—''and you know better than I by the way you feel here.'' His hand slid down between her breasts and began stroking her flat tummy.

''N-no,'' she said through a sudden gasp. ''S-stop it!''

Jacob's laugh was hoarse as he said,. ''Your voice and the look on your face do not match your words, crazy one. Let me show you what it is to be truly a woman.''

Dominique pushed at his big hands as he grabbed her hips and dragged her beneath him, but it was no use. He was as strong as an enraged bear and twice as intent on his mission. Filled with indecision as he stretched his big body above the full length of hers, she opened her mouth to beg for mercy, but her parted lips only provided access for his driving tongue. He pressed himself down on her, bruising her, cutting off her breath with his massive chest as his passion flared to frenzy.

His strong hands were suddenly everywhere, punishing and rewarding her at the same time. Fingers of liquid heat pulled one of her breasts over the top of her low-cut dress and began kneading her nipple, surprising her with a surge of desire. The fingers of his other hand, tipped in flames, slid under her dress, singeing her thighs as they traveled to her center on a search for the treasure buried beneath her golden mound. Hampered by her drawers, Jacob's educated fingertips probed blindly, lighting small fires wherever they touched, as he sought entrance to the uncharted valleys of her sweetness.

Dominique bucked, moaning with pleasure and surprise as his touch threw open the doors of raging desire. No longer the lady, the properly educated daughter and the pristine niece, Dominique was raw, pulsating flesh, demanding gratification, consumed for the first time by the needs of a full-grown woman. She was desperate for some unnamed fulfillment, frantic to ease the agonizing pressure building inside her. Instinct made her snake her hands along Jacob's hips, then sent them slithering beneath his breechclout to his nude buttocks. There, her roaming fingers dug into his rigid flesh. She pulled him down toward the white-hot ache between her legs, grinding her hips against his, cursing the barrier of clothing between them.

"Oh, damn!" she cried out. "Damn it all, Jacob—*stop* a minute!"

Her writhing hips and agonized moans, the sight of her golden hair hanging loose and unkempt against the buckskin dress, inflamed him beyond reason even as her words jolted his conscience. She was desperate, not with passion but with fear. In her terror, her frantic attempts at escape, she'd nearly torn the skin from his backside. What was wrong with him? He'd almost taken her in a rage, used his passion for her as a tool of domination instead of an instrument of love. He was behaving like a lowly beast. He was no better than the wildest of animals to ravage an innocent like Dominique. Small wonder, if his behavior had been repeated by others, that the white man had labeled Indians savages. Control returned to Jacob in a wave of disgust. He rolled off her and onto his back.

Fighting for air, Dominique struggled to a sitting position. What had happened to Jacob? Where had he gone? Still panting, she turned her head and stared over at him. He lay on his back with one arm draped across his face. His chest rose and fell in short, rapid movements, and droplets of sweat glistened in the shallow valley below his breastbone, spilling down along the trail to his navel. Her gaze followed that course to his hips, where her eyes held, then widened with surprise. The pouch beneath his breechclout strained to harness the huge swelling she'd heard about but never before seen. How could this be? How could such a monster fit inside even the largest of women? What *had* she been thinking of a few moments ago?

With a startled gasp, Dominique averted her face. Overcome by the sight, her own bold desires, and the dark forbidden thoughts running rampant in her mind, she covered her mouth and fought a sudden girlish urge to giggle.

At the sound, Jacob lowered his arm from his eyes and looked up at her. She was hunched over, her delicate shoulders trembling like those of a frightened rabbit. Knowing she must be horrified at his outrageous assault on her, probably crying as well, he ground his teeth and sat up behind her. "Dominique, please—please forgive me. I did not mean to— I thought you were . . . I thought I could— Oh, please understand. I meant you no harm." The trembling increased, and she turned her lovely face even farther away from him. Snarling with self-loathing, he lightly touched her shoulder. "Rest now. I will not disturb you again this night."

When she collapsed onto the blanket, Jacob lay down beside her, careful not to make any physical contact. He stared at her back, the icy blast of his own scorn freezing his muscles into tense cords, and exhaled heavily. How could he have touched one of such purity and naïveté so violently, so intimately? He had to remember that she was white, and white women were frightened of such things, found little or no pleasure in the most natural acts. He would have to move slowly with her, treat her as he would a young filly in need of breaking. Maybe, he thought, finding a glimmer of hope for the future, if he informed her of his plans and told her he intended to make her his wife in an effort to protect her from the others, she would react differently, accept him more easily.

Jacob practiced the gentle words he would use when he broached the subject in the morning. Then he thought of her barbed tongue and the probable response. First she would laugh at him, tell him she needed more protection from him than from the others. Next she would spit on him and tell him she could never agree to marry an animal such as he. So how should be proceed?

Thinking of the ceremony from every angle, it occurred to Jacob that she probably wouldn't even wonder what was happening if he went ahead with his plans. Marriage was a simple, private thing between two people in the Dakota nation; what had transpired would never even cross the mind of a white woman. She would not know that she was his wife. He would not tell her. The day he did would be the day she could look into his eyes without wanting to spit in them. Satisfied with the solution, Jacob prayed to the gods for sleep—and for the strength to ignore the woman lying next to him, the woman he wanted so badly.

But thoughts of Dominique, of her soft ivory skin and rounded curves, of how very close he'd come to making that softness his own, kept the ache in his loins at high tide. Grumbling to himself, Jacob tugged the blanket around his shoulders and began counting the dwindling Plains buffalo.

Even as she struggled to bring her breathing under control, Dominique continued to fight the urge to laugh. What was wrong with her? There was nothing funny here, not one single moment a woman of her breeding could find even remotely amusing. Yet here she was, still fighting the urge to giggle, panting as she wondered what it would have been like if Jacob hadn't stopped fondling her. Cursing him because he had stopped, she squirmed against the buffalo rug, seeking some unnamed relief, then rolled to her side.

Sleep. Perhaps if she could force herself to sleep, the inappropriate thoughts would vanish. She would stop thinking of Jacob and the new exciting sensations his touch ignited in her, forget the strong urge to reach out for him and beg him to ease her torment. She would think of Monroe, her papa, the lush greens of spring in her own hometown. Sighing to herself, Dominique rolled over on her tummy and began counting the ducks lining up for their morning treats along the banks of Lake Erie.

When she finally dropped off, the relief she sought was not to be. Her mind returned to Jacob and his experienced mouth, Jacob and his fiery hands, Jacob and the fascinating swelling that branded him as a man of passion. Her mind brought her body back to the heights he'd shown it; then suddenly her imagination carried her a step further. She was tossed inside a wildly gyrating kaleidoscope of passion she'd never guessed at or dreamed of before. She fluttered, with Jacob's hands and tongue as her wings, ever higher through the spectrum of colors until a brilliant explosion of scarlet and platinum shattered her dreams and eased her suffering. Then she sank into the dark, endless depths of slumber.

The following morning Dominique awakened refreshed from the first good night's sleep she'd had since her kidnapping. Then she realized her drawers were damp. Horrified, only vaguely aware of the sensations she'd experienced during the night, she jerked upright. What had happened to her? Why did she feel so alive, so . . . strange? Dominique twisted her head to the side as a new, equally terrifying thought occurred to her: Did Jacob know? Had she cried out his name during the night? But he was gone. With a sigh of relief, she lay back down and stretched, curiously happy and satisfied. Then the flap opened, and Jacob stepped inside.

''Well,'' she said, unable to look into his eyes as she sat up, ''this is a surprise. I would have thought you had to run back to the cavalry and pretend to be a soldier by now.''

Spurred on by what he assumed was sarcasm, Jacob added some of his own. ''That is no problem yet. Your

dear uncle was quite happy to send me scouting two or
three days ahead of the troops. In fact,'' he added as he
crossed over to where she lay, ''since I'm the nincompoop
who managed to lose you, I think he encourages me to go
on these trips of great bravery in the hopes that I will be
shot or scalped.''

''My uncle Armstrong is a very intelligent man.'' Dominique set her chin in a challenge, hoping he would accept
it and continue his teasing, say anything as long as he
didn't mention last night. But he ignored the invitation and
instead tossed a buckskin dress across her lap.

''Put this on,'' he ordered, forcing his features to remain impassive. ''Then we will eat.''

Dominique glanced up at him, her eyebrows arched,
then examined the garment. It was just another dress, but
the hide was pure white and as soft as any flannel she'd
ever touched. ''Is this for something special, a party or
something?''

''No. One of the women gave it to me. It is newer and
cleaner than the one you wear now.'' To make sure she
would change into it, he baited her. ''Be quick about it.
You are beginning to smell bad.''

''I am not! If anything stinks around here, it's you!''
She pushed up to her feet, intending to continue her tirade,
''In fact, if—''

''Removing your tongue is a job I have been looking
forward to since you first flapped it at me,'' he said, interrupting her. He fondled the handle of his knife and
grinned. ''If you'd like to keep it, I suggest you put it back
in your mouth and get dressed. I will wait outside, but
only for a minute. Be quick.''

''Oh, very well!'' she said with a stomp of her foot.

After he closed the flap, she studied the dress more
closely. Not only was the hide white but the sleeves and
hem were embellished with rows of thick fringe. The
neckline, cut in the shape of a V instead of the round
shape on the dress she wore, sparkled with decorations.
Porcupine quills, sewed to echo the lines of the V, covered

the entire front. Between these oblique lines were clusters of shiny blue beads along with a few scattered shells painted in bright colors.

Dominique quickly shed the tattered garment she wore and donned the beautiful new dress. Smaller than the previous buckskin, this one fit snugly across her hips and ended a good two or three inches above her knees. She laughed as she pictured her indecent image descending the elaborate staircase of her home, then shrugged. She had much bigger things on her mind, couldn't afford to concern herself with modesty and the conventions that bound a young lady in white society. Her only priority now had to be survival—and escape. Dominique snatched the porcupine-quill brush off the rug and pulled it through her tangled hair.

She thought of Jacob's warnings about the jealous squaws as she smoothed her naturally wavy locks, but decided to adapt his orders to fit her own sense of style anyway. How could the other women hate her more than they already did? She braided a length of hair from either side of her head, then tied the two plaits together at the back of her head. This left the rest of her long red-gold hair to spill down her back, unfettered and free, a gesture of defiance of sorts, in contrast to the fact that the rest of her remained a prisoner. She topped the look off by plucking an eagle feather from Jacob's lance and jabbing it into the knot where her braids met. Then she positioned a length of hair across her shoulder, coaxing it to slip off the tip of her breast at just the right angle, and tore back the flap of the tipi.

When Dominique stepped through the opening, Jacob was unprepared for the change in her—or for his gut-wrenching reaction. He'd half expected to feel at least a small trickle of pain running through his heart when he first saw Dominique in Lame Fawn's wedding dress. No small creek, but rivers of emotion, of love, raged through his veins instead, threatening to flood his arteries like a thousand spring thaws.

There was nothing in Dominique to remind him of his first wife, to bring even the slightest ache to his heart. The dress fit her as if it had been stretched over her curves while wet, became new to his eyes as if it had never touched the flesh of another. Dominique was incredibly beautiful—sun-kissed from the top of her brilliant gold-red hair to the tips of her white-moccasined toes. She looked like no other. No other could ever hope to resemble such beauty. Her radiance choked Jacob, cutting off his air and strangling his mind. He stood there, gawking at her as if he'd never seen a woman before.

"Why, Mr. Redfoot," Dominique clucked, familiar with his expression, immensely pleased to know she was the cause. "It's not polite to stare, you know." She batted her lashes furiously, posing haughtily as she asked, "Is something wrong? Do I have a smudge on my cheek or something?"

"N-n—" Jacob cleared the enormous frog that had mysteriously taken over his throat, then said, "Ah, no. You look fine." In control again, or at least in as much control as he would be able to muster on this day, he forced a taciturn expression and walked to her side. He unfolded the blanket he carried, preparing to move along with the required courtship, but Dominique gasped, halting his movements.

"Oh, Jacob, what's happened to you? Your hands and arms, they—they're all covered with bruises and cuts, and—"

"It is nothing. I fell from my horse." Trying his best to ignore her, he wrapped one end of the blanket around his shoulders and the other around hers.

"What are you doing now?" She demanded, stepping back. "I'm not cold."

"Please," he said, still not daring to look into her eyes, "do not question what I do. Unless it is your wish to pleasure every man in the village, you will follow my instructions. I am trying to show the other warriors that you are my woman and persuade them to leave you alone when I am gone.''

Dominique quickly ducked back under the shelter of his blanket. Maybe she should have braided all her hair, she thought with more than a little panic. Maybe she should have left the old tattered dress on and told Jacob this one didn't fit . . . and maybe now was the time to ask some questions of the man who would know all the answers. ''What else should I do to make sure they leave me alone?''

''Only follow me''—he turned, finally staring into her big brown eyes—''and see if you can't find a way to keep your lovely mouth shut.''

Dominique bit her lip and lifted her chin, but allowed him to walk her through the camp to the community fire. There he nudged her into a sitting position, then sat down beside her, the blanket still in place. As they nibbled on pemmican and jerky, Jacob occasionally leaned close and whispered short choppy sentences that made no sense. When she'd ask him to repeat them, he would shrug and say, ''It is nothing. Finish your meal,'' then continue to ignore her until the mood struck to whisper in her ear again.

Tired of the game, the next time he leaned in close, she turned on him. ''All right, that's it! What are you doing and why can't I understand a word you're saying?''

''I'm sorry,'' he lied, ''but I have much on my mind. I will try to remember to speak English. Come,'' he said, getting to his feet, pulling her up with him. ''Let's take a walk down by the river.''

Keeping the blanket and his arm firmly across her shoulders, Jacob made a deliberate stroll through the camp, then disappeared into the trees at the edge of the village in full view of any who cared to observe them.

When they reached a suitable spot, under the shade of an oak tree whose branches would shade them from the sun as well as protect them from a threatened storm, Jacob spread his blanket on thick grass and stretched out, urging

Dominique to do the same. Propping himself up on his elbows, he stared out at the muddy waters and considered the course of his own life.

The banks of the Little Missouri, one of several tributaries to the Missouri River, were only forty-six miles from the fort. The Seventh Cavalry, slowed by its sheer numbers, would need another two days to reach this area. By then the Dakota would be several miles to the west—four days and nearly fifty miles for the troops, and yet this day seemed to be hundreds of miles and another lifetime away from Jacob's experience as a soldier in Custer's army.

Today was his wedding day. He'd done the required show of courtship by wrapping Dominique in his blanket and whispering into her ear. There wasn't a soul in his village who wasn't aware of his intentions—if one didn't count the bride. After spending the afternoon by the river, he would simply walk her back through camp, blanket still in place, and take her to his tipi. Once they stepped through the portals of his lodge, they would officially be as one. He would be husband to the woman he loved. And more alone than he'd ever been in his life.

"Jacob," she said, her voice piercing his musings like a sudden bolt of lightning. "How long have you lived with the Sioux?"

He jerked his head toward her, then glanced back out to the swiftly moving current. "Many winters—years. Since I was eleven."

Sensing he was troubled, but not sure why, she tiptoed into another question. "How did they get hold of you? I mean, were you kidnapped, too, or— Look, if you'd rather not talk about it, I'll understand."

Jacob glanced over at Dominique, really looking at her for the first time since she'd stepped out of his tipi. The radiant beauty was still there, but he was able to stand the glare as he noticed the compassion reflected in her dark eyes. He pushed up and sat cross-legged beside her, then began his tale. "I was not kidnapped, crazy one; I was saved."

"Saved?" Dominique wrinkled her nose. "From your own family? I find that hard to believe." She cocked a light auburn eyebrow. "Are you pulling my leg?"

Jacob looked at the long legs she'd curled up beneath her, and grinned. "No, you can see that I'm not. Would you like me to?"

"No, silly! I was trying to ask you if you're lying to me."

"Oh." He shrugged, trying to understand what dishonesty could possibly have to do with another's limbs, then said, "I did not lie. The Dakota saved me from certain death. My family—my mother, father, brother, and two young sisters—were attacked and murdered by a band of Crow Indians as we searched for a home in the Black Hills."

"And they chose to spare you?"

"No, impatient one. They would have taken my scalp along with those of the others had they seen me. A coincidence saved me from that indignity." He laughed at her creased brow and explained. "I was hidden from view, squatting behind a bush, when the attack came. Fear froze me to the spot as I watched the members of my family fall one by one."

"Oh, my God, Jacob. How perfectly awful." Dominique closed her hand over his and squeezed. "If you'd rather not go on—"

"It is all right. I have long since ceased to think about it, or to remember the horror. I've chosen to have my recollections begin with a great warrior on a tall painted horse." He closed his eyes and thought back to that fall day nearly twenty years ago. Smiling at the memories, he said, "That Indian was Chief Gall of the Hunkpapa Dakota. He and a large number of warriors drove the Crow off into the hills, then returned to the site of the ambush to help themselves to whatever might be of use. That was when Gall's sharp eyes found this agonized little boy."

"Agonized? But I thought you said you were spared from the attack."

"From the attack of the Crow, yes, but not from the wrath of the red ants whose home I destroyed when I stepped upon it."

Dominique began to chuckle, then burst into full-blown laughter when she put it all together. Before Jacob had a chance to go on, to explain what had become obvious to her, she said, "Wait, let me guess! That's how you got your Sioux name, Redfoot."

Joining in her laughter, he entwined his fingers with hers and nodded. "Yes, crazy one, that is why I am called Redfoot. My foot was swollen, itchy, on fire with pain, and completely useless for a week after Chief Gall pulled me up on his pony and called me his son."

Dominique's gaze turned thoughtful and pensive. She stared down at the fringe shading her knees, and frowned.

"What is it, *wi witko*?" he asked softly. "What troubles you?"

"I—I don't know how to put this. I don't want to offend you, but there's something I don't understand."

"We've exchanged enough angry words these past two days. You will not hear any more from me this day. What do you wish to know?"

"Well . . . what the chief did—I mean, saving you and all. I thought—that is, Uncle Armstrong and Aunt Libbie have told me a lot about the Sioux and their bloodthirsty ways. Why did Gall save you, Jacob? Why didn't *he* kill you and take your scalp?"

Jacob's blue eyes darkened to match the storm clouds above, but he kept his temper as he had promised. "There are a lot of things your uncle, the general, does not know about my people. He is wrong about many of our ways. The Dakota do not kill for sport, Dominique. There was no need for them to kill me. I represented no threat to their security or their way of life."

She shook her head. "I still don't understand. The general has told me about some perfectly awful things, about the terrible attacks on homesteaders and the mutilation of the bodies and other atrocities I can't even mention. Should

I believe you or him? It sounds almost as if you're talking about two different groups of people.''

"At times we Dakota are forced to be just that. Most often, we are put in that position by people like your uncle.''

Dominique pulled her hand away. "That's not fair. He's working for the government trying to clean up the West. If your people would stop fighting him and do as they're told, none of this bloody business would be necessary.''

Do as they're told. Jacob worked his jaw, trying to keep his temper—and his promise. How would she feel if he informed her of just a sample of the horrors her precious golden-haired uncle had visited on the women and children of the Dakota nation? Would she believe him if he told her the Long Hair had sent his troops in with orders to kill them all—infants as well as adults—and then had done just that? Probably not.

Jacob let out his breath in a long whistle and reclaimed her hand. "Let us not speak of this any further. It is a subject we can never agree on.''

Dominique pursed her lips and frowned. "Oh, all right, but there is something else I have to know about your people, about you and your sense of . . . fair play.''

"Ask your question, but I will not be drawn into an argument.''

Dominique tried to pull her hand away again, but this time he held tight. She looked at him with pleading eyes and said, "I'm worried, Jacob—and a little confused. What happened after you hit me? Barney and Hazel—''

"They both are fine,'' he said with a smile. "After I hit you—and again, I apologize—I left a warning and then rode straight for my village.''

"But why didn't Barney come after us? Why would he just let me disappear like that?'' she cried, suddenly feeling insignificant.

"I said I left a warning. If we feel we are being persecuted by the soldiers or by other hostile tribes of Indians, the Dakota stick a pole in the ground and tie a flag and a few locks of hair at the top. That is our warning, our way of saying, stop—come no farther or we will fight.'' He released her hand and took a length of her hair between his fingers. ''I had no pole, so I broke a large branch from a tree and striped it of its leaves. The flag was torn from your petticoat, and the lock of hair—'' Jacob held up his hand. ''Haven't you noticed?''

''*You* did that? I thought I felt a hole back there, but I was sure I must be losing my mind! Couldn't you have been a little neater about it?''

''Sorry,'' he said with a chuckle. ''But I was in a hurry.''

''I suppose I should be grateful you didn't take it all.'' She felt him stiffen at her words, but she went on. ''So Barney and Hazel, and I guess my whole family, think I was captured by the Sioux. Why haven't they tried to rescue me?''

''They are on the march,'' he said grimly. ''But they will not seek us out only for your benefit. Your uncle does know the dangers of chasing after a small band of renegades. Besides, I believe he thinks you have killed yourself by now.''

Dominique's brows shot up and tears leapt into the corners of her eyes. She turned her head away, swallowing hard, and said, ''And you, Jacob? How is it he allows you back in his army? You can't tell me it's because he doesn't care about me! I know my uncle Armstrong loves me very much. Why, I can't believe he hasn't had you shot for this!''

He put his arm around her shoulder, seeking the appropriate words of comfort. ''I believe if the general could find a legal way, he would have had me shot. As it is, he seems to be hoping the Sioux will do it for him. He misses you very much, Dominique. He allows me to ride with him only because he believes I was attacked by the Indians who were chasing you. That is why I carry these wounds. My good friend did this to me to make certain the soldiers would believe my story.''

Dominique's mouth was in the shape of a perfect circle. She whirled around, staring wide-eyed for a full minute before she finally said, "You did all that on *purpose*? How could you stand it?"

"The safety of my friends and family is worth a few moments of discomfort. I'm sure you could do the same if necessary."

"Oh, I don't think so, Jacob." Dominique examined the deep wound running the length of his arm and shuddered. "No, I don't think so at all."

She turned away from the sight and stared out at the river. She'd learned much in their talk, but instead of feeling enlightened, Dominique was more confused than ever. Why had he saved her when she'd cost him so much? He'd said when he first left her at the tipi that he loved her. Was it true? Could he possibly love her enough to risk his people's freedom? Or did he keep her for another, more sinister end? Was she to be an instrument of barter sometime in the future, or would she perhaps be saved for some larger, more ominous purpose on down the road? Dominique imagined her dead body tied to a pole—the ultimate Sioux warning—and shuddered.

She stole a glance at Jacob and found that he, too, stared out at the churning waters. But Jacob's expression and thoughts were as unreadable as the rapidly darkening skies. She turned her attention back to the Little Missouri and its ragged, twisting banks, and sighed. He hadn't saved her for love at all. If he truly loved her, she thought with a pout, he wouldn't have brought her here where she would surely die. And die she would if he left her in this place much longer.

The first drops of rain, huge and fat like drops of clear pancake batter, began to fall, soaking them in a matter of minutes. Without another word between them, Jacob took her hand and pulled her to her feet. Then they dashed back to the village beneath the shelter of the wedding blanket, trudging along the already muddy path leading to Jacob's tipi, and ducked inside.

Now Dominique's legal husband in the eyes of the Dakota, Jacob took the blanket from her shoulders and issued his first order. "Sit and warm yourself by the fire. I will return before dark." Then he stepped back into the coolness of the blinding rain and headed for the warriors' lodge where he would help preside over a council of war.

Dominique shook her hair, hoping to speed the drying time, but stopped abruptly as a bit of pink caught the corner of her eye. There, lying on the rug near the back wall, lay a crumpled piece of her stationery.

She stared at it for a long moment, trying to understand that message it seemed to be sending. She thought back to her conversations with Jacob, the feeling of closeness, the trauma he must have felt as a young lad torn from his family, and she finally understood.

Jacob hadn't ignored her or her invitation. The youth, Jacob Stoltz, had never learned how to read. Not only had his family, his childhood, been stolen from him, but he'd also been robbed of the precious gift of the English language. Why did he choose to remain part of this savage world?

Chapter Fourteen

FULL OF ANTICIPATION, DOMINIQUE WAITED FOR JACOB'S return over the next few hours. She carefully planned the words she would use to tell him she understood his deficiency and his reluctance to admit it. Her next move would be to temper the shock of that knowledge with what she hoped would be an offer he would gladly accept—to allow her to teach him to read the written word. Once they were back in civilization, of course.

He finally returned to the tipi at twilight. "I bring you food," he said as he passed by the fire and handed a small bowl to her. "Eat and then get your rest. The days to come will be difficult for us all."

When he turned as if to leave, Dominique set the bowl aside. "Jacob, wait! I want to talk to you."

But he kept his back to her, unable to look at his new bride without acknowledging her as such. "I must return to the warriors' lodge now. We still have much to discuss. Sleep well." Then he disappeared into the stormy night.

Dominique pushed out a heavy sigh. Jacob was gone, but he'd left a cloud of gloom in his wake, a feeling of despair she couldn't identity. With a disinterested palate, she ate her meal, then curled up on the rug to await his return.

A few feet away in the biggest lodge, Jacob spoke to the elders, his voice cracking with irritation. "The soldiers seek Sitting Bull and those who would follow him along the Little Missouri. Their intentions are to follow us all the way to the Rosebud Creek where Red Cloud's people wait. These are the weapons we have been issued for the fight." He held up his government-issue Springfield 1873 single-shot carbine and a Colt six-shot revolver. "I have yet to receive instruction on how to fire either of the guns."

The men laughed, slapping their knees. "Do they know of our great assortment of weapons?" asked Chatanna. "Do they guess we can kill them fifty ways before they can even reload?"

Jacob joined in the laughter, even though his heart was not entirely in it. Between the Dakota and the Cheyenne, they figured to have over forty different types of guns, ranging from sixteen-shot repeating Winchester and Henry rifles to pistols and other rifles. To a weapon, they were all obtained as a result of the United States government's generosity to the Indian traders. Now these guns would be turned on the men who had supplied them. Jacob thought of some of the friends he'd made in his short term in the cavalry—Barney in particular—and slowly shook his head. When the time came, would he be able to cut his friends down? Could he ever face Dominique again if he should be forced to bring down the general or one of his brothers?

"My son." Chief Gall's voice was warm with concern and understanding. "I can see your mind is elsewhere this night. Perhaps you think of your bride, alone and waiting in your wedding lodge? Go now. You have supplied us with much information."

And because there was no way he could tell his father why he was in no hurry to return to his tipi and the long lonely night ahead of him, Jacob gave him a counterfeit smile of thanks and rose. "Good night, my father. Tomorrow we march on toward the Rosebud. Maybe when the solders discover our numbers, they will use this wisdom to its fullest advantage and call for a retreat."

"The nincompups will never retreat!" Chatanna exclaimed. "And neither shall the Dakota! We will fight until all the white eyes are nothing but pieces of flesh scattered across the plains!''

This incited the other men to a rousing cheer. Jacob stepped from the lodge, his mind burdened by a glimpse of what the future might hold for them all. He entered his tipi quietly, relieved to see that Dominique had been lulled into a deep sleep by the steady rain tapping lightly against the buffalo-hide walls. He stood staring down at her for a long moment before joining her on the rug. She still wore the white buckskin dress, still possessed an almost ethereal radiance, even in slumber. Would they ever have an opportunity to know each other as husband and wife? he wondered. Would the differences between their people, the deep-seated hatred, tear them apart before they had a chance to explore the love he felt, the love he suspected she kept hidden inside for him? He lay down beside Dominique, keeping several inches between their bodies, and tried not to think of her warmth, her softness, and the fact that, as of tonight, she belonged to him.

When he finally fell asleep, Jacob had short vivid dreams of such intensity that they jackknifed him off his blanket with their violence. Each nightmare was equally vicious and bloody, each with its own theme of murder and mayhem. But most horrifying, the thing that brought sweat to his brow and tremors to his hands, was his body and the clothing he wore. In one dream, he would be streaked in war paint and covered with eagle feathers. In another, he was dressed in a full regulation cavalry uniform. In some of the nightmares, he would be a combination of both. Many of the images were obscure, muddied, but their impact on his mind was crystal clear: Jacob no longer knew who he was.

The following morning when Dominique awoke, Jacob was already gone. She spent the day helping the other women pack up camp in preparation for the march farther west. Not once during that entire period did she ever lay eyes on Jacob or his father, Chief Gall. That night after a meal of greasy, tasteless soup and buffalo jerky, Dominique sat in the tipi, wondering how long she would be alone this time, how long would she remain safe.

Then Jacob stepped through the flap. "I go now," he announced as he gathered his cavalry uniform.

"Go now?" Dominique jumped to her feet. "What do you mean, go now? You just got here, Jacob. Please don't leave me alone again. I'll go crazy if you do."

Jacob smiled as he stepped into his regulation trousers and buttoned them over his breechclout. "You mean you are not crazy already?" He tore off his breastplate and reached for his cavalry shirt, but Dominique stepped between him and the garment.

"I'm not laughing, Jacob! I don't see one damn thing that's funny here. Take me with you. I simply cannot stay here without you another day."

He stared into her defiant brown eyes, careful not to become lost in them, and grinned as he slid his index finger under her chin. "Will you miss me so much, *wi witko*?"

Dominique slapped his hand away and stomped her foot. "I'm serious. I'm not staying here!"

"I'm afraid you have no choice." Jacob's expression sobered and he tugged her into his arms. "Neither do I. I must go now. I have to ride under cover of night and return to the army. You know that; I have explained the reasons to you. Why do you insist on making my life so difficult?"

"*Your* life difficult? Mine hasn't exactly been a stroll through the park since I met you, you know." She lifted her chin and stuck out her bottom lip.

Her expression was the end of his control. Jacob's mouth closed over that bottom lip, parting it from its mate as he searched for the delights he knew lay beyond. He indulged his hands, allowing them to roam over her back and down to her firm round bottom where he clasped, then crushed her to his hips. There, in spite of the promises he'd made to himself, he lingered, even as his need grew huge and hot, even though he knew she would realize how much he wanted her.

Concern for her fears finally coaxed him into releasing her hips, but only long enough for his hands to slide up and cup her face. His mouth only inches from hers, he murmured between nibbling kisses along her cheeks, "My love, my little one, I shall miss you."

Directed by sheer instinct, Dominique's head arched back, exposing her throat and the pulse hammering there. Jacob took her cue, letting his mouth cruise to the spot, teasing the sensitive flesh along the route with his talented lips. She gasped, then moaned, "*Mon Dieu*, Jacob, *mon amour, mon trésor*."

His mouth still caressing her, he moved back up her throat, then nipped the tip of her ear. His breathing erratic, he whispered, "What names do you call me now, *wi witko*?"

"You first," she said lazily, her eyes feeling sleepy, drugged somehow. "Who is *widko*?"

"*Wi witko*." He laughed. "Crazy one. You." He kissed the tip of her nose, then sought her mouth again. Pulling at her bottom lip with his teeth, Jacob nibbled and teased, flicked the upper with the tip of his tongue before ending the agony and plunging deep inside her sweet mouth. He wanted to plunge inside every soft damp part of her, feel her respond to him, want him as much as he wanted her, and forget about white men, red men, and war. But some measure of reason returned.

Jacob released her and stepped back. "I must go now, but first tell me—what names did you call me?"

Dominique stood alone, dazed and off balance. She looked into Jacob's eyes, knew the spell was over and that he really did plan to leave her. Her kisses, as much as he seemed to enjoy them, weren't enough to persuade him to stay. If anything, she'd only managed to delay his departure. How could she tell him she'd called him her love, her treasure? *Why* had she even thought of him in those terms?

Angry, sad, and frightened all at once, Dominique puckered her mouth and began to cry. "I called you an idiot, a stupid, mean dolt, and . . . and," she sobbed, "a d-dirty rotten b-bastard for bringing me here."

"Stop that." He pointed at her cheeks, wet with tears by now, and repeated the order. "I mean it, Dominique. Stop that right now. You know I do not like this."

"I don't c-care what you like, you s-savage! I w-want to go home." She stomped her foot and squeezed her eyes, working to bring as much moisture to her cheeks as possible.

Perplexed, Jacob reached down and picked up his shirt, never taking his eyes off her. "Please, stop that," he said softly, trying a new tack. As he buttoned the shirt, he began to back away. "I must leave, please don't do this anymore."

"D-don't leave—please don't l-leave," she cried, increasing the volume of her tears and raising the pitch of her voice.

Unable to stand it any longer, Jacob ducked outside the tipi and jerked the flap closed. He lowered his voice, speaking in his most authoritative tone: "Stop that at once, woman."

From inside the lodge, the wails increased followed by a resounding, *"No!"*

Jacob glanced around the campsite. Several warriors stood around, their heads cocked, their expressions a mixture of curiosity and disbelief. Jacob closed his ears to his bride's sobs and straightened his shoulders as he strode through the village. His voice gruff, he explained as he passed by his peers, "My woman has burned herself on the fire. She will be quiet in a short time. I have ordered her to do so." Then he continued on toward the horses, hoping to God he was right.

Inside the tipi, Dominique abruptly stopped crying and listened at the wall. Jacob was gone. "Bloody hell!" she muttered, looking around for something to break. She spotted Jacob's lance resting against the wall and stomped over to it.

Grabbing both ends of the wooden handle, she slammed

it downward and lifted her right leg. The lance split in half. Dominique dropped to the ground, howling in pain.

"Damn, damn, double bloody hell and damnation," she cried, a flood of authentic tears pouring down her cheeks as she cradled her injured leg.

The following morning when Dominique awoke, she found a bright blue welt running across the width of her leg just above the knee. When she stood up, her pulse pounded against the engorged area. She bit her lip and moaned, "Damn your bloody eyes, Jacob Stoltz."

Hopping on one foot, she did a pirouette, but as she got halfway though the second circle, she stopped and her mouth dropped open. Spotted Feather stood at the entrance of the tipi, her lip curled with malice.

"You are a poor excuse for a dancer, white devil. Do not waste your feeble energy on such nonsense. There is much work to do in our camp."

Her eyes like cold flat stones, Dominique quietly said, "Get out and leave me alone."

Spotted Feather advanced a step, her fists clenched, but stopped when she realized the futility of such a move. This pale-faced woman was now the wife of Redfoot, *her* Redfoot. And while she could hardly wait to deal with this intruder, the deed would have to be done in a manner that would not cast suspicion her way. Attacking the white filth, killing her in broad daylight, in her own tipi, would be a very foolish act.

Spotted Feather grinned, knowing she would have her chance, hoping that chance would come along very, very soon. Not bothering to cover her hatred, she spat, "Even though Redfoot has stupidly chosen you for his woman, you still must do your share of the work around camp. Follow me. I will show you what you must do."

And because she knew ignoring the Indian's orders would only add to her considerable pile of troubles, Dominique set her jaw and trailed along behind the nasty-tempered squaw.

When they reached the tipi with many poles leaning against it and several pouches scattered along the ground, Spotted Feather stopped. She turned her head and shot a wad of spittle near one of the pouches. Pointing to the spot of damp earth, she said, "Stand there, dog face."

Hiding her disgust, Dominique lowered her head and obeyed. As she stood, the Indian balanced a long pole across her shoulders, then hung a pouch on either end. Again a beast of burden, feeling like an ox harnessed for a day's plowing, she meekly followed Spotted Feather as she wove her way through the lodges and out of the camp.

She limped along, sidestepping sagebrush and prickly pear cactus as the Indian led her down into a heavily wooded ravine, then on to the banks of the Little Missouri River.

Motioning for Dominique to approach the water's edge, Spotted Feather spouted her orders: "Take the pouches from your shoulders. Fill one with water and hang it from the branch of that tree. Fill the other; then put it on one end of your pole. After you have done that, hold it with one hand and take the other from the tree and put it on the pole. When you come back to camp, I will show you where to dump the water. Then you will come back and fill them again. Do you understand, stupid white dog?"

Through clenched teeth, Dominique said, "Yes, I think I can manage that," *stupid red bitch*.

Spotted Feather sneered and said, "We shall see. Fill the pouches. I will watch to see that you *manage*."

Dominique grabbed a pouch and dropped to her knees. Leaning forward tentatively, she balanced herself on a small boulder and reached into the rapidly flowing current.

"Put the pouch into the water, stupid dog!" Spotted Feather gave her a shove. "You will take all day like that!"

Dominique cried out and pushed away from the current. "Don't do that!" she gasped.

"What is wrong?" The Indian woman laughed. "Are you afraid of a little water?"

Dominique averted her gaze, returning it to the river, then stared down at the grass-covered banks.

"You *are* afraid," Spotted Feather said. "So white women do not swim, is that it? Are you afraid of getting your precious white skin wet, dog?" Again she laughed, but stopped abruptly as a solution to her problem bloomed in her mind. The white she-dog could *not* swim! Nature would be her ally and help her to kill this woman who had blinded Redfoot with her golden hair.

Through another burst of laughter, Spotted Feather said, "Fill the pouches and bring them back to me quickly. Do not make me wait too long." Then she whirled, laughing into the wind, and hurried back to the village.

More hesitant and unsure than before, Dominique inched back to the water's edge. As she lowered the pouch, she stared into the muddy water and trembled at the memory of another muddy river—wider, faster, deadlier. She turned away and filled the pouches as quickly as she could, then limped on back to camp. As she promised, Spotted Feather was waiting by a large cooking pouch made from the lining of a buffalo stomach.

"Dump them in here," she ordered loud enough for the other women to hear. When Dominique finished, the squaw gave another order as loud as the first. "Now go back to the river and fill them again. When you return, I will show you where to dump them."

Still the obedienct prisoner, Dominique returned the pouches to the pole and stumbled off toward the river again.

Waiting until the white woman was out of sight, Spotted Feather glanced around the village. Everyone was busy with chores. None looked in her direction. This time holding in her laughter, she dashed behind a tipi, then quietly made her way through the trees on a path that ran parallel to Dominique's.

Silent and anxious, the Indian crouched a few feet from her quarry, waiting for the perfect moment. When Dominique finally crawled to the edge of the bank and leaned over, Spotted Feather leapt from her hiding spot and sprinted toward her victim.

Dominique heard the footsteps at the same time she felt a tremendous blow between her shoulderblades. She flew up and over the bank so fast that her scream was still lodged in her throat when she hit the water.

Chapter Fifteen

THE TURBULENT WATERS OF THE LITTLE MISSOURI RAGED onward, cutting a zigzag gouge in the Dakota countryside as it raced to merge with the Missouri. Bobbing along in the fast-moving current, a cloud of golden-red hair stood out like the first crocus of spring.

Frantic and wild-eyed, Dominique kicked against the water. She flapped her arms up and down in a vain attempt to save herself, but the river kept pulling her under. Her lungs screaming for oxygen, she finally opened her mouth and gulped for air, but the banquet she brought her starving lungs was nothing more than a cupful of muddy water.

Beyond panic, she opened her mouth and blew, hoping to push the liquid from her system. It was no use. She was dying. Tiny spots, flickering on and off like a thousand fireflies, appeared behind her eyelids. Her arms and legs grew heavy despite the buoyancy of the water. She was becoming numb, unable to feel the sharp sting of rocks and twigs scraping against her thrashing limbs. Then the current slammed her against a boulder protruding from the river's edge.

The impact caught her just below her breastbone, forcing the water from her lungs, sending a veritable fountain spewing out through her nose and mouth. Stunned, still unable to draw the breath she so badly needed, Dominique clung to the boulder, even as the river tried valiantly to snatch her away again. When she was finally able, she took in air, a teaspoon at a time, until she could breathe in large gulps.

Once her appetite for oxygen was sated, Dominique grabbed at anything she could find—twigs, clumps of grass, half-buried rocks—and used them as tools to help her crawl up onto the bank and out of the water. She lay panting in mud and grass still damp from an earlier downpour. Clinging to the last thread of sanity, Dominique tried to get her bearings, to understand what had happened to her, to determine if she was still in danger. Then she heard it.

The snapping of twigs and branches, the ominous sound of something much bigger than she was, crashing through the trees. Still exhausted, her energy depleted, she found just enough strength to turn her head toward the noise. What she saw transformed her heart to stone, her mind to clay. Dominique rolled her eyes to the heavens and passed out.

Twenty miles to the east, the Seventh Cavalry examined the remains of the Hunkpapa camp.

"Good work, Stoltz." Custer leaned down and tore a rawhide thong from the thistles on a shrub. "They're getting a little sloppy."

"And their numbers are growing," Jacob added, supplying information that was not part of the Dakota plan. "Did you have a chance to look at their grazing circle? This camp supports at least five hundred horses now."

"Well, then," Custer replied, slapping the leather holsters containing his pair of snub-nosed English revolvers. "I guess that's just five hundred more Indian ponies we'll have to shoot."

"And five hundred more Sioux?" Jacob said, barely able to keep the sneer from his lips.

"I doubt that, Private." Custer ran his hand across his ragged auburn beard as he studied the evidence. Then he turned to the group of scouts, amending his orders. "I think it's about time for us to gather up a few of the guides and maybe four companies of men for a little scouting party up river. I'm going to put to rest once and for all these rumors about large bands of hostiles joining together. I have a feeling we're chasing more shadows than Indians.'' He turned back to Jacob with his final orders. ''Private, tell Captain Ruffing I want two more scouts plus you. We'll ride in the morning at five. Go now—be quick.''

Jacob saluted, then returned to his mount. He kicked Hammerhead in the flank before he was fully seated in the saddle, then galloped off to the main body of troops. As he rode, he thought of the new danger to his people, of the excellent tracking and trailbreaking instincts the Long Hair possessed. Custer and a small group of men could easily cover fifty miles in one day. The Dakota camp was no more than twenty miles ahead. How could he make certain the scouting party didn't stumble over his people? Over Dominique?

He thought of her, safe and warm in his lodge, and ached to hold her in his arms, to call her his wife. He'd been so sure when he married her that he'd found the perfect way to ensure her safety. Had he instead plunged her into danger again?

To the west, Dominique came to with a start. She was lying face down in the dirt and mud. Her legs felt as if she'd rolled through a cactus patch. Her arms ached and burned; one of them seemed to be covered with something damp and sticky. She opened her eyes, but saw nothing. Thinking back over the day, Dominique guessed that she'd fallen in the river at midmorning, not more than an hour or two ago. Why was it so dark? What was that dank, feral odor? A low growl, coupled with the swishing of leaves and shrubs, refreshed her memory. The last thing she remembered before passing out on the muddy bank was the sight of a huge grizzly lumbering in her direction. If what she had heard above her was that same bear, he was about to bury her alive.

Instinct, and a strong urge to live, clamped her teeth together, cutting off an impulsive scream. Her system shut down, limiting her breathing to a few shallow puffs between long periods of total inertia. Dominique's ears and frantically pounding heart were her only fully functional organs.

When at last the swishing sounds grew fainter and the crashing of branches and tree limbs signaled the bear's retreat into the wooded ravine, she finally allowed herself to take a deep breath of air. Exercising extreme caution, she opened her eyes to survey her surroundings. Dominique turned her head and looked up. Daylight sparkled in filigree patterns through the dirt and leaves covering her.

In a sudden panic, she pushed up on her hands and knees and arose from her shallow grave. Knees knocking, she looked around. She was several yards away from the river. How far had the beast dragged her through the forest after she had lost consciousness? How soon would he return? All was quiet, save for her thundering heartbeat. Terrified the silence would suddenly be broken by the grizzly's return, she quickly made a decision. With no time even to examine her body for injuries, Dominique forced herself to take cautious steps in the opposite direction from which she'd last heard the bear.

She stayed on course, with panic supplying the necessary adrenaline, for over an hour. Then the rain began. Light sprinkles fell at first, dropping just enough moisture to streak the dirt on her face into a kind of hideous war paint and soak her drying buckskin dress again. Then the skies opened up and she was in the middle of a full-fledged Plains thunderstorm.

Dominique collapsed against the base of a gnarled oak tree and contributed to the drenching of the earth. Her tears fell every bit as hard and relentlessly as the raindrops, and she gave in to her misery. How could God let these things happen to her? Why hadn't he just let her drown in the Missouri the day she first set foot in this savage land? She cried for her papa and her dead mother, and grieved for the loss of her perfect life. She lamented the ruination of her pampered future and the children she would never bear, and the tears fell even harder. What would become of her now? Who would save her?

Then, as quickly as it had begun, the storm passed and Dominique slowly pulled herself together. She looked around, trying to get her bearings, then plotted her next move. She could sit right on this spot and wait for the bear to become hungry again and track his runaway supper.

She could return to the riverbank and toss herself in, completing God's apparent plan for her.

Or she could save herself.

She could pull herself up on her own two feet and go in search of the closest thing she would find by way of protection in this harsh land—the Hunkpapa camp.

Knowing this was her only real option, Dominique struggled to her feet and made a quick survey of her battered body. Rivulets of water ran off the hem of her dress and down her scratched and scraped legs, but she was able to stand and walk with just the slightest pain. She tried to raise her right arm, and winced as the muscles running up along her shoulders balked. She slid her hand across the back of her neck and found it tender and swollen. Where had she received that injury? Further investigation revealed several deep clefts, but none felt as if her skin had been pierced. Had the bear clamped her in its mouth and dragged her by the neck? She shuddered at the thought, at how close it had probably come to snapping her fragile bones.

A stickiness in her bent elbow diverted her attention, and she finally looked down at her arm. Angry grooves of torn flesh still weeping bloody teardrops greeted her vision. The bear had clawed her. Repulsed, Dominique shuddered again, then looked away from the wound. She would have to resume her journey now or die. The scent of her blood, her fear, would soon bring the scavengers— and probably the grizzly as well. It was time to go. Time to think about her life and the strange turns it had taken of late, time to wonder what part she would allow others to play in her suddenly uncertain future, however short it might be.

Using the river as her guide, Dominique trudged through the hills and valleys and the impossibly crooked trails running parallel to the Little Missouri. As she walked, the unseasonably warm sun beat down against her damp hair and buckskins, giving her an eerie ghostlike appearance as clouds of steam rose up from her body. By the time she found her way back to the camp, Dominique was not only dry—she was also in control of her own destiny, and she had made an unshakable decision about the course of her life.

Pausing at the outer perimeter of the camp, she caught her breath and searched through the village for the one face that had given her the strength to go on. When she found it, she straightened her shoulders and held her head high. Then Dominique Custer DuBois marched through the center of camp and headed for the group of squaws standing around the cooking fire.

As a rapidly approaching figure got within range of her vision, Spotted Feather looked up and gasped. "Many Quills! I thought— We were certain you . . . you had fallen into the river! I thought you had drowned!"

"I'm sure you did, you lying red bitch!"

Then Dominique drew back her fist and drove it into the Indian woman's chin.

The other women backed away, buzzing among themselves, but none offered to help their fallen friend, and none thought of attacking the crazy white woman.

Taking advantage of Spotted Feather's confusion and her loss of equilibrium after the stunning blow, Dominique leapt onto the squaw's chest and straddled her body. She grabbed her wrists and pinned them to the ground, then drove her knee into the woman's throat. Keeping enough pressure on the spot to cause Spotted Feather to choke for air, but not enough to kill her, Dominique held her firm.

"Listen to me, you red bitch, and listen good! Your answers will determine whether you live or die, understand?"

Gagging as she tried to make a reply, Spotted Feather managed to nod.

"Good," Dominique spat. "I'm here to tell you I've had it with you and your miserable back-stabbing friends!" She shot a vicious glance at the others, knowing if they didn't understand her words, they could certainly understand her mood. Then her scathing glare dropped back down to Spotted Feather. Increasing the pressure of her knee, she said, "Do you have any idea how easily I could kill you right now? Do you know I'm within one inch of snapping your scrawny neck, you bloody red—what is it you like to call me—*dog face*?"

With considerable difficulty, Spotted Feather again managed to nod.

Unmindful of the crowd of warriors as well as squaws who had gathered around, Dominique went on. "Then if you value your life, you'll listen up and listen up good. I'm not interested in killing anyone, not even a piece of garbage like you, but I guarantee if you ever look, touch, or talk to me again, you had better be prepared to do a better job than you did on me at the river. *Understand?*"

Dominique stared down at the squaw, waiting for an answer, then noticed the bulging eyes and protruding tongue. She eased her knee back and shook the woman's wrists. *"Understand that I'll kill you if you ever come near me again?"*

Through a hoarse gurgle, Spotted Feather said, "Y-yes."

"You'd be wise not to forget it." Dominique released her and got up off her body, shooting an afterthought at the squaw as if it were a spear: *"Bitch!"*

Again straightening her shoulders, Dominique lifted her chin and began to stomp through the camp. "I've had it with all of you!" she shouted at no one in particular. "I'm not taking any more orders or doing any more of your disgusting jobs—*you hear*?'' As she passed by a crudely constructed drying rack with strips of buffalo meat draped across it, she lashed out with her bloodied arm and sent it flying into the mud, jerky and all.

Continuing her tirade as she approached Jacob's tipi, she raised her voice a notch. ''And if any of you don't like it, that's just too damn bad! I invite anyone who disagrees with me to come to Redfoot's tipi! I'll be more than happy to tangle with any one of you yellow-bellied cowards!'' She turned and punctuated the announcement by kicking a parfleche across the campsite. As if blasted from a shotgun, buffalo chips scattered in all directions. With a triumphant nod, Dominique whirled around and stepped through the opening of Jacob's tipi.

Once inside, she felt her bravado waver. Legs wobbly, her breath coming in short gasps, Dominique sank down onto the buffalo rug. She sat there trembling, and prepared to meet her end. Surely when the others, Spotted Feather in particular, got over the shock of what she'd done, they would come for her. They would string her up, perhaps stake her to the ground, and practice unspeakable tortures on her. In spite of the grim thoughts, Dominique smiled. She was ready for them now. She hadn't been before. They couldn't hurt her anymore.

And then a tall figure appeared at the entrance of the tipi. In a voice that sounded very much like that of Chief Gall he said, ''Please come outside, crazy one. I wish to speak to you.''

The end was near. Dominique slowly got to her feet. After stopping a moment to smooth her tousled hair, she took a deep breath and adopted a solder's stance. Then, her manner reflecting nothing but pride, she stepped through the flap.

''What is it?'' she said crisply.

Wrapped in his summer blanket, a necklace of bear claws protruding through the opening, Gall stared at the white woman. The setting sun seemed to funnel up from her glorious halo of hair, lighting the afternoon skies with streaks of red and gold. Smiling his appreciation, he finally said, "You have had some trouble today."

Through a short chuckle, she said, "If you could call being attacked by a totally insane squaw and an enraged grizzly, trouble, then yes, I guess I had some trouble today."

Gall's thick brows drew together at her words; then he scanned her body. Seeing the deep grooves on her arm, he let his breath out in a whoòsh. "You have been set upon by a great bear?"

She shrugged. "Looks that way, doesn't it? I don't know what really happened. I saw a bear coming, and I fainted. When I woke up, he was burying me. Then he left."

"You must have great medicine to have survived such an attack," he said, his awe complete.

Again she shrugged. "Maybe he didn't like the way I tasted." Cocking her head from side to side to ease the ache in her neck, she pressed on. "Surely you didn't stop by to inquire about my health. What do you want?"

"I come about your troubles with Spotted Feather. She has admitted her attack on you at the river."

Dominique's breath whistled out through her teeth. Here it comes, she thought, staring down at the damp earth.

Accepting her silence, Gall went on, trying to explain. "She had hoped Redfoot would bring his marriage blanket to her. When my son chose you for his wife instead, even I wondered about the wisdom of his choice."

"His *wife*?"

Unaware of the reason for her confusion, he nodded solemnly. "Yes, daughter. On the night he wrapped you in his marriage blanket and took you to his tipi, I prayed to the gods that all would be well in your union. I see now the wise choice my son has made. You are a very strong, brave wife for a warrior such as he. You and my son will create many fearless children."

Her head spinning, Dominique couldn't speak, could barely think. She scanned her memory, trying to remember something, anything, that would have given her a clue about a marriage between them, but she was blank. Jacob had said only that he wanted to protect her, that he would make certain the others knew she was his woman. If what Gall said was true, he'd certainly done that.

Shaking her head, she said, "I—I don't know what you want of me, what I'm supposed—"

"I come to make things right for the wife of my son. That is all."

She cocked her head. "Sir?"

"I come to inform you that Spotted Feather has been severely punished. Her jealousy has nearly cost the life of my son's wife. We are at war now. We have no time for jealous women in our camp. I have banished her from our village." He pointed to a spot near a stand of trees.

Turning slowly, for suddenly every joint and muscle in her body seemed to cry out in pain, Dominique searched the perimeter of the camp. Finally she spotted the lonely figure of a woman sitting hunched in a ball.

She looked back at Gall. "How long do you plan to make her stay out there?"

"She is banished. She may not return to our camp, ever."

Dominique wheeled around for another glimpse of the figure, then back to Gall. "B-but the soldiers are coming! She'll die alone out there!"

"Spotted Feather has her knife. She will be able to choose when and how she dies."

"No! You can't do that, it's—"

"I am Gall, chief of the Hunkpapa. I do what I must."

Dominique slammed her hand onto her hips and began tapping her toe, in spite of several sharp jabs of pain. "And I," she began to lie boldly, "am the crazy white woman who wrestled a grizzly bear and won. Think about that! I had a monster by the throat, screaming the worst imaginable threats in his face, and he ran away!"

Dominique waved her arms in spite of the pain, hoping to convince Gall, "I scared the hell out of that bear, don't you get it? I *do* have powerful medicine; I just didn't want you to know about it. You shouldn't argue with a powerful person like me. It's bad medicine! Let me take care of Spotted Feather. I'm the one she hurt—I should be the one to carry out her punishment. I demand the right to be in charge of her.'' She set her jaw and narrowed her eyes, daring him to disagree.

Gall worked at his sternest expression, but his eyebrows wavered between confusion and amusement. Women, white women in particular, never spoke to him in such a manner, never dared even to think the thoughts this one had just voiced. He ought to banish her along with Spotted Feather. It was his duty to teach her a very important lesson: to hold her busy, busy tongue. But as he stared at her, at the determination in her big brown eyes, he knew he would never be able to do it. How did Redfoot manage with this one?

Gall broke into a grin and slowly shook his head. ''I fear I am growing old when I cannot deal firmly with a silly white woman. I fear also that I did not wish my son nearly enough luck for his future with you. He has chosen your name well, crazy one.''

Dominique let his last remark slide, knowing she would have to figure out what to do about this ''marriage'' before Jacob returned. Instead, she addressed the business at hand. ''Then you agree? Spotted Feather is mine to punish?''

''Against all the Dakota stand for, yes. I give her to you to do with as you please. But understand this—I will not hear any of your complaints regarding her again.''

''It's a deal.'' Dominique stuck out her hand, but the big Indian merely cocked his eyebrow. She withdrew the offer, then leaned over and kissed his cheek instead. ''May I go talk to her now and bring her back to camp?''

The naturally reddish hue of Gall's skin deepened to a rosy burgundy as he gruffly said, ''Yes. Begone now, and do not speak to me of this again.''

''Thanks, Chief,'' she said as she whirled around, feeling curiously lighthearted and happy.

Dominique hurried to the edge of camp, but as she approached the trees, she slowed her pace and quietly approached the dejected woman. Spotted Feather's legs were drawn up close to her chest, and her face was pressed between her knees.

Slowly sinking to the earth beside her, Dominique quietly said, "I think the clouds have finally rained themselves out, don't you?"

The Indian turned her head slightly. One large black eye stared at her visitor, widening with surprise, then she buried her face again.

"Ahhh." Dominique breathed a sigh. "Would you look at that sunset filtering through the storm clouds? Funny," she went on, talking as if she spoke to a rapt audience. "When I lived in Monroe, I hardly ever noticed the sunsets. Watching the sun come up over the water is the thing to do where I come from. Now, it seems the farther west I get, the more dramatic and beautiful sunsets seem to be. I wonder what it must be like to watch the setting sun from the California coast. Why, it must be absolutely spectacular to see a fireball of sunlight dipping below the ocean waves, crashing and—"

"What do you want?" Spotted Feather cut in, her voice a dull, flat monotone.

Acknowledged at last, Dominique came right out with it. "Do you love Jacob? Is that why you tried to kill me?"

Her dark eyes suspicious and mistrustful, the Indian raised her head and stared at her enemy. Then, with a tiny shrug, she shot a wad of spittle near her foot and stared back down at the ground.

Dominique bristled. "You mean to tell me you shoved me in that river and damn near drowned me on the chance, the meager *chance*, that you might be in love with Jacob?"

Spotted Feather raised her head again, but kept her suddenly fearful gaze on the cottonwood trees. "No, no. I did it because—because I do love him."

"Well, I love him, too," Dominique said softly, surprising herself with the admission.

Anger and hurt flared in the Indian's black eyes. She raised her proud chin and said, "How you feel does not matter to me!"

Dominique shrugged. "I can understand that—I'm not too crazy about you either. But what about Jacob? Doesn't the way he feels count for anything?"

Spotted Feather shot her a sideways glance, then bit her lip. "I—I do not know how he feels," she finally said in a low whisper. "We have never spoken of such things."

Her voice as low, but misted with tenderness, Dominique admitted, "I know how he feels. Jacob has told me he loves me."

The Indian's head whipped around, and tears sprang into her midnight eyes. She stared at Dominique for a long moment, chewing on the inside of her mouth, then looked away. "Redfoot is Dakota," she choked out. "He needs a Dakota wife. You cannot make him happy the way I could."

"Jacob is also a white man. I admit that I don't know much about making any man happy, but maybe neither of us can meet all of the needs of a man like Jacob."

More dejected than ever, Spotted Feather stared down at her thumbs. Then her eyes brightened as a new solution occurred to her. "Perhaps the only way for him to be happy is to take two brides! One red, one white."

"Ah—no, dear. I don't think so." Dominique reached out to the Indian and rested her hand on her knee. "As long as there is still some craziness left in me, and since I seem to be married to Jacob, I'm the only wife he's going to have. I wouldn't wager your moccasins on things being any other way."

Spotted Feather frowned, then looked away and sighed. "It does not matter anyway. I am banished and cannot live with my people any longer."

Dominique swallowed hard, knowing the next thing she said might open the doors to more danger for herself, knowing also that if she didn't do so, she could never live with the guilt of Spotted Feather's death. "Your banishment is one of the reasons I wanted to talk to you. I have spoken to Chief Gall, and he has given me permission to bring you back into the camp.''

Spotted Feather jerked her knee from under Dominique's hand, and moved away. "You—you lie, white dog! Father will never let me return to our people. Why do you *lie* so?''

"Listen, lady," Dominique said, the embers of her own temper sparking, "I'd appreciate it if you'd stop calling me all those dog names—in fact, I must insist that you stop. The chief said . . . well, roughly, he said that I could do with you as I pleased. Your punishment is up to me.''

"This is *true*?" the surprised woman said through a rush of breath. At Dominique's affirmative nod, the squaw's voice took on a note of disbelief. "And my punishment? What is my punishment to be?''

"I—I really haven't thought about that." She leveled a thoughtful gaze on the Indian and said, "I think I'll just sentence you to being nice to me for as long as I'm part of this camp. No more names, no more laughing and saying nasty things about me, and most definitely, no more making me tan hides and fetch water. Sound fair?''

Spotted Feather's mouth dropped open and again her incredulous eyes became moist with tears. She turned away from the white woman, at a loss for words, unwilling to let Dominique see the weakness controlling her.

Dominique reached over and squeezed her trembling hand. "I'll take that as a yes." When the Indian's trembling increased, and the beads decorating her buckskins began to clatter, Dominique inched closer and put her arm around the other woman's shoulders. "You must be cold. Come on, let's go back to camp and stand near the fire with the others." When she tried to coax Spotted Feather to her feet, the Indian balked.

"No, wait," she said in a voice strangled with unshed tears. "Please—tell me why. Why do you do this for me? I am your enemy.''

"Enemy? I see no enemy here. We are two women who

love the same man, and I think we both want him to be happy. How can we possibly be enemies?"

"I—I do not know," Spotted Feather said with a nervous chuckle.

"Nether do I. Come on, now," she said, pushing up to her feet, then pulling the Indian up along with her. "Let's go eat. I'm starved!"

When they reached the campfire, Dominique stood back and allowed Spotted Feather to inform her friends of her restored status and of the curious circumstances that had led her back to them. After much laughing and hugging, the women turned to Dominique and encouraged her to sit in a place of honor. Then Spotted Feather went to the cooking pouch and filled a bowl with the evening's meal.

"You shall have your food before the others," she said as she handed the bowl to her newfound ally. "Please fill your belly."

Wishing she could have watched the other women eat first to make certain none died from the new offering, Dominique graciously accepted. She peered into the bowl, noticing the greasy slick covering the broth, then popped a chunk of meat into her mouth. Although it was terribly fatty, a deliciously familiar flavor tantalized her taste buds. "Ummmm, it's been ages since I've had pork. Where on earth did you find a pig? Do they run wild out here?"

"A pig? We have no pigs. You eat beaver tail."

"Beaver tail?" Dominique peered into the bowl and muttered, "Beaver tail, huh? Pass the béarnaise sauce, if you please." Still staring down at her dinner, she went on. "Maybe you'd better pass the wine sauce, too. Oh, hell, if you can find some, I'd appreciate it if you'd just pass the wine."

The following morning Spotted Feather appeared at the entrance of Jacob's tipi. "Have you risen, Redfoot's woman? I bring some food."

Dominique crawled to the flap and pulled it aside. Cracking a bleary eye, she peered up at the Indian. "Oh, ah, thanks, but if you don't mind, I thought I'd sleep in today. I had a tough time of it yesterday. I could use the rest.''

Although she still had to force a smile for the white women, the Indian managed a pleasant expression and a halfhearted apology. "Oh, I—I am sorry."

Spotted Feather stood on one foot, then the other, looking as if she couldn't quite decide what to do. Dominique pushed out a sigh, wondering exactly what she had created, then pulled into a crouch, and stepped outside. Yawning as she stretched, she said, "What a beautiful day! I suppose now's as good a time as any to get up." She peered into the bowl the Indian offered, wondering if the meal had been ladled from the community pot, or if the squaw had prepared something special just for her.

Dominique wrinkled her nose. "What do we have for breakfast this morning—badger toenails?"

The Indian grimaced. "We do not eat badger. They are evil. I have brought you soup."

Her stomach still slick with a lining of grease from last evening's meal, Dominique didn't have to lie when she said, "Well, whatever it is, thanks, but I'm not hungry this morning. I think—"

Her words were cut short by the crack of rifle fire.

To a person, every man, woman, and child in the Hunkpapa village froze.

When three more shots were fired, the village exploded in pandemonium.

Chapter Sixteen

WATCHING WITH DISBELIEVING EYES, JACOB SAW CUSTER and his brother Tom fire another shot above the head of their younger sibling, Boston. Hooting and hollering, the Custer boys fired off another round, then collapsed in hysterics behind the hill with the other men in their group.

Jacob inched forward and peered through the tall grass. Boston Custer was riding his horse full out across the plains. He was obviously terrified, unable to find the rest of the scouting party, and most probably sure the entire Sioux nation was right on his heels.

Jacob looked back at the general and said, ''Your brother runs like the wind. Perhaps someone should stop him and tell him about the joke you've played.''

''Don't worry about it, Private. Teasing Bos is our favorite amusement.'' But he looked over to his other brother and said, ''Better ride on out and get him before one of those imaginary Indians does.''

''Now?'' Tom complained. ''I was kinda looking forward to forming a search party when he couldn't find his way back.''

''Now,'' Custer reiterated. ''We've a lot more country to explore today.'' He glanced at Jacob again, and said, ''Don't look so worried, Private. Sometimes we all need a little lesson. Believe me, Boston will think twice before turning his back on us in terrain like this again. Besides, he's used to our little jokes. Why don't you relax? You'll need your strength later on. The ride we're facing from here on out will put us in land never stepped upon by white men. It could prove to be quite rough." Then he spun on his heel and strode down the hill among the rest of his men.

Jacob spit at the ground, then looked back through the grass at the profusion of small buttes—little mountains among which a man could easily be lost for the rest of his life. For that reason, the Hunkpapa had chosen this area for their temporary home. The scouting party was very close to that site. Had the Custer brothers' foolishness actually alerted the Dakota to their presence, or would this small group of soldiers stumble over them by surprise? In Jacob's lowly position among the whites, he could only hope his people had heard the shots and taken the necessary precautions.

Jacob cursed the general and the orders that kept him close by his side. It was increasingly difficult to break away, to report to Gall and inform him of the soldiers' plans. Custer liked to join the scouting expeditions himself, and he led his men with an arrogance suggesting there wasn't another who could do the job as well.

Again Jacob spit into the grass. He would have to get away soon. News had reached him of yet another column of soldiers coming in from the north. If what Jacob heard was correct, these troops would soon come across the main Dakota and Cheyenne camps hidden in the Tongue River valley.

Jacob took a deep breath and decided to follow his commander's orders. He lay back against the sweet spring grass and closed his eyes. Then he thought of Dominique and the way she'd looked the last time he saw her. Her beautiful brown eyes were flowing with tears as she cried and begged him to take her away with him. She was utterly helpless, vulnerable, and terrified. All that and more. His heart lurched, then left a terrible ache in his chest when he thought of the misery and terror she must be enduring.

All because of him. Someday, he vowed, if there was any way possible, he would make it all up to her.

For now, Jacob thought with a heavy sigh, he could only pray that she would somehow be able to endure her ordeal.

Several hours later, and many miles farther to the west, Jacob's woman hummed as the final rawhide thongs secured her lodge for the night.

"Put it over there," Dominique said, pointing to a spot near Jacob's tipi.

The young girl dropped a fresh supply of buffalo chips into the parfleche, then turned expectantly and waited for her next order.

"Thanks, Yellow Flower. Now would you please bring Spotted Feather to me?"

Bowing, practically kissing the white woman's feet, the youngster scrambled off on her new errand. Dominique stood back and surveyed the new camping spot. After the shots were fired in the morning, the village had been dismantled immediately. Before Dominique could even ask where they were going or who had been shooting at them, Spotted Feather appeared with Peaches and urged her to mount up. She was not asked to carry anything or even to pack up her meager belongings.

Now that they were settling in for the night, the first tipis erected had been the warriors' lodge followed by the one she shared with Jacob. Dominique had nothing to do now but wait for the remaining tipis to be raised and supper to be cooked. She took a deep breath and exhaled, thinking how different her life had become in just one day. Then she saw Spotted Feather sprinting toward her.

Out of breath, the Indian gasped, "Yes? What is it you wish now, crazy one— Oh! I am sorry. I did not—"

"That's all right. Crazy one is a name I'm used to, thanks to Jacob. I didn't mean to interrupt your chores, but I wonder if you could help me out. I'm bored."

"Bored?" Spotted Feather cocked her head. "Sick?"

"Only in the head." She laughed. "I just want something to do that won't scare the hell out of me or turn me into an old woman. What can I do to help out?"

"*Work?* But you should rest. The chief tells us you are recovering from the attack of a great bear. He has ordered that you rest and become well."

"I am well," Dominique insisted. "The wound doesn't bother me near as much as the boredom does. Now, please, there must be something I can do beside tan hides. I can't stand sitting around doing nothing."

Spotted Feather wrinkled her brow, but glanced around the village. Then she looked back at Jacob's tipi, to the very lodge she'd hoped to decorate herself one day, and sighed. "If you like to paint, you might as well work on Red—your husband's lodge."

Dominique glanced at Jacob's tipi, then around at the others. Of those that were completely erected, most were covered with hunting and war scenes, painted either as stick figures or in crude, childlike terms. Jacob's tipi was unadorned. "What do the pictures mean?" she asked, suddenly intrigued.

"Some tell of a warrior's coups, others, of his great hunts or years of prosperity. All reflect the warrior's life."

Dominique pressed her fingertip to her mouth and swayed as she considered the possibilities. "Are these paintings a means of identification?"

"I do not know what is identification."

"The paintings—do they tell us the name of the warrior who lives in the tipi?"

Spotted Feather shrugged. "I suppose it is so."

Dominique's grin was huge as she studied the large buffalo-skin canvas before her. Although she was none too proud of her scholastic records during her years at boarding school, she'd always enjoyed—and excelled in—art classes. Maybe there was a way to use this talent to please her man after all.

She turned back to Spotted Feather, the natural light in her eyes bright with excitement. "Tell me about the paints and the brushes. Where do I get them?"

Grumbling to herself, Spotted Feather disappeared for a moment, then returned with the equipment. "This brush is made from a piece of buffalo shoulderblade," she explained as she passed the tool to Dominique. "For smaller things, you can make many little brushes from this porcupine tail."

Squatting down, the Indian opened the large parfleche she carried and took several small pots from it. "These are your paints. They are made from the juice of berries and baked earth of many colors. If you wish to have more colors than these, you can mix them together." She pointed to a pot, explaining, "If you mix this one with the one—"

"I think I understand," Dominique cut in, eager to begin. "Thanks for your help."

With a barely contained sneer, Spotted Feather returned to her chores.

Dominique stood back and surveyed her giant canvas. After visualizing, then discarding many subjects, she finally settled on the perfect one. Then she painted until dark.

Two days of travel and two temporary villages later, the Hunkpapa settled down in a ravine near the Powder River. They were now eighty miles closer to their rendezvous with the other hostiles waiting at the Rosebud, and more than thirty miles beyond the reach of Custer's army.

While the other women finished setting up camp, Dominique finished the first scene on the tipi. Using her lips and tongue, she shaped the end of her small brush into a fine point and added a dash of white to the large sapphire eyeball she'd painted earlier. Then, as she stood back to make certain she had the correct angle on the highlight, Spotted Feather approached.

"Oh," the Indian sighed, her jealousy overridden by astonishment. "This is truly magnificent."

"Do you really think so?" Dominique glanced at the squaw, then back up at the giant eagle she'd been working on. Perched above the flap of the tipi, the bird's image was one of strength, of boldness, from the tip of its open beak to its wide-stretched wingspan. Dominique had blended the paints, then shaded the canvas so precisely that each feather was clearly defined.

Below the bird's body, one foot, its talons sharp and threatening, gripped the limb of an oak, but the other hung free, swollen and useless. Beneath this blood-red foot, a column of ants led down to the small mound painted at the base of the tipi.

Laughing at the symbolism, Dominique turned to Spotted Feather, asking, "What do you think Jacob will say about this? I hope he won't think it's too silly."

"Not silly," she breathed, still shaking her head in awe. "Oh, no. Redfoot with think it is . . . truly beautiful." Her mouth open, she continued to stare at the expert depiction of the eagle.

From the distance, several yips reached their ears, then echoed throughout the village.

Spotted Feather turned to Dominique, her eyes wide. "He has returned! I must prepare his food."

"Who?"

"Redfoot, crazy one! I must go prepare his food!"

"He's my—" She paused, still unable to believe it, but managed to say, "My husband. I'll prepare his supper."

Spotted Feather glared, in spite of her promises, then turned and marched toward the fire. Dominique followed along behind the Indian, uninterested in the squaw's instant lack of respect. She suddenly had bigger things on her mind. Over the past three days, she'd done little but paint and think about what she would say to Jacob when she saw him again. She'd rehearsed angry speeches, indignant demands, and accusing phrases. Now she couldn't seem to remember even one of them. She stood beside Spotted Feather at the cooking pouch, more hindrance than help as she absentmindedly stirred the stew and tried to recall the slightest word that might trigger her memory.

Then, too soon, Dominique saw him at the fringes of

the village. Jacob walked through the smoky ribbons of
twilight, his carriage proud, his thick German body shad-
owing those of his smaller Dakota brothers. His head bent
low, he listened to one of the warriors, then responded
with quiet animation. As he talked, he transferred his
broad-rimmed hat and rifle to one hand, and worked at
unbuttoning his gray regulation shirt with the other. When
he stopped to give the hat and gun to his friend, Jacob
finally looked up toward the center fire ring. Then he saw
his woman. He froze, locking her eyes with his.

From across the short distance, his intense gaze hit
Dominique harder than his fist ever had. She took a backward step, stunned by the raw emotions running rampant
inside her. And then he began to move again. Slowly, his
eyes never leaving hers, he peeled off his shirt and added
it to his friend's bundle. Then, his steps deliberate and
calculated, Jacob advanced on her.

By the time he reached the fire, Dominique had given up
the search for forgotten speeches. Instead, she struggled just
to form the syllables and say one word: "H-hello."

"Dominique," he breathed as he reached for her hand.
"Are you well and happy? Have you—" Jacob's words
evaporated as he noticed the healing wounds running the
length of her arm. "What has happened to you?"

"It—it's nothing."

But Jacob pulled her closer and began a thorough inspection. He found not only the claw marks on her arms,
but the bruises on her neck and the scratches on her legs.
"You have been mauled, and more! How has this happened to you?" he demanded.

Spotted Feather shouldered her way against him, but the
blend of envy and love vanished from her eyes as she
listened to Jacob's questions and understood the response
the answers might bring. The crazy one would tell him
what had happened. Redfoot's anger would not be with
the white dog but with her. And worse, if he really did
feel some love for this she-devil, he might be *very* angry.

Spotted Feather hunched her shoulders, making it look as if she were shrinking inside her dress, and backed away from them.

The movement wasn't lost on Jacob. He glanced at the Indian, then turned his suspicious gaze on his wife. "Well? I do not wish to ask you again. What happened?"

Dominique peered out of the corner of her eye at the woman she'd befriended, then straightened her shoulders and found her voice. "Like you, I've been a little clumsy. I fell off my horse."

Jacob's eyes narrowed. Again he looked from Dominique to Spotted Feather and back to Dominique. "I don't believe you have told me all there is to tell. You did not receive these wounds falling off a horse. I want the truth."

At his words, Dominique found a lot more than her voice—her memory returned. "That's as much truth as you deserve. It's certainly as much or more than you've ever told me."

After glancing around at his people, he looked back at Dominique, his gaze a distinct warning. "The only words I want to hear from your flapping tongue, woman, are the answers to my questions. Do you understand?"

"Perfectly," she said, setting her chin. "And the thing I understand best is that you are two-toned, two-faced liar."

Taken back, Jacob raised his brows and said, "*What?* Why do you dare talk to me this way?"

"Because I, too, seek the truth, Mr. Redfoot." She lifted her chin and stood on tiptoe, bringing her shoulders level with his chest. "Why don't you start telling me the truth, *husband dear?* Maybe then you'll get a few honest answers from me."

"Oh," he whispered quietly, "you found about . . . *that.*" Jacob released her arm, then stepped aside. "Perhaps we should continue this discussion later in my—*our* tipi."

"Perhaps, dear husband, that is one of the more clever things you have thought of in a long time." She put her hands on her hips and leaned forward. "I think now would be an excellent time for our conversation, don't you?"

Jacob stared into her eyes, into what might have been the sable depths of insanity, and considered his options. He could stand his ground, as any Dakota warrior would, and order her to the tipi where she would have to wait until he was good and ready to talk. He took a quick survey of the other villagers. Yes, that was what he *ought* to do. Then he thought of the possible consequences and of Dominique's probable reaction.

The idea of the tears and sobs that would most likely accompany her expected response, the fact that her reaction would occur right out here in front of the other warriors, drove him to say, "Now may be the best time for us to talk. Yes, we will talk now. Into the tipi, woman. Go now."

Flashing a triumphant grin, Dominique whirled around and sashayed off toward the lodge.

So intent on choosing the correct words to explain their "mystery" wedding, Jacob directed his full attention to Dominique's retreating figure—and to her cute round bottom straining at the fabric of the white buckskin dress she still wore. After that taut behind disappeared into the tipi, Jacob started to follow her inside. Then he froze in midstride. Surely that was not the eye of some monstrous bald eagle staring him in the face! He stood back, staring up at the painting and gasped, "Ayee!"

Dominique poked her head out through the flap. "Well, I had to do *something* to keep busy around here." When he ignored her words and continued gawking at the painting, she added, "Didn't I, Jacob?"

But still he didn't answer. He stood there staring, twisting his head this way and that, then brought his hands to his cheeks and sighed in amazement.

Anxious, Dominique said, "Well, what's the matter? Haven't you ever seen an eagle before? Jacob? I thought we were going to talk."

"Yes. Yes, we must talk," he said, still transfixed by

her work. "We have much to talk about, too." Then he finally ducked through the flap and joined her inside. "*You* painted my tipi? By *yourself*?"

Dominique blew out a sigh and stalked over to the fire. She grabbed a long stick and began stirring the embers, complaining, "There are a few things I'm capable of doing, Jacob. Things, I might add, that I can do extremely well. Painting is one of them. Don't you like the eagle?"

"Oh, yes," he said in a whisper. "I like it very much. It is very beautiful—like you."

Immensely flattered, her anger melting, she mumbled, "I—it's not that good. I'm a little rusty."

"I have never seen a painting of such perfection. But the thing I like best about it," he added, his voice a soft low caress, "is that you did it for me." He started toward her, a sensual glaze clouding his eyes.

Using all of her resolve, the last of her strength, Dominique pulled the stick from the fire and held it between their bodies, narrowly missing his exposed navel with the red-hot tip. "Oh, no, you don't," she warned, backing up. "None of that, Mr. Redfoot. We came in here for one reason and one reason only. Now, talk. You have a lot to explain, my darling husband."

Chuckling to himself, Jacob gave her a slow, lazy grin. Hooking his thumbs over the waistband of his cavalry trousers, he said, "Sorry if I'm having trouble remembering why we're in here. I've had many things on my mind these past few days—you in particular. I have been worried about you. I see by your many injuries I had cause."

"Don't change the subject. You know what we're here to discuss. Tell me all about this wedding I didn't know I was at. Who said 'I do' for me?"

He cocked his head. " 'I do'?"

Exasperated, Dominique threw the stick to the ground. "How in God's name did you manage to marry me without my knowledge? Can you answer me that? And please tell me—*why* did you marry me? I mean, was this absolutely necessary, or did you think—"

"I see your tongue has suffered no injuries in my absence," he sliced in.

Grumbling inwardly, Dominique produced her best pout and stared up at him with mournful eyes.

Knowing from experience those beautiful eyes would flood with tears any minute, Jacob held up his hand. "Please—don't do that. I will try to explain."

The pout vanished. "Well? Go on. I can't wait to hear your newest lie."

"I have no need for more lies. I did what I had to do in order to protect you from the other warriors. If I hadn't married you, they would have used you for their own pleasure while I was away."

"Thanks for that much, Jacob, but couldn't you at least have *asked* me? Don't Dakota women usually know when they're about to become someone's wife?"

"Dakota women, yes," he said with a smile. "And I did mean to speak to you before the ceremony, but I'm afraid your flapping tongue left me no choice."

"I see," she said, her eyes glittering. "So you just wrapped me in your blanket, took me to your tipi, and bam! We're married. Is that it?"

"Pretty much."

"Some ceremony, Jacob. Very impressive. How do you intend to divorce me? Unwrap your blanket and spin me out the front door?"

Choking as that image flashed in his mind, he said, "Divorce is a little more complicated, but not much. I must say to you in public that I divorce you. Then the marriage is no more."

"Just like that?"

His expression solemn, he echoed, "Just like that."

"I see," she snapped. "And how do I divorce you?"

"You cannot. Divorce is not your decision. You are my wife until *I* say the marriage is no more."

"Not where *I* come from." Dominique looked away from him, no longer interested in or amused by the strange customs. Her tone low, accusing, she said, "It doesn't sound to me like the Dakota take marriage very seriously.''

"They do," he said softly. "I did."

She jerked her head up to meet his gaze and saw the naked truth in his deep blue eyes. They seemed to be saying that he considered their marriage real, that to him the fact that she was his wife meant much more than a simple act to protect her. Could she believe him this time? Or was this just another in a series of deceptions?

"Jacob," she began, biting her lip between words, "when you brought me to your tipi—the second time, that is, several days ago—you said . . . when you . . . you—" Dominique hesitated, searching for the right words, gauging his expression. She found an intensity in his gaze that shook her, knew that he was willing to stand there and let her babble on—flap her tongue, as he would put it— without making any attempt to rush her. With an awkward grin, she finally spit it out. "Y-you said you loved me. Was *that* true, Jacob?"

His smile deepened and grew warmer as he said, "Except for a few necessary lies, I always speak the truth."

"Now what's *that* supposed to mean?" she demanded with a stamp of her foot. "It sounds like another of your lies, and it doesn't make a damn bit of sense."

"It does to me." He shrugged.

Dominique narrowed one eye and stared at him a long moment before she said, "Maybe it makes some sense to me after all. I think I understand: You don't love me at all. You just—"

"I have put the entire Dakota nation, not to mention my life, in jeopardy because of you," he cut in, his tone cool. "After doing that, if you cannot understand how much this man must love you, then it is you who have managed to deceive me. I had thought you to be very smart in the head."

Tears stung her eyes and a huge lump blocked Dominique's airway. The words swimming through a tiny sob, she said, "Oh, Jacob. What's going to become of us?"

The anguish in her eyes, the look of what he hoped was a hint of her love for him, was too much for Jacob. He took two large steps and crushed her to his chest. "I don't know," he breathed against her golden hair. "I wish I could see the future like our great medicine man, Sitting Bull, but I cannot."

Dominique accepted the comfort of his strong arms and basked in the warmth of his love. Her senses drenched in his essence, in the heady scent of raw power and horse-flesh, of sage and all that was nature, she pressed her mouth to his chest and murmured against the silken mat protecting his heart. "Why, Jacob? Oh, why does it have to be like this? Why couldn't we still be at the fort, dancing and having a good time, falling in love the way I've heard it should happen?"

Laughing in spite of the tender moment, Jacob pulled back and tilted her chin up to meet his gaze. "You mean there is a special way it should happen and we have not followed the correct order?"

"Oh, you know what I mean." Her cheeks grew warm, and Dominique knew they must be flushed. She lowered her gaze and shrugged. "I thought falling in love was supposed to be easier than this."

Again he forced her to look into his eyes. "Is this what has happened to you, *wi witko*? Have you fallen in love with me?"

Dominique puckered up her mouth and glanced around the tipi. She wasn't ready to tell him, couldn't seem to bring herself to say the words. She searched the walls, following the seam up to the skylight, then down the other side, cocking her head from side to side as if she were trying to decide how she felt.

Jacob released her and stepped back. "Perhaps you will know when I return from the warriors' lodge. I must go now. The Father awaits."

Dominique gasped. "All right, I'll say it: Jacob, I love you."

With an indulgent grin, Jacob pressed his hand to his

chest and said, "I'll believe those words from your mouth when they start from here. Perhaps when I return you will understand what I mean."

"B-but you can't go. I—we're not done talking yet."

"I am done for now. And I must go. I am not going to return to the cavalry tonight. I will come back to you. Surely your questions can wait until then."

Her expression coquettish, her dark eyes full of mischief, she said, "Well, I suppose most of them can, but there is one little thing I've been wondering about since I found out I'm your wife."

"Tell me what it is. Then I must go."

"I just wondered. I mean, if I've been your wife for the last four days and during that time you spent not one but two whole nights with me in this tipi, how come I'm still . . . you know. Why haven't you . . . Shouldn't you have tried to . . ." She shrugged and rolled her impish eyes. "By now?"

Jacob leaned back and roared his laughter. Through his chuckles, he finally said, "Oh, crazy one, you are wondering why I haven't lain with you on our marriage blanket? Is that it?"

Again Dominique shrugged. "I guess that's what I mean."

Jacob dragged her back in his arms and slowly fit his mouth to hers. The kiss was brief and tender, an expression of love. Then he whispered against her full lips, "This blanket business is something we will have to discuss in detail when I return. For now I will answer your question the best way I can. I've left you to your own blanket for the same reason I do all that I do since I met you—I love you." He kissed her again, then released her. "Now I must go. You rest. We may have to discuss this important question of yours for a very long time tonight." Then he gave her a roguish grin and stepped through the flap.

Dominique hugged herself and whirled around in a circle. For reasons she wasn't entirely sure of, she was supremely happy and tremendously excited. Tonight something special and wonderful would happen to her. Tonight, if Jacob still desired her, she would finally know what it was to be a woman.

Licking her lips in anticipation, she tried to imagine an act she knew little about but had thought of often over the past months. She pulled off her buckskin dress, then unwound her heavy braids. Giggling as she tried to equate lovemaking with the simple stories she'd heard in boarding school, she fluffed the lace edging around the low neck of her camisole, and smoothed the legs of her drawers. Then Dominique picked up the porcupine tail brush and sat down at her blanket.

As she thoughtfully dragged the brush through her long wavy hair, a sudden idea froze the movement. What about Jacob? What would he expect of her, *from* her? She thought back to her conversation with Spotted Feather and shuddered. Would she be able to please him the way a Dakota woman could? Or had she fought the squaw for a prize she didn't deserve, and for a man she couldn't possibly please?

Dominique stretched out on the buffalo rug and pulled the thin blanket up over her shoulders. She thought of Michigan, of her beautiful mother and her premature death, and softly sighed. She had never missed her quiet wisdom more. In the Dakota village, there was no one to help her with this dilemma, no woman in this camp who would tell her what to do for a man like Jacob.

With another, heavier sigh, Dominique rolled over on her back. How could this be? How could she suddenly be feeling so inept? A nonswimmer, she'd somehow managed to pull herself from the river and avoid drowning. A city girl, unused to animals and the wild, she'd found a way to save herself from the jaws of a grizzly.

Would the so-called natural act of mating be her undoing?

Chapter Seventeen

JACOB FEIGNED A YAWN, THEN SHOOK HIS HEAD AS IF TO clear it. He'd been sitting with the council for hours now, going over the same ground, planning strategies, and making arrangements to rejoin Sitting Bull's group at the Rosebud. But he'd been thinking only of Dominique.

He contemplated her final question over and over, wondering if it had been an innocent observation or a blatant invitation. If, as he dared to hope, it was the latter, what had happened to her earlier fears? Jacob remembered her trembling shoulders and frightened gasps the night he'd nearly taken her. He was a fool to think she'd changed her mind so quickly and offered herself to him. Why couldn't he dismiss this feeble hope? He shifted his position, wondering how much longer he could stand the heaviness in his loins, the incessant throbbing that had once been a sweet ache for the crazy one.

". . . by the next moon?" Gall looked up from the fire, waiting for an answer, then noticed the glazed look in his son's eyes. "Redfoot? I have asked how long before the Long Hair's army reaches the Rosebud. Do you not have this information?"

Jacob snapped his head up. "Oh, forgive me. My mind wanders. Our troops are badly slowed by the large wagon train. Custer's cavalry is not what we need to worry about. Others, Major Reno and General Crook, are much closer to finding our lodges and attacking them." This time when he yawned, Jacob added some dramatics and stretched his arms high over his head.

Gall nodded. "We have kept you too long, my son."

Rubbing his eyes, Jacob said, "It is not you. I have been riding with the general's scouting party for two days and have had little sleep the past few nights. I will be here for another night. We can finish our talks tomorrow."

"Go, then," Gall urged. "Sleep well. We will talk tomorrow as we move onward."

"Tomorrow, then." With that Jacob rose and bade them good night. He stepped outside the warriors' lodge and inhaled the crisp night air, hoping to put his tortured body and mind at ease. Still he thought of Dominique. Still he dared to dream she might want him as much as he wanted her.

Tugging to release the buttons of his dark blue army trousers, Jacob strode across the campground and headed for his lodge, for his woman. He lifted the flap quietly and stole inside. As he worked his troop boots down over his calves and off his feet, he glanced at the outline of Dominique's form. She rested on her side, her back to him. Was she asleep or simply ignoring him? Jacob slid his trousers off and discarded them. After looping the rawhide lace securing his breechclout around his finger, he hesitated. Then he noticed Dominique's shallow breathing, the rigidity of her tense shoulders. She was awake. Without another thought, Jacob jerked the piece of rawhide, and the final garment dropped to the ground.

Taking tiny sips of air, Dominique listened to the rustling as he disrobed. When she felt him slip beneath his own blanket on the rug beside her, she shivered. He was so close, yet so far. Her breathing ceased altogether when he placed his hand on the back of her head and began stroking her hair.

Separating a thick ringlet from the bulky waves, Jacob pulled it high, then watched, fascinated, as the silken strands floated down to her shoulders. "By the firelight, your hair loses its golden color and becomes one with the flames. Have you decided to become one with me, *wi witko*?"

"Oh, Jacob," she gasped, taking a huge gulp of air, "I—I don't know." Dominique rolled onto her back and stared up at him. He rested on one elbow, his blanket draped loosely across his hips. He looked into her eyes; his gaze was intense and demanding, but his thoughts were unreadable. She suddenly didn't know what she wanted, what to say. "I—I've done little but think about us and what's to become of us since you left, but still, I'm not sure."

"Ah," he sighed. "I have thought of us, too, even while the council spoke of war. You and the short time we have together fill my mind. My people can run no more. We must turn and fight the soldiers. I worry what will happen to us."

Alarmed, Dominique sat up. As she spoke, her blanket slid down from her shoulders and pooled in her lap. "Does that have to be, Jacob? Isn't there some way to avoid a war?"

His eyes imprisoned by the sight of her taut nipples pushing against the sheer fabric of her camisole, Jacob said, "I do not see a way to stop the bloodshed between your people and mine. But let us not speak of war tonight. Let us finish our earlier conversation—let us speak of love."

Her bottom lip trembling, Dominique confessed what she'd known all along. "Love is what I feel when I think of you. I suppose that does mean I love you, Jacob. Right or wrong, I love you, but I don't know if I should, if we have the right to . . ." She let her words trail off and lowered her head.

Gently coaxing her back down on the blanket, Jacob stretched across her waist and stared down into her lovely features. She glowed with innocence, curiosity, and the love of a woman for a man. Deeply touched, Jacob struggled for the right words, fingering the satin ribbon woven through the ivory lace at the neckline of her camisole. He finally said, "You are my wife, *wi witko*. I am your husband. Where is the wrong?"

Intensely aware of his touch, of the fire in his fingertips as they skipped over the soft rise of her breasts, she said, "Our m-marriage may be legal to you, but to me, it simply didn't happen."

Jacob lowered his head, directing his mouth to trace the path of his hands, and spoke against her silken flesh. "You need only to say the words—but it is you who must say them now. Say you wish to be my woman, and we will be as one." As he waited for her reply, Jacob punctuated the statement by dragging his fevered lips across the fabric to her nipple where he teased the hard crown, leaving a damp circle in the cotton.

"I want to, really I do," she said through a sudden groan.

His big hands skimmed over her breasts and down her shoulders, leaving wakes of desire in their trail. "Then say the words," he encouraged, maneuvering his mouth along that same path. "Say them now and you will be mine."

"Oh—*oh!*" she gasped, assaulted by the exhilarating sensations, the curious blend of strength and tenderness in his touch. "Oh, yes, Jacob, yes. I do want to be your woman. Show me what to do. I don't know what to do."

"What of your fears?" he said, forcing a calm, even tone.

"Fears?" She was swimming in confusion, aching to be touched everywhere at once. "About what?"

"I know I have frightened you with my desire. I realize you have never lain with a man. How can I put your fears to rest?"

Unable to understand, unwilling to take the time to analyze his thoughts, Dominique said through a tremor of anticipation, "I'm only afraid that you will be disappointed in me, that I won't know how to make you happy."

"Oh, crazy one," he groaned, taking her face between

his hands. "You need do nothing to make me happy. Because you exist, I am content."

Before she could answer or change her mind, Jacob brushed her mouth with his, teasing her lips apart with the tip of his tongue. "Be mine, *wi witko*. Open yourself to your husband," he commanded as he stretched out full length beside her. Taking her mouth, plunging deep inside her with the same rocking movement he would use to make her his, Jacob coaxed the ribbon loose and gently pulled the camisole apart. When she tried to close it again, he took his mouth from hers and slid his hand between her breasts. "Relax, Dominique. Let me love you."

When he looked into her eyes searching for signs of compliance, what he saw instead nearly tore him apart. Dominique was laid bare, the windows to her soul as clear as the first raindrop of spring. Her trust in him was complete; her love was immeasurable. Nearly choking on a surge of emotion, uttering an unfamiliar sob, Jacob turned away from her and laid his head in the crook of her neck. Murmuring against skin so soft he thought he must be touching the clouds, Jacob finished unlacing her camisole. "Raise your arms, Dominique. Help me with this tangle of clothing," he managed in a strangled whisper.

Eager to reach the next plateau, Dominique obeyed, but as soon as he lifted the garment off her body, she clasped her arms across her exposed breasts.

"Why do you cover yourself, *wi witko*? I have seen your beauty before—remember?" At her nod he, too, thought back to that first day, to the sight of these small firm breasts. Then they were taut from exposure, the nipples hard from the icy water. Now they stood rigid, not from the cold, but from the heat of his touch. Jacob lowered her arms to her sides and assaulted those taut peaks with his tongue, circled and teased until he had the response he sought.

She was twisting, turning, working to bring every part of her body into some kind of contact with his, making him the crazy one, challenging his rigid control. Jacob left her breasts then, working to gather himself. Trying not to think of where his lips touched, he slid a wet trail down her trembling ribs to her navel where he hovered, teasing, tantalizing, driving in and out of the shallow indentation with his tongue until her cries and the strangled sound of his own name nearly drove him insane.

In need of a break, of a moment to himself, Jacob leaned back, and stared up at her with clouded eyes. She lay there panting, twisting her head from side to side. Dewdrops of perspiration had replaced his mouth, kissing the skin between her breasts and forming a trail down to her hard flat stomach.

"Hurry, Jacob," she gasped, her eyelids fluttering, even though they were closed. "Please don't stop now."

"I've only begun, my love. There is no need to hurry this night," he said, suddenly unsure if it was a promise he could keep.

Jacob leaned over and tugged at her drawers, but this time, after he'd slipped the cotton undergarment down over her feet, she didn't try to cover her exposed body. She waited, biting and sucking on her smallest finger, and watched him through half-closed eyes as he began a sensual journey up her legs. Nibbling and teasing her soft skin as he made his way to the source of her heat, his kisses, and the maddening caresses of his tongue, ended abruptly at midthigh.

Lifting himself alongside her body, Jacob pressed his own throbbing need against her hip and whispered in her ear, "How do you feel now, *wi witko*? Are you still afraid of me?"

"I, ah, no," she gasped, suddenly reminded of the embarrassing dream she'd had, painfully aware of the wonderfully strange sensations that had led to the release of her frustrations and inhibitions. Was it about to happen again? Could she stop it? Did she even want to try? "Touch me," she begged. "Please don't stop touching me."

"Where would you like me to start?" he whispered, moving his fingertips around in lazy circles, tracing a crooked path down to her navel. When those fingers skittered across the apron of her golden meadow, he lingered there, asking, "Is this a good spot?"

Dominique was beyond any thought of self-control, nearly incapable of speech as the powerful conclusion of the dream loomed ever closer. "Oh, Jacob, please—something's happening." Higher and higher her body raced, past her ability to halt the unexpected response. Her hips writhing on their own, making the decision for her, she made one last feeble attempt to explain. "Ohh, I—I'm sorry, I don't know what's happening, I—" Dominique's body took over then, cutting off her speech, shutting down her mind.

Stunned at first, surprised she'd peaked before he'd even touched her woman parts, Jacob quickly slid his hand between her legs and helped bring her agony to an end. As the spasms ebbed, when he felt her pulsating heat lurching against his fingers, Jacob's own need grew huge, threatened to claim what was left of his fragile control as well.

With a sharp intake of his breath, he rolled over on top of her, spreading her legs with his knee as he lowered himself to her damp, nurturing nest. He thought of warning her, of giving notice he would soon enter her, but when he looked into Dominique's eyes and found them swimming in pleasure not part of this world, he drove into her, past the thin barrier, and up to her very center. There, battling some primeval instinct, fighting the potent urge to thrust his maleness in frenzied, rhythmic strokes, Jacob forced himself to lie still. And wait. For her pain to diminish. For the tight untested walls of her sheath to relax. For her words of encouragement. Then, he swore to himself, and only then would he begin the movements as ageless as time, bring her to new heights she couldn't have imagined, and take himself to the exquisite brink of those heights. And then, because he had no choice, he would spill his seed onto the ground.

"Jacob," she softly said, her voice drowsy with pleasure, "are we one now?"

"Yes, *wi witko*," he whispered against her ear. "Now you are my woman. When your pain is no more, move your hips against mine, and I will show you what it truly means to be my woman."

But her pain, if she'd had any at all, was a vague memory. Dominique immediately tested this strange new union, slowly pressed up against him, then pushed her bottom back down to the buffalo fur. The sensations whetted her appetite for more. Awkwardly testing her new skills, she ground her hips against him again, but this time when she came up off the rug, Jacob filled his powerful hands with her derriere.

"Easy now," he said hoarsely. "Let me show you the rhythm."

And then he took her to where she'd never been, showed her through the gates of a new, more agonizing pleasure. All her senses were drenched with Jacob, each nerve ending alive and begging for the slightest attention from him. Her arousal more intense than ever, the demand for gratification, deeper, fuller somehow, Dominique fell into the rocking motions, matching Jacob's movements, demanding as much as she gave. This was no dream, and the culmination would never be lost in hazy memories. She knew now that the dream and the experience she'd had just before he'd made her his own could only be considered a prelude, a simple release of pressure. Dominique knew what he offered now was much more than physical gratification, a greater gift than she would ever receive again. Jacob made love to more than her body—he stroked her very essence, filled her mind and her being with a feeling so exquisite that she felt as primitive as her surroundings, as wild and as free.

Faster and faster they rode, higher and higher, but no one gripped the reins of this passion. Somehow, somewhere, Jacob had lost his proud control, his mind. He was consumed by her, mad from her cries and from the erotic sound of his name as she begged him to stop the torment, then urged him to go on. He would never be the same again, never be the self-possessed, stone-hearted warrior he'd trained himself to be. Jacob understood all that, and still he plunged ahead, caring little if he should drown in her sweetness. When Dominique slid her fingers through his hair, gathered the thick waves into her palms, and pulled him to her as she bucked and twisted in the throes of ecstasy, he was completely lost.

Through the thick sensual fog his mind had become, Jacob recognized his own release was imminent, knew what he must do to protect her, but her spasms were the only source of control now. Dominique's body owned him, milked him of life's precious fluid, then left him lying on top of her, dazed and incoherent.

Dominique struggled for breath as Jacob lay sprawled across her breast. Squirming, she wriggled her torso free and gulped the cool night air. When her pulse finally slowed and some measure of reason returned, she inclined her head and gazed lovingly at her husband. His eyes were closed and his breathing was still erratic, the shallow breaths taken in short choppy gasps. Dominique smiled and ran her hand across his shoulders. His skin, slick with perspiration, felt hot to the touch, feverish. If she were at home, she thought with a delicious giggle, heat like that would signal a dire sickness, bring a visit from the doctor at the very least.

Thoughts of home, of her previously comfortable life, gave Dominique pause. Would this union, the consummation of her marriage, her love for Jacob, have been the same if they had been tucked away in her cozy bed back in Michigan? Or even at Fort Lincoln?

She pictured her frilly, feminine room at the Custer house and remembered another day—herself as another woman. Dominique began to laugh.

Jacob's voice, groggy and cracking with emotion, cut into her musings. "I thought I had pleased you well. What is so funny, my crazy wife?"

"Oh, Jacob," she moaned, still stroking his slick back.

"You must know how well you pleased me. I'm not laughing about you—it's *The Ladies' Oracle*."

"The what?" Concern for her well-being eclipsed the urge to remain buried deep inside her. Jacob rolled over to his side and cradled her in his arms. "Have I injured you in some way?" Again she laughed, her sweet voice sprinkling the air like a thousand chirping robins. Jacob shook his head, soothed by the sound, and said, "Forgive me, then. Your husband must be a very stupid man. I still don't see what is so funny."

"You couldn't possibly know," she managed, controlling her chuckles. "The *Oracle* is a book, a fortune-telling book. It predicted this would happen, but I didn't believe it at the time."

She remembered back to the day spent in her room with Libbie, thinking how terribly long ago it all seemed, and recalled some of the questions she had asked of her aunt. Dominique glanced up at Jacob, giving him a shy smile, then nestled her head in the crook of his arm. No wonder Libbie wouldn't tell her about the intimate matters between herself and the general, she thought, this time stifling the urge to giggle. How could any woman explain what had happened to her here? She would never be able to put into words the way she had felt as Jacob made her his, couldn't even bring herself to discuss the myriad emotions tingling throughout every pore in her body, with the very man who'd made her feel that way. She only knew she'd never been more contented or more satisfied with herself as a woman.

With a sigh of pure pleasure, Dominique kissed her husband's damp breast and said, "You're anything but stupid, Jacob. I think you're absolutely wonderful, and I love you so much right now, my insides hurt."

"Then I *have* injured you?" He started to rise, but Dominique pressed her hand to his chest and coaxed him back down.

Her words swimming through another bout of laughter, she said, "You've got to stop taking everything I say so literally. I mean that I hurt here"—she laid her fingertips against her left breast—"because I'm so very happy. Do you understand?"

A wave of raw emotion washed over him, welling up past his throat, threatening to spill out from his eyes. Jacob crushed her to his chest and buried his face in her hair. What was happening to him, to his careful reserve? He'd never been moved to such depths, not even when he said his final good-bye to Lame Fawn. Would loving the crazy one mean the end of his sanity, his brave facade? Jacob took several deep breaths, searching for a way, any way at all, to regain some measure of control over himself.

But he had no more control now than he'd had as he made her his own, he thought, furious with himself. Now, because of his inability to harness his passion, his seed swamped her system, searching through her secret folds for its mate, frantic to fulfill the creation of life. His anger damning the flood of earlier emotions, Jacob lay back against the buffalo rug and cleared his throat.

"You must talk to one of the other women in camp," he said briskly. "Someone who will teach you about the powders and herbs necessary to prevent the creation of a child. Have you made such a friend here yet?"

Blushing at the thought of discussing such an intimate matter with others, or even with Jacob, Dominique shrugged and looked away. Her voice unnaturally low and shy, she said, "No one around here seems interested in being my friend. The closest, I suppose, would be Spotted Feather, and she"—*tried to kill me*—"well, she doesn't like me very much."

Jacob rested his weight on one elbow. Staring down at her, he examined her wounds. "You and Spotted Feather have had some trouble. This much I know. Tell me what's happened; explain your many injuries."

"Look, if you don't mind, I'd rather not. Besides, none of them are too—"

"Tell me now, Dominique. Too much has passed between us for secrets. What happened to you? What has Spotted Feather done to cause these wounds?''

The luster in her dark eyes dulled as she tried to think of a way out of the conversation. She gave him a quick glance, then averted her gaze. ''It wasn't her fault. I was getting water down by the river, and I . . . fell in. My legs were injured when I tumbled downstream and then again as I climbed out of the water.''

''So you fell into the river again?'' he said, amused.

Dominique frowned. Why was she protecting that nasty squaw? Then she thought of Gall's idea of punishment, assumed Jacob's sense of justice would impose an even worse penalty, and said, ''Yes, that's pretty much the way it happened.''

''And this?'' he asked, his tone suspicious as he pointed to the turquoise and yellow rectangle above her knee.

''This,'' she laughed, ''happened the night you left me crying in your tipi. I, ah . . . dropped your lance.''

Puzzled, he glanced from her leg to the far wall. The weapon no longer hung from its rawhide thong. Looking back at Dominique, he turned his palms upward, but before he could speak, she explained. ''When I dropped it, ah, well, it landed pretty hard across my knee, Jacob. I'm sorry, but I'm afraid it broke in half.''

A slow grin lit his features as he began to understand. ''You *dropped* it, crazy one? Perhaps what you did was more like a temper—''

''That's my story, Mr. Redfoot. Take it or leave it.''

Jacob pulled her into his arms, laughing and kissing her all at once. Then he sobered and ran his fingers along her arm. ''This was no accident, *wi witko*. Did someone— Spotted Feather, perhaps—attack you with the claw of a grizzly?''

''No.'' She laughed again, relieved she could still tell him the truth. ''I'm afraid those claws were still attached to the bear when that happened.''

''Dominique,'' he warned, ''I mean it. No more lies will pass between us. How was your arm injured?''

"But I'm not lying, Jacob. I swear it." She related the story, down to her burial and the terror she had felt. When she finished, her eyes were moist. Jacob pulled her back in his powerful arms and began rocking her.

"You were very fortunate," he said, his voice splintered and ragged. "Not many live to tell of such an encounter."

Dominique pushed back, dotting wet kisses along his cheek as she moved. "But it's all true, Jacob. That's all there is to my wounds. No secrets, no problems."

"And Spotted Feather?" he said suspiciously.

"She doesn't like me," Dominique hedged. "But I know why, and I even understand a little. She told me she hoped to be your wife one day. In fact, she actually thought you should marry her, too, so you could have *two* wives, one red and one white."

"And you?" he asked. "What do you think of this idea?"

"I think it stinks!" she pouted. "Even if I'm not woman enough for you, if you think for one minute I'd allow another woman, Indian or white, in your bed now, you've got another think coming, you thick-headed . . . nincompup!"

"Poop," he choked out through his laughter. "The word is nincompoop!"

"Not around here it isn't," she said, working to keep her indignant expression. "And don't try to change the subject. I've seen the way your people live. Do you think I haven't noticed your greedy chief and all his wives? Maybe one woman isn't enough for him, but I know I can learn to please you, Jacob. If you give me a chance, I'm sure I'll be enough for you."

His love growing deeper by the minute, filling parts of him he hadn't been aware of till this night, Jacob slowly shook his head and whispered, "What makes you think I'll ever want anyone but you, crazy one?"

"That's easy enough—Spotted Feather. She says you

are Dakota and you need a Dakota woman to make you truly happy.''

''I need only you,'' he said softly, following the outline of her ear with his fingertips. ''I worry only that I will not have the strength to handle you.''

Dominique blinked back a sudden rush of tears. ''Really, Jacob? I mean, wasn't I a little . . . Did I manage to make you happy?''

''You are what I believe your people call 'spoiled,' '' he said with a low chuckle. ''But so shall I spoil you this night. Tomorrow and other nights I will show you how to touch me, and I will allow you to discover for yourself what it is that arouses my passion.''

''Oh,'' she said on a quiet sigh. ''Then you weren't—I mean, I didn't, you weren't . . . pleased?''

But how could he tell her how deeply he'd been moved, explain that even though thoroughly sated, his body ached to join with hers again? Jacob simply smiled and said, ''You have pleased me so, still I cannot think straight.''

''Oh, Jacob,'' she sighed, resting against him. ''You make me feel so happy, so cherished. How long can these feelings last? What will happen to us when I return to my family? How in God's name will I ever explain this to them?''

Unable to look into her eyes, unwilling to stain their union with any more deceptions, Jacob shook his head. ''I do not know how to answer your question. I am not even sure you *can* go back to your people.''

Dominique bolted upright. ''What do you mean, I can't go back? Of course, I can. I *must*.''

Pained more than he ever could have imagined, Jacob stared into her frightened eyes, and settled on an offering of hope. ''I will do what I can to see you are returned to your family. That is the best I can offer.''

''Jacob?'' she whispered, her voice barely audible, her heart at a standstill. ''You said 'you'—surely you meant to say 'us.' We belong together. We are husband and wife now.''

Jacob dropped his gaze to the blanket and sighed, "I belong here with my people."

"But you're white," Dominique cried, suddenly gripped with panic. "You can fit in with white society, I've seen you do it! You were a soldier just like any other, Jacob. I know you can do it again for me. Can't you? Jacob?"

He'd guessed this conversation would take place some-day, sometime, but never had he imagined it would be so difficult. His expression tormented, his eyes filled with pain, Jacob softly said, "I cannot expect you to under-stand so easily, *wi witko*. I can only tell you that even though the skin you see is that of a white man, it protects the heart of a Dakota warrior. It always will."

"Oh, Jacob," she softly cried through a throat suddenly tight. "My God, Jacob, what are we going to do?"

"I—" Overcome himself, Jacob gathered her in his arms and gently eased her down on the rug.

Too filled with emotion to speak, Jacob answered his bride the only way he could. He made love to her as if this time might be the last.

Chapter Eighteen

Ϻ

Montana, June 18, 1876

MORE THAN THREE WEEKS LATER THE MAIN BODY OF THE Hunkpapa council rode into the valley of the river they called the Greasy Grass. Accompanying the group on one of his increasingly rare visits, Jacob rode beside his bride of nearly a month. When the Hunkpapa band turned toward the south and headed down through the valley to set up camp, Jacob nudged Sampi's flanks and held Peaches's bridle.

"Come, *wi witko*," he said. "Follow me."

Dominique's sturdy little mount trailed after the larger stallion, carefully picking her way among the rocks and shrubs scarring the ragged bluff. They plodded along to a wide grassy hill rising up over two hundred feet from the valley below. There Jacob slid down off the stallion, then lifted Dominique from Peaches.

Still holding her in his arms, he walked to the summit of the hill. "I brought you here so you could understand," he explained as he gently set her on her feet. "Look. See what your uncle and his army face."

A sense of foreboding sent a sudden shiver up her spine, but Dominique wheeled around and stared out at the magnificent view. Along the skyline in the distance, the Big Horn Mountains, still wearing a crown of winter snow, provided a scenic backdrop for the terrain to the west. Below the ragged bluffs, the Greasy Grass River, swollen with spring runoff from these mountains, snaked through thickets of cottonwood trees. A huge valley carpeted in thick grass played host to an immense band of grazing Indian ponies. But most impressive, even frightening somehow, were the seemingly endless circles of tipis. Stretching on for miles along the river's path, they seemed to fill every available parcel of land comprised by the quiet pastoral scenery.

Dominique gasped. "Jacob, my God! How many—"

From behind her, Jacob pressed his hips against her bottom and wound his arms around her waist. Resting his chin on her shoulder, he quietly said, "I wanted you to see this so you might understand. I want you to know that these are all my people."

Extending his arm across her shoulder, he pointed out the separate camps. "Most of the circles are Sioux." Then he named each tribe. "Oglala, Miniconjou, Sans Arc, Blackfoot, Two Kettles, and Brules. Soon our own Hunkpapa camp will join them. At the other end of the valley, to the north, over a hundred Cheyenne lodges unite with us."

"But, Jacob," Dominique said, her voice barely a whisper, "what happens if Uncle Armstrong finds them? What will your people do if the cavalry comes across this—"

"Come," he said softly. "We must talk."

Taking her hand, Jacob led Dominique to a grassy furrow running along the top of the knoll. Sitting down with his back against a small hill, he stretched his legs out and motioned for his wife to sit across his lap.

"This is as far as my people will go, *wi witko*," he explained. "The Dakota will run from soldiers like your uncle no more. We are not animals to be hunted for sport."

Dominique stared into his eyes, hoping to find just a spark of humor, the hint of a joke, but she saw only a great sadness mingled with a heartbreaking sense of helplessness. She lowered her head and spoke in a flat, cold tone. "Surely you must know there will be a war if your people stay."

"Yes," he agreed, his voice resigned, dispassionate. "That seems to be the only solution."

"But *why*? Why does it have to be that way?" Dominique hooked her arms around his shoulders and pulled, hoping to shake some sense into him. "Why can't your people do whatever it is the army asks of them and be done with it? Why do they have to fight?"

"That is a question you wouldn't ask if you understood what the whites demand of us."

"Then help me, Jacob. Help me to understand what could possibly be worth the terrible price the Dakota will pay if your people don't surrender."

Expelling a heavy sigh, Jacob slid down away from the hill until he and Dominique were sprawled side by side in the deep grass. He tried to explain. "Many winters past—eight, I think—Red Cloud, chief of the Oglala, signed a treaty with your government. He agreed to take his tribe and other Dakota, and some Hunkpapa, too, to a reservation on our own land in the Black Hills."

"I've heard of the Black Hills."

"I'm sure you have," he muttered, his jaw tight. Unable to talk just then, Jacob kissed the top of her head, then stared down at her golden-red locks. Hair very nearly the same color covered the scalp of a man he'd vowed to kill. How could he hate one of the Custers so much, yet love another with every fiber of his being?

Dominique lifted her head and gazed up at her husband. "Jacob? Is something wrong?"

"Only everything, crazy one. Only the fact that I love you, and that love has become a very difficult thing in my life."

"Maybe it has nothing to do with your love for me at all, Jacob." Dominique looked him square in the eye. "Isn't it possible that I've only been some kind of beacon, a light showing you who you really are?"

"I no longer know who I am."

"Oh, I think you do. You're two people, Jacob. One, the warrior Redfoot, who wants to protect his people and their way of life. The other, Stoltz, who would probably like to honor the memory of his murdered family and, I hope, keep the love of his wife.'' Dominique's heart ached as she watched a painful self-examination flickering in his eyes. ''What I think, Jacob, is that you are having a very difficult time choosing sides.''

''It is more than difficult,'' he whispered, his throat tight. Jacob slid his big hand behind her neck and crushed her to his chest. Again kissing the top of her head, he said against her hair, ''It is impossible.''

Jacob's heartbeat accelerated, thundered against her ear. A sudden rush of tears swamped Dominique's eyes, but she squeezed them back, choked on them, and swallowed. After a deep breath, she managed to say, ''Tell me about the Black Hills, Jacob. Are they as beautiful as I've heard, and are they really blue?''

Jacob waited a long moment, grateful for the change of subject, then said, ''Often, on hazy mornings in particular, they appear to be one with the sky.'' The ache in Jacob's chest gradually eased as he thought of the land in which he'd spent so many summers. ''And they are truly the most beautiful mountains I have ever seen. Running all through the thick forest are creeks so thick with fish a man need only reach into the water to catch them. There is so much game that even the poorest hunter need never go hungry.''

Again Dominique lifted her head and stared up at Jacob. The pain was gone from his eyes, and a lazy contentment seemed to glaze them, a look quite close to what she'd often seen after they made love. Dominique smiled up at her husband. ''It sounds as if you love those mountains as much as you love me.''

The statement pulled a short laugh from him. Jacob rumpled her hair, murmuring, ''I could never love anyone or anything as much as I love you, but yes, *wi witko*, I do love the Black Hills. All Dakota do. That love for the land is one of the things that has brought us here to this place.''

''Are you talking about the treaty?''

"That, and the lies. Red Cloud and those who joined him were guaranteed control of their land and promised that no one, not even the government, would pass through the boundaries of what they called the Great Sioux Reservation without permission of the Dakota."

"And someone did?"

"Oh, *wi witko*," he sighed, cupping her face. "Come up here to me."

Still lying next to her husband's body, Dominique rolled onto his chest, then lowered her lips to his for a brief tender kiss. "What is it, Jacob? Don't you know you can tell me anything?"

"I don't want to see you hurt any more than you have to be."

"I need to understand what is going on here. I think I've earned the right to hear it all."

After a slow resigned nod, Jacob fit his mouth to hers again, then said, "Against all that is fair, all that is right, your uncle violated the promise of the United States government and brought his troops into the Black Hills two winters ago."

"Uncle Armstrong?" she gasped. "Oh, Jacob, he wouldn't do that. He couldn't have—" But Dominique cut off her own words as she thought back to evenings around the fireplace in the Custer home. She really didn't know what the general was capable of, didn't have much more than a passing acquaintance with the uncle who'd rarely been part of her life. Fourteen years her senior, he was off to West Point, then engaged in the service of the United States Army by the time she was old enough to recognize him. What she knew of George Armstrong Custer she had learned from adoring family members and hero-worshiping neighbors. Hardly an unbiased panel.

Jacob gave her time to digest his words, to consider them, then said, "The fact is that he did violate the treaty, *wi witko*. He and his army boldly marched into our land, slaughtered our game, and even shot at those of us who dared protest his presence. When he left, after he'd had his fill of wild cherries and strawberries, he returned to his government carrying tales of gold. It didn't take long for the whites, soldier and civilian alike, to come to the Black Hills and begin taking from the Dakota what was rightfully theirs.''

"Oh, Jacob," she cried. "I'm so sorry."

"You have nothing to apologize for. Even an apology from your uncle would serve no purpose now. We have lost the Black Hills to seekers of gold and greedy government agents. We will not lose our dignity as well.''

She didn't have to ask Jacob what he meant by that. Dominique already knew that, to a man, the Dakota would hold their ground, fight to the death if necessary to prevent their families from being dragged off to some new land the whites would designate as their reservation. But she had to make an attempt to change his mind. "Why don't your people give surrender a try? Maybe the new reservation wouldn't be so bad.''

"You forget," he said, grumbling. "Red Cloud and his people did give it a try before the Black Hills were taken from us. The government expects our warriors to become farmers. What do we know about farming? What do we *care* about farming? The Dakota are hunters and wanderers. We do not stay in one place too long.''

Dominique nestled her head against his shoulder and neck, and sighed. "There has to be a solution to suit everyone somewhere.''

"I have spent many days and nights looking for this solution, but it doesn't seem to be there. You have lived with my people long enough to know them, to understand many of their ways. How well do you think they would do on a reservation?''

Again she sighed, then shrugged.

"On a reservation our warriors would turn into old men, grow weak and fat. They are not farmers, will never be farmers!''

"I—I don't know what to say.''

But Jacob did. "What about the children?" he went on.

"My father tells me you have spent much time with the children. How will they ever learn our ways if they are trapped on government land?"

"I guess they probably won't," she said as the full impact hit her. "I suppose after a generation or two, their heritage and way of life will be lost forever."

"Then you finally understand."

Angry tears stung her eyes, and again Dominique had to fight to keep them in. She understood only too well. But did he? Did Jacob understand that more than the Dakota way of life was at stake? Did he realize that both her husband *and* a large chunk of her family might very well be taken from her before this senseless hostility between the Indians and the soldiers ended?

Unaware of her turmoil, Jacob stroked her hair as he thought back to some of the things Chief Gall had told him. "My father says you spend many hours drawing in the dirt with the children. What do you show them?"

Pushing her dark thoughts to the back of her mind, she said, "How to draw more precise pictures, like the eagle I painted on your tipi. They are very bright and eager to learn." Lifting her head and looking into Jacob's eyes, she added, "I've also begun teaching them the alphabet. I could do the same for you, if you're interested."

Lost in her expressive brown eyes, touched by her offer, he raised his brows and whispered, "So you know."

"I figured it out after I found my note in your pocket. Why didn't you just tell me you couldn't read?"

Jacob shrugged. "I thought about it, but then I would have been forced to explain, to think of more lies. I have no stomach for lies."

"Hah!" she exclaimed. "Then you must have an ulcer the size of Lake Erie."

He grinned and amended his statement. "I have no stomach for *unnecessary* lies. Tell me about this lake you speak of. Where is it?"

"Lake Erie? My home in Michigan is very near its shores."

Jacob's features softened, and his eyes grew narrow as he listened to her. "This home on the lake—do you miss it terribly?"

"Not as much as I used to," she admitted. Lowering her lashes, trying to hide a sudden surge of guilt, she added, "Since becoming your woman, not near as much as I should."

Jacob slid her chin into the V between his thumb and forefinger and forced her to look into his eyes. "Have you grown unhappy as my woman? Do you wish for me to set you free?"

"Oh, no, Jacob!" Her large eyes grew even bigger as she tried to explain. "If I have any wish at all, it is for your safety and the safety of my family. I do understand how you feel about your people, really I do, but I'm afraid you've forgotten about mine. What about my family and their way of life? Would you have your people shoot them without a thought for me?"

"I have not forgotten about you or your family." Jacob stroked her cheek as he slowly shook his head. "I don't wish to see you or even your fierce uncle the general hurt in any way, but it is not my people who chase him. He chases us."

"Oh, damn it all!" she complained with a heavy sigh. "I know that. I just . . . I wish we could all be safe and happy, that we could all find a way to live together in peace."

"That is a very big wish, my crazy wife."

"I know," she whispered softly. "But I am asking that you do everything you can to make it come true."

Not one to make idle promises, Jacob gazed into her eyes for a very long moment before he finally said, "I will do all that I can, *wi witko*. If I have to go to your uncle on my knees, I will. I give you my word that I will do whatever is in my power to keep us all safe."

This time, when the tears erupted, Dominique's efforts to stop them were fruitless. She tried to turn away from him, but Jacob's grip on her chin tightened and he kept her face within inches of his.

"Why do you find it necessary to do this to me, crazy one? You know how it upsets me."

"I—I'm s-sorry," Dominique sobbed. "But this time I can't h-help it. You've just made me the happiest woman in the w-world."

Jacob released her chin and began brushing the tears from her cheeks. "First you tell me I make you so happy you hurt inside; then I make you happy enough to cry. I fear that one day I might do something that will make you so happy you will drop over dead."

Dominique's sobs dissolved into laughter. She threw her arms around Jacob's neck and pressed her cheek to his. "I love you so much," she breathed into his ear. "No matter what happens, always remember that I love you."

"And I you, *wi witko*," he whispered back. "You will be with me in spirit wherever I go, whatever becomes of me."

The urge to cry stronger than ever, Dominique abruptly sat up, straddling her husband's hips, and looked around. She blinked, pushing back the tears, wishing a simple blink of her eyes would make her problems disappear as easily, then continued to glance around the beautiful countryside.

The midday sun burned bright, kissing the lush greens of the long grass and low bushes. The scent of late spring and rebirth was all around them even as they spoke of death and the end of life as they both knew it. Dominique trained her vision to the west, staring out at the low grassy hills and benches, and thought of the valley two hundred feet below.

If she ignored that valley, the overwhelming size of the Indian villages, and their ominous threat, Dominique could almost believe that she and Jacob were the only two people on earth. She could forget their troubled future and concentrate only on the present. She had Jacob's promise, knew if there was any way to end this terrible conflict, he would find it. She could ask no more of him.

Her attention caught by the sounds of low, soft nickering, Dominique looked over at the horses. Sampi stood, almost protectively, at Peaches's side and nipped playfully at her withers. The mare's response was a high-pitched squeal—and a swaying movement that brought her flanks in contact with the stallion's.

Thinking back to the night Jacob had made her his—spoiled her, as he put it—Dominique realized her time for asking was at an end. It was her turn to give. "It seems, my wonderful husband," she said with a mischievous smile, "that our horses have a much better idea of what to do on this beautiful sunny day than we do."

His grin equally mischievous, Jacob said, "I have not run out of ideas where you are concerned, crazy one." Then he pushed up on his elbows, preparing to lift her off his hips, but Dominique pressed her hands against his chest and forced him back down in the grass.

"No," she ordered. "Save your energy for your long ride back to the cavalry in the morning." At his cocked eyebrow, she seductively said, "Since I'm already here, I'd like to practice a few of the things I've learned from riding Peaches. How would you like it if I spoiled you for a change?"

"Oh?" Jacob's eyebrow inched up another notch, but he turned his palms up in submission.

Using exaggerated movements, taking her time, Dominique stretched her arms high overhead and pulled off her buckskin dress. Slowly, almost imperceptibly grinding her hips against Jacob's as he lay expectantly on a bed of grass, she tugged at the satin ribbon on her camisole. Delighted to see her husband's deep blue eyes darken with desire, she ran her tongue across her upper lip as she removed the undergarment.

And then she sat there, acting for all the world as if she had no audience, and allowed her fingers to slide down her breasts and off the tips on a journey to the drawstring of her drawers. Squirming against him, she played with the bow, loosening it the barest inch at a time.

Jacob reached for her. "That's enough," he said gruffly.

Dominique slapped his hands away. "No, it's not. I'll let you know when it's enough."

"Maybe you will," he warned, pressing his hips against her bottom, "and then again, maybe you won't."

"Jacob," she countered as she rose and stepped across his body. "Get a hold of yourself. Let me have some fun."

"You can have all the fun you want, crazy one," he said as he watched her remove her drawers. "I do not know how long you'll have to enjoy it."

Stripped now, Dominique stepped back over Jacob's body. But instead of lying down with him, she stood above him, bracketing his hips with her long legs. She looked down at him, shocked by her own boldness, tremendously pleased by his reaction, and said, "Aren't you a little over-dressed, husband dear?"

With a hoarse gasp, a low moan, Jacob fumbled around with suddenly inept fingers as he tore at the rawhide thong securing his breechclout. Unable to turn away from her even for an instant, he let his glassy-eyed gaze follow the curves of her cream-colored legs to her auburn forest, where it lingered, first seeking, then adoring her secrets. His breath coming in short puffs now, the words thick with passion, he managed to say, "If it is your wish to make me as crazy as you are, I think you should know—it is working."

Increasingly self-conscious about her indecent posture, Dominique impatiently said, "Have you gone and tied the strings in a knot?"

When he didn't answer, but continued to stare up at her as he struggled with the garment, she slowly sank to her knees, hovering just above his upper thighs. "Here, let me do that."

"No," he choked out. "Stay back—this will keep us apart no longer." Then he reached for his hunting knife, slipping it from the sheath, and cut through the rawhide laces securing not only the breechclout but the holster as well.

"Oh, Jacob," She laughed as he tossed the ruined garment into the furrow. "How are you ever going to get back to the village?"

"I don't know, and I don't care," he said with a tongue suddenly too big for his mouth. "All I care about right now is you. Get down here and teach me this lesson you speak of."

Dominique grinned, inching her knees along the sweet grass, but stopped just short of touching him. "You're sure you're ready for lesson one?"

"You can see that I am, woman."

"All right," she said, her own breathing erratic. "First we'll start with the letter A. A is for Apache. An A is nothing more than a tipi with a lance drawn through the middle. Now, B is for buffalo—"

"Buffalo *hides*!" he threatened. "And if you don't tend to your husband—*now*, woman—you'll be tanning them for the rest of your life!"

Her laughter deep and throaty, Dominique slowly lowered herself on the man she loved, the only man she would ever love.

Later that evening after a supper of barbecued antelope, Jacob and Dominique strolled hand in hand through the Hunkpapa village and headed down to the river.

The sound of the pretty stream, its cold waters trickling a little song as it made its way to the Big Horn River, the gentle rustling of the cottonwood trees in the light summer breeze, all provided stark contrast to the unrest all around them. But still intent on enjoying his wife, of committing to memory what might be their last night together, Jacob sat down on the grassy banks and pulled Dominique onto his lap.

"The Greasy Grass River reminds me of the Black Hills," he commented, struck by nature's bounty.

"Ummmm," she sighed. "It's so peaceful and lazy. If all the streams in the Black Hills are like this, I can't wait for you to take me there. You will someday, won't you?"

"If I can."

Dominique raised her head up from Jacob's shoulder and looked into his eyes. "What do you mean by that?"

"We must make some plans now, *wi witko*." He took her trusting face in his hands and explained. "After tomorrow, when I return to the cavalry, it may be a long time before I can return to you."

Trying to keep the fear from her voice, the tears from her eyes, she said, "How long?"

Jacob shrugged. "I do not know. I only know it is time for us to make some . . . arrangements for your safety if I cannot be here to take care of you."

"Stop it, Jacob. I don't like the way you're talking to me or the things you're saying. Stop it this minute."

"But I must," he insisted, still holding her face. "Surely you don't want me to go away from here with thoughts of you heavy on my mind."

"No, of course not," she cried, flinging her arms around him and burying her face in the side of his neck. "But please don't talk as if you're never coming back to me. I can't stand to think about that."

"Then don't think at all. Just listen to what I say and promise you will do as I ask." When he got no response, he gently said, "Dominique? You must promise that you will do as I ask."

And finally she did, with a sob she couldn't swallow and a light nod.

"Good, then." Jacob raised his hand to her hair and stroked the silky waves. "If I cannot prevent a battle between your people and mine, you must do all you can to protect yourself. No one will do it for you. Do you understand this?"

Again, a slight nod.

"If the soldiers come into our camp, show yourself and go with them. They—"

Tearing free of his hands, she sat up. "But Jacob, I'm not leaving here without you. I'll wait until—"

"You promised," he cut in with a finger to her mouth.

"Listen and do what I say. Go with the soldiers. Understand?"

Through a miserable sigh that was half sob, she said, "Oh, all right."

"The soldiers will be looking for you if they come into camp," he continued. "Some of them hope you are still alive, especially Barney and the uncle you call Boston. I have a very difficult time around them when they talk of you and your unfortunate ordeal."

In spite of her heavy heart, Dominique managed a small chuckle. "I suppose you have to stifle the urge to tell them just how alive I am, don't you?"

Joining her laughter, Jacob pressed his mouth to her hair, whispering, "I believe at least one of them would claim my life if he had that information."

"Please," she moaned, saddened again, "don't even talk about your life in those terms."

Jacob's entire body stiffened at Dominique's words. After easing her to the grass beside him, he quickly sprang to his feet and walked to the water's edge.

Alarmed, Dominique pushed up off the bank and tiptoed up behind him. "Jacob?" she whispered softly. "What is it? What did I do?"

She'd merely pointed out what should have been obvious to him all along. The only way he could hope to prevent this looming conflict, his best chance at convincing either side of the futility of the coming battle, would be to place himself in dire jeopardy. And if he had to go to these extremes in order to keep his promises, there was every possibility they would never see each other again. He would not let what could be their last night together be spent with heavy hearts.

Jacob turned and pulled her into his arms. Rocking her, squeezing her so tight neither of them could breathe, he said against her hair. "Come, *wi witko*. Tonight is ours and we will talk of the future no more. Come with me, my wife. Our tipi beckons."

Chapter Nineteen

%

Yellowstone River at the mouth of the Rosebud, June 21, 1876

"JESUS, STOLTZ," BARNEY REMARKED AS HE APPROACHED Jacob. "You look like hell."

Raising tired bloodshot eyes to his friend, Jacob shrugged.

Barney sat down beside him on the wooden dock where a steamer, the *Far West*, was tied, and leaned back against a sack of grain. "How come you keep letting the general send you out on these fool missions?" he asked. "You're gonna get yourself killed—that is, if you don't drop dead of exhaustion first."

Again Jacob shrugged, too tired to think of anything except the conference going on among the army officers aboard the steamship.

"Does it have something to do with Dominique?" Barney ventured, his voice low and sympathetic. "Is that why you keep volunteering for Sioux target practice?"

Jacob glanced at him, then looked away. Able to tell his friend most of the truth for a change, he allowed a weary smile and nodded. "I suppose she has a lot to do with it. Everything that has happened to her is my fault."

"Look, buddy, you can't go on blaming yourself." Barney began spinning the brim of his hat around in his hand. "I can see how you must feel about that gal. I know— I think I can understand, feeling the way I do about the widow Swenson, you know, what you must be going through." Feeling as awkward as he'd been that first night with Hazel, he stumbled onward. "Look, you really should think about something else. Try to, you know—"

"My friend," Jacob said, his smile warm and grateful. "If you're trying to make me forget about Dominique, you're doing a poor job of it. In fact, you're beginning to sound just like her."

Barney blew out a heavy sigh. "I know I ain't too good with words, but what I'm trying to tell you is that you should just forget her. Bury her."

Jacob's sluggish eyes popped open. "*Bury* her?"

"You know, pretend like. That poor gal has been with those savages for over a month now. You might be better off spending your time and energy hoping they've killed her. Believe me, if she's still alive, what's left of her ain't gonna be worth saving."

The breath whooshed out of Jacob, but he stifled the urge to laugh, not to gasp in horror. Averting his gaze, he covered his face with a big hand and shook his head.

"Sorry, buddy," Barney said. "I didn't mean to upset you. I just thought it was time you looked at the facts."

Jacob lifted his head and gave the lieutenant another grateful smile. "Thanks, Barney. I know you're trying to make things better for me and I do appreciate it, but I'll never bury Dominique—in my mind or otherwise. I just know she's alive and well. I know it in here." He pressed his hand to his chest, and again he smiled.

"Stoltz, don't do this to yourself. It ain't healthy."

"My friend," Jacob said, feeling the significance of the word for the first time with a white man. "I appreciate what you are trying to do for me, but it is—"

Jacob cut off his own words as a group of officers ended their conference and began marching down the gangplank from the steamer. Generals Terry and Gibbon disembarked first, followed by Custer and an officer Jacob had never seen before. He jumped to his feet, saluting the officers as they passed by.

"Lieutenant Woodhouse?" Custer called out, ignoring

the private. "We march on up the Rosebud tomorrow. Follow me to my tent. We've a few things to go over."

"Yes, sir!" Barney snapped, saluting as he followed the officers through the dusty trail.

Tagging along, hoping to remain undetected, Jacob fell in step, but when the men reached Custer's tent, the general turned and furrowed his brow. "What is it, Private?"

Jacob was running out of time, left with few choices if he hoped to find a way to prevent the imminent war. He removed his hat, struggling to sound suitably respectful, and said, "I wish to speak with you, sir."

Custer raised a thick auburn brow and shook his head. "Later, Private. Can't you see I'm planning our next strategy?" He turned to step inside, but hesitated, adding, "Maybe you heard me say that we'll ride in the morning. Go get some rest. You look like hell." Then he disappeared into the tent.

Three days later, a full twenty-four hours earlier than planned, Custer's command reached the well-worn Indian trail leading from the Rosebud to the Little Bighorn Valley. There was no doubt in Custer's or any soldier's mind, that they had at last found their quarry.

Jacob rode up alongside the general as he gave orders for camp to be set up. He took a deep breath, realizing he was so close to his own village he could almost smell the evening meal cooking and the hint of lilacs in Dominique's hair. In spite of that, Jacob somehow managed to say, "General Custer, sir? May I have a word with you?"

"Private Stoltz?" Custer frowned, then stared back out at the wide path. "What in hell do you want?"

"A word. A private talk."

Custer heaved a tired sigh. "Do you have any idea how close we are to rounding up those hostiles? Can you guess how very occupied I am at this time? Please go help the others set up camp and leave me to my thoughts."

But Jacob had finally run out of time. He couldn't afford to be put off again. "I am sorry, sir, but this is very important. I have information for you regarding these hostiles.''

''Oh?'' His attention drawn, Custer glanced at the soldier. ''Well? If it's something you think I should hear, spill it.''

''You need to hear this, sir.'' Jacob narrowed his steel blue eyes, adding. ''But it is most important that our talk be heard by no one else.''

Custer regarded him for a long moment, then shook his head in frustration. ''Oh, all right, Private. This is highly irregular, but I could stand to sit down on something besides this horse for a spell.'' He dismounted, encouraging Jacob to do the same, then strode across the river valley to his tent.

Once inside, he showed Jacob to a low box taken from the supply wagon, then sat down on another. ''All right, Private. What's this all about?''

''You cannot lead your men farther up the valley.''

''Excuse me, Private? Are you trying to tell me and the best military minds in the army that you know better how to run this campaign than we do?''

''No—yes—that does not matter. What I know about this foolish mission, I have learned from the Sioux themselves.''

''Oh, have you, now?'' Custer said, his thick mustache twisted in a smirk. ''Say something I can use now, Private, or get out.''

Jacob swallowed hard, knowing his next words might land him in the brig—or worse. ''I have seen the hostile camp firsthand. You face not a few warriors but the entire Dakota nation. They stretch the full length of the Greasy Grass River.''

''The *what*, Stoltz?'' Custer narrowed one eye and leaned forward. ''Are you aware that 'Greasy Grass' is the Sioux name for the Little Bighorn River?''

Jacob averted his gaze for a moment, then went on. ''I know only that you face many more warriors than you would suppose.''

Suspecting now that he spoke to a madman rather than a soldier with valuable information, Custer decided to humor him. He rose and said, "Well, thanks, Private. I'll be sure to take this information under advisement. Now if you don't mind, I have several hours' worth of work to accomplish."

"But I do mind!" Jacob exploded as he jumped to his feet. "I mind that you will not listen to me, that you do not care enough for my people or your own to try to understand what I'm trying to say!"

"Private," Custer warned, "you are within one word of getting yourself arrested, even as we stand on the eve of war. Don't think for a minute just because we face a few hostiles, our rules and regulations will be relaxed."

"And I say, respectfully, sir, to hell with your rules and regulations!"

"You're out of order!" Custer made as if to stomp from the tent, but Jacob stepped between him and the opening in the tent.

Custer's determination and inborn arrogance wavered as he stared into the eyes of the private, this madman who made nearly two of him. Lowering his tone, yet trying to keep an underlying threat in his words, he said, "What you're doing here can be considered insubordination, at the very least, Private. Perhaps you're overwrought and have been pushed too hard the last few weeks. If that's the case, I can make some allowances for what's happened here, but I will not tolerate any further—"

"Why won't you listen to me?" Jacob cut in, no longer interested in protocol or his own safety. "I tell the truth. There are over nine hundred lodges in the valley. Do you know how many warriors await your arrival?"

Custer's small eyes grew round, their centers hard, as he made the calculations. If what the private said was even close to the truth, he faced not a few hundred, but a few *thousand* hostiles. Where had this green soldier gotten his information? Could he believe even a little of what the private had to say?

As he stared into those intense sapphire-blue eyes, warm trickles of foreboding suddenly skittered across Custer's chest. He took a backward step. "I—I don't see why I should believe you. How could you possibly have obtained such information and lived to tell about it?"

"I told you," Jacob said quietly. He was out of options, and he knew what he had to do now. Harboring no regrets, thinking only of his promise to Dominique, he admitted, "All I know I learned from the Dakota themselves. I have lived among them for almost twenty winters. They are my family."

Custer's heart began to pound as he studied the man for signs of deceit. He could find none. "That's just ridiculous. I don't believe you for a minute."

"I have spoken the truth. I ask only that you send your men back to the fort and let my people go. There is no need for bloodshed."

"I make the decisions around here," Custer said, his arrogance overriding his uncertainty. "And I think you've gone crazy, running scout for me so much. That's not so unusual." He wiped a damp palm across his mustache and went on. "I'm going to make it easy on you and have you sent back to the *Far West*. You can accompany the wounded back to the fort, with no questions asked. I'm offering you a way out, Private. You'd best take it."

"And you, sir, had best listen to what I have to say. Retreat while there's still time."

Custer stared at the private, his mind spinning with possibilities. There was something here, some little thing he ought to believe, but what was it? What if the madman *was* telling the partial truth? Maybe he did have some kind of friendship with the Sioux, Custer suddenly thought, but what if his warnings were meant to *protect* the hostiles because there were so *few* instead of so many lodges waiting on the banks of the Little Bighorn?

His confidence again on the rise, Custer raised his chin. "Thank you for the information, Private. I'll be sure to consider all you've told me here. In the meantime, I'm going to have to place you under arrest. When we return to Fort Lincoln, you will be subject to a general court-martial.''

"Fool!'' Jacob spat, down to his last chance of convincing the bullheaded soldier of what he faced. He grabbed a handful of the general's shirt and hauled him close to his face. "If you attack the Dakota, you will also attack your own flesh and blood! Dominique lives! She is with these *savages*!''

Custer's naturally pale skin blanched even further as he listened. Then he drew his snub-nosed revolver and drove it into Jacob's throat. "Take your hands off me, Private.''

Jacob released the material, but didn't move, didn't avert his suddenly menacing gaze.

"You've made a lot of mistakes here tonight, Private,'' Custer went on between clenched teeth. "But one of the biggest was even mentioning the name of my niece in connection with this wild tale about the Sioux.''

"I am sorry you feel that way,'' Jacob answered, his jaw tight. "But I thought you might want to know she is well and happy—and will soon be caught in your gunfire.''

"Lies,'' Custer spat, "all lies! Dominique, even if she is alive, couldn't be happy in a Sioux village. Do you take me for an idiot? Now tell me the truth! If you have seen her, tell me when and where, soldier. I want the truth *now*—that's an order!''

A hot glare of loathing passed through Jacob's eyes, shook his thick body down to his boots, before he was able to say, "I have most recently seen her—alive and *happy*—in my very own lodge.'' Without thinking, he recklessly added, "I have taken Dominique as my woman.''

Custer buried the barrel of the gun into Jacob's throat. "You son of a bitch!'' he screamed, grinding his teeth. "Take that back this minute or I'll blow your goddam head off!''

"Go ahead,'' Jacob sneered. "Shoot me, but be sure

to tell Dominique of this conversation. Tell her what her husband tried to do before you murdered him."

Enraged beyond any fury he'd ever experienced, Custer pulled the hammer back on the gun, but at the last minute, some small ration of logic kept him from pulling the trigger. Custer himself had once been court-martialed, for something very close to the act he was about to perform. Was this lying private worth his career? And perhaps the presidency?

Still grinding his teeth, he lowered the gun to Jacob's chest and shoved. "Turn around, Private. That's an order!"

Jacob assumed the general was finally considering his warning. Understanding that if he wanted to see Dominique alive again, he must obey the general now, Jacob made a slow circle. Before he completed the arc, the gun crashed against his temple. Jacob dropped to the ground.

Custer backed out of the tent, calling to the first officer he spotted. "Lieutenant Woodhouse, get over here—on the double!"

Barney loped to his commander's side. "Yes, sir?"

"I've found it necessary to place Private Stoltz under arrest. Get a length of rope."

"My God, General, sir! What'd he do?"

"That's no concern of yours, Lieutenant! Get the rope now. Be quick about it before he comes to and I have to shoot him."

Barney gulped, then dashed off to the supply wagon.

While he waited, Custer kept one eye on the big German lying on the floor of his quarters as searched the campground for his officers. Finally spotting Major Reno, he called to him, "Reno, bring Benteen. Be quick. We have a change of plans."

Barney returned with the rope then, gasping and out of breath, and stood there waiting for his next order.

"Tie him," Custer said. "Bind his hands behind his back as tight as you can; then do the same to his feet. It wouldn't be a bad idea to connect the hands and feet with another length.''

"My God," Barney muttered again, near tears as he began to tie his friend. "What'd he do, General?"

"He's insubordinate, and he's a traitor, Lieutenant. Those are the charges for now." He glanced up, watching for his officers, and added, "I suspect when I return from the battlefield, I'll be adding more."

"A *traitor*, General?" Barney choked out. "I can't believe that of Jacob. He's—"

"You are not to second-guess me. You are to guard this tent and guard it with your life. Is that understood, or would you like to join the private?"

"Understood, sir." Barney snapped off a salute, then marched to the opening in the tent. Taking up a position just outside the flap, he observed as the general joined two other officers a few feet away.

"We have to ride out tonight," Custer said to the surprised officers.

"Tonight? But the men and horses are exhausted," Major Reno complained.

"And we're already ahead of schedule," Captain Benteen said, trying to sound respectful to a man he abhorred. "Maybe you have forgotten that General Terry warned us not to get greedy about this. He said we're supposed to wait until Sunday when we're at full manpower and go in all at once."

"There's no time for that," Custer barked, impulsively adding a statement that wasn't entirely true. "And General Terry isn't in charge of you men—I am. I say we go tonight and take them by surprise. I have word the Sioux know we're here, and they also know that we don't plan to march on them for a couple of days."

Major Reno's brows shot up. "Where'd you hear—"

"That doesn't matter," Custer sliced in. "What does is that we get our plans straight. Here's what we'll do."

The three men hunkered down and Custer began to draw a diagram in the soft earth with a stick. "I think it'll be best if we separate into three groups and surround the Sioux. There will be no running away from us this time. Reno, take your men to the southern end of the Little Bighorn Valley. Benteen, you go straight to the southwest. I'll take my group up north along the bluff. That ought to do it.''

"That ought to do it," Major Reno echoed, exchanging glances and a disgusted shake of his head with Benteen. "That might just do it all right."

The following afternoon Dominique walked along the banks of the river, remembering the conversation she'd had with Jacob just six days ago. She gazed into the water, so clear the pebbles lining the bottom stared back at her like little eyeballs, and wondered if he had managed to do the impossible. Had Jacob found a way to turn her uncle's army back?

She glanced up and noticed a large dirty cloud rolling toward her from the south. A dust storm? she idly wondered. Then Dominique heard the screams of women and children, the shouting of a general alarm. She jumped to her feet, her heart in her throat, and began running toward the great dust cloud.

As she neared the rolling apparition, soldiers suddenly appeared through the earth-colored fog. Dominique slid to a stop and buried her fist in her mouth. *"N-nooooo,"* she screamed, strangling on her knuckles, her fear. "God, no!"

Dominique stood there, paralyzed by her terror and by the unwillingness of her mind to accept the message her vision sent.

Then she witnessed the unspeakable.

Amid the rifle fire, the screams of terror and agony, she watched a United States Cavalryman run down a fleeing woman, a squaw she recognized as one of Chief Gall's wives, and then fire point-blank into her unprotected back. The bullet passed through the Indian woman's body and through that of the child she carried in her arms as well.

Dominique swooned, nearly fainting, but her anger, her rage, quickly cleared her head. Able to propel her legs again, she charged the soldier, screaming as she ran. "Stop it! Stop it, you bastard!"

As a screaming woman approached him, the soldier turned in his saddle and raised his rifle. When he peered down the sights and positioned his finger on the trigger, a cloud of beautiful red-gold hair filled the sights. "Huh?" he said, startled, as he looked up from the gun. "Well, I'll be damned."

She was upon him now, and before the soldier could say another word, Dominique grabbed the barrel of the rifle and jerked it out of his hands. Swinging it as hard as she could, she arced it upward and cracked the soldier alongside the head with the butt of the weapon.

After the man hit the ground, Dominique tossed his rifle toward the river, then pulled herself up onto his horse. Wheeling the animal around, she plunged headlong into the dust cloud, screaming as she rode, "Who's in charge here? Where is General Custer? Take me to the general!"

Surprised soldiers parted, making way for the mad-woman as she galloped through their ranks, but none tried to stop her until a horse veered up alongside her and a big hand reached out and grabbed her reins.

"Whoa, now!" Major Reno called out. "Easy, now."

Dominique glanced over at the officer, but didn't really look at him. She repeated her demands. "Take me to General Custer. This must stop now!"

"Dominique? It is you, isn't it?"

Catching her breath, working to slow her rapid pulse, she studied the officer more closely. "Major Reno? For God's sake! Stop this!"

"Take it easy, girl. I'll get you to safety."

"No! Where's my uncle? Make him stop this!"

In spite of her protests, Reno kicked his mount in the flanks and began leading her away down thorough the col-umn to the rear. "He's not with this group," he shouted above the din, "but he's going to be mighty thrilled to see you. I'll have a soldier take you to safety."

"But I don't want to go to safety!" She grabbed at the reins, but Reno held fast. "I want this stopped, you murderer! Stop it now!"

"Dominique, I'm sure you've been through hell these past weeks, but I can't take time to explain anything to you right now." He beckoned to a soldier, a sergeant major he trusted implicitly, then said to her, "Go with this man. Your uncle will explain all this later if you're still interested."

She opened her mouth to object, to complain about the outrageous cruelties she'd witnessed, but then Dominique remembered Jacob's words: "If the soldiers come into our camp, show yourself and go with them." She'd promised him that she would.

Swallowing hard, fighting the urge to look back at the Hunkpapa village, Dominique bit her lip and allowed the sergeant major to lead her away from the battle.

All through the night and into the next day Jacob worked to free himself from his bonds. Finally, as bright sunlight trickled in through the crack in the tent flap, he pulled a raw and bleeding wrist through the loop and quickly removed the rest of his bindings. His head pounded and he was disoriented. Crawling on his hands and knees, he silently made his way to the opening and peered out. All was quiet, save for a few summer birds singing their love songs. Jacob stuck his head through the flap, then ducked back inside. Barney sat on a chair to his right. From his quick observation, the lieutenant appeared to be asleep.

Jacob rubbed his aching temple. A Dakota warrior wouldn't even have to stop and think. He would simply reach through the opening and break Barney's neck. But Jacob could no longer think like a warrior, could barely think at all. There had to be another way out.

Again peering through the opening, Jacob inched the flap open. He studied his sleeping friend for a moment;

then he struck. He whipped his arm around Barney's head, firmly clasping his palm across the surprised soldier's mouth, and dragged him inside.

"Do not fight me," Jacob implored in a whisper. When Barney's struggles ceased, he relaxed his grip but kept his hand over Barney's mouth. "I am sorry, friend. But I do what I must. Do you understand?"

Wild-eyed, confused, Barney nodded.

"I cannot explain everything to you now," Jacob went on. "But I must go after the general and try to stop him. This war cannot happen. Please forgive me for what I must do now."

And before Barney could understand or have any sense of danger, Jacob smashed him across the back of his head with his own gun. "I am sorry, my friend."

Jacob quickly bound him with the ropes he'd just escaped from, then checked his pulse. Relieved to feel life surging through Barney's veins, he whispered, "Rest well, my friend. Enjoy your long and happy life." Then he stole from the tent.

The camp was nearly deserted. On cat feet, Jacob crept over near the supply wagon where the surplus horses grazed. After choosing the fittest animal, Jacob silently coaxed it through the dense timber and heavy undergrowth, walking alongside the horse until he was well out of earshot of those who were left behind. Then he mounted up and urged the horse into a gallop.

He rode hard and fast, stopping only to allow his mount to rest. Hours later, Jacob pulled up and listened to distant echoes. Off to the south, where his own Hunkpapa village lay, he could make out the vague popping of occasional rifle fire. Ahead, to the north along Custer's path, tremendous bursts of gunfire resounded. There could be only one decision.

Heartsick, he galloped toward the northern bluffs. As he rode, the wind carried an ominous warning, a message of death to his ears, and a deep sense of failure nearly overcame him. Still, Jacob forged ahead.

By the time he reached the battlefield, an eerie silence had settled over the valley. Jacob rode to the top of a small bluff, then groaned as he made a visual sweep of the area. Puffs of dust and gun smoke rose above the dead, a shroud of sorts protecting the lifeless skin from the sun's burning rays. Sickened by the carnage, the mountain slopes carpeted with the bodies of red men and white men alike, Jacob slid down off his mount and fell to his knees in despair.

"*Why?*" he screamed, pounding his fist into the earth. "Why didn't anybody listen to me?"

In shock, unable to accept what his eyes told him, Jacob got to his feet and began walking through the field of bodies. Even in his dazed condition, he began to understood the futility the soldiers must have felt as their numbers were overwhelmed by his people. Many of the men died behind barriers constructed with the bodies of their own horses, shot no doubt by their loving masters in a last ditch effort to save themselves.

Jacob called a halt to his journey and sucked in a huge gulp of air as he caught sight of a thatch of red-gold hair. As he moved toward the fallen leader, Jacob's shoulders slumped and he groaned in frustration as he looked down on Custer's almost peaceful features. A small bullet hole near his temple and a dark stain at the side of his blue shirt were the only hints that the great general had not simply fallen asleep.

Again Jacob cried, "Why? Why couldn't you have listened to me?" He rubbed his eyes, then glanced around. Boston and Tom Custer lay nearby, their faces much more gruesome in death, the loss of their lives somehow more terrible. Thinking of Dominique and the white burial custom, Jacob looked around for a tool with which to dig a common grave for the Custer brothers. For her, he would try to save them from the final indignity.

Then up ahead he noticed movement. When he looked toward the ridge, he saw several warriors descending the slopes. His people would return to the field now to collect their wounded and dead. Then, to complete the final ritual they would strip, scalp, and mutilate their enemies to prevent their passage to the heavens.

As the Indians drew closer, Jacob recognized his father, Gall. Wearing his full headdress, he was a regal sight, a dramatic antithesis of the testament to death all around him. When the chief waved, acknowledging and greeting his son, Jacob's response was to turn his palms up and shrug, mutely asking the same question of his father that he'd asked of his wife's dead uncle.

From behind Jacob, a dying Cheyenne warrior caught the movement through hazy eyes. Spotting Jacob's cavalry uniform, determined that not even one of the soldiers would live to tell this tale, he raised his rifle.

"Death to all Long Knives!" he screamed as he began firing.

Jacob turned at the sound, but he was too late. He caught the full impact of the first round against his skull.

Two other bullets slammed into his body as he fell to the bloodied earth, but Jacob never felt them tear open his flesh.

Chapter Twenty

June 27, 1876

DOMINIQUE PACED UP AND DOWN IN HER SMALL CABIN ON
the steamship, the *Far West*. As she walked, she loosened
the collar of the shirt she'd borrowed from an officer, then
eyed her buckskin wedding dress, which lay on the bunk.
The heat was especially stifling in the confines of the cabin.
But here she was, decently covered in a man's long-sleeved
flannel shirt and a skirt hastily thrown together from one
of the ship's fine tablecloths. Again she eyed the more
comfortable buckskins, then sighed and crossed over to
the porthole.

Where was Jacob? she asked herself for the thousandth
time. What had become of her uncles? She stared out at
the Little Bighorn River and at the calm waters and un-
scarred landscape where the ship was docked. Only a few
miles upriver, the battle still raged. The memories of the
horrors she'd witnessed added to the perspiration on her
brow. Hoping to catch a gust of fresh air, Dominique
pushed the porthole open. The minute her fingertips
touched glass, the crew below began shouting. She froze.

A horse burst through the bushes near the water's edge.
Dominique lurched against the glass panel, her heart thundering in her ears, and strained for a better view. Then
she noticed the lathered animal carried a naked Indian.
Dominique watched, dry-mouthed, as the savage waved
his rifle, but she slumped with relief when the crew members surrounded him in greeting.

"Sioux, Sioux, Sioux!" the Indian screamed as he fell to the ground.

Dominique ran out of her room to the top deck of the steamship. Leaning outward, she shouted down at the men below. "Captain Marsh! Please, Captain Marsh! What's happened? Is there word from the Seventh?"

The ship's pilot turned and regarded the panic-stricken woman. Holding up his hand to her, he whispered to a crew member so that Dominique would not hear his words. "What's Curly trying to tell us, Baker?"

The crewman shrugged as he studied the stick figures the Indian was drawing in the dirt. "I'm not sure, Captain. He—"

"Sioux, Sioux! *Absaroka!* Boom, boom," the savage shouted, stabbing his finger into his chest. "Boom, boom, *absaroka*!"

"Oh, Christ, Captain. He's talking about the cavalry. I think he's trying to say we've been whipped!"

Marsh glanced up at Dominique, then shook his head. "I can't tell her that on the word of a half-crazed Indian, especially after what she must have gone through in that Sioux camp. Try not to look so damned upset. Pretend he's just babbling on about nothing of any consequence."

Changing expressions as he turned back to the ship, the captain smiled up toward the railing. "It's nothing, Miss DuBois. Just one of your uncle's Crow scouts who got separated from the main group. You go back to your cabin and rest now. I'll be sure to inform you when I hear any news about your family."

But Dominique knew there was something more, some horrible news the Indian was trying to tell them about. Disheartened, she turned and slowly walked back to her cabin. Beyond tears, she stretched out on the narrow bunk, and tried to find a way to escape from the nightmare her life had become.

She slept in snatches, always alert to the slightest sound, and worked at filling her mind with hope. When the dawn broke, Dominique rose and crossed over to the porthole.

She was staring out, remembering her past, wondering what was left of her future, when again the quiet was shattered. A single frantic rider exploded through the willow thickets. This time the stranger wore the uniform of a soldier. And this time she was unable to move.

Certain she couldn't bear to hear his message, Dominique waited in her quarters. Her eyes dull, her hopes reduced to a bare flicker, she observed as the crew helped the exhausted man from his horse.

After a few moments, Captain Marsh looked up toward her window. He quickly turned away, then started up the gangplank.

Dominique swallowed hard, knowing he would soon bring her the news she'd been dreading. Holding her head high, she marched to her door and opened it, then stood there waiting to receive him.

Captain Marsh approached the cabin and uttered a gasp as he realized the door was open. "Oh, Miss DuBois, I—ah, excuse me, I don't mean to intrude."

"Please come in, Captain. I've been expecting you," she said, her voice sounding as if it belonged to someone else. "I have a feeling you finally have some news for me."

Marsh removed his hat, bowing his gray head as he tried to find the right words. "Yes, I'm afraid I do. Why don't you have a seat?"

"I'd rather stand, if you don't mind. Please, just tell me what you've found out. What's happened?"

"Well, I, ah—it's just terrible, ma'am. I don't know how I can even tell you after the dreadful experience you've already been through as a captive—"

"Why don't you forget about what did or didn't happen to me in the Sioux camp, Captain?" she said angrily. "I have. Now please tell me—do you have news of my uncle, of the Seventh?"

Unable to look her in the eye, Captain Marsh took a deep breath and finally spit it out. "I'm afraid that, to a man, your uncle's troops were wiped out. I'm sorry I couldn't bring better news.''

Dominique choked back a sob. ''What do you mean, to a man? Where's my uncle Armstrong? I demand to see him at once.''

''Please, Miss DuBois. Please sit down. Let me get you some water.''

''I don't want water, I want my uncle!'' *I want Jacob!* Dominique swallowed another sob.

''Please, ma'am. If you'll just sit—''

''Captain, I said I want to see my uncle.''

''Yes, ma'am I know you did, but I'm afraid you didn't hear me. You uncle—*uncles*,'' he corrected, ''are all dead, killed by the Sioux.''

Dominique sucked in a breath so painful she thought it might crack her ribs. She pressed her hand to her mouth and turned away, speaking through her fingers. ''And Boston? Boston, too?''

The captain brushed his hand across his eyes as he gave her a slow, painful nod. ''Both Boston and Tom. I—I thought I had talked Bos out of going. He told me he'd stay behind and play poker with me on the ship. I don't know what made him decide to mount up and ride off with the rest of them. I—I really liked that boy.''

''And Cousin Autie?'' she managed through a throat barely able to perform. ''Was he with Uncle Armstrong's men?''

''Autie Reed? Yes, I'm afraid so. He's gone, too,'' he said quietly.

A sudden rage swooped over her, spun her around, and sent her flying at the captain with talons of fury. ''How could you let Autie and Boston go?'' she demanded through a heart-wrenching sob. ''They were so young, so full of fun! They never had a chance to live—don't you understand? *They never lived!*''

The captain just stood there, allowing her to pound her fists against his chest until she'd exhausted her anger. When she finished, and stood before him panting for breath, Marsh held out his arms to receive her trembling body.

Dominique took a step back and lowered her head. "Please forgive me. I—I had no right to take my anger out on you. I realize you had no control over my uncle or his men."

"That's all right, Miss DuBois. I'm damn near as upset as you are by all this. I got to know several of those boys, especially the members of your family, over the last few weeks. I can't tell you how it grieves me to learn of their fate."

Marsh stared at her, pulling on his fingers as if he were stretching taffy, then began to make his way toward the door. "If you think you'll be all right now, I should get back to my crew. We have a lot of preparations to make before we can transport the wounded. Will you be—"

"*Wounded?* I thought you said they were all dead. Which is it, Captain?"

"In your uncle's group, there are no survivors," he reiterated. "But he divided his command three ways. I've been told to expect some wounded from Major Reno and Captain Benteen."

"Oh," she said softly.

"If that's all?"

"Yes, I suppose that's all. Thank you for coming to me as soon as you heard. If you receive any further word of—"

"You will be the first to receive any news, I promise you."

"Thank you, Captain." Barely aware of Marsh's reply or of the sound of her door closing, Dominique moved over to the porthole. *Jacob.* Where had Jacob been through all this? Riding with the Seventh Cavalry? Or attacking it with his Dakota family? Was he still alive or—

"No," she sobbed against the glass, refusing to think of him in any way except filled with vitality. "You can't be dead, my love. Jacob, please, let me know you're

alive—please. Are you out there somewhere looking for
me?''

South of the Little Bighorn, Jacob struggled to clear his
bruised and battered mind. He felt as if he were clawing
at something, swimming against the frigid current of some
raging river. Was it real? The muddy waters were dark
and icy, thick with the ashes of those who'd died at the
Little Bighorn. He was exhausted.

He tried to move his arms and legs, but his brain
couldn't make the connection. He felt himself being
dragged downstream again, swirling away into a starless
abyss, to the murky depths of hell. It was then that Jacob
realized he languished in a hell born of his shattered logic,
swam in a river of his own pain. He knew that now. He
also knew he was dying. Jacob renewed his battle against
the current, knowing he would have to fight his way out
of this imaginary river if he was to survive. His reward
was a distant light, a tiny beacon of encouragement. He
put forth his mightiest effort, and the light grew stronger.

''Dominique,'' he cried out, sure the light was the halo
of her golden-red hair. With superhuman strength he navigated the powerful waters using determination as his only
compass. When at last the colors of life, of springtime and
renewal beckoned, Jacob managed to move his arms. He
thrust his way out of hell for a moment and clung to the
banks of consciousness. He fought and struggled, desperate to pull himself onto the grassy plains of sanity, to lie
in the rays of a nurturing sun. To feel warm again. To live.

''Dominique,'' he called out again, but this time her
name was a distant gurgle in his throat.

Jacob's strength failed him. His arms grew numb. He
slid back into the frigid river of his mind, too weak to
cling to safety, too far gone to care. Fingers of ice pulled
him down into the cold dark waters and guided him back
to its frozen lair.

* * *

The following morning, Dominique leaned over the railing of the *Far West* and watched as the last of the wounded arrived. Some of the men walked, but many more were carried on stretchers or in the arms of the survivors. Numb in body and mind, Dominique observed the proceedings with weary eyes. Suddenly a soldier, limping slightly, caught her attention. She blinked, trying to awaken her senses, and pressed harder against the rail. The soldier's head was swathed in bandages, but his features were easily recognizable even in the vague light of dawn—*Barney Woodhouse!* But how was that possible? her incredulous mind asked. He'd always been a part of the general's command, directly attached to Custer's own company.

She stared harder, making certain of the identification, then allowed herself to hope. If Barney had survived, then maybe the captain had been wrong about the others. Maybe, she thought, her senses reeling, just maybe he'd been wrong about many of the stories he'd told her!

A surge of hope propelling her, Dominique twirled and ran along the railing to the gangplank. She hesitated a moment, suddenly overcome by the suffering, the terrible wounds of the surviving soldiers, then she plunged headlong through the able-bodied men until she found the one she sought.

"Lieutenant Woodhouse! Oh, Lieutenant!" she cried out, running across the muddy grass.

Barney looked up, surprised to hear a woman calling his name, then nearly fell over as Dominique threw herself into his arms. "Miss DuBois?" he gasped. "God almighty, you're alive!"

"Yes, yes, and so are you!" She pulled back from him, and stared into his haggard features. "What about Jacob? Have you seen him? Is he all right? Was he with my uncle? Please, Barney—is Jacob all right?"

Unable to look into her hopeful brown eyes, Barney turned his aching head as he took her by the arm. "Come on over here out of the sun and away from the others," he said in a whisper as he started for the cottonwood trees.

Barney glanced at her as they walked, wondering how he could tell her, how to explain the miracle of his rebirth. "Have you been told? Do you know what happened—"

"To the Seventh? Yes." She nodded, swallowing hard. "Captain Marsh said everyone was killed, but here you are! I thought he might be wrong, that maybe Jacob and the rest of my family were—"

"Don't," he said softly. "Please don't. The general and his men were wiped out two days ago. There's no doubt about that."

"But you're here!" she cried. "And you haven't said a word about Jacob. Please, Barney, if you know, tell me. Where's Jacob?"

He hung his head and slowly shook it. Then he told a half-truth. "I'm sorry, Miss DuBois, but the last time I seen Jacob, he was riding out after the general."

"But I don't understand!" she said, gripped with panic. "How come you're here if everyone in the Seventh is supposed to be dead?"

He took her trembling shoulders in his hands and told the story he'd settled on. The one he would tell for the rest of a life that had been miraculously returned to him. "Just before the Seventh pulled out, your uncle assigned me to guard a prisoner. I—I got stuck on guard duty watching some guy I never seen before. The general didn't even bother to tell me what the prisoner had done wrong, just told me to watch him till he got back."

"B-but," she sputtered, eyeing the bloody bandage wrapped loosely around Barney's skull, "you're wounded. If you didn't go with them, how—"

"I didn't say I was too good a guard. The prisoner got loose somehow, then split my scalp open when he made his escape. I got a lump the size of my fist on the back of my head."

But Dominique wasn't listening to his woes. She was frantic with worry, desperate to learn where Jacob had been during the battle. Had he been fighting against his own people, the Dakota, alongside her uncle Armstrong?

Or had he ridden into battle as a soldier, only to turn on the cavalry once the battle erupted? Or had he lurked on the fringes of the battleground, unable to do either? Dominique swayed against Barney's chest.

"Let me help you back to the ship, Miss DuBois," he offered as he noticed the glazed look in her eyes.

"What's happened to Jacob?" she said in more of a wail than anything. "Where do you think Jacob is now?"

"Honey," he said solemnly, "I think you'd better forget about him. I think he went the way of your family."

At his words, Dominique's tears finally fell. Jacob *was* her family, as much a part of her as the Custer blood chilling her suddenly frozen veins. A painful flood burst from her, splattering the front of Barney's shirt, soaking her own. She allowed the tears to fall for several minutes, gave in to the feelings of hopelessness and anguish. But then, as she thought of Jacob, of his strength, and of the love they'd shared, her tears ebbed as quickly as they'd begun.

Dominique stood erect, her shoulders square and proud. She glanced back toward the ship, heard the moans of the dying men, and wiped the final tear off her cheek.

"If you can manage that bump on your head by yourself, Barney," she said, her voice curiously distant, "I'd better go see what I can do to help the wounded." Then, without waiting for his reply, she turned and marched back to the gangplank.

"Well, I'll be damned," Barney muttered, thoughtfully stroking his straggly mustache. "If she don't beat all."

Then, as he'd done almost continuously since Jacob cracked his skull, Barney continued talking to himself, "Either that gal is a bigger chip off the ole Custer block than I thought or she's gone totally insane from living with those danged Sioux."

Although every available inch of space was occupied by over fifty wounded men, the *Far West* was assigned the unenviable task of speeding up the Yellowstone River, then on to the Missouri River to deliver the terrible message to Fort Lincoln and the world. In record-setting time, the steamship plowed through over seven hundred miles of water in only fifty-four hours. It was nearly midnight on July 5 when the overworked engines of the *Far West* finally shut down.

Sequestered in her cabin for some deserved rest after tending to the injured men for yet another full day, Dominique sat bolt upright on the bunk. The silent engines, producing more noise than her troubled mind could bear, coaxed her to place her aching feet on the floor. She stood, wobbly and dizzy, and staggered over to the porthole. The streets of Bismarck swarmed with men from the ship and townsfolk roused by their excited voices.

By the light of dawn, she would be transported to the fort. Too soon she would have to face her aunt, find a way to palliate Libbie's grief and endure her own.

Dominique took a breath of the stale night air. She'd grown strong over the past few weeks, she thought, wondering how she would handle this latest test. Finding a way to assuage Libbie's loss, and control her own feelings about losing the general and the others would be difficult but not impossible. What would she do with the part of her she would have to hide? Who would help her bear the loss of her own husband? Who was there to care?

Dominique rested her forehead against the glass as a new wave of panic swelled up in her throat. Still she thought of Jacob. Still she dared to dream he was alive.

"Jacob?" she said in a smothered whisper. "Jacob, please hear me. Please remember that I love you. Jacob . . ."

To the southwest, deep in the Bighorn Mountains and farther from Dominique than either of them could have imagined, Jacob struggled for lucid thought. Unable to remember how he'd been saved from his own confused mind, he realized that he'd somehow been pulled from the icy waters of his nightmares. Now he fought another element, one even more frightening than the cold death he'd faced.

Somehow his skin had become parched, felt as if his body had been buried in the scorched earth of the summer plains. He tried to move his limbs, to crawl along, digging into the blistering dirt and sand with his fingers on a search for life-giving fluids.

His tongue, swollen and cracked, filled his mouth. And still, though his voice was feeble, he managed to call for his woman. "Dominique."

A vast nothingness surrounded him, yet flames reached out, stabbing his fevered flesh at will, burning his already blistered body unmercifully. Jacob tried to open his eyes, struggled to get his bearings, but when he finally managed to crack one eyelid, the shock of the bright light sent a spiraling flame through his head. Never before had his pain been so overwhelming, so intense. But still he fought, still he struggled to find the way to his sanity, to his life. To his woman.

"Dominique," he whispered thickly, again renewing his fight.

His cries and struggles were suddenly tethered as strong hands swooped down on him, pinning him against the blistering earth. He opened his mouth to cry out, but his efforts filled his lungs with the same flames licking his body.

"Bring more water. His fever rises," a deep masculine voice ordered.

"He will die!" a woman wailed through an anguished sob. "He will die!"

"Silence!" the man said. "Get the water!"

Jacob heard those excited voices, wondered if the footsteps accompanying them belonged to an angry god. But then his battered brain gave up on him again. The flames of hell sucked him back into the abyss.

Chapter Twenty-one

Bismarck, July 25, 1876

BARNEY WATCHED LIBBIE CUSTER WALK OVER TO THE boardwalk; then he turned back to the rig. Holding out his arms, he smiled and said, "Now it's your turn, Miss DuBois. Lean over and put your hands on my shoulders."

With no outward emotion, still as unresponsive and tight-lipped as she'd been over the past two weeks, Dominique did as she was told and allowed Lieutenant Woodhouse to lift her from the buggy.

"There you go, honey," Barney said as he set her on the street. Still trying to get through to the nearly catatonic woman, he suggested, "Why don't you go stand over by your aunt and get out of the hot sun until your train is ready to leave?"

With a blank stare and a shallow breath, Dominique lifted the hem of her black silk mourning dress and followed his instructions.

Behind her, his heart breaking for both of the unfortunate women, he babbled on, even though he knew no one listened. "That's right. You get on out of the sun. I'll just go back to the buggy and unload all your luggage."

As Dominique neared the boardwalk where her aunt paced restlessly, a whoosh of steam caught her attention. Slowly turning, she glanced at the train that would carry her back to Michigan, back to her father—and away from what might have been.

The heaving machine beckoned, drawing her anguished

mind to a lovely day in May. She'd stood in very nearly the same spot then, watching Jacob. Loving him. Soothed by the memories, Dominique wandered over near the tracks. Even though billows of steam jetted toward her, adding to the discomfort of the miserably hot morning, she continued, caught by the shiny black engine. As she approached, she thought back to Jacob, to the wonder in his eyes, and to the child she could see exposed in them that day. Suddenly feeling close to him again, wanting only to share some small part of him, Dominique reached out to touch the engine, mimicking the action she'd seen him perform so long ago. The hot metal seared the pads of her fingers.

"Oh!" she cried out, as much with pain as with a sudden flash of insight. "Oh, my God!"

Reality shattered her reverie, drove its point home as if on the tip of a saber. And finally Dominique understood what her heart and body had been trying to tell her for the last two weeks.

Jacob lived! Not as her husband, not as the lover she ached to hold in her arms again. His life had been returned, continued, through a gift, a miracle of love. Jacob's fire still flickered, grew even larger—within her womb.

Through a sudden rush of tears, of joy, Dominique stumbled backward, lurching in a half-circle as she tried to regain her footing, her composure. *Jacob, oh, Jacob, did you know? Could you have guessed what you were leaving behind?* Overcome by the surge of emotions, drowning in a sudden wave of love, Dominique reached out, searching blindly for her balance.

Libbie watched, terrified that her niece would fall face down in the street. She called to Barney as she hurried down the boardwalk. "Lieutenant! Lieutenant, quick! Grab Nikki. She's going to faint."

In a daze of another kind now, Dominique barely noticed the strong arms supporting her or the dainty hands guiding her along the boardwalk to a bench. She sat when

Libbie gently pushed her shoulders down, but she stared at the train, her eyes moist and trancelike.

"There, there, dear," Libbie comforted as she sat down beside her. "It's going to be all right. Someday it's just got to be all right again." Struggling to hold in her own tears, Libbie lifted her handkerchief and began to fan her niece.

Flushed with joy, blooming with the first bud of happiness she'd felt since her last night with Jacob, Dominique allowed her lashes to flutter down on her florid cheeks.

Alarmed, Libbie looked up at Barney. "Well, don't just stand there, Lieutenant! Quick, go get a glass of water. Hurry!"

Then she turned back to her niece and tried to put her own pain aside. "There, there you poor dear. Don't let your grief or the horrible memories of your time as a captive overcome you. You must be strong. Autie would want it that way."

The sound of Libbie's voice, the words she knew must be terribly painful for her to speak, brought Dominique out of her trance. "Oh, Aunt Libbie, please don't worry about me. It's not that I'm so upset or that—"

She cut off her own words as she realized what she'd been about to say. How could she possibly tell Libbie about Jacob, about her love for the man she also called Redfoot? Her aunt would never understand. Dominique had no one with whom to share this moment of joy. She would have to hide her happiness at discovering the knowledge of her destiny, the newfound purpose in her life. Now that existence, her future, would include the birth of Jacob's child, she thought, suddenly radiant. She could go on with her life, fulfill this obligation lovingly, and perhaps deliver a special message as well. How could she ever explain what she must do now to her family?

She needed more time to think. Dominique's head slumped and her eyes closed as she feigned another dizzy spell.

"Oh, please, Nikki," Libbie cried. "Hang on. Be strong." She turned her head, peering around the corner, and muttered, "Where is the lieutenant with your water?"

Prepared now, Dominique straightened her shoulders. "I'm all right, really I am. It's just, well, I've finally realized that I can't leave here. I can't go home with you."

"What? But of course you can. You have to, dear."

"I—" Again she hesitated, more sure than ever what she must do, still uncertain exactly how to do it.

Finally settling on a half-truth, Dominique worked to produce the necessary distress in her voice. "W-we haven't talked about this before, but while I was a captive in the Hunkpapa village, certain things happened to me, things that—"

"No, Nikki." Libbie pressed a finger to her niece's mouth. "I understand these savages practice unspeakable abominations on white women. There is no need for us to discuss this. I've taken it for granted that you were badly used. It's best if you try to forget it."

"That's not possible," she answered with heavy innuendo in her tone. "We have to talk about it. You need to know that I was the woman of a warrior called Redfoot."

Color flooded Libbie's cheeks. She lowered her voice, insisting, "We don't have to discuss this, either, nor shall we. If these things still trouble you after we get back home, there are doctors who can help you get over it. Until then, you must try to put that degrading experience out of your mind."

"Putting it out of my mind isn't the problem, Aunt Libbie." Dominique took a deep breath and squeezed her eyes shut. "Putting it out of my body is."

Libbie screwed up her brow. "I don't follow you, dear."

Dominique expelled the breath and came right out with it. "Things haven't been normal with my body since I was kidnapped. I've been feeling ill and bloated. I thought it was because of, you know, all the changes and terrible things that happened, but— Oh, Aunt Libbie, I'm going to have Redfoot's baby.''

Libbie's head wobbled, and her breathing became rapid and shallow. When her eyes rolled to the back of her head, then closed, Dominique snatched the hanky from her hand and began to fan her brow.

Barney barreled around the corner at that moment, offering the expected glass of water. ''Here is it, Mrs. Custer. Sorry it took so long, but—'' His tongue froze to the roof of his mouth as he studied the women.

''Thanks, Barney,'' Dominique said as she accepted the offering.

''Ah, you're welcome,'' he said slowly, scratching his head. ''I'll just go finish . . .'' He let his words trail off as he backed down the boardwalk, a look of utter confusion flickering in his expression, ''The water y-you . . . she . . . I'll just go get the luggage.''

A smile tugging at her heartstrings, Dominique lifted the glass to her aunt's mouth. ''Take a drink of this,'' she encouraged.

Libbie gulped greedily, then sat up, waving Dominique and the glass off. ''I'm all right. It's just so hot today, and I—I'm a little . . .'' She turned and looked into her niece's eyes, and her own filled with tears. ''It's so awful!'' she burst out. ''So unfair! I'd give anything to be in that way, to have that much of my husband to keep with me always, but instead—instead, some stinking savage has—has—''

''Please stop it,'' Dominique cried, knowing exactly how Libbie felt, wishing not for their roles to be reversed, but that they could both be filled with the same joy.

''I'm sorry, dear,'' Libbie finally said, regaining her fragile control. ''Of course, I don't mean to suggest this is your fault in any way or that there was anything you could have done to prevent these circumstances. It's just all so unfortunate.''

''As unfortunate as it may be, it's a fact,'' Dominique went on, eager to end the increasingly uncomfortable conversation. "But now, at least, you understand why I can't go home. Why I can probably never go home."

But Libbie didn't agree. She patted her hand and said, "Now, now, dear. It's not as bad as it seems. After all, your condition is not entirely . . . irreversible."

"Aunt Libbie?" Dominique breathed as pinpricks of foreboding stabbed at her scalp. "What do you mean?"

"Just what I said. There are several chemicals—aloes and cathartic powders—we can obtain fairly easily. If that should fail, we can—"

"No!" Dominique jumped to her feet, horrified at the thought of losing Jacob's child. "You're talking about a miscarriage, about taking my baby away from me! I won't let you do it! I won't let anyone do it!"

"Nikki!" Libbie whispered between clenched teeth. "Sit down. You'll cause a commotion."

Dominique glanced around, then took a seat several feet away from her aunt. "I won't do it," she insisted. "You can't make me do it."

"All right." Libbie shushed her, waving her hands. "Just think about it, then. You'll come to your senses when you're not so overwrought."

"I am *not* overwrought. I'm pregnant."

"Nikki! Such language!" she said, louder than intended. "I must insist you get hold of yourself. You still have the Custer name to uphold. Please don't dishonor it with such talk, and don't even think of staining it by bearing the child of a savage."

Dominique's mind suddenly became that serene spot in the ocean at the eye of a storm. She moved closer to her aunt and folded her hand in hers. "I appreciate and understand your concerns, really I do, but the child is mine, too. This baby carries Custer blood as well as its father's. I can't bring any harm to it."

"Oh—oh, Nikki," Libbie cried, weeping for herself as much for as her niece. "You simply can't have this child! Whatever will you do? How can you possibly face your—"

"I lived with the Sioux—remember?" she said with a smile. "I can face anything. Here." Dominique returned her hanky. "Don't cry for me. I'll be all right."

"But how can you be? How—"

"All aboard!" the conductor hollered. " 'Board!"

"Oh, dear," Libbie sniffed. "We'll talk about this later. Come on, Nikki. We have to go now."

Dominique rose and walked down the boardwalk with her aunt, explaining as they neared the passenger cars, "I meant what I said. I can't go back home with you. Not now, anyway. Please give papa my love and tell him I'll write the first chance I get."

"But you have to return with me! Where will you go? How will you live?"

"I've been thinking about that." Her smile secret, manipulative, Dominique turned and watched Barney approach with their luggage. When he set the trunks down, she gave him a broad grin. "Thanks, Lieutenant."

"You're welcome, Miss DuBois. It's great to see you looking like yourself again before you leave."

"Oh, I'm not leaving. In fact, I'm hoping you and Mrs. Woodhouse won't mind some company—just until I can get a place of my own, you understand."

"Huh?"

"Oh, I realize you two are on your honeymoon, so to speak, but I promise not to be in the way too much. I'll just be a little mouse in the cupboard until I can sweet-talk a few of the soldiers into building a little place for me."

"Well, I don't know. That may be against the r-rules, and . . . Jeez, Miss DuBois, I—I don't know what to say."

"You don't have to say anything, Barney. I think I can still get what I want from the soldiers—at least for a couple more months anyway," she added, laughing to herself. "Are the Indian scouts still living at the fort?"

"Well, sure."

"And don't they have families—children?"

Barney scratched his head. " 'Course."

Explaining to both her aunt and the confused soldier, she said, "During my stay with the Sioux, I discovered that despite the language barrier, I was able to work with the little ones, teaching them art and even some English. I'll wager the army wouldn't mind putting up a little house for the new schoolmarm. What do you think?"

Barney shrugged. Libbie dabbed at a final tear.

"Well," Dominique went on, undaunted. "Even if they're not convinced at first, I believe they will be. I think it's about time *everyone* knew what these treaties say. Maybe next time the Sioux come to the bargaining table, they'll have some idea of what they're gaining—and what they're giving away."

"Last call!" the conductor warned. " 'Board!"

"Oh, dear, oh, dear me," Libbie fretted, filled with indecision.

"Come on, Aunt Libbie. You'd better get on that train before we both miss it."

"I don't know, Nikki, I just don't know if I should leave you here like this. What will your father say? He expects us to come back home together—and the danger you'll face! I just don't know."

"Barney and Hazel are going to take care of me." She whirled around, "Aren't you, Barney? Tell my aunt she doesn't have a thing to worry about."

Barney chewed on his lips, not sure where his allegiance should lie or what Hazel would say. He finally shrugged and said, "Well, sure, I don't see why the missus and I can't take care of her a bit if she just has to stay on. I wouldn't worry none about her, Mrs. Custer. We'll make sure she's all right."

"Oh, I just don't know . . ." Libbie wrung her hanky, twisting the fancy lace into little knots.

With an affectionate smile, Dominique leaned over and kissed her cheek. "Good-bye, Aunt Libbie. Be sure to give my love to Papa and Grandpa Custer." Then she pushed her up the steps and into the railroad car.

Dominique and Barney stood looking for Libbie's face to appear in a window, then waved as the stricken features of the general's widow appeared.

When the train finally began its journey east, Dominique started making plans. "Now, then," she said, taking Barney's arm. "Don't you think I could use Hazel's sewing room as my bedroom for a couple of weeks? It shouldn't take a couple of big strong soldiers more than a week or so to put a small house together for me, should it?"

As they strolled toward the buggy, she continued. "I thought just two rooms would suffice. I want my bedroom to be private, but I think the kitchen and living room can all be rolled into one. After all, what's a single girl going to do with more room than that? Barney? What do you think about a fireplace? Will a cook stove be enough for heat? Barney . . . ?"

Several weeks later, still deep in the Bighorn Mountains, Jacob heard the calls of wild geese overhead. His mind began to return in bits and pieces. His body, vague, still detached from his brain somehow, rested in a great warm nest of quiet pain.

Where was he? What had happened to him? He thought of Dominique, of clouds of hair the color of maize at sunset, and he was content. Slowly, languidly, he pieced together his memories of the short time she'd been his. With sudden clarity, he remembered their last afternoon together. She'd brazenly straddled his hips and stared down at him, her expression lusty and wanton. How different she was that day from the nervous young woman on the night they'd become one—how brave, how bold.

Or was she so different? he suddenly wondered. He thought back to long ago, to the night he'd brought life back to her frozen limbs. How brave she'd been then, how bold, as she spit in his face and kicked at his crotch. Jacob laughed out loud, then groaned as twin arrows of pain shot into his ribs.

A woman's voice, tender and full of concern, hummed to him. Soft hands stroked his brow. Jacob reached up, encircling the small wrist, and said, "Dominique?"

"It is I, Spotted Feather. Have you awakened from your deep sleep, Redfoot?"

Jacob released her, then gradually inched his eyelids open. The sun was low, shuttered in shades of tangerine and persimmon through ribbons of wispy white clouds. He managed to keep his eyes open long enough to adjust to the light, then glanced up at the woman.

"What has happened? Where am I?"

"You recover from terrible wounds, Redfoot. You rest in the big mountains with a small band of our people. You will live."

She reached for his brow again, but he caught her wrist and said, "Where is Dominique?"

Spotted Feather jerked her hand away and sat back on her haunches. "She is where she belongs—with the Long Knives. It is *I* who have cared for you, not the crazy one."

"I thank you for your trouble, woman. Now, tell me—is our father here, too?"

"Yes. He waits for your mind to return."

"Then go fetch him and say that I must talk to him."

The berry-skinned woman got to her feet, grumbling to herself, then stomped over a small hill and out of sight.

Jacob closed his eyes and waited. Dominique was safe and well, he thought with a sigh of relief. Unlike her foolish uncle, she was most likely on her way back to Fort Lincoln by now, and then—on to where? Would she wait for him to seek her out? Or blame him for the slaughter of her family members?

At the sound of approaching footsteps, Jacob opened his eyes again, this time without pain, and saw his father sink cross-legged into the grass beside him.

"Spotted Feather tells me you have decided to join us at last," Gall said, his voice low and tight.

Jacob drew his brows together, noticing the new grooves

at the corners of the chief's eyes, the deep anguish buried in their centers, and said, "How long have I slept?"

"Since the great war of the Greasy Grass, two moons have passed."

"Two moons!" Jacob abruptly sat up, the jolt of pain following him and snapping inside his head like the crack of some giant whip.

"Lie down, son. You are not yet well."

But Jacob forced himself to remain sitting, rode each new wave of pain as if he were breaking a wild pony, until the pounding in his head became a dull ache he could manage. How could he have been unaware of his own existence for so many weeks? he wondered. Could he hope even in his wildest dreams that Dominique still waited for him?

Jacob groaned as that terrible Sunday returned to his memory. He saw the hundreds of bodies strewn across the slopes of the Little Bighorn Valley, remembered the face of the general as he lay staring up at the sky for all eternity, and called up a hazy recollection of the Cheyenne warrior who mistook him for the enemy.

His heart heavy, he said, "I remember many dead soldiers that day. What of our people?"

Gall shrugged. "We lost some warriors, but it was a day of victory for the Dakota. A day the Long Knives will not soon forget."

"From what I saw," Jacob said, unable to hide the disgust in his voice, "you did not leave anyone to remember."

"I admit that we did not show them mercy, but the Long Knives brought that on themselves." At his son's raised brow, Gall explained. "Before we knew they were upon us, before we could hide our families, the soldiers came into our camp firing at all who moved. I lost two of my wives and three of my children to their guns before we were able to drive them off."

"Oh, my father," Jacob groaned. "I am sorry."

Gall waved him off. "After that, I fought with a bad heart. I admit this."

"There is no need to explain. I would feel the same." At his own words, a sudden fear shook him. What if Spotted Feather had not spoken the truth! What if she thought to ease his troubled mind with a lie? Jacob quickly looked up at Gall. "What of the crazy one? Did you see her to safety?"

Gall shook his head. "I did not see your woman, but Drooping Belly tells me he watched her attack one of the Long Knives, then steal his horse. He said she rode off screaming at any who would listen. As for her safety, there is no way to know for sure." At Jacob's frown, he managed a rare smile and said, "Do not concern yourself with the safety of your crazy wife. She had the women of our village shaking whenever she passed by—and, I must admit, even a few warriors as well. You would spend your time better worrying about those who might cross her path."

Jacob let out his breath in low chuckle, wincing as the wounds below his ribs complained about the movement. "I believe she has probably survived this war better than I."

"Better than most," Gall agreed.

Now that his initial concern about Dominique was eased, Jacob worked at concentrating on the ruins of his memory. "Spotted Feather also tells me I am among a small number of our people. Where have the rest gone?"

"All councils have split and gone in separate directions. The Long Knives did not learn their lesson at the Greasy Grass. Still they hunt us."

Jacob thought back to the carnage, to his memories of life among the soldiers, and groaned. "Now they will hunt you in bigger numbers than ever. I feel sure they will not stop hunting you until they have avenged the death of their great leader, Custer, and his men."

"Ah," Gall sighed, "then we did battle the Long Hair.

None of those who viewed the bodies could be sure. He was among the dead?''

Jacob nodded. "I saw him myself before one of our friends shot me."

Satisfied with that much, Gall nodded, then proclaimed, "The Long Knives will send new leaders to take his place, but we shall battle and subdue them as well. The Hunkpapa will never be ruled by the whites."

"These are foolish goals for any of the Dakota! Where do you think this will all end?" Angered and sickened by the memory of those who'd died, white and red man alike, Jacob struggled to his feet. His legs as weak as those of a newborn fawn, he stood on his own and waited for the pounding in his head to ease.

"My son," Gall said, joining him, "do not try to move. We have until the next moon to rejoin Sitting Bull and move onward toward the grandmother's land. You must rest."

But wobbly as it was, Jacob stood his ground, then took a couple of steps toward the crest of the hill. "It is your intention to go to Canada?" he asked of his father.

"That is where Sitting Bull goes. That is where we will join him."

Jacob looked out at the hills, beyond the forests and to the east. "That may be where you go, but you do not go of your own choice. Still you run. Still your people are afraid."

Gall stepped up beside him, a thousand questions glittering in his eyes. "*My* people, son? What of *our* people?"

Jacob turned sad blue eyes on his father. "They are your people, not mine. Go, run to the grandmother's land, but do not count me as one of your warriors."

"Ah, so then it has come to pass. Your heart has returned to the people of your birth. You have become one of them."

"I belong to no one!" Jacob said, the force of his words exploding shells of pain in his head. "I have tried to understand both the Dakota and the soldier, tried to find a

eason to do battle with either side, but I cannot under-
tand!''

"My son," Gall said gently. "You have been ill, your
mind is—"

"My mind is hurt, but it is from the foolishness I have
een all around me, not from this wound! This war has
been a terrible thing, can you not see this?'' But he wasn't
interested in Gall's reply just then; he cared only about
he answers his fragile brain had saved and then unraveled
or him.

"The Dakota," he went on, "fight for the land they
call theirs, for their sense of honor. I see this, I understand
his. The Long Knives battle in the name of their government, for the right to take your land as their own, and I
think because they wish to gain ultimate power over the
earth. I see and almost understand this also. What I cannot
see, what I will never understand, is why no one thinks to
fight for *peace*! *Why does no one fight for peace?*''

Jacob raised his hand to the side of his head, soothed
he angry valley the bullet had seared into the side of his
head, and waited for the throbbing to ease. At his side,
Gall stood, open-mouthed, deep in thought.

Finally after several moments of silence, the chief
spoke. "You ask many honorable questions. I do not have
he answers you seek. Perhaps after a long winter of councils, we will find some of these answers for you."

Suddenly weary, barely able to keep his eyes open, Jacob rested his hand on Gall's shoulder. "Find the answers,
but discover them for the Dakota, not for me. When I am
ready to travel, I will go to the east and search for my
woman. After that, I cannot be sure where my life will
lead me."

Clearly disturbed, Gall gripped Jacob's shoulders. "You
plan to ride into the soldiers' fort? Do they know your
identity? Do they know yet that you wore the uniform of
a soldier but hid the heart of a Dakota warrior? Will they
be pleased or angry to see that you live?"

Jacob shrugged, unable to remember at that moment.

Gall persisted. "Do not be foolish, my son. Try to think back to that terrible day. On whose side did you fight the afternoon your life was nearly given up to the Great Spirit?"

Jacob smiled and managed a few last words as a sudden fog enveloped his brain. "I fought on no man's side that day. I battled for only one thing: I was a lonely warrior waging a fight for peace."

Then the fog thickened into a great dark storm cloud. Jacob fell to the ground.

Chapter Twenty-two

✠

October 25, 1876

"WHOA, SAMPI, MY FRIEND," JACOB SAID, PULLING THE big stallion to a halt.

From behind, Peaches ignored the man's command and continued walking until she stood beside the big sorrel. After nudging the rider's thigh, she lifted her head and emitted a shrill whinny.

Laughing, Jacob said, "So you know how close you are to home, is that it?"

Still chuckling, he looked over to the stand of cottonwood trees, to the spot where he'd hastily set up the Sioux warning pole the day he'd kidnapped Dominique. That was so long ago, and yet the memories of her, of her laughter and her touch, seemed fresh and alive within him. If he should find her again, would she accept him as she once had? he wondered again, as he had throughout his long journey. Had she gotten over the loss of her family, been able to forget and forgive the fact he'd been unsuccessful in his quest for a peaceful end to the battle?

Jacob pulled off his buffalo robe and tossed it over near the trees, exposing his cavalry uniform. Then he reached into the pack strapped on Peaches' back, took out his broad-brimmed hat, and carefully positioned it on his head.

The time was near to seek answers to his many questions about Dominique. But first he had to make peace with the army. Jacob kicked Sampi's flanks and tugged on the lead line attached to the mare. In a short time the blockade was in sight. Less than an hour later, Jacob arrived at the outer perimeters of Fort Abraham Lincoln.

As the weary trio approached, a guard called out, "Who goes there? Stop and identify yourself."

"Private Jacob Stoltz, Company C, Seventh Cavalry, reporting, sir."

"*Company C?* But that's impossible. Company C was with the general at the Little Bighorn, and there were no survivors. That ain't—"

"It is a very long story, sir. One I wish to repeat only once. Will you please tell me where I can find Lieutenant Barney Woodhouse? I would like to report to him."

The man continued to stare at Jacob, awestruck, but finally said, "Just ride on up to Officers' Row, over yonder. *Captain* Woodhouse has the place next door to the schoolmarm's little house at the end. You can't miss it."

"Thank you." Jacob saluted, then continued on his way. When he reached Barney's quarters, he slid down off Sampi and tied him and Peaches to the rail out front. Then, knowing full well his visit might result in an arrest, a court-martial, and even a death sentence, Jacob walked up the stairs and rapped the brass knocker against the wood.

When the door opened, Barney's lean form blocked the entrance. Grinning at the man he hoped he could still call friend, Jacob said, "Private Stoltz reporting, Captain, sir."

Barney gasped, and his eyes bulged. "*Stoltz?* Is it really you?"

Jacob removed his hat. "It really is—what's left of me, anyway."

"Oh, Jesus, Stoltz! Get on in here!" Barney hauled him through the doorway, clasping him in a quick bear hug before he closed the door and caught his breath.

"I can't believe this! I mean, I really can't believe you're alive. I was sure, you know, the way you left and all . . . and then the battle . . . I didn't see how you could possibly have gotten through that mess and—Jesus, Stoltz! You look like hell!"

"How nice of you to say so. I am very happy to see you again, too, Barney—or should I say Captain?"

"Oh, Stoltz," Barney muttered, strangling on a dose of brand-new and very unfamiliar pride. "Get on over to the couch and sit a spell. We got lots of catching up to do."

"Thank you," Jacob said, unable to hide the weariness in his voice. He sank into the cushions slowly, trying to ease the inflammation the long ride had brought to his wounds, then took a deep breath and said, "Why don't we get the military explanations out of the way first? Which officers should I see, and what charges am I to defend? Is there to be a court-martial?"

"For what?" Barney said, wrinkling his nose. "Living through the battle? That's the only explanation anyone's going to be looking for. How in hell did you do it?"

Jacob's gaze narrowed, then became hopeful as he listened to his friend. His voice alive with surprise, he said, "What about my arrest and escape? What about my attack on you?"

"I don't know what you're talking about, Stoltz," Barney muttered, the words short and choppy. "My only memories of the Little Bighorn are brief. The general asked me to guard a prisoner—I don't remember the man's name or his crime. Then the fellow escaped, knocking me out in the process. I have no idea what became of the man after that."

"That's it?" Jacob gasped, incredulous. "You have said nothing more?"

Barney screwed up his features, then shrugged. "That's about the size of it, buddy."

"But why? Why do you do this for me with no explanation? Didn't you wonder why Custer arrested me? Didn't he tell you that I was—"

"I'm curious," Barney jumped in, knowing his best defense of Jacob would be complete ignorance of his deeds. "There's no doubt that I'm curious, Stoltz, but I think it'll be healthier for us both if I don't know any more than I do. I just feel mighty indebted to you, so let's call it even.''

Now Jacob's curiosity was piqued, and he screwed up his own features. ''I don't understand, my friend. I think I almost killed you. For this, you wish to thank me?''

Barney laughed. ''I suppose you could have been a little more gentle, but yes, Stoltz. I do thank you. You saved my life, you know. If I hadn't got stuck watching over you, I'd have died in the battle with the rest of my company. I never would have come back here, married Hazel, and made captain if it hadn't been for you. Thanks, friend.''

Jacob accepted his outstretched hand and shook it as swells of emotion crested in his chest. He cleared his throat and managed to say, ''I want you to know this much: The only thing I did to anger the general was to try to save him and his men from their fate.''

''You don't owe me any explanations, Stoltz. I mean that.''

''And I thank you, but I want you to understand—I tried to convince Custer it would be foolish to go on ahead. I scouted for the general. I went into places no other could, and I told him how many warriors he faced.'' Jacob hung his head and sighed. ''He would not believe me. He would not listen. That is why he is dead.''

Uncomfortable, vaguely disturbed by some of Jacob's explanations, Barney changed the subject. ''That's enough talk of Little Bighorn. It's a closed book as far as I'm concerned. What happened to you? Where've you been all this time?''

Jacob looked up at his friend, twinkles of mischief playing hopscotch in his deep blue eyes. ''I have been camping with the Sioux.''

''Oh, come on, now, Stoltz. Give me the truth.''

''That is the truth, friend. After I escaped from you, I followed the general, but I did not arrive in time to save him. As I walked through the battlefield, a Cheyenne warrior saw me and emptied his rifle into my body. When I awakened from a long and terrifying sleep, I was being cared for by the very Indians the cavalry had sought to kill.''

"Jesus," Barney breathed. "Why in hell would they do that?"

Jacob shrugged. "I cannot pretend to know what is in another man's mind, but I like to believe the Dakota are trying to learn and understand the whites. It may be time for us all to try to find a way to live in peace with one another."

"Sounds like a lot less bloody solution than we've tried so far." Barney stared at his friend for a long moment, then jumped to his feet as if slapped. "I don't know what's wrong with my manners. Here you been riding for days, I suppose, and I ain't even offered you a bite of food or a warm drink. How about some coffee? Hazel will be back soon, so I'll let her feed you. She's got something cooking that'll warm your innards."

Jacob nodded, inhaling the aroma of slowly roasting beef, the clear scent of a woman lingering throughout the house, and his mind returned to an earlier statement Barney had made—and the main purpose of his journey. When the new captain returned carrying two cups of steaming coffee, Jacob accepted his, then said, "Thanks, friend. Please tell me about your Hazel. Did I hear you say you were married?"

"Yep. Right after I got back from the Little Bighorn. That sweet gal is the best damn thing that ever happened to me. Better than making captain any day."

Jacob nodded, smiling as he stared into the cup. "And Dominique?" he ventured softly. "Does Hazel keep in touch with her?"

"Keep in touch? Oh, Stoltz! I forgot about you and, ah, her."

Jacob's head snapped up and his brows slammed together. "What? What is it? Has some harm come to Dominique?"

"No, I—it ain't exactly that." Barney stumbled around, searching for a way to tell his friend, then shook his head and turned his palms up. "I told you once to forget her, to bury her. I don't suppose you took that advice."

"No," Jacob said, his expression stern. "And I'm not going to take it now. What's happened to Dominique? Where can I find her?"

"Aw, hell, Stoltz," he muttered. "Don't you remember that she was, you know, captured? I don't have to remind you of that, do I?"

"No, you do not."

"Well, she come back. Reno's bunch found her at the Little Bighorn, and she come back on the steamer with the wounded. I—well, Jacob, I don't know how to put this, exactly, but she's not the same, if you know what I mean."

Losing patience, sudden concern driving him, Jacob said, "I don't know what you mean. Please tell me—where is Dominique? What is wrong with her?"

His eyes shadowed, fearful, Barney chanced a look at his friend. "She's here, Stoltz. She didn't go home to Michigan with Mrs. Custer."

"Dominique? Here at Fort Lincoln?" Jacob leapt off the couch, spilling the hot coffee on his trousers. The burning sensation stinging his legs was no competition for his pounding heart, and he went on, oblivious to the discomfort, "Where is she, Barney? Take me to her at once!"

"Easy now, Stoltz." Barney stood up, staring at the stains on his friend's pant legs, wondering how he'd been able to stand the pain, and said, "I got to tell you about her, explain that she just ain't the same gal."

Now Jacob's eyes narrowed, but the twinkle in them was no longer mischievous or good-natured. His voice low and dangerous, he said, "I wish to see Dominique and judge this for myself. Take me to her."

Barney's chest flattened as he saw Jacob's expression. "She'll be coming along with Hazel 'fore long. But you got to listen to me before they get here; you got to understand what I'm trying to say." Barney scratched his head, then fiddled with his mustache as he tried to find a delicate way to put it. "For God's sake, man, she was taken in by one of them warriors—don't you get it? He kept her to himself, you know, like she was his own little—toy.''

The tension vanished from Jacob's body. He sucked in a breath of cool air, unaware he'd stopped breathing. ''This doesn't bother me, Barney,'' he said quietly. ''I just want to see her.''

''That's right big of you, Stoltz. I'm sure Dominique will appreciate that much. As for the rest—''

Jacob raised his brow. ''The rest?''

''I—I—'' Barney stared at his friend, studied his big thick body, and sighed. Even though Jacob appeared gaunt and weaker than usual, he still looked to be strong enough to snap a man of his own build like a toothpick. Someone else would have to explain to the big German that the sweet gal he loved carried a half-breed baby in her womb, the child of a savage. But it would have to be someone he wouldn't want to hurt—a woman, perhaps. Feeling more than a little cowardly, but unable to do anything else, Barney said, ''I believe I'd best let the missus explain the rest.''

Outside the house, while Jacob tried to make sense of Barney's puzzle, a buggy rounded the corner and made its way to Officers' Row. Riding behind the driver on the bench seat, Dominique leaned in close to Hazel, trying to hear what she had to say.

''. . . getting too big for discretion. Besides, next month the snow will start falling, and you'll have to stop going up to the scouts' quarters anyway. Tsk, tsk, all this running around in your condition is highly improper.''

''What?'' Dominique asked. ''I didn't hear everything you said.'' Straining against the sudden gusty wind, she cocked her head. That was when she noticed two strange horses tied at the rail.

''Looks as if you have company,'' she shouted to Hazel. ''Come over to my place later, and we'll talk about—'' Dominique's words stuck in her throat and her heart seized up as she stared at the horses. ''Peaches?'' she said in a strangled whisper. ''And . . . Sampi?''

"What?" Hazel shouted back. "What are you talking about?"

But Dominique focused only on the horses, heard only the sound of her own heartbeat hammering away in her throat. "Stop!" she screamed at the driver. "Stop this instant!"

The startled soldier reined in his team, but before the buggy came to a halt, one of his passengers leapt over the side of the rig and ran on ahead of him.

"Dominique!" Hazel shrieked from the bench. "My Lord, what can you be thinking of in your condition? Dominique!"

But she was beyond the sound of Hazel's voice, past the point of considering her body or its limitations. Dominique flew to the mare's side and buried her fingers in the long black mane. "Oh, *mon Dieu*!" she said in half-sob. "It *is* you—Peaches!"

She glanced at the big stallion, swaying as a wave of dizziness swept over her, and choked out, "And Sampi, too. My God, it's really Sampi!" *Jacob's here,* her mind whispered. *Jacob? But how? Where?*

She clutched at her throat, unable to call out his name for fear the hope would evaporate. What if it was true? What if Jacob was waiting just inside the door?

"Jacob?" she cried in a muffled sob. "Oh, Jacob, please be in there." Then, forcing her stricken limbs to move, Dominique grabbed at the hem of her skirts and bounded up the stairs two at a time. Throwing her shoulder against the wood, she turned the knob and crashed through the door in the same instant.

The noise startled Barney and his guest. Turning toward the sound, both men gasped.

"*J-Jacob,*" she managed in a constricted sob. "Oh, God, it is you!"

"Dominique," he breathed through a relieved sigh.

Jacob covered the distance between them in two long strides. Then, faster than he could blink back an unexpected tear, he gathered her into his arms.

"Oh, Jacob!" she cried against his neck, her own tears flowing like the Missouri in May. "You're alive. You're *alive*!"

"Yes" was the best Jacob could manage as his warrior's armor began to crack and peel. Behind his eyes, something hot pulsated, demanding release, threatening to expose him as a man whose heart now ruled his head. Unable to stem the burning tide, unwilling to allow anyone to witness this ultimate lack of control, Jacob pushed Dominique's bonnet to the back of her head and buried his face in her hair.

They were entwined as one, their bodies fused so tightly it was difficult to tell where one started and the other left off, when Hazel burst into the room.

"Oh!" she gasped, stumbling onto the sight. "Oh, my— Barney? What's going on here?"

"Come here, sweetheart," he managed, his own tears at high tide.

Guessing at, but not believing the identity of the man holding Dominique, Hazel kept her gaze fastened on the pair as she slowly made her way to her husband. "Is that who I think it is?" she asked in a whisper as Barney put his arm around her shoulders.

"Yep." He nodded, still too choked up for intelligible speech.

"Oh, but, Barney, this is highly improper, terribly indiscreet. I must insist that you—"

"Hazel," he said, cutting her off, "just be quiet and give 'em a minute."

And because her husband rarely *told* her to do anything, Hazel glanced up at him, biting her lip, then looked back to the overt display of affection. Dominique and Jacob were swaying in each other's arms, whispering mindless words against a backdrop of happy sobs.

When Jacob finally felt in control again, became able to patch up the cracks in his armor, however temporary the repair work might be, he slid his hands up either side of Dominique's head and pushed her away from him. "Let me look at you, *wi witko*," he whispered for her ears alone.

Swallowing a sob, Dominique wiped at her tears, but they continued to fall as he untied the ribbon at her throat and tossed her bonnet aside.

Struggling once again to chill that burning sensation behind his eyes, Jacob removed the pins from her hair, then drew his fingers through the burnished gold strands. Pointing to her damp cheeks, he grinned and scolded, "Stop that at once. You know I do not like it."

Laughing and crying all at once, Dominique let her tears fall even harder. "Oh, Jacob," she managed just before she collapsed against his chest again. "God, how I've missed you."

Glancing over the top of Dominique's head, Jacob saw that Barney's wife had joined him. He gave the couple a warm smile, then noticed the suspicious expression in Hazel's eyes, the knowing look of a highly perceptive woman. He released Dominique and urged her to step back.

Her tears more of a light spring rain now, Dominique looked up at Jacob and smiled. "Welcome home, Private. What took you so long?"

Keeping the Woodhouses in view, he smiled back. "It is a very long story. Do you really want to hear it all now?"

"I want to know everything, every tiny little—" Dominique choked on her words as her vision cleared and she got her first good look at the man she loved. "Jacob! What's happened to you? You look as if . . . as if you've been—"

"Looks like hell, don't he?" Barney supplied.

"Thanks again," Jacob shot toward his friend. He glanced back at Dominique, at the concern in her moist brown eyes, and shrugged. "It is nothing. I fell off my horse."

"Oh, Jacob," she cried out, her eyes again filling with tears. But this time, when she moved back toward the comfort of his arms, he sidestepped her, taking her hand instead.

Aware of the tension and disapproval radiating from across the room, Jacob said, "Mrs. Woodhouse, hello. It's good to see you again."

"Jacob," she said, her mouth tight. "Nice to see you, too. Why don't we all take a seat and try to sort through this in a more . . . comfortable fashion?"

Dominique glanced at Jacob, gasping on a deep breath, then said, "I suppose she's right. Let me hang up my cloak first." As she slowly walked back to the entry, a slow, wicked grin spread across her face. Dominique whipped off her coat and hung it on the rack, exposing her shapeless gray silk and wool tattersall frock. Then, hiding her triumphant expression from Barney and Hazel, she turned sideways and draped her hands across her swollen belly.

"Dominique?" Jacob gasped, unable to believe his eyes. "You—you are with child?"

Still trying to hide her expression from Hazel, Dominique lowered her head in a suitably shameful posture and said, "Yes, I am, Jacob. The baby is due in four months."

"But how can that be?" he bellowed, crossing the room, no longer interested in anyone's opinion but his own. "Dominique!" he said, gripping her shoulders. "How can this *be*?"

Caught off guard, frightened by what she saw in Jacob's eyes, *hoping* the message he sent was an act, a way to keep the others from knowing his true identity, Dominique was beyond speech. "I—"

"Private," Hazel said as she started toward them, "don't be so quick to judge. She has been through a lot of—"

"Sweetheart," Barney sliced in as he took Hazel by the arm. "Why don't we give Dominique and Jacob a few minutes to themselves? I believe this conversation should be held in private."

"But, Barney, this is highly irregular, terribly improper. I don't—"

"Darling," he warned, "I think it's time we took our nightly walk around the compound, don't you?"

Alarmed by her husband's aggressive behavior, but warmed by it as well, Hazel looked to Dominique. "Will you be all right, dear?"

"Yes," she said, finding her voice. "Please don't worry about me. Barney's right—I think we need a moment alone."

Jacob's intense gaze never left Dominique as the older couple slipped into their coats and made their departure. When the door closed and they were truly alone, his expression didn't change, didn't soften. Still he stared at her with a mixture of anger and disbelief.

"Jacob," she said softly, her alarm growing. "Why are you looking at me like that? You don't think— I mean, surely you must realize this is your baby."

"Of course I do!" he said, slamming his fist into the palm of his hand, as angry with himself as he was at her.

Confused, ready to burst into tears again, she said, "Then why are you yelling at me? Why are you so angry?"

"Because you did not do as I told you! Because you did not seek out the herbs my people know about that would have prevented . . . *this*."

"But, Jacob," she said, still perplexed, but not as alarmed, "*this*, as you put it, is our baby—the best of you and me. And I did get those herbs after our first night together." She laughed, adding, "But I'm afraid taking them then was a little like closing the barn door after the horses got out—don't you think?"

"I see nothing funny here," he said, his expression defensive, desolate somehow.

"What's wrong, *mon amour*? I don't see why are you so angry. Don't you know this baby is the only thing that's kept me going? I thought you had died at the Little Bighorn."

"Oh, *wi witko*," he said as he pulled her into his arms, "I am not angry with you. It is my own deadly seed that angers me so."

Dominique pushed away from him. "I don't understand what you're talking about. What is it you're trying to say to me?"

Jacob closed his eyes, thinking back to long ago, then pulled her close again. "I am trying to say something that I should have told you before now, but didn't because I thought I could prevent this." He pointed at her belly. "It is the story of Lame Fawn, my Dakota wife."

"Your . . . *wife*?" she said, nearly strangling on the word.

"Many years before you," he whispered, sliding the backs of his fingers across her cheek.

"And so?" she said, her voice the barest of whispers.

"Look," he explained, bringing her hand up in front of her face, then pressing his palm against hers. "See how big I am? See how small and frail you are? Lame Fawn also thought to have my child, but when her time came, the baby had grown so large, she could not expel it."

"Oh," Dominique sighed, her heart numb. "Lame Fawn died giving birth?"

Jacob nodded. "She and the child."

Dominique rested her head against his chest, gauging both his and her own feelings, choosing her words with care. She finally lifted her head, then held his hand to her mouth. "I'm sorry for the pain you must have suffered when you lost them, and for the anguish you're obviously feeling even now, but—"

"I have long since ceased to feel their loss. The anguish I feel now is for you. If I should lose you in the same way, lose you for any reason, the pain I'll suffer will never go away. I cannot lose you, Dominique. I will not take the chance."

"But, Jacob," she said with a soft laugh, "you and I don't have any choice now. Look at me."

He glanced at her round belly and shrugged. "There

must be some way to relieve you of this burden, something that will not put your life in danger.''

"There is," she said quietly. "It's called childbirth, and it's going to happen in February." Before he could argue, Dominique began running her lips along the hills and valleys of his knuckles, kissing him, soothing him.

Then she nipped at the back of his hand with her teeth. "You're going to have to do a lot more than get me in the family way to lose me, soldier," she said, giving him a reassuring wink as she backed away.

Spreading her arms, she slowly circled, commenting, "Look at me, Jacob. I'm no frail little flower. I'm strong and healthy, and the doctor says my hips are just made for having babies. Why don't you just trust me, Jacob? I know I can do this."

"But, Dom—"

"I mean it," she cut in, gliding back into his arms. "You kept asking me to trust you, to put my faith in you, and I did. I did everything you asked, believed you when you said you'd do all you could to stop that awful war and save my family. Now it's your turn to trust in me."

Her words triggered another memory, and suddenly he couldn't wait to explain. "I want you to know about your uncle and his brothers. I did try to—"

"Not now, Jacob. Please not now. If I didn't believe you had done everything you could to save them, I wouldn't be standing here talking to you." She rose up on tiptoe and fit her mouth to his in a brief kiss. "Please, we've both been through so much. Let's have no more talk of death and pain today. We have so much to celebrate, so much of life to experience. Can't we just enjoy each other and rejoice in the fact that we've found each other again?"

In spite of his misgivings, Jacob smiled, then cupped her face in his hands. "My woman has the wisdom of three old chiefs."

"And she has love enough for her husband to be fifty of his wives. Hold me, Jacob. I've missed you so."

He crushed her to him, his heart bursting with love, and

whispered in her ear, "Where do you sleep, *wi witko*? Do you stay here with Barney and Hazel?"

She shook her head against his chest. "I live in the small house next door."

"Then let us go there now and celebrate our reunion without benefit of all these clothes."

Dominique laughed and pulled out of his arms. "I wish we could, husband dear, but we're not in your Hunkpapa camp now. As far as everyone around here is concerned, I'm a single lady and I carry the bastard of a sex-crazed savage. I'm afraid that, until we're properly married, I'll have to sleep alone."

"Oh, really?" he said, his mind working to find a way around this policy.

"Really," she answered back, looking for a solution to the same problem.

"Then let us step outside now, announce our intentions to marry and be done with it."

Again she laughed. "Would that it were that simple, Jacob, but I'm afraid it's not. Before we can be married, we'll either have to wait for a preacher to come here or go to Bismarck and look one up. That will take a couple of days, at the very least."

"I see," he said, still looking for a solution. Then suddenly his sapphire-blue eyes lit up and a lusty grin tugged at the corners of his mouth. Raising his brow, he asked, "This house next door—you say you live there alone?"

"I do." She nodded, pretty sure they'd arrived at the same conclusion.

"This may be a good thing," he said advancing on her. Jacob slid his big hand around her neck. "And what would you do," he asked suggestively as he began to rub his thumb up and down, caressing the length of her throat, "if a half-naked savage should appear outside your window after you retire this evening?"

Dominique's breathing accelerated at his touch. Goose bumps sprang up all over her body, inside as well as out.

"I would probably open my window," she said in a breathless whisper, "to see what was going on."

"And if this savage should come inside your house and lie down on your bed?" he added, his mouth watering at the thought.

"I—I would go to him as a friend. I—" Dominique closed her eyes and shivered as spurts of desire raced throughout her body. "I would try to help him in any way I could, perhaps give him some . . . English lessons."

"English?" Jacob growled, his voice thick with emotion. "Still you think to give me English lessons?"

"I don't recall you complaining the last time I tried to instruct you," she said with a lazy seduction in her voice.

The sudden image of Dominique standing nude above him sent shudders throughout Jacob's body, melting cords of muscle here, hardening others with an agonizing stiffness there.

Delighted by his reaction and by the glazed look in his eyes, Dominique went on. "A is for Apache—"

"B is for buffalo hides," he cut in impatiently.

"And T is for tired," she said, ending the game. "I'm exhausted. I think I'll turn in early tonight."

Chapter Twenty-three

✖

JACOB PACED BACK AND FORTH IN FRONT OF THE WINDOW. He stopped long enough to cock his head toward the bedroom door and listen for a moment; then he resumed his incessant marching.

"Jesus, Stoltz," Barney complained. "Will you sit down? You're making me dizzy."

"I cannot. Something is wrong. The child should have been here hours ago."

"Give the poor gal a chance, Stoltz. She hasn't been in labor but a few hours. I think it takes a little longer for the first one."

Jacob halted again, this time bending down and staring out across the compound at the riverbanks. "Where is the doctor?" he complained. "He should have been here by now!"

"You got to take it easy and relax, Stoltz. I'm telling you, you're just this side of wearing me out. Doc will get here when he's darn good and ready to get here." But Barney didn't believe those last words himself, knew the doctor wouldn't be in any big hurry to come back from town just to deliver a baby—the child of a private's wife, no less.

Using up his rapidly waning creativity, Barney tried once again to change the subject. "So what have you heard from the government? Anything new?"

Jacob stopped in midstride and drew his brows together. "The government? What do you mean?"

"About your job. What's the latest?"

"I believe you know the latest," Jacob grumbled as he resumed pacing.

"No, I don't think so. Fill me in. Have you got the job for sure?"

Jacob heaved an exasperated sigh and explained—again. "You know I have. You know that after the spring thaw, when Dominique is able to travel, we will move on to the Red Cloud Agency at Yellow Medicine Creek. There I will become the Indian agent and Dominique will continue teaching English to the Sioux and others who will sign the treaty of peace. Do you understand this yet, or do I have to write it down for you?"

"I get it." Barney laughed. "It just feels so good to hear you talk about it. You and Dominique might really make a difference for them Indians, what with your uncanny instincts about 'em and the way those little savages flock to her. Maybe your dreams of peace aren't so far-fetched after all."

"I hope to persuade the government to return the Black Hills to the Sioux. That would go a long way toward ensuring peace between the people of—" A loud moan followed by Hazel's excited voice cut into his thoughts and through his head. Jacob stomped across the room, shouting, "That's it! I cannot take this any longer."

Barney watched, wide-eyed, then jumped to his feet when he realized Jacob's intent. "Wait, Stoltz! You can't go in there!"

"I go where I must," he insisted, reaching for the doorknob. "I will not stand out here any longer and do nothing while my woman dies!" He kicked the door open and barreled into the bedroom.

"Oh, my Lord!" Hazel gasped as Jacob reached the bed. "You can't be in here! This is . . . *highly improper,* terribly indecent at the very least! I must insist—"

"Leave him be, Hazel," Dominique said, her voice strained even though she languished between contractions.

Jacob sank to his knees and leaned across the bed. Mopping her damp brow with his hand, he asked, "Is the child too big? Are you—"

"Everything is going as it should, Jacob. Please don't worry about me."

"But I heard you cry out in pain!"

"Well, damn it all, Jacob, this *hurts*!" she managed just as a new contraction loomed up from nowhere, first crushing her against the mattress, then lifting her as her back arched in agony.

Terrified, Jacob glanced at Hazel and shouted, "Do something, woman!"

But before Hazel could say a word, Dominique turned on him, her voice hoarse and guttural. "Shut up and give me your hand, you nincompoop! I—I need you, Jacob. I need your strength."

Feeling utterly helpless, Jacob placed one hand on her brow and the other on her breast. Dominique laced her fingers around his wrist and began twisting and squeezing, pulling his flesh as she bore down in the final stages of labor.

"Push, honey," Hazel encouraged, no longer taking notice of the frantic soldier. "Come on—I can see the head! One more time, Dominique. Give it all you've got."

Jacob watched his woman, his wife according to both Sioux and white law, and squeezed back the tears that seemed to be a part of his life now. *Please don't die,* he said in a silent prayer just before he leaned in close to her ear and whispered, "I love you, *wi witko.* I'll always love you."

Then Jacob looked down in time to see his son slip out of his mother and into his rightful place in the world.

"Oh, Dominique," Hazel cried, "look at him! It's a beautiful little redheaded boy!"

Still struggling to get her breathing under control, Dominique inclined her head, then collapsed against the pillow. "Jacob, did you see him? We have a son."

But Jacob was overcome with emotion, too shaken to form even the simplest of words. For the last four months he'd done nothing but worry about Dominique and love her. Never once in that time had he allowed himself even to think about the child, imagine it as a person, or wish for a son to carry on his name. Now that the child was here, now that physical proof of his union, the love he shared with Dominique, rested inches from his big hands, he couldn't move, couldn't talk. He leaned his elbows against the mattress and stared, a stone man, as Hazel finished cleaning the infant, then placed him across his mother's abdomen.

"Look, Jacob," Dominique whispered, aware of her husband's turmoil. "He takes after his father."

Jacob's gaze followed the path of hers to their son's writhing body and the fully erect symbol of his sex. The baby howled his displeasure at the rude interruption in his life, then shot a stream of urine into the air.

Startled out of his trance, sprayed by the child as well, Jacob leaned back, his chest swelling with pride, and said, "Dominique, speak to this little nincompup! Tell him he must have respect for the man who will be his father."

"The little nincompup!" Hazel objected. "What kind of name is that to call a newborn baby?"

Dominique laughed and reclaimed her husband's hand.

Jacob grinned, his mouth lopsided, and said, "It is a good name. It means this child is a . . . a baby nincompoop."

Then he burst out laughing, joining his wife in hysterics as Hazel looked on, her eyebrows alternately rising and falling.

"Highly irregular, extremely indelicate," she muttered as she wrapped the baby in a quilt. "Nothing about this has been the least bit proper."

Lifting the infant from his mother's tummy, Hazel leaned over and placed him at her bosom. Tiny fingers groped for Dominique's breast, instinctively seeking the life-sustaining fluid within.

Hazel gasped, and tears sprang into the corners of her eyes as she observed mother and child. "Oh, my Lord, would you look at that!"

Dominique studied her son, smoothing his damp hair, branding his scent into her memory, then looked back up at Hazel. "He's beautiful, isn't he?"

"Oh, my dear, he's much more than that—he's white! With that red hair and pale skin, no one will ever guess his father was a Sioux Indian! This is truly a day in which to give thanks."

Dominique exchanged a loving glance with her husband, both of them harboring a secret smile, then said to Hazel, "His skin may not be red, but always remember this: That white flesh is there only to protect the heart of a great Dakota warrior."